Born Bad

BARRY HOFFMAN

LEISURE BOOKS   NEW YORK CITY

Who else, but for my children,
Dara, David and Cheryl—
my love and constant inspiration.

A LEISURE BOOK®

November 2000

Published by

Dorchester Publishing Co., Inc.
276 Fifth Avenue
New York, NY 10001

ISBN 0-8439-4793-4

Other *Leisure* books by Barry Hoffman:
EYES OF PREY
HUNGRY EYES

ACKNOWLEDGMENTS

I am indebted to the many people at the University of Pennsylvania who helped make the campus become a character in this book: the many tour guides who answered countless questions and the campus police—from the Commissioner himself, on down to patrolmen who worked the campus. Thanks, too, to Richard Chizmar of Cemetery Dance Publications for his support and friendship, and Don D'Auria, editor of Leisure Books for his faith in me. Finally, a word of appreciation to Ray Bradbury—your plots and characters have always inspired me; "The Small Assassin," "The Burning Man" and "Hail and Farewell" for this particular tale.

AUTHOR'S NOTE

The University of Pennsylvania portrayed here is the University of 1995. As with many campuses, in the five years since I wrote *Born Bad* there have been changes. New buildings sprout up all the time. But the flavor of the University remains: the folklore and stories that make each campus unique. Most landmarks mentioned remain. So nitpickers needn't bother bitching about petty inaccuracies. This is the University of Pennsylvania as perceived by its students; the University of Pennsylvania of 1995.

Born Bad

Prologue

The pain was excruciatingly exquisite; *almost* enough to overcome the gangrene of a soul ravaged by crack.

She lay spread-eagled on her bed as another contraction hit with a wave of pain that nearly overcame her lethargy. Her scream pierced through the open door, and brought a profane response from a fellow crackhead down the hall.

Earlier that morning, Cherese had promised to be there with her; to take her to the hospital when it was time. A while ago . . .

—Ten minutes? An hour? *The entire morning?* She wondered, unable to recall.

Cherese had gone to the store for a pack of cigarettes . . .

—Or maybe a dime rock they would both share.

"I'll be right back, sugar," she'd said, garbling her words on the thick wad of gum in her mouth. "Promised I'd be there for you, and I will. Watch some TV. Just needs to get me some smokes . . ."

After Cherese left, she'd stared listlessly as some mothers and their daughters tore into one another on some fool talk show. Limp in her chair, like a wilted plant, she couldn't summon the energy to move, though she had to pee. Pee real bad. Then she remembered the rock in her purse. She'd promised herself . . .

11

Barry Hoffman

—No, promised her unborn child.

. . . no more drugs so close to going into labor, but she felt so down she wanted to cry. Felt so low, she began to weep, tears streaming down her face. One hit. What could be the harm? Just a taste.

Her hands shaking, she lit up and took a drag. Inhaled deeply, and the world exploded in front of her. The worn drab green carpet erupted into the deep green of a lush lawn. The sun, barely visible through the dust-caked window, now almost blinded her with its intensity. The muffled sound of the television now exploded; a haggard teen's head seemed to lunge through the tube to command her attention. She could almost feel the spittle on her face as the youth bellowed; smell the onions on his breath from a hoagie. She imagined her child somersault within her as the drug raced through her body.

"I hear you knocking, little one," she said aloud, "but you can't come out." Then laughed hysterically. "Can't come out till Aunt Cherese be back," she said in a singsong voice, then laughed again.

Her oversized dress felt constricting in the oppressive heat, so she slipped it off. She wore no underwear beneath. She smelled herself and almost gagged. "You stink, girl," she said aloud. " 'Nuff to make one puke." Then laughed some more.

The baby knocked again.

Invigorated now, she left the room and waddled down the hall, her coffee-colored skin glistening with perspiration. She was careful not to step on needles that littered the floor, or the dog shit that smelled every bit as pungent as she did.

She knocked on the first door she came to, knocked again and without waiting for a response yelled, "Jesus, I'm gonna have me a baby. Sweet Jesus, I'm gonna have me a baby."

From beyond the closed door, a muffled voice answered. "Shut the fuck up, bitch."

She giggled. "No. No. No," she answered. "Gotta tell the world. Having a . . ." She frowned, unable to grasp the rest of the thought.

A door opened down the hall and a head peered out. She cradled her bloated belly in her hands. "Ain't it a wonder. Me. Having a . . . *having a baby*!" she cried triumphantly.

A man gawked at her. "Shit, lady. Ain't no one give a fuck." Like a turtle, he withdrew his head and slammed the door shut.

The high dissipating, she realized her thighs were wet. Had she peed on herself again? Good God, she thought, seems I spend half my waking hours peeing. Before she could consider the thought, her belly was wracked with pain.

A contraction. Oh, shit, her mind screamed, I *am* having a baby. *Now!* She banged on Cherese's door.

"It be time, Cherese. I need you, honey. You promised. You promised to be there when I needed you. You promised . . ." Her eyes again clouded with tears. "Fuck, you promised," she muttered, and almost sat down right then and there, the fatigue weighing on her like a sack of rocks.

Later, she lay naked on her bed, not knowing how she'd gotten there, as yet another contraction came. She half expected the child to burst through her stomach, like in that movie *Alien,* stare at her with indifference, then abandon the useless shell that had nourished her. Abandon her . . .

—Like Cherese.

Almost against her will—for she was deathly afraid her unborn child would loathe her—she crawled deep within herself. To her womb. To the child. *Her* child. When on crack, she could venture anywhere; even into the realms of her own body. She had never gone to see the baby, though. Afraid it

13

would be deformed or hideous because of her sins. But now, curiosity got the best of her.

A little girl, she saw; so tiny it could fit in the palm of her hand. *Too* tiny. Against its will being thrust into a world that would shower her with contempt. The child suddenly opened its eyes and focused on its mother. She stifled a scream. The eyes weren't accusatory; didn't condemn her for poisoning her body with crack, heroin and alcohol the past seven months. She could have lived with that. Worse, there was only a flicker of emotion—irritation. The child was pissed. Its thoughts pierced her mind.

"I've been living in this cesspool too long, and it's time to get the fuck out. *Now, Mother!* Before this shit kills me."

Ungrateful little bitch, she thought, as another contraction sent her scurrying away from the vile creature.

She had tried, tried so hard to stay clean once she'd become pregnant, but the drug was like the first tentative kiss of a lover. So filled with promise, she needed more. The drug was a hill that had become a mountain. At first, she'd easily been able to scale it and experience the ultimate high. Then she'd needed more and more, yet she could never again reach the top. And as she stubbornly sought the orgasmic climax of those first hits, she had taken larger amounts of the drug. A dozen or more hits a day. When money ran out, she'd traded her body for a few dollars for another rock. One of those faceless men had fathered the child who now demanded its freedom.

Once pregnant, she *had* stopped . . . for a while. But the weight of the world was too much to bear. Her parents would have nothing to do with her. Friends she had borrowed—then stolen from—now shunned her. Only Cherese had grudgingly taken her in.

—Only to abandon her now.
—Promised . . .

—Be there for you.
—Promised.
—Be there . . .

A taste, from time to time, was all she needed, she told herself. But a taste never got her to the mountaintop. And now the baby demanded to escape the poisonous stew within her.

She thought she had drifted off, or perhaps passed out, for as her eyes fluttered open she was aware of a presence on her bosom. *The child . . .*

—*A screaming child.*

Still tied to her by its umbilical cord. It shook uncontrollably for a few moments, its little hands flapping like the flippers of a seal. Then it lay quiet and still . . .

—Dead?

Then within minutes, without warning, the baby began to wail again.

A spider scurried across the infant's buttocks. She flicked it away, aware for the first time the room was crawling with vermin. Though she felt drained, she was determined to remain awake to protect her child from the insects that seemed attracted by the baby's scent.

She felt like she had to pee again, and laughed at the thought. Did pee. But the flow wouldn't cease. She raised herself gently, for fear of disturbing her baby, who for the moment seemed too tuckered out to cry, and saw a river of blood cascading down her legs. So much blood. *Too much blood.* She had to hang on. Hope that . . . Cherese, yes, hope Cherese would . . .

—Would what? She tried to grasp the thought.

Would come back to save her, that's it. No, *not her*. Come back ... to save her ... *her baby*! Yes, she had to hold on. Hold on for her baby.

Chapter One

Looking at the tarp-covered body of the young coed, Ariel could feel the patter of feet dancing on *her* grave. It could have been her. Yes, she thought, but for the grace of God ... and all that shit, fifteen, sixteen, even seventeen years earlier *it could have been her*. Not seriously, but there had been days. *There had been days.*

Ariel had considered suicide at one time. Most adolescents had, she knew, statistically speaking. For most, like her, it was a whim, a fleeting thought at a time of extreme vulnerability. But only a thought; one that had never led to even an attempt as a cry for attention.

She wondered, though, what made someone cross that narrow line between thought and action. What could have been so horrible to kiss it all good-bye at nineteen? Why hadn't her friends—her roommate, for God's sake—seen it coming?

Ariel looked at her partner, with his receding hairline and pasty complexion. Fortyish, he sometimes wore a mustache, depending on his mood, or if he'd had an argument with his wife. He'd shaved it the day before; yep, an argument with his better half.

The little man—five-feet-four, though he swore up and down he was five-seven, even five-eight—was in his element. *This* was his kind of case. A no-brainer; a case closed quickly where imagination was unnecessary.

Doug Thiery *lived* for such cases, as well as domestic disputes that got out of hand; also quickly and relatively effortlessly solved. Interrogating a suspect or recalcitrant witness, he could be doggedly relentless. His less-than-forbidding demeanor caught others off guard. A wuss, nerd, geek; a *pushover*. He cultivated the image, then pounced upon those who underestimated him. She had to admit he got results.

But it wasn't because he was a good homicide detective. Give him a whodunnit with no simple answers, and he was adrift at sea; totally helpless and dependent on her. He gladly deferred to her in those cases that made it all worthwhile for her. Cases not closed within the magic forty-eight-hour window when evidence was freshest and clues plentiful. Cases without any clear direction. Cases you couldn't operate on automatic pilot, when you had to use your mind; even get into the mind of the perp to get results.

Did such a partnership make for a good marriage? She doubted it, but steady partners in homicide were few and far between when you were female and neither black nor white, fish nor fowl. She was a mutant, as she recalled another biracial acquaintance describe her. Any children she might have would be lighter than her, if that was possible, or one of the many shades of brown, depending on the father.

Only gays were treated worse in the Boys Club that made up the Philadelphia Police Department. Doug Thiery was her partner, not on his merits, but because he wore quickly on other detectives who could go to their Sergeant and request an amicable divorce. Ariel had no such pull with her superior. So, she had Doug Thiery.

Doug quickly took in the scene, as Ariel remained in the background, all but invisible. She didn't mind. He wasn't dismissing or disrespecting her. It was just the way he worked. Ten minutes later, he consulted his notes and approached her.

"Seems cut-and-dried. Sharon Ingster . . ." He paused and checked his notebook. "Age nineteen. A freshman, from some hole-in-the-wall town in Minnesota. No witnesses."

He closed the book, and made eye contact with her.

"I'm going to check her room for a suicide note. Why don't you speak to the campus security guard who was first on the scene?"

"No problem," she answered. The University of Pennsylvania had its own police force, so *she* knew she wouldn't be speaking to a lowly security guard, but a trained cop. No sense, though, in making her partner look foolish, she decided. She was about to ask where the "security guard" was, but he stopped her with an afterthought.

"Oh, by the way, we haven't found the roommate yet. If you get a chance . . ." He left the thought hanging.

"I'll look into it, Doug," she finished for him, taking him off the hook. God, what a wuss, she thought. Couldn't ask. Couldn't *tell* her what to do. *If you get a chance* . . . The king of the dangling sentence. She could imagine him with his wife.

"You want to . . . you know. . . ."

She could see his wife looking at him disdainfully.

"What, Doug? Go to the movies? See a play? *Fuck me?* Spell it out, dear."

He turned, and this time she stopped him. "Doug, where is this dude you want me to talk to? You know, the first one on the scene."

Not picking up on her sarcasm, he pointed behind her. "The black guy, over there. Standing alone, like he doesn't know what to do with himself."

She turned. "Fuck," she said, just under her breath. Lucius Jackson. Her ex-husband. All she needed to make the evening complete. First, a nothing case, just before her four-to-midnight shift ended. Now Lucius, whom she had managed to keep at arm's length for eight years.

If there was a God, he was having a good laugh tonight.

At her expense.

Chapter Two

Lucius Jackson had spotted his ex immediately—with that little dweeb of a partner who'd given him the once-over, and dismissed him as nothing more than a glorified crossing guard. For the moment, though, it was the gaggle of students taking in the morbid scene that held his interest.

Sharon Ingster had killed herself in The Quad, where most freshman lived their first year. These students, many away from home for the first time, would be even more traumatized than older students who had gotten used to living on their own. For that reason, Lucius spent an inordinate amount of time at The Quad, getting to know the *fresh meat,* as some of his colleagues labeled them. Just as importantly, he wanted them to get to know him, not as just another cop out to hassle them, but as someone they could confide in.

He had always been able to read people—except for Ariel—which made him so good at his job on campus, and had doomed his first marriage.

He now searched the faces of the youths gathered within shouting distance of Sharon Ingster's body. With each face he read doubts, fears and insecurities. Not voiced, but he saw it in some of their eyes.

"Could have been me."

19

"Should have been me."

"*Will* be me."

Saw it in *too many* of their eyes.

Amy, ungainly and self-conscious. Standing alone. Still bundled in a winter coat, though the early March night was almost balmy. Terribly vulnerable. Lucius would have to keep an eye on her.

Mia, with her short-cropped brown hair, remained aloof though she was in the midst of the crowd. Average height. Average weight. Everything average. Cute? Well, neither hideous nor gorgeous. Someone who blended in with the masses. Ask twenty people, tomorrow, who had been at the scene, and no more than one or two would remember Mia. Almost as if she didn't merit a second glance. Neither her posture nor the blank look on her face betrayed her emotions. Shock? It was a shock to them all, Lucius decided, but Mia was a closed book. Fragile? No, he decided. She had long ago come to terms with herself. One of a group, never the focal point.

He smiled as he spotted Shanicha. Also average height, but with baby-smooth ebony skin, every bit as dark as his. Her hair, styled differently every few days, was now tied in a ponytail and wet. The different ways she wore her hair utterly changed her appearance. There were times, at first, when he thought the girl passing him was Shanicha's sister visiting her on campus.

She wore a bathrobe and probably nothing underneath, he thought. She must have been taking a shower, but she wouldn't have missed the action for the world. She made her way through the still-gathering throng. She appeared jazzed, almost predatory, he thought, devouring every comment, yet not uttering a word of her own. The next day, she'd be talking up a storm, though. She didn't hang out with any one group, but seemed to be everywhere.

His girls. But they were all his girls. He got close with

20

the guys, but they seemed less vulnerable than the females. The boys would boast of their conquests, but it was the girls who would share their innermost fears with him. And now one, Sharon Ingster, lay like a broken sparrow. He took her death as a personal defeat. It should never have come to this. She should have sought him out. *He* should have known she was in peril.

Some girls were in tears. He was no shrink, but Lucius thought those were in less danger than a number of others who were subdued, even awestruck by the prone figure lying before them.

Some of these kids might glorify the finality of Sharon's final statement to the world, he thought. Sharon no longer had to study. No longer had to make herself look attractive to get a date. No longer had to please her parents. No longer had to decide whether to give in to boys looking to get into her pants. A way out others might consider. The thought made him shudder.

Now Ariel approached. Lucius, at six-foot-two, was not much taller than she. He felt like he'd been in a time warp. Even after eight years, neither one had changed much.

He was dark-skinned and heavyset. Not fat, but he had a big frame. He kept in shape. Had to. In the Philadelphia Police Department you could let your body go to flab, but patrolling the campus daily, an out-of-shape officer would quickly lose the respect of college kids; become the butt of whispered jokes and barbs.

When he'd begun to lose his hair, a few years before, he'd shaved his head à la Michael Jordan and Charles Barkley. The style was in vogue. He feared it made him appear intimidating and unapproachable; someone else for college kids to fear. But, surprisingly, the girls in particular found him cuddly; possibly because of the engaging smile he flashed eagerly and often. A good listener, he quickly gained their confidence.

21

His mind focused on Ariel. Statuesque, even in jeans and a denim shirt, tied in a knot at her stomach. She looked more like a college coed than a thirty-four-year-old homicide detective. A *white* coed, her face the color of bone; someone who'd been at the beach three or four days earlier, whose tan was rapidly fading. Flashlights that crisscrossed illuminated her long wavy hair. Not quite black, but the darkest of browns, with a hint of red in just the right light. A curl hung down each side of her face, at her ears. She exuded sensuality and self-confidence, which he imagined still hid her deeply rooted insecurities. A beautiful *white* woman, possibly Italian: Few who didn't know her realized she was *black*. That she didn't consider herself black—nor white for that matter—had destroyed their marriage.

Deny it as he might, she was a sight for sore eyes.

Chapter Three

You're a professional, Ariel, she told herself as she neared Lucius, so act like one. Get the information you need to close this fucking case, and hope something juicy lands on your plate tomorrow. Don't get personal. Don't let your emotions take over.

Don't let your emotions take over.

Don't . . .

Before Ariel could speak, Lucius did.

"I knew her," he said.

"Sharon Ingster? You fucking her, Lucius?" she heard herself ask. Well, she thought, there goes the best-laid plans, and all that shit. Now that she'd opened the can of worms, there was no turning back.

"I thought time heals all wounds," Lucius answered, shaking his head. "Guess you're still bitter."

"You didn't answer my question."

"I don't sleep with white women," he said bitterly.

It had been meant to hurt her, but Ariel wasn't easily intimidated.

"You slept with *me* for three years," she shot back.

"Not the white you."

Ariel smiled derisively. "The same old Lucius. In your dreams you slept with your Nubian Princess. In reality you slept with me—the black me *and* the white me. You can't have one without the other, sorry to say."

Lucius raised his hands in resignation. "I'm not getting into a pissing contest with you, Ariel. I never cheated on you when we were married, so this shit about sleeping with Sharon Ingster is uncalled for."

"You looked, though. Black, white, green. See a pretty face, nice tits and a pert ass, and you were color-blind."

"Still am. And I *still* look. But never touched any then, and never would now. My job—no, my *career*'s too important to me. Don't be laying your insecurities on me."

Ariel began to respond. Though she'd said it often enough, she had never really thought Lucius had ever been unfaithful. She had been—shit, she still was—insecure, and with ample justification. But her suspicions hadn't been what had led to their divorce. It was her color—or lack of it, to be more precise, and *his* insecurities that made divorce inevitable.

Eight years later, she thought, and they were still rehashing that same tired argument, as if they'd never been apart.

Stop it, she told herself. Stop it and do your job.

"I don't want to argue with you, Lucius," she said instead.

He raised his eyebrows in disbelief, and she laughed.

"Well, maybe I do. I've got a lot of pent-up resentment,

23

but let's not get into that pissing contest you mentioned. Can you help me close this case?"

"How about we go for a walk. It's a bit too public here, with all your lab technicians and uniforms traipsing around."

His voice was husky. Could be commanding, even intimidating, Ariel knew. But now he was asking, not trying to bully her.

They walked a short distance to a statue in what he said was the Baby Quad, and Lucius calmly shooed away a few students who had gathered there.

"You were always more ambitious than me," he started. "You're a better cop. . . ."

He held up a hand when she tried to interrupt.

"You *are* a better cop. I'm a people person, Ariel. Left the force because it was too impersonal. Here, I get to know the kids. I'm not a faceless policeman coming on a scene only *after* a crime's committed."

He paused.

"What are you trying to say, Lucius?" she asked, as if seeing him for the first time.

"I'm telling you why I know the Sharon Ingsters of this campus intimately, without having to sleep with them. Why I'm partially responsible for her death."

"You've got my attention."

"I'm not just a campus cop, Ariel, is what I'm saying. I'm a social worker. A priest. A friend." He laughed. "Don't be looking at me like I'm crazy. It's difficult to put into words. I'm not here to enforce the law. Don't get me wrong. *I do*."

She looked at him, confused.

"Talking in riddles. I know. Look, let me give you an example. Couple of weeks ago we caught some kid sneaking into other kids' rooms stealing CDs, watches, cassette tape recorders. Could have, maybe should have, turned him over to you guys for prosecution. But the guy's a freshman with problems. Counseling's what he needed, not a police record.

Born Bad

So we came to an understanding. He's getting the help he needs, he's still a student in good standing, yet he knows he steps out of line again and he's history."

He took out a piece of gum, offered it to Ariel, who politely refused, and popped it in his mouth.

"Can't smoke around them," he said. "Sets a bad example. Gotta have something in my mouth, though."

"I'm impressed," she said, and when she saw his skepticism, added, "Really. You're not just giving me the U. of P. line. You believe it. And I *am* impressed."

He smiled, then went on. "The freshman are the most vulnerable, like that boy I was telling you about. For good reason they're naturally wary of cops. Their contact with the police has been mostly adversarial. I have to show them we're not to be feared. We're here to protect them. To guide them. We try to intercede *before* they've gone too far. You know, before they're entrapped in the criminal justice system.

"I let them know they can bend my ear, if the spirit moves them, and what they say goes no further. Look around, Ariel. This is my principal domain—The Quad."

As she looked at the three- or four-block row of dark brownstone buildings, Lucius told Ariel that most of the freshmen spent their first year in The Quad. Each room with windows ten feet high. Many were open. In some places the buildings rose three floors; in others four. Sharon Ingster had plunged from a fourth-story window.

"Did she?" Ariel asked.

"Did she what?"

"Bend your ear?"

"Not at first. She spent a lot of time the first semester out here on the grass, under this statue, as a matter of fact. Kids here stake out their own territory—here at The Quad, at Houston Hall, on Campus Green, Locust Walk, at sororities or frats. This was Sharon's turf. Usually alone, but sometimes

25

with a few others. She wasn't a loner, first semester, but she wasn't Miss Congeniality either."

"But she did open up to you." It wasn't a question.

Lucius looked at her suspiciously.

"Hey," she said, "I'm not implying anything improper. Looks like I'm not the only one who's overly sensitive," she said with a smile.

"Sorry." He shrugged. "With you, it's a habit to question your tone." He paused. "Yeah, she opened up . . . a bit. Her mother—Vicki or Victoria—wore the pants in the family. Leastways, when it came to child-rearing. Pops worked, came home to a few beers, a good home-cooked meal, and then adjourned to the tube. Sharon's mother had everything all planned out for Sharon and her sisters."

"How many sisters?" Ariel asked.

"Four. Three older. Two had gone to a local college within driving distance. Graduated, married and began raising a brood of children. That was the plan for Sharon. Only, she applied here on the sly and got in. Got an attractive financial aid package, and wouldn't be talked out of leaving the homestead."

"No cause for suicide, though," Ariel said.

"Not in and of itself. But her mother never accepted her betrayal. Wrote her these poison-pen letters. Called her every name in the book. Really venomous stuff."

"She showed them to you." Again, not a question.

"One. Before she even opened it. It was three or four days after a heated argument they'd had over the phone. She gets this letter and won't open it. Gave it to me and her hands were shaking. Told me to read it to myself. If it was really horrible, she said, just put it back in the envelope. It was. I did, and she burst into tears."

"Did she keep the letters?"

"If I say yes, you'll ask how I know . . ."

"You went into her room before we came," Ariel said,

interrupting. "I know you, Lucius. You may practice and believe in this New Age crap . . ."

He began to protest, but Ariel stopped him.

"Sorry. Figure of speech. No matter what you believe, I know you to be a cop at heart. Fuck protocol. You went into her room. So what? I won't tell, if you don't. Now what about the letters?"

"In a shoe box under her bed. Dozens. I didn't read any. I'd seen one, and that was enough. But I could tell she'd read them more than once. There were dried tearstains on some."

"So, to get back at her mother, she takes a plunge?"

"I don't think it was as simple as that. As I said, she opened up. I think she eventually came to terms with the letters. She toughed it out and got decent marks first semester—mostly *C*'s with a few *B*'s. But she proved she could hack it here."

"So why the belly flop?"

"With winter there is less contact with the kids. But I'd bump into her. Last five, six weeks I noticed a change. I'd say hello. She'd reply weakly, head down, and rush off like she had something to hide. Something *had* happened, and I didn't pursue it. I thought there might have been an incident at home during semester break, but I let it slide. That's why I blame myself."

"You're not a social worker, Lucius, and you're not a shrink."

"But I sensed a problem and let it pass. Something at home, or that time of month, I thought, or just the winter blahs." He shrugged.

"She the only one who exhibits strange mood swings?"

"Course not."

"You help all the others, whether they want it or not," she said.

"Point taken," he said with a weak smile.

27

"Bottom line, then, was she suicidal?"

"Until the past six weeks, no. When she clammed up, I don't know. It's a sign. An indicator of depression. Yeah, she was capable."

"Suicide note?"

Lucius looked at her. "You ask about a suicide note, I say yes and my career's in your hands. I don't know if I want that."

"If it's there, my partner will find it. I want *your* insight as to its authenticity. Was it her note or someone else's handiwork? And don't be petty," she added, shaking her head in exasperation. "Look, Lucius, whatever our problems, I never took it to work when we were married. Never back-stabbed you."

"Sorry. You know I don't mean it," he said, and paused. "Yeah, next to her desk are one, maybe two dozen balled-up letters. Flawed attempts to explain what she planned to do. On her desk a short note." He took out a small notebook and read from it.

Fuck it. I'm a screw-up. Can't even express myself the way I want. I'm sorry, but it's for the best.

He closed the book. "Never should have come to this, Ariel. She was a sweet kid. Never should have come to this."

Ariel put a hand on his shoulder. "I'm sorry, Lucius. No bullshit. You've changed. Least in some ways. Changed for the better."

He looked into her eyes with just the trace of a smile. "Least in some ways."

She gave his shoulder a squeeze and let go. Snapped her fingers, remembering something she'd meant to ask. "Shit, do you know where I can find her roommate?"

Lucius scanned the crowd, which had grown considerably. He pointed. "See the girl with the green pea coat? The one

28

with the scraggly dude draped over her? Kelly Lewis."

From his tone, Ariel didn't think Lucius approved of the couple.

She turned to leave, then turned back again. She didn't quite know the words, but gave it a try anyway. "I'm sorry about your wife, Lucius. I heard she was good people. I . . ." She'd run out of words. Then. "If *you* want to talk—not about us—just need someone to talk to, call me. I mean it. I'm not just trying to be polite."

Before he could answer, she turned and trudged off to get Kelly Lewis's spin on her roommie.

Chapter Four

Kelly Lewis didn't look particularly broken up by her room-mate's death, Ariel noted as she took the measure of the girl. From her complacency, she could have been watching a parade, her boyfriend in tow squeezing one of her formidable braless breasts.

Ariel noted that breasts were Kelly's chief physical endowment. But she certainly wouldn't be auditioning for *Playboy*'s University of Pennsylvania college coed issue. Her face was long and narrow, like Silly Putty stretched to its limits. Her prominent chin reminded Ariel of Jay Leno. She wore no makeup to mask an ashen complexion adorned with zits; so many that they might be mistaken for a severe case of chicken pox. Her stringy dirty-blond hair—dirty both in color and in need of a shampoo—hung limply. She wore oversized jeans and a T-shirt several sizes too large, which almost, but

Barry Hoffman

not quite, obscured her large breasts. Her eyes showed no emotion whatsoever.

Her boyfriend could have been her brother in appearance. At a little over six feet, he towered over his woman, but the shape of his face, hair and complexion were almost identical. Like a leech, his hand seemed permanently attached to the girl's breast, his fingers kneading her nipple. Kelly, however, seemed oblivious.

Ariel unceremoniously flipped her shield and introduced herself curtly. After Ariel asked for some privacy, her boyfriend reluctantly shrugged and peeled himself away. Kelly starred impassively at Ariel, a slight pout on her lips, as she scratched her now-vacated nipple.

"You broken up by your roommate's death, or relieved to have the room to yourself?" Ariel asked. She had learned to ask the unexpected to keep witnesses and suspects off balance. Knowing they'd be interviewed by a cop, most had rehearsed responses to imagined questions. Her haphazard, brazen and often random line of questioning reduced the effectiveness of prepared answers. Kelly Lewis was clearly caught off guard by Ariel's approach.

"What's that supposed to mean?" she asked in a high-pitched squeaky voice.

"The two of you tight, is what I mean, or did a computer match you up?"

The girl shrugged indifferently. "We're both freshmen. We don't choose our roommates. We got along okay, but we weren't bosom buddies."

"She get along with her parents?" Ariel asked, abruptly changing the subject, like a rabbit eluding a fox.

"Her mother was a bitch," the girl answered with just a trace of emotion. "Sent her letters which made her cry."

"Who'd she hang with?"

"Nobody—leastways not since she broke up with her boyfriend."

30

Now it was Ariel's turn to be surprised. "What boyfriend?"

"Wayne. You know, like in *Wayne's World*—the movie. Wayne Fontes."

"Were they sleeping together?"

Kelly giggled and unconsciously touched one of her zits. "Sharon and Wayne in bed together; that would be a sight. Wayne *wanted* to get in her pants, but Sharon was saving herself for Mr. Right. *Saving herself*—those where her words. She didn't talk much about her sex life. Considered it coarse and unladylike." Kelly mimicked her roommate with disapproval.

"They broke up because Wayne tried to cop a feel once too often," Kelly added.

"This a surprise to you?" Ariel asked, pointing to the body of the girl's roommate, covered by a yellow tarp.

"She hadn't been herself lately." Kelly surprised Ariel with some insight. "She cried a lot, for no real reason at all, and wouldn't talk about it. Stopped opening her mother's letters. Starting cutting classes for the first time. Had trouble sleeping. She'd be sitting in her chair when I'd get in at night, and be sitting there when I woke up in the morning. Spooky stuff."

"She confide in you about *anything*?"

"Not after Wayne dumped her. She retreated into herself." Kelly smiled. "Heard that in a movie once, and been aching to use it myself."

Then her face clouded over.

"Got so bad I'd get down just being around her. Last month or so we were like ships passing in the night." She smiled again.

"Heard that in a movie, too, right?" Ariel asked, beating the girl to the punch.

"Yeah. Ships passing in the night. That was us. She'd come in after class, and I'd vacate the premises."

"She drink or use drugs?"

31

Barry Hoffman

The question seemed to amuse the girl, as she giggled again.

"Sharon was a real straight arrow," she said when she'd recovered. "Warned me . . ." She stopped abruptly, as if suddenly remembering she was talking to a cop.

"I'm not out to make trouble for you, Kelly," Ariel said soothingly. "Don't hold back on me, though," she said with the hint of a threat.

Kelly shrugged. She seemed to do that a lot, Ariel thought. Kind of like a nervous tic.

"I *experimented*. Hey, that's what college is all about," she said, playing with a zit on her nose.

"And Sharon?"

"Preached about the dangers of alcohol and drugs. Look, just between the two of us, I think she was more like her mother than she would have liked to admit. Didn't even drink coffee. Only hot chocolate and soda, and *that* had to be caffeine-free. Honest."

"What about the last time you saw her? How was she?"

"Brooding."

"When was that?"

"This morning. She was in her chair. Brooding. I got dressed, split for class and went out with my boyfriend after. I just got back."

"Anything else that will help me get a handle on her?"

Kelly scrunched up her face in concentration, then found another zit on her chin to examine with her fingers. "Can't think of anything."

Ariel gave her a card with her office number on it. "Something comes to mind, give me a call, okay?"

"Sure. Look, uh . . ." She seemed unsure of herself. "I don't mean to sound insensitive, but like, do you know when I can get back to my room? I mean, I can find another room to crash for the night," she rushed on, "but I've got some books I need. . . ."

32

"And a change of clothes would be nice," Ariel finished for her.

"Yeah. Sure. That, too," Kelly said, but Ariel had the feeling she could care less about a change of clothes.

"It's best if you find somewhere else to stay for the night. Soon as we're done with the room, though, I'll make sure you can get your books, a change of clothes—whatever you need."

Ariel asked Kelly to come down to the station the next day to give an official statement, thanked her, then went off to find her partner. Unless Lucius had overlooked something—and this she doubted—Sharon Ingster's death appeared to be just what Doug Thiery would have wanted: a clear-cut suicide with no loose ends.

Chapter Five

Her partner couldn't have been happier with Ariel's report. He had a suicide note, along with dozens of aborted attempts scattered across the dead girl's floor. Sharon Ingster was clearly a disturbed young woman. And there was the recent breakup with her boyfriend; the final blow to the woman's fragile psyche. It all fit like a preschool jigsaw puzzle. Doug was beside himself. Another case put to bed; better yet, in less than two hours.

Ariel cautioned him. "Let's wait on the toxicology, okay? We don't want egg on our face, just to set a new land-speed record."

"Of course," Doug agreed, but she could tell he was miffed.

"One more thing," she said. "Could you ask the ME to check if she was a virgin?"

"Why?" was all her befuddled partner could respond.

"Humor me, Doug. It lends credibility to the roommate's story. She's a bit of a weird duck. I'd like the confirmation."

"If it makes you happy. But *only* if I get to drive back to the station *without* you smoking."

Ariel pinched her partner's cheek. "What I give up for you."

Chapter Six

The crowd began to disperse when the police removed Sharon's body. Not wanting to draw attention to herself, Shanicha reluctantly left. She felt like the power behind the throne, and self-satisfaction at the influence she wielded was far more significant than appearances.

She'd been in the midst of a shower when news of Sharon's plunge spread, and Shanicha still felt dirty. As she lathered—the shower to herself—she replayed the events of the evening.

Satisfying, so very satisfying.

Almost as if she had orchestrated what had occurred. She laughed. *She had,* no almosts about it.

Just as when she was eleven, at the fires, now she couldn't get enough of the crowd reaction. Talking about Sharon. About themselves. But really talking about *her*. Everyone was talking.

"I hardly knew her. Such a waste, though . . ."

". . . goose bumps. I mean we've all got problems."

34

Born Bad

". . . thought about it once, but to *actually* do it . . ."

They'd be talking about it for days, Shanicha knew. About Sharon. Really, though, about *her*. If only they knew. To be able to convince someone to take her own life. Such incredible power. Such a shame to remain silent. To be able to share the knowledge would have been the ultimate high, but she wouldn't get carried away. Never had. No letters to the police or newspapers. No cryptic clues. Getting away with murder was its own reward.

The hot water flushed the suds from her breasts. Rid herself of the sweat, dirt and grime . . .

—And the spiders.

She lathered her genitals. One couldn't be too clean. She'd learned to take her customary forty-five-minute showers either before others awoke, or late at night. She didn't care that others would bitch she was hoarding all the hot water. She just didn't want to draw attention to herself. Be part of the woodwork, was what it was all about; a fly on the wall. There, but unnoticed. The unseen hand that makes the puppets dance to *her* tune.

Showers were essential, though—two, and sometimes three a day . . .

—Her smell would attract them, and their loathsome webs.

. . . but she couldn't be viewed as neurotic or obsessive.

She had sought out Sharon Ingster for the explicit purpose of convincing her to kill herself. Her motive? For kicks. Simple as that. To see if she could pull it off. She had always been a manipulator. But to convince someone to take her own life—it didn't get better than that.

She had finally found Sharon, and others like her, at group counseling sessions for the clinically depressed. Their common denominator? All had been victims of acquaintance rape. At the hourly sessions, held two times a week, each of the six participants spilled her guts, when she felt comfortable. Shanicha had fabricated a story, but made it seem she wasn't yet prepared to bare her soul. She was allowed to indulge herself in silence.

She quickly focused on Sharon as being the most vulnerable. Sharon had told them about her overbearing mother, who could never be placated. If she came home late on one of her infrequent dates in high school, she was accused of promiscuity. If she hung with girls, she was a lesbian. She tearfully read some of her mother's letters, letters always harping on Sharon's inadequacies, and comparing her unfavorably to her older sisters.

Weeks before, Sharon had talked about how upset she'd been when Wayne dumped her for not putting out.

"I wanted to get back at him," she'd told the group. She had gone out with his best friend to hurt him, but found they had nothing in common.

"I had to see the date through." She tried to make them understand. "Wayne had to know I was . . . I don't know." She paused in thought. "*Desirable*. That's the word. Desirable to others. We were at a party and he offered me some punch. I knew it was spiked with alcohol, but it tasted so sweet—like fruit juice. Pretty soon, I was wasted. I must have dozed off, 'cause next thing I know I'm in a bedroom at the house, and I'm half-naked. He was sucking my breast," she said, her arms unconsciously covering her bosom as she described what had happened; her eyes closed, as if fearful of the rebuke she'd see in the other's eyes.

"I told him to stop, but it was like he didn't hear me. He slid his hand up my dress, into . . ." She stopped, and began rocking back and forth, wracked by sobs. Finally, she was able to continue.

"No one, no one, *no one* had ever touched me there before.

36

I was so ashamed. Not just because I felt violated, but . . . I liked it," she said just above a whisper. "God help me, but I liked it. I had such conflicting emotions."

She opened her eyes. The others were shaking their heads or nodding in *sympathy*. She smiled, as if an awful load had been lifted, then rushed on.

"I let him undress me. No more protests. Then he took his clothes off and made me touch him. No," she said, shaking her head, as if recalling the exact moment. "Didn't *force* me to touch him. Guided me. It was like an out-of-body experience. I was doing things that repulsed me, but *I was doing them willingly*. But I didn't ask to be raped. When he first tried to"—she again seemed to search for the appropriate words—"uh . . . enter me, it was like a slap in the face. Up to then I admit I hadn't protested—except at the very beginning. But I didn't want to be . . . be *fucked*. I tried to push him away, but it only turned him on more. 'Fight me baby. That's it.' He thought I was toying with him—playing some coy game. You know, 'No, no, don't,' when I meant, 'Yes, yes, fuck me.' "

A few of the others girls uttered their assent, like they'd all been through it themselves. Most of them thought they had, Shanicha realized.

"Before I could get him to understand, he was in me," Sharon continued. "A few seconds later he . . . ejaculated. *He raped me*," she yelled, "but it was my fault," she said quietly, winding down. "My fault. My fault. My fault."

During the rest of the session, the other girls told her it *wasn't* her fault. *No meant no,* whether in regard to foreplay, or all the way up to the act itself.

Gibberish, thought Shanicha. While no slut, she was no novice either. She didn't necessarily enjoy sex, but she didn't *not* enjoy it either. But it didn't rule her life, like so many others she knew. And those that didn't do it *talked* about doing it almost nonstop.

Barry Hoffman

But when she got down and dirty with some guy, she knew there was a point of no return. You can't expect to turn guys their age on and off like a faucet. Inertia, if nothing else, took over at some point. She likened it to a roller coaster. Once it reached the top, there was no turning back. To expect a guy to respond to foreplay, then stop in the midst of the act itself, was akin to stopping the roller coaster on its descent. It was absurd to blame the guy; to call it rape.

But Shanicha fawned on Sharon with all the others.

After each session, the girls all went their separate ways; as if purposely avoiding one another. *I can't be seen with her. They might know she was raped. Then they'd know I was raped, too.*

That night, though, four weeks earlier, Shanicha followed discreetly behind and with the others out of sight, she caught up with Sharon.

"Are you sure you're okay?" Shanicha asked. "I'm worried about you."

"That's sweet, but I *had* to get it out. Everyone was just so supportive, I'm beginning to believe I can put this behind me. Come to terms with it, you know."

"But what happens when you turn the lights off tonight," Shanicha asked. "He'll be back, won't he?"

"How do you . . ." she started, then slapped her palm on her head. "I was going to ask how you knew. What a schmuck. You've *been* through it. You know what it's like when the lights go off." She shuddered.

Shanicha knew Sharon's roommate almost fled the room whenever Sharon was there. Since the rape, Sharon had closed herself off from everyone—except the group at counseling. Shanicha had heard Kelly Lewis bitching about life lately with Sharon.

"Like a fucking zombie, sitting in that goddamn chair. There when I go to sleep. There when I wake up. She comes in, I'm outta there."

38

It was just what Shanicha was looking for. Someone who'd be alone, where her presence wouldn't be noted.

"We should talk," Shanicha told Sharon. "I mean, if you want to. Maybe keep the ghosts at bay a bit longer."

Sharon had smiled, said her roommate left as soon as she got back and, yes, she'd like to talk.

And Shanicha knew all the buttons to push. Three weeks ago she had first broached suicide with talk about past-life memories.

"It doesn't all end with death, Sharon. I don't believe in heaven or hell. But I believe in coming back."

"Get out," Sharon said.

"Don't mock me," Shanicha said, with just the right amount of hurt.

"I'm sorry. It's just so . . . I don't know. Farfetched. Yeah, just so way out there."

"Maybe, but think about it. Most people call it déjà vu. A place they recognize. A conversation they swear they already had. At times I find myself looking at books I've picked out of the library at random. Books about places I've never been. And I'll see a picture and say, 'I've been there.' Sometimes, I can almost grasp someone lurking inside my mind saying, '*We were there*.' "

"Get out." This time there was awe in Sharon's voice.

Slowly, Shanicha drew a picture of possibilities for Sharon. Suicide isn't the end. Just a jumping-off point for a new beginning. In their case a *better* life.

She was subtle. No pushing or prodding. After all, the fun was getting there. Driving them to the abyss. Sharon's death would be anticlimactic, and would provide little exhilaration. The thrill, the *challenge,* was stealing Sharon's will. Making her putty in Shanicha's hands.

"Jump, Sharon."

"How high?"

"Roll over. Fetch. Play dead."

And in her mind, Sharon would comply. It was better than sex. Taking a shower, after, she'd replay how compliant Sharon had become and achieve orgasm. Rewind and play it again, while lathering with soap, and come again.

That evening, at the counseling session, Sharon had provided the final missing piece.

The girls had been talking about sibling jealousy. Sharon had been unusually reserved. Then out of the blue, interrupting another girl, as if she weren't there, Sharon bitterly tore into her older sister Mary.

"I saw Mary with another girl. A week before her marriage."

The room grew still.

"She and her best friend were in her room. The door was open a crack. No one else was home. I was supposed to be at the library, but I'd fallen asleep reading a homework assignment. Woke up to some giggling. I was going to their room to ask if they wanted some pop.

"Through the crack, I saw them on the bed naked. Sitting up, gently touching one another. My *perfect* sister. The one my mother lauded over me. 'Mary pulls her own weight. She gets good grades, yet holds down a job and gives her earnings to the family.' She was pretty. I was plain. She was an athlete. I was a klutz. Her friends were so considerate. 'Well, guess what, Mother,' I could hear myself telling my mom, 'your precious Mary and one of her considerate friends *are playing with each other*.' "

Sharon paused, wiping a tear from her eye.

"I should have been repulsed. Should have burst right in and told them to stop. Or I should have run away. But I was fascinated. And, God forgive me, I was turned on. I watched, transfixed. For forty-five minutes. Maybe more, until I heard my mother's car pulling into the driveway. They heard it, too." She shrugged. "A week later, Mary was married."

Sharon went silent for a few moments.

"I don't know what was worse," she finally added. "Seeing what my sister did or being aroused by it. I mean, what did it make me? I had dreams. Not often, and not just then—but all the way up until the rape—that I was with my sister. And who was I supposed to confide in? My mother? A guidance counselor? A friend? What if she turned on me. So I kept it bottled in, until now."

For the rest of the session the psychologist tried to peel the guilt from Sharon. The other girls all commiserated. One or two even admitted to homosexual fantasies of their own.

Bullshit, Shanicha had thought. All bullshit. If one of the girls said she was visited by an alien, some of the others would say, they, too, had had such an encounter. The sharing was so cathartic. Bonding. They were bonding, which would lead to healing. Well, if the counseling was so cathartic, Shanicha thought, why did they all traipse in looking so miserable each session? This baring and sharing and bonding were like opiates. Lasted a while, then you hit rock bottom again. Had to come back for another fix to get you through the week.

Shanicha, though, now had what she needed. Sharon was beginning to bore her. Poor child. Mother a bitch; sister a bit kinky; Sharon fucked so she could no longer save herself for her true love. Sharon felt guilty, all right. Guilty because she enjoyed it. Fucked, *not* raped. Admit it and she could get on with her life. But she wouldn't. The bitch actually felt better being miserable, feeling sorry for herself.

At least she had a mother, Shanicha thought. A *real* family. A home where you didn't have to worry about dodging the stray bullets of rival drug dealers.

Shanicha now had the key to Sharon Ingster. For weeks now she had nudged Sharon toward the precipice. Tonight, she'd push her over.

After the counseling session, the two girls went about their usual routine. Shanicha went to her room and waited. Within

41

ten minutes, her phone rang once. *Their signal*. Sharon was alone.

Sharon was sobbing in her chair when Shanicha entered. She was pretty, Shanicha thought—for a white girl. She was big-boned, but not fat, with a nice set of jugs. It was no wonder Wayne so insistently tried to cop a feel. Her face was a little too round, her blue eyes a bit too large. Her short brown hair could have used a bit of styling. She was no knockout, but with some makeup to give her face some color and clothes that accentuated her more favorable attributes, boys would be lining up to date her.

Shanicha sat on Sharon's bed, and beckoned to the girl.

"I'm so ashamed," Sharon said, sitting stiffly next to her friend. "I don't know what got into me. All of a sudden it came out, like I had no control. Do you think, I don't know . . . that I'm some kind of freak?"

Shanicha put her arm around Sharon's shoulder, and drew her close. "Such a silly girl. Why would I think you're a freak." She stroked Sharon's face with her hand, and gently kissed her on the lips. Sharon didn't draw back, and Shanicha smiled to herself. She kissed her again, this time using her tongue. Again, Sharon responded in kind.

She unbuttoned Sharon's top and unhooked her bra. Gently she caressed the girl's breasts, kissed them and let her tongue dance around her nipples.

Sharon's breathing quickened. She yanked at her skirt, while Shanicha's fingers pinched her other nipple; just hard enough to make Sharon sigh. Sharon began to remove her panties, but Shanicha stopped her.

"No, let me."

With Sharon's panties off, Shanicha's fingers probed her genitals. With each tentative touch, she could feel Sharon getting worked up to a fever pitch.

Then Sharon sought Shanicha's breasts.

42

Yes! Shanicha said to herself, and drew back from the other girl.

"What's wrong?" Sharon said.

"I'm not like that."

"Like what?"

Shanicha could hear fear creeping into Sharon's voice.

"I don't want to be touched."

"You mean by anyone, because of what happened to you, right?"

A bit of panic there, Shanicha thought.

"No. Not by a girl."

"But you kissed me. Touched me." She seemed to suddenly realize she was naked, and covered herself with a pillow. Her voice was tinged with hysteria.

"It's what I thought you wanted," Shanicha said calmly, "to make you feel better."

"You think I'm a lesbian!" she said, shaking her head. "I'm not. I just got caught up. . . ." She broke off, and with her arms cradling the pillow, began silently swaying back and forth; withdrawing into herself.

"I'm sorry. I misunderstood," Shanicha said. "Of course you're not a lesbian." She mouthed the words, but gave them no feeling. "Look, I better be going. We'll talk, though. Tomorrow. We'll talk. Okay?"

Sharon said nothing. Just rocked back and forth.

Shanicha made sure no one was in the hall as she left. She most definitely needed a shower. It was a bit early, but she had to get Sharon off her.

She had been showering twenty, maybe twenty-five minutes when all hell broke loose. She put on her robe. What could it be? Tiffany Green bumped into her as she came out of the girls' room.

"What's all the fuss about?"

"Someone jumped."

What a shame, Shanicha thought. Wonder who it was. She laughed to herself.

Now, as Shanicha lathered, she saw in her mind's eye Sharon sprawled on the concrete below; dressed in her Sunday best. Shanicha's body wracked as she came. Shaking, as she reached orgasm again, she focused her eyes on the girl's shattered face. And one last time, as first one girl screamed, then a second, then what seemed like a chorus of horrified shrieks.

Music to her ears.

Chapter Seven

Back at the Roundhouse, the department's central headquarters, which housed the homicide unit, one of the detectives on the night shift told Ariel and Doug their Sergeant wanted to see them.

It didn't surprise Ariel that Russ McGowan was still in his office an hour and a half after his shift had ended. Promoted six months earlier, he was an upwardly mobile kiss-ass, satisfy-his-superiors-at-any-cost political animal. He made no secret of the fact his stay would not be lengthy—a year, eighteen months max—then he fully expected to make Lieutenant. And from there . . . one could fill in the blanks. He had the pulse of the department; a managerial style that endeared him to the brass; and he was smooth, good-looking and media-friendly. The whole package—*superficially*.

What galled Ariel was the man wasn't overly competent. He could network with the best of them, though, she had to grudgingly admit. He spewed forth the latest law enforcement jargon at the drop of a hat, and read voraciously to impress his superiors with his knowledge of the most recent developments in procedure and technology in the field. Moreover, he was glib, able to maneuver his way out of what for others would be the most embarrassing of setbacks. A Teflon man; he always found a fall guy, so nothing stuck to him.

Once in command, he had quickly jettisoned most of his predecessor's unit, replacing them with officers loyal to him. Loyal not out of respect, but because they knew he was going places and their advancement was dependent on his goodwill. If you didn't kiss McGowan's more-than-ample ass, he'd most assuredly come back to haunt you, as he had a razor-sharp memory, especially when it came to holding a grudge.

Ariel would have been long gone if she hadn't been the lone female in the unit. A *black* female, no less. It was not yet politically expedient to get rid of her.

She held him in contempt because he was so manipulative and didn't give a fuck about those who served under him. Her responsibility, he made it clear, was to advance *his* career. "Get with the program," was his credo. Russ McGowan's program was clearance. Get a case, solve it and do so quickly. If an incompetent Assistant District Attorney couldn't convict, it was no hair off his ass. He'd done his job. Someone else had screwed up and would have to be held accountable. That, if allowed more time, a stronger case, built on supporting evidence, could guarantee conviction didn't mean squat to him. Clear the case and go on to the next. If an ADA demanded more, he'd get it. Those who didn't were left to their own devices.

Even the late hours McGowan put in were due more to inefficiency than dedication. He attended so many conferences, and spent so much time on the phone networking and kissing ass, he *had* to stay late just to keep up with the paperwork.

Unfortunately, Russ McGowan embodied the management style currently in vogue. He would get his promotions, and the department would be worse off for it, Ariel thought.

Ariel, though, had no desire to impress the Russ McGowans of the department. Unbeknownst to her superior, Ariel was where she wanted to be—in homicide. It had taken an often arduous twelve years. She had paid her dues, and then some, but she had no desire for further advancement. The next rung up was supervisory and Ariel was no administrator. She wanted hands-on work; cases from the mundane suicides and domestic homicides that bored her to the infrequent mysteries that proved so challenging.

As long as she did her job—even if not quite the way or with the speed her Sergeant demanded—she wouldn't have to kowtow to anyone. And, while being a woman had definite drawbacks in the still-chauvinistic police department, it had the advantage of guaranteeing her employment as long as she could take the shit dished out.

Doug wanted to make a beeline for McGowan as soon as he heard they were wanted. Ariel was in no hurry.

"I've gotta pee," she told him. "Cool your heels for a few minutes," she instructed, and left him without waiting for a response.

Even after two months teamed with her, Ariel was well aware that Doug was still uncomfortable working with a female. At the beginning, he would open their squad car door for her, and insisted on doing all the driving. He treated her as he did his wife—with courtesy; civility owed her as a *woman*. That she found such treatment degrading never seemed to dawn on him.

To make matters worse, she couldn't tolerate his driving. Doug slowed at every yellow light; stopped completely at every stop sign and *never* exceeded the posted speed limit. His sense of direction was also for shit. More than once he'd gotten lost—in Center City, no less.

Ariel had exploited one of his many weaknesses to get the reins of the car. A nonstop talker while driving, he'd once gone on a ten-minute monologue about how much smokers irritated him.

"Had a partner once was so bad I had to keep two extra changes of clothes in my locker. Come back from a call and had to stick what I was wearing in a plastic bag . . ."

Ariel had stopped smoking two years earlier, but to gain control of the car, she'd started again. Doug had tried everything to persuade her to stop; haranguing her on the evils of smoking; leaving pamphlets with picture of blackened lungs in her locker; running the air conditioner in the winter. Finally, they'd struck a bargain. When she drove, she wouldn't smoke. She feared her sometimes reckless driving might irritate him more than her smoking, but while he'd close his eyes as she drove through a yellow-changing-to-red, he had held his tongue.

Another small battle won.

Now telling him she had to pee, which in fact she did, left him flummoxed. As if taking a leak was a woman's thing.

In homicide, there was no separate locker room for the lone woman in the squad. While in uniform she'd had to change in a closet—literally; one that had been assigned to her with a straight face and good intentions. What they didn't understand was their effort to afford her privacy was another form of exclusion. Relationships form in locker rooms, and information is disseminated. The advantages of being with her colleagues in the locker room far outweighed her lack of privacy.

One day she'd knocked on the locker room door, asked if everyone was decent and walked in. She chose an unused locker and stripped off her uniform; clad only in a bra and panties with a dozen eyes fixed on her. She'd turned and confronted them.

"Fuck, you see more skin on the beach. Grieve, if you

want, but from now on this is *my* locker room, too, whether you like it or not."

One uniform, Chavez, shrugged and stripped down to his jockeys. Seeing his fellow officers staring at him, he shot back at them.

"Consider it a bathing suit. I've got no problem, as long as she doesn't."

An uneasy truce ensued. Some of the patrolmen refused to enter until she had left. Others, however, joined Chavez. Nobody filed a grievance. Another barrier broken.

Here in homicide, her battle had been over the lone stall with a door, but no lock. One day she had eaten something that didn't agree with her and had stunk up the place something awful. The next day a hand-scrawled placard lay on her work area: "Bombs Away! Dampier on the pot. Enter at your own risk."

Now when she used the stall, she hung the sign. It was far better than any locks, and showed she could take the barbs of her colleagues in stride.

Coming out of the locker room now, she saw Doug in McGowan's office. McGowan saw her and beckoned her over. Pissed, Ariel put on her best face and complied.

"ME's on the phone. Come on over soon as you're done," he told her.

When she returned to McGowan's office, she was even more annoyed. The ME hadn't told her anything about the cause of death, but Sharon Ingster had not been a virgin. It probably meant nothing, but she'd wanted to check it out. Now, she didn't know if she'd be able to.

There was but one chair in McGowan's cramped office besides the Sergeant's. Doug quickly vacated it and offered it to his partner. She accepted, but *not* in response to his civility. No, she wanted eye contact with her superior. Wanted it, because he loathed it.

McGowan didn't like being stared at. Maybe he considered it a challenge to his authority. Maybe he feared his eyes betrayed inner thoughts he wanted to hide. Regardless, all in his command, except Ariel, avoided direct eye contact with him. When pissed, as she was now, she glared directly at him. If he didn't like it, he would have to tell her so. She knew, though, he had too much pride.

"Doug was just filling me in," he said, avoiding her glance by looking at her partner. "I just told him I'd gotten a call from the University. Justifiably, they don't want a lot of unwanted publicity. If we could wrap this up quickly, they would be grateful.

"It's too late for the story to make the morning papers," he continued. "The University can live with a day's worth of television coverage, but hopefully we can expedite matters here—unless, of course, circumstances dictate otherwise."

He paused to allow Ariel to comment.

She said nothing.

"Anyway," he went on, "Doug's brought me up to speed. You've done a thorough job—*both* of you," he said, but was clearly directing his praise at Ariel. Not because she'd earned it, she knew, but to assure compliance. Transparent, she thought, he was so utterly transparent. He *was* smooth, though, she had to admit. It was all the more galling. Slick without substance.

"A clear-cut case of suicide; note and everything," he continued. "Your interviews reinforce the conclusion. Unless you have any objections, I'd like to let the University know there won't be any undue delay."

Ariel had learned to pick her battles carefully. She didn't like this being ramrodded down her throat, but even she had to agree Sharon Ingster's death was suicide; her not being a virgin notwithstanding. So she remained silent.

"Fine, then. Doug, I'll leave it to you to wrap it up. Please close the door when you leave."

Dismissed. Don't let the door hit you on the ass on the

way out, Ariel could imagine him thinking. Within moments, he'd be on the phone earning himself Brownie points with superiors for *helping* to protect the University's precious image.

Outside, Ariel got into Doug's face, close enough so she could smell the breath mint he'd probably popped into his mouth before going to see McGowan.

"Into the locker room, Doug. *Now!*"

He looked confused.

"I don't want the night shift hearing us air our dirty laundry in public."

She turned and he obediently followed. Once in the locker room, he asked lamely, "What's got your nose so bent out of shape?"

"What's the rush, Doug?" she asked, ignoring him.

"You heard the Sarge wanted this cleared quickly. What's the harm?"

"The harm is we'll look pretty salty if toxicology indicates foul play. And the ME called. Ingster was no virgin, which contradicts part of her roommie's story. Probably means nothing, but *I* would have liked to look into it."

She closed her eyes to keep from totally losing it, then continued.

"I don't mind your ass-kissing—"

"That's uncalled for—" he interrupted.

"But my credibility is on the line, too," she finished, ignoring him. "Get this straight, Doug, once and for all. Have the courtesy to check with me before calling a case closed. And *don't* try to butter me up by giving me the credit. The egg's on my face, too, if you're wrong."

Doug shook his head sadly. "Why can't you work with the man, Ariel? We both know that politics dictates a quick resolution to what's a clear-cut case, but you're so intent on butting heads with McGowan, you could care less what the facts indicate."

"All I ask is you don't go behind my back," Ariel shot back. "I don't buy this *let's all be good soldiers shit*. It would have killed you to wait five minutes until I'd taken a piss? You want your Brownie points. Fine. But *not* at my expense." Done, she turned to leave.

"What about the paperwork?" he asked, trying to sound conciliatory.

"I'm going home, Doug. Our shift is long over. You can stay and do the damned paperwork, but I won't sign off until toxicology comes back."

She could have—*should have*—left well enough alone. She'd made her point, but she was still angry and the temptation was too great. Before leaving she'd give him something to think about.

"I'd reconsider staying, if I were you, though. Irene might think we're having a one-night stand. 'You getting some black pussy, honey?' "—she mimicked his wife. "Is that what you want her asking you when you get home?" With that she left.

She should have regretted emasculating him, but she didn't. A backstabber, he deserved it. And she knew she had hit all the right buttons. A man's worst nightmare, when teamed with a female, was his wife's reaction. Working in such close proximity, with their lives literally in each other's hands, more than a few had given in to temptation. Worse, for every one that did, it was suspected a dozen more had. That for the most part it was just so much bullshit meant little. Perception was everything, and Doug certainly didn't want his wife suspicious.

The gutter talk—*black pussy*—was also intentional. Ariel had been brought up speaking proper English, and street talk hadn't come easy. She'd made it part of her working vocabulary, however. Doug could never handle vulgarity from a woman; even from a hooker who had cut up her pimp after

51

one beating too many. Five minutes into the interrogation, he had turned it over to her.

And being a *black* female had its own sexual ramifications. That Ariel didn't look black, that she didn't perceive herself as black, meant nothing. To all but black officers, she *was* black, and everyone knew how attracted white men were to the forbidden fruit of sex with a black woman.

Leaving the building, Ariel knew she had overreacted. Knew why, too. It wasn't her partner. He didn't merit her attention. It wasn't McGowan. She'd come to terms with what drove the man. It wasn't the case. It was Lucius— seeing him for the first time in eight years. It brought back too many memories; not all of them bad.

Chapter Eight

Imitation is the sincerest form of flattery. The cliché expressed the awe she felt for Shanicha. Shanicha had done it *again,* she marveled. One day *she* would show her gratitude in a way only Shanicha would appreciate.

Except for Shanicha, she alone knew Sharon Ingster hadn't committed suicide. Shanicha Wilkins hadn't pushed her from the window. But she had pushed her to the edge, where suicide appeared the only option.

Now she sat with two other girls, in a cramped dorm room, discussing what drove someone to suicide. About how fragile they all were. About how it could have been any of them.

Just what Shanicha had envisioned. Had scripted.

Again.

Everyone talking about *her*, without even being aware. It

had been that way in grade school, in high school and now college.

That she wasn't taking part in the discussion, but appeared aloof and distant, didn't faze the others at all. She'd long ago gotten used to being forgotten, as if she'd never been there.

She had always been one of those kids who could spend an entire year with a single teacher, in grade school, then pop in the first day of school the next year only to have the teacher look at her blankly. The face was familiar . . . but the name. What was her name? She could read it in their faces as they talked to her, but never called her by name. Some even tried subtle tricks to get her to reveal herself, but she never fell for it. Let them feel like fools for forgetting who she was. She cared—cared more than she dared admit—but didn't let it show. She *hadn't* forgotten, though.

Once on a school trip to Linvella Orchards, she'd even been left behind while browsing in a gift shop. The bus was halfway back to school, she found out, before anyone noticed she was missing.

She hadn't forgotten she'd been abandoned.

She considered herself a work in progress. She had seen, more than once, the havoc Shanicha left in her wake. Seen the attention she commanded. She pulled strings without being seen, and sat there like an innocent while repercussions erupted around her.

Shanicha would never be forgotten. Shanicha was a presence. Long after Sharon Ingster's suicide was little more than a memory on campus, her parents would still be living with the consequences of what Shanicha had wrought. Imagine, she thought, a whole family so affected. Even Shanicha might never know the full impact.

Yes, it was truly awe-inspiring.

Meanwhile, she watched and learned, without Shanicha's knowledge.

Unbeknownst to Shanicha, she had spied on her as she

53

manipulated the girl. Being invisible, she found, did have its rewards.

She wasn't about to turn Shanicha in; never had, though the opportunity had presented itself before. She had learned much. Would learn more—then do her one better.

Payback. For those who had forgotten.

Chapter Nine

Entering her apartment at two-thirty in the morning, Ariel shed the armor that shielded her daily from the indignities of her job, and life in general. It was like a second skin that, after years of practice, she now easily slipped in and out of.

"Hi, Boss," a voice greeted her. It was Chanda, a fifteen-year-old runaway who'd been living with her for close to six weeks. Chanda, who loved to get under her skin. Chanda, always testing, pushing the envelope. Tonight she wore a bra and cutoff jeans; trying to get a rise out of Ariel, just like addressing her as "Boss" knowing she detested it.

That she was wearing anything at all was the result of one of the many compromises they had reached. Ariel had come home one night to find Chanda camped out on the couch watching Letterman in the nude.

It was an attempt to be outrageous, Ariel knew. To see how far she could go—and possibly a bit farther. The girl wanted desperately to stay; wanted just as desperately to be sent packing.

The two of them had parried—they never fought or really argued—over appropriate attire.

"What if I brought someone home with me, with you naked on the couch?" Ariel had asked.

"When you come in, announce yourself," she'd retorted. "I'd be in my room before you got through the door."

"Why should I have to announce myself in *my* own home?"

"You said to consider this *my* home as well," she'd answered with a sly smile. "I like to be comfortable in *my* home."

The girl could be infuriating, but she'd finally agreed to no nudity. The bra—which accentuated Chanda's breasts, already the equal to Ariel's who was not particularly endowed—was another test. Ariel was too preoccupied with thoughts of Lucius to make it an issue. No objection, she knew, would be taken as acceptance. Without comment now, Ariel couldn't later protest with any credibility. She decided to let Chanda have her victory. There would be more significant challenges, she was certain, if Chanda decided to stay. Just as at work, you pick your battles.

"I'll cook you a burger," Chanda volunteered after Ariel had taken off her coat.

"No, thanks. I'm not really hungry. I need a shower and some time to be with myself," she said, and smiled.

"Really into ourself tonight, aren't we?" Chanda said scathingly.

"What's gotten into you?" Ariel asked, suddenly confused.

Chanda gently tapped Ariel on the forehead. "Knock. Knock. Anyone home? It's after two in the morning, and I could be asleep."

"So?"

"I stayed up for you and you trounce in and want some quality time with yourself. Maybe *I* have a problem I want to get off my chest."

"Do you?" Ariel asked hopefully, surprised the girl might finally open up to her.

"No, but I could have," she said sullenly, sporting a pout.

"You're infuriating. And you know it. That's what galls me." Ariel paused, putting Lucius out of her mind for the moment. *This* was important. If she was flip about it, she could antagonize and lose Chanda for good.

"Look," she finally said. "Let's compromise. I *really* do need a shower. A burger, though, sounds good. I *am* hungry, come to think of it. Then, if you're intent on being bored, I'll tell you about Lucius."

"Who's Lucius?"

"First the shower."

"A new man in your life?" she said with a big grin.

"Not another peep out of you, young lady," she said, not able to hide her amusement, and went to her shower.

As she showered, her thoughts remained on Chanda. While she was loath to admit it, Ariel desperately needed Chanda to stay. Since the breakup of her marriage to Lucius—and even before—she'd needed constant companionship. She'd had more affairs—or live-in lovers—than she could remember; none truly satisfying. Some lasted a few weeks, two as long as six months. None were serious. She had no intention of remarrying *until* she found a man who could deal with her dualism; if such a man existed. Yet she despised being alone.

Having been excluded by both whites and blacks much of her life, she had no *best* friend to confide in and console her, and she wasn't tight with anyone on the job. So, as sick as she was with her little flings, she feared loneliness even more. When Chanda entered her life, she'd grasped at the opportunity like a drowning woman for a life preserver.

The youth had been brought in as a witness, with two other women, when two pimps got into an argument; one ending up dead, cut up like Swiss cheese.

It was Doug's kind of case, so Ariel followed his lead. He thought he'd have more success interrogating the youngster, but within five minutes he'd turned her over to Ariel.

"She punctuates every sentence with *F* this and *F* that," he told her. "Could you . . . ?"

Another of his dangling sentences. But she could and did. A foul-mouthed little brat didn't bother her one bit. Ariel kept her sitting and stewing for forty-five minutes while she interrogated one of the other two witnesses. She finally came into the room, bare save for a table and two chairs, and just sat, just looking at the youth.

"I could use a cigarette," the girl finally said.

"You on drugs?" Ariel asked, ignoring the request.

"Fuck, no," she said, showing Ariel her arms. "See, clean. Now how about a smoke?"

"What if I asked you to take off your shoes? Would I find needle marks between your toes? Or maybe behind your knees?"

"No!" she shot back sullenly. "I don't do drugs."

"Grantham your pimp?" Harvey Grantham was the pimp who'd been killed.

"Don't have no pimp either."

The banter went on for half an hour. While never admitting the dead man was her pimp or that she was a prostitute, she told Ariel what had happened and fed her the name of someone Grantham had called his attacker.

Ariel rewarded her with a cigarette.

"I'm not going to ask your age. You'll lie, but I'd bet my shield you're a minor."

"What of it?"

"And if I work at it hard enough, I can locate your parents. See, runaways don't come to Philly unless it's the closest big city. You going to make it difficult for me, or act mature and tell me who you are and where you came from?"

The girl pulled her knees to her chest, hugging them, and began to shiver. "I'm not going back. Never!" Then silence.

Ariel was pretty certain the youth was from a middle-class home; her tone of voice, fashionable haircut and bearing.

57

"Your parents catch you with your boyfriend and ground you? That your story?"

She glared at Ariel, then smiled. "Want to send me back? Try this on for size. My father—my *real* father, not some stepfather—began fucking me when I was twelve. Slapped me around if I protested."

She never broke eye contact with Ariel as she spoke.

"He'd lay with me for hours at a time. Relieve his needs, then make me cuddle with him. Then he'd fuck me again."

She took a drag on the cigarette, swallowed, then went on.

"The worst thing is my mother knew. I could hear her crying next door. I never told her because I *knew* she knew. She couldn't look at me."

She finished the cigarette, and Ariel gave her another without her asking.

"Six months ago," she went on, "he brought a friend with him and they both had a go at me. One watching the other; both getting drunk as a skunk. I snapped and broke one of their bottles. I slashed his friend across the balls and my father in his face. It cut so deep, I could see his tongue through his cheek. I ran and never looked back."

She closed her eyes, as if reliving the experience.

"No way I can—*would*—go back to that household. No way I'm going to be stuck in some orphanage or foster home. I can fend for myself."

"By letting men fuck you for money," Ariel said.

"Not much of a choice. Got no skills. No degree. Just a decent bod," she said with a shrug.

"I find that unacceptable," Ariel said.

"Fuck you, then."

"Don't you want to make something of your life?" Ariel asked, ignoring her comment.

"Wanting and doing are two different things," she said sullenly.

"What if you were given a chance?"

"What kind of chance?" she said guardedly.

"Live with me. Go to school. Get some skills and a degree. Make a life where you don't have to literally sell yourself."

"What do you get out of it?"

"Companionship," Ariel said without hesitation.

"Like you're wanting, right. Give me a fucking break."

"You don't know anything about me," Ariel said. "Appearances can be deceiving. Stay with me and I'll tell you about it."

"I won't be a prisoner. I come and go as I please."

"There'll be rules," Ariel countered. "*But* we'll negotiate them. You won't be a prisoner. I won't be your mother. But stay in *my* house, eat *my* food . . ." She paused. Then. "Live by rules *we* agree to. If it doesn't work out, you're free to go."

"Why me?" she asked with what seemed like genuine curiosity.

"Without me you'll be back on the street, no matter where you're put. That's a given. You'll soon be dead, on drugs, sick with AIDS or stuck with some pimp just as bad as your father. I'm no good at living alone. And I've had enough with men for a while. So, let me help you and I can bore you with my petty problems."

She shrugged. "Why not. On a trial basis," she added hurriedly.

"Chanda's not your real name," she said, looking at the paperwork Doug had begun, pronouncing the *Ch* like *Charles*.

"My parents lost the right to name me. I chose Chanda— the *Ch* is pronounced *Sh*, like *Shark*. I like the look of the *Ch*, though."

"What about a last name?"

"Just Chanda. Like Cher, Madonna or Roxanne."

"Cher, Madonna and Roxanne don't have to go to school." She shrugged again. "Your last name's fine—*for school*."

Ariel pulled some strings and had the girl released to her custody; a witness who might have to testify in a murder investigation. She hadn't given her age, so Ariel put down eighteen, so no one would come snooping around.

Rinsing her hair now, Ariel recalled the first time Chanda had seen her apartment. Everything in the sparsely furnished living room was black and white: a couch, two easy chairs, a TV, tape deck and CD player, and an end table with only a black phone, a *TV Guide* and small fishbowl on it.

"Bitchin'," Chanda said. "You don't have any stuff."

Ariel laughed. "A reaction to my parents. Both . . . how can I put it," she said and thought, "collect things. And never get rid of anything. You had to hold your breath walking from one room to another or you'd knock something over."

Chanda laughed for the first time. "All the rooms like this?"

"All except my workroom. Same color scheme, but plenty of clutter. My clutter room, I call it."

"Why black and white? You got something against color?"

Now it was Ariel's turn to laugh.

"Remember when I told you appearances can be deceiving?"

Chanda nodded.

"Look at the picture on the television."

Chanda picked up the picture, looked at it, then at Ariel, back to the picture, then to Ariel again.

"These your parents? Your *birth* parents?"

"Yep."

"You're black!" She came over and put her arm next to Ariel's face. "You're lighter than I am."

She was, Ariel thought. Chanda was tawny, like someone with a good tan.

"Actually, I'm not *black*. Society considers me black because of my mother. My father's white—Jewish. I live in both worlds."

Chanda looked bewildered.

"See, it's like a wardrobe. I have just three or four outfits that match, but I can mix them to make seven or eight. Being biracial is the same. I'm not less black because I'm half white. But I'm not less white because of my blackness. I'm more than the sum of my parts, is what I'm saying. Others can't accept it. There is a need to categorize. I'm either black or white, as far as others are concerned. And, to white society, I'm most definitely black, even if I don't look it."

"So, by your color scheme, you're saying, 'Fuck them.' You're neither black nor white, but both."

"You got it."

Chanda walked over to a small fishbowl with two black fish. "Even the fish match the color scheme." She laughed.

"Not just that," Ariel said. "The fish are like me."

Chanda stared at her, waiting for her to explain.

"They're goldfish," Ariel explained. "I always thought *goldfish* were *gold*—hence the name. But I learned goldfish came in all colors, and most aren't gold. These, Salt and Pepa, like the singing group, are like me. Outsiders in a world defined by society. Black goldfish. Sounds pretty stupid, doesn't it?"

"Bitchin'," Chanda said. "You're right. You're not what you appear to be."

Ariel finished her shower and put on a robe. The past six weeks had been a tug of war at times; skirmishes punctuated by cease-fires—the latter becoming more the norm. Chanda hadn't opened up any more about her personal life, but didn't seem to mind a set routine. Deep down, Ariel was pretty sure the youth wanted rules with consequences for breaking them. Ariel had to be careful, though, not to mother the girl. Habits like smoking and flaunting her body galled Ariel, but she refused to totally stifle the youth. Ariel knew if she came on too strong, Chanda might just pack up and leave.

And now, after a burger, she'd be telling her about Lucius.

Maybe it was for the best she didn't have to brood about him alone. Chanda, after all, was insightful and a good listener.

She almost laughed out loud as Chanda watched her devour the burger. Chanda was so bursting with curiosity, Ariel could almost feel the girl willing her to finish. As soon as Ariel was done, Chanda pounced.

"So who is this new guy?"

"Not a new guy. I met my ex-husband today. First time in seven years." She grew silent, trying to think how to begin.

"You two getting back together?" Chanda asked, misreading her silence.

Ariel frowned. There was a trace of fear in Chanda's voice. Of course, she thought. What a fool I am. If we got back together, where would that leave her? Back on the streets, she probably figured.

"Hardly. It brought back memories, that's all."

"I don't understand."

"First you have to learn about me. I'm mixed. Biracial. You know that, but not what it means. I'm much more like my father—he's Jewish—than my mother. We have the same build. I have his blue eyes. His temperament. But there's a lot of my mother in me, too. Just as my father told me of his heritage, so did my mother. And while I was never religious, I spent a lot of time in church. The music . . ."

"Right!" Chanda said, as if she'd had a revelation. "Your CDs are all R&B, jazz and gospel."

"The music in my mother's church had power, a hold on me I couldn't deny. *Didn't want to deny.* And I could sing. *Really sing,* not just carry a tune."

"Really?"

Ariel nodded. "When I was nine, I was in the choir at church. I'd get wrapped up in the music. The rest of the world that could be so cruel would disappear. No kids who made fun of me. No kids who fought me. No kids or adults who wouldn't let *me* be *me*. All gone when I sang.

"One day—I can't even remember the song—but all of a sudden it was just me singing; belting out this song while everyone else had stopped. When the song was over everyone was clapping and whooping it up. I felt like crawling under a rock, I was so embarrassed. At the same time, I couldn't contain my joy. From then on, I was the only one who had solos." She smiled. "I rocked the place. I really did."

Chanda lit up a cigarette, and Ariel gave her a cold stare. Chanda shrugged and put it out.

"To make a long story short, I was truly biracial. I had black days. I had white days. I had days when I could come to grips with my duality. Unfortunately, others were constantly forcing me to choose one or the other."

Ariel got up and took out two sodas from the fridge, giving one to Chanda.

"I met Lucius at the Police Academy. I was at another crossroads where I had to choose an identity. Whites—not all, but most there—wouldn't accept me. To them I was black, plain and simple. Worse, when I associated with them, many thought I was trying to *be* white. At the same time, if I hung with some of the whites, I'd lose face with the black cadets. Trying to pass, they'd say behind my back, but it got back to me."

Ariel took the pack of cigarettes Chanda had left on the table and took one. She usually only smoked when she was with her partner, but talking about herself and Lucius, she felt the need for one now. Chanda took one as well, but there was no way Ariel could deny her and not look like a hypocrite.

"A classic no-win situation," Ariel said after lighting up. "So, I chose to be black out of self-preservation, all the time feeling twinges of guilt and unease when the other black cadets would put down the white cadets solely because of their color."

She put the cigarette in an ashtray, popped the top of her soda and took a swallow straight from the can. Then she took another drag on the cigarette.

"When Lucius and I married, he thought he was marrying a black woman who happened to have one white parent. But even he was insecure. We'd go to a party where just about everybody was black, and not five minutes passed before he made a comment to make sure everyone knew I was black. Some were pretty lame. 'Looks like cream, but my woman's pure coffee.' Shit like that."

Chanda laughed with her mouth full of soda, and spat some out in a stream, unable to contain herself. Ariel had to duck to avoid being hit. Then she, too, burst out in laughter.

"Finally," she said after regaining control, "he found a line that worked. He'd talk about my mother's collection of African artifacts. Anyway, if I had denied my white side, everything would have been fine. I couldn't. Wouldn't. I was, after all, my father's child, too, and I was as proud of his heritage as I was of my mother's. Maybe it was because he was Jewish. He didn't talk about white people, but of the oppression Jews faced long before Africans had been brought to this country. Obstacles they had to overcome just to stay alive. Prejudices they still faced. It's not something I could deny. It's what I am."

She got up, and while telling the rest of her story, paced back and forth like a caged tiger.

"I refused to hide my feelings from Lucius, and of course, we'd argue. It came to a head when I got pregnant. I was just out of the Academy and on the streets. Lucius wanted me to have an abortion. 'You're young. Quit now and you'll regret it forever. You'll never be able to be a cop *after* raising a family.' He was right. I wanted a career, so I had an abortion.

"Problem was, Lucius was full of shit. He wanted the abortion because he feared he'd father a light-skinned son or daughter. He wouldn't come out and say it, but later—after the abortion—when we talked about a family, he talked about putting it off. I could see the fear in his eyes."

Ariel stopped pacing and faced Chanda.

"I never regretted the abortion, but I couldn't cope with Lucius's racism and hypocrisy. Sooner or later he'd turn on me. At least that's what I thought. We divorced. He remarried—a real dark-skinned woman—and that should have been the end of it. She died, though, about six months ago. Ovarian cancer. It didn't mean anything then. Really, I never gave it a second thought."

"So what changed?"

Ariel told her about the suicide. About seeing Lucius again, hearing him talk about his job.

"Through all our wrangling near the end, I'd forgotten why I'd been so attracted to him in the first place. He was a decent person. I realized that again tonight, as he blamed *himself*, in part, for the girl's suicide. I love my job, don't get me wrong. I wouldn't trade places with him. But I deal with death and the vermin responsible. He builds bridges with people. He does more in a semester than I've done in my entire career."

"That's bullshit," Chanda said.

"No, it's the cold, harsh truth."

"Then why am I here?"

Ariel began to answer, then realized she had no response.

"You took me off the streets. Probably saved my life, though I'll regret admitting it tomorrow," Chanda went on when Ariel was silent. "Why do you have to put yourself down to build him up? He may be a great guy, but sounds like he's got flaws. He never met you halfway. He wanted . . ."

"A Nubian Princess," Ariel finished. "Called me that when we made love. I was his Nubian Princess. He couldn't accept me as anything else."

"So what now? You going to see him?"

"No," she said firmly. "I'd be setting myself up for a fall."

"What if he's changed?"

"I doubt it."

"You've come to grips with yourself. Maturity, they call it," she said with a smile. "Maybe *he's* matured."

Ariel shrugged. "Doesn't matter. Didn't seem like he wanted anything to do with me. But it did bring back memories."

She looked at the clock in the kitchen.

"Hey, it's after three, young lady. I can sleep till noon, but you've got school tomorrow. It's time we called it a night."

Chanda scrunched up her face in annoyance, but for once didn't argue.

"Chanda," Ariel said as the youth got up and stretched. "You were right. It was better talking it out than wrestling with it myself. Thanks."

Chanda flushed, clearly pleased with herself. She went to her room with a bounce in her step after saying good night.

Ariel, for her part, hadn't fully come to terms with her thoughts about Lucius. She went into her workroom and slipped a CD by Chante Moore in a player she kept there. Turned it down so as not to disturb Chanda. There was a song, "Am I Losing You?"—a soulful ballad she'd played a number of times over the past six months—thinking of her tumultuous last days with Lucius again, after hearing of his wife's death.

In hindsight, she thought their marriage was doomed from the start. He was a proud *black* man who'd married an equally proud woman. Not *the* black woman he thought he was getting, though.

The bumpy road their marriage traversed had made her come to grips with herself. Made her finally accept the fact that she had been a fraud. To accept the fact she was black *and* white. And when they'd divorced, as far as she was concerned, it was *his* loss, not hers.

The song told of a love between two people so powerful, it could never be recaptured with another. That had been the case with her, but not for Lucius. He had found someone to fill the void in his life, and deny it all she might, she was envious. While she went from one man to the next, he had found his true love; only to have her taken away by cancer.

It was the chorus that brought tears to her eyes, the song's very title, "Am I Losing You?"

Truth be told, they had lost one another. Didn't matter how much he'd matured, she now told herself. No way he could ever accept her as she now perceived herself.

It didn't lessen the hurt, though. There were times she resented her parents for their selfishness and naivety. A freak of nature. A *mutant*. She'd lost the one man she wanted to spend her life with. Unless she gave up one half of herself, she feared she'd never find true happiness. And she couldn't—*wouldn't*—abandon either part of her. Many—most—had. Society labeled you black, so black you were. But identifying themselves as black rang hollow to her. Deep down, the conflict within simmered, and she knew any number of biracial women who thought they'd defined themselves by their blackness only to become involved in self-destructive relationships. These were bitter, angry women—filled with self-loathing that they tried to deny. She'd wrestled with her identity, much as they had, but she finally had come to grips with her duality. Regardless of how she *was* perceived, she refused to allow others to dictate who she was. That it had cost her husband, and countless friends, had wounded her deeply, but at least she was at peace with herself.

She played the song again, this time singing along with it.

After it finished, she said aloud, "I didn't lose you, Lucius. You lost me."

She sat in thought, then shaking her head in resignation, said aloud, "So, why do I feel so miserable?"

Chapter Ten

Up until that night—early morning, actually—Chanda had felt like a boarder; much like a foster child on trial. She considered staying with Ariel as no more than a rest stop along the way. No way Ariel would want her to stay for good. No way Chanda wanted to be tied down. The streets gave her freedom. Deep down, though, she knew sooner or later they'd lead to her demise.

Still, staying with Ariel was a matter of convenience. Thoughts of a more permanent relationship had crept up on Chanda slowly. There were days she'd get home from school and feel good about herself; feel *almost* at home. Think maybe, just maybe, she'd stay and get her degree.

To her credit, Ariel had been true to her word, no matter how Chanda tested her resolve. She constantly pushed the limits of the woman's tolerance, not because she wanted to leave or be booted out, but to make sure, early in the game, that Ariel wasn't a fraud.

Well, Ariel wasn't a fraud, she'd found out quickly. They butted heads, but Ariel was adept at the art of give-and-take. And Chanda had toned down her act accordingly. On the streets, gutter talk was a defensive necessity. But even profanity lost its power when used to begin or end every sentence. And with Ariel, there was no need for profanity, so she tucked it away for the most part.

Walking around naked gave her a sense of freedom she hadn't had on the streets. It hadn't begun as a test of wills with Ariel. On the streets she'd worn most of her clothes, no matter what the weather. Whatever you couldn't carry with you would soon be gone. Anything you weren't wearing might disappear while you slept. While many homeless lived by an unwritten code, there were those who had no scruples whatsoever. She got so tired of wearing *everything* she owned, she literally took it all off once she'd been at Ariel's a while.

That evening when Ariel found her on the couch naked, it hadn't been to intentionally incite her. Chanda was just making herself comfortable. But once Ariel made it an issue, she was determined to see how far she would bend. In the end, she'd agreed to wear clothes outside her room.

"If you want to be stark naked, do so in your room. If you want to sleep in the nude, it doesn't bother me. It's *your* room. I won't intrude," Ariel had said. True to her word, Chanda's room was truly her own, and Ariel never entered without permission.

That afternoon, she'd been beat when she got home from school and had just taken off her top. Again, it wasn't intended as defiance, but she could see from Ariel's eyes *she* took it as another test. Yet, she'd let it pass.

Tonight, though, could have spoiled everything. All her life she'd met others' physical needs. What *she* wanted never counted. When Ariel had called her from the crime scene at the University of Pennsylvania, there had been something in her voice. Something that instinctively made Chanda think there was something Ariel might want to talk about. So, she'd stayed up until Ariel returned. Then she came in and dismissed Chanda. Just like everyone else. She wanted to be with *herself*.

Barry Hoffman

Again, though, Ariel had surprised her. When she saw Chanda was upset, she did confide in her. Literally the first time that had happened in Chanda's life.

She'd been surprised that someone so seemingly in control of herself harbored demons of her own. Chanda was so into herself, she thought only she had lived a wretched existence. But Ariel had had it tough growing up. She still wasn't totally comfortable with herself. That someone so *old* would have some of the same insecurities she did was eerie, yet comforting at the same time.

Chanda had also been fearful at first that Ariel and Lucius might reconcile. That would put her back on the streets, for why would a couple want a teenager hanging around? It was insensitive of her to think in those terms, but she was beginning to like Ariel. Like her a lot. Thoughts of leaving, which had always been on the surface, were now buried. Yet, Lucius could ruin everything.

Ariel, though, had read her mind. Chanda took her at her word, that even if they reconciled, she would have a place here. Would be welcome. She also knew that Ariel needed a man, whether it be Lucius or someone else. Not just to screw, but to be there for her on nights such as this. She knew, too, that Ariel still had strong feelings for her ex-husband, no matter how she tried to mask them.

Tonight *could* have spoiled everything. Instead, she felt more at home than ever. With her door closed, she undressed, then donned a pair of pajamas; a secret she'd keep from Ariel because . . . well, because *she* wasn't ready to lay herself bare yet.

It wasn't her only secret. Trivial compared to one. This was not the time, though, to dwell on the past. She let the warmth of the evening wash over her as she heard Ariel singing in her clutter room; had scarcely put her head on the pillow before she was asleep . . .

—In *her* bed. In *her* home?

Chapter Eleven

Shanicha sat in front of her mirror, brushing her hair. She was naked. Her roommate went to bed early and slept like the dead. More or less alone, she could indulge in her eccentricities. Brushing her hair each night in the nude, admiring herself, much as the boys she had slept with had. Her coffee-colored skin, so smooth—the only blemish the thinnest of scars below her right eye from a fight with one of her brothers. Her oval brown eyes smoldered. Her nose was turned up a bit; her lips full, but not too thick. Her breasts taut and firm, her body finely chiseled. And her hair long and the deep black color of newly poured tar. She changed the style every few days—sometimes daily—as it expressed her ever-changing moods.

In her mind's eye she saw Sharon Ingster step toward the window . . .

—She ran the brush through her hair once, twice, a third time.

Saw the young woman close her eyes . . .

—She quickened the pace of her brushing.

. . . pause in a moment of indecision . . .

—She glistened with sweat, her nipples hardened, as she brushed faster yet.

. . . then plunge, her terror-filled eyes opening as she realized there was no turning back. A calm settled over her just before she hit the concrete below.

—Gasping for breath, she reached orgasm at the moment of impact.

She'd have to take another shower, she knew. Much as she loved her scent, so did the spiders, and she must not leave a trail for them to follow.

For now, though, she resumed her brushing, and a different picture emerged from the mirror. Sometimes, like now, she believed she could picture her birth. Her adoptive parents had told her she had been a crack baby; along with two other adopted children in their family.

They had told her so she would understand the mood changes she experienced, and her sometimes aberrant behavior in preschool and kindergarten. Told her so she'd understand why one moment she'd be quietly coloring and the next throwing her crayons and tearing her designs to pieces. Told her so she could understand the sudden tantrums that all but overwhelmed her at times.

It had all been explained to her. She'd been told over and over it wasn't her fault. And, there was nothing wrong with her that she wouldn't outgrow. And by first grade she'd learned to control her emotions. Fit in. She *had* to fit in, for even at six she had urges to hurt others. But to act on these urges she had to blend in, because she had no desire to get caught when she did something bad. Self-destructive she wasn't. She didn't want to be sent to a special class or special school for children with emotional problems.

In the mirror, her birth mother's face was shrouded, like the electronic images they used on television to protect the identity of a rape victim. She could see herself lying on her mother's stomach, some instinct drawing her to her mother's breast for nourishment. She couldn't move, though, and her mother didn't understand this primal need she possessed.

The woman—almost as dark as she—stroked her face, trying to calm her as she cried and shook uncontrollably from cocaine withdrawal.

The hand fell from her cheek, and she knew she was alone.

Forever alone.

Robbed of her mother at birth. Robbed of her identity. She longed for her mother. Hated her mother at the same time.

Tears ran down Shanicha's face as she continued to brush her hair.

She longed for her mother, yet reviled her. Longed for her touch, to hear her voice. Hated her. Hated *everyone*.

Chapter Twelve

Ariel felt a strange sense of déjà vu five weeks later as she saw the body of a young coed who had plunged to her death in The Quad at the University of Pennsylvania.

Sharon Ingster jumped from what was called The Baby Quad, the western-most portion of the freshman living area. Monique Dysart took her dive from the Lower Quad—to the east. Lucius had again been first on the scene. Almost on automatic pilot, Ariel went to speak to him while Doug surveyed the victim's room.

"We have to stop meeting like this," Ariel said with a sad smile when she'd approached Lucius.

He was silent. Ariel noted he looked the worse for wear; tired, with bags under his eyes. He seemed deeply shaken.

"Did you know this one, too?" she asked, already knowing the answer.

He looked at her, as if for the first time.

"Knew all three. It's a fucking nightmare."

"Whoa. Back up a minute," Ariel said. "You said *three*. This is the second suicide here."

He smiled, but Ariel noted it was devoid of humor.

"Your second. My . . . *our* third."

"I don't understand."

"There was one last week."

"We weren't called," Ariel said. "Weren't notified. I saw nothing in the papers." She was exasperated. It was like pulling teeth with Lucius tonight.

"The second was discovered at four in the morning. Not your shift. A coed hung herself from a pole in one of the showers. Much like the first, pretty open-and-shut. Suicide note and all. The detectives were . . . let's say, cooperative," he said derisively. "The University obviously didn't want the publicity. From what I gather, some calls were exchanged and it all but disappeared. Being a suicide, there was no reason to drag you in, I assume." He shrugged. "A plague on both their houses," he added. "University wants to hush it up, and you guys are more than accommodating. With some publicity, maybe this could have been avoided," he said, looking at the covered body of Monique Dysart.

"With just a week between this and the last one, no way they can hush this up now," Ariel said, as much to make Lucius feel better as to state the obvious.

"A suicide cluster," Lucius said, as if he weren't paying attention.

She looked at him questioningly.

"The head of Psych Services told me suicidal thoughts can be contagious. Like dominoes. The first leads to the second, which spurs another to action. There were Crisis Intervention Counselors after the first two suicides, but it was all low-key. Now, from what I've heard, they'll put on a full-court press. We're to report *anyone* we think *might* be troubled. Right now, I'd say it's half the fucking freshman class."

"So nothing suspicious here," Ariel said, ready to wrap things up.

He looked at her long and hard. "Something bothers me about this one. Don't get me wrong. There's nothing overtly suspicious. But . . . well, for one thing, there was no suicide note. Monique thought herself a poet. Pretty dreadful stuff if you ask me, but she was a prolific writer. If anyone was to leave a note, it would be her."

"Anything else?"

"You might have your ME check the back of her head." He gave Ariel a tight smile. "I checked things out before the cavalry arrived. Anyway, she fell facedown, but I noticed a slight contusion on the back of her head. Obviously, I didn't see her jump. She may have bumped her head on the window frame or the ledge, but you asked."

"Was she a candidate for suicide?" Ariel asked, aware that Lucius's suspicions were contagious.

"I've been second-guessing myself since the call went out. So many of these kids are having problems, but no different from last year's freshmen or the class before that."

He paused, as if debating how to go on.

"I don't want this to come out wrong, but the prettiest thing about Monique was her name. It may sound insensitive, but the truth is she doesn't look much worse now than before she jumped."

Ariel grimaced. "That bad, huh?"

"She was a wild, outgoing kid. I think it was to compensate for her looks. She even made fun of herself. Kind of a preemptive attack. *You won't call me ugly if I call myself ugly first.* Know what I mean?"

Ariel nodded.

"She'd been withdrawn lately. You used to find her at

every party. She was a flirt. Maybe a tease. On the other hand, there hasn't been much partying recently—especially after the second suicide. Everyone seems into themselves. So I might be off in left field with Monique. You know, looking for something that isn't there because she jumped."

"What about her roommate?" Ariel asked.

Lucius shook his head. "Lived in a single. Her parents were loaded."

"Any close friends? Someone with some insight?"

"She knew a lot of people, but she wasn't tight with anyone in particular. If you want, I'll ask around. Find a couple of kids who knew her better than most, if it's important."

Lucius stopped talking and looked at the crowd that had gathered. He frowned.

"What's wrong, Lucius?"

"The reactions of some of the kids. Different from the first, even the second suicide. There's one girl who'd prowl the crowd—almost eavesdropping. Tonight, she's transfixed. Another who's usually aloof, tonight she's jazzed. Others, who were curious before, look scared shitless now. I don't know, maybe it's me. You know, looking for something to make sense of it all; projecting my perceptions. It's tough, though, waiting for the other shoe to drop."

"What do you mean?" Ariel asked.

"Wondering who'll be next."

"You think there'll be others?" Somehow the thought hadn't occurred to her. She reacted to events, didn't try to foretell them. It came with the territory of being in homicide.

"Cluster suicides, Ariel. Dominoes."

Ariel was worried. Concerned about Lucius. He was taking this so personally and talking a lot of gibberish. He seemed to be in shock himself. It was so unlike him. Well, so unlike the man she'd known eight years earlier.

"Just one more thing," she said. "Maybe I should speak to

the head of Psych Services. Get his insight. What do you think?"

Lucius shrugged noncommittally. "Name's Stanley Isaacs. A piece of work." He laughed at the expression on her face. "You'll find out for yourself." He took out his notebook, paged through it and read her a phone number where she could reach Isaacs. "Want me to round up some of Monique's friends?"

"Let's take it one step at a time. I'm just backup on this. I'll have to check with my partner, and we'll both have to speak with our Sergeant—who's probably on the phone with someone from the University as we speak. I know," she said, seeing his expression. "A plague on both their houses. Look, I'll give you a call, all right?"

He nodded and gave her his card. "Office and beeper," he said tonelessly, once again fixated on the crowd.

"You take care of yourself, Lucius. And don't go blaming yourself. Promise?"

"Sure," he said, but she was certain he was no longer listening to her.

Chapter Thirteen

Confused, surprised, though not in the least displeased, Shanicha merged with the crowd trying to see the body of Monique Dysart.

She wasn't responsible for Monique's suicide. Or was she? She'd most definitely had a hand in the death of Jocelyn Rhea the week before, but she hadn't even chosen a new target yet. Probably wouldn't have chosen Monique, even though the girl was also a member of the acquaintance-rape counseling group.

I've created a monster, she thought, carefully hiding a smile that threatened to betray her feelings. Had it gotten to the point where all she had to do now was sit back and watch the weak drop—or take the plunge, to be more precise? Would it become an epidemic? The thought excited her. The feeling of power, literally controlling life and death, was exhilarating.

The only fly in the ointment was the cop; the bald black dude scanning the crowd; looking at *her*. He'd been at the suicide scenes before, taking the pulse of the crowd. He'd been around a lot all the way back to the first semester, getting to know the incoming freshmen. She had steered clear of him, but she'd felt his eyes on her when she and her friends played touch football in the mud or just sat around shooting the breeze.

Other campus cops were there, mainly for crowd control, but he was the only one actually checking out the crowd.

She'd thought he'd focused on her the first time; then tossed it away as creeping paranoia. She was sure he was taking her in now. Not *just* her, but as his eyes swept the gathering group, his gaze rested on her the most; left, then returned to her. And now he was talking to some white bitch—a *real* cop.

—Talking about *her*.

The woman cop had been there before, too, when Sharon jumped. It was nothing to wet her pants over, but Shanicha tucked it in her memory for future reference.

Her mind turned back to Monique. The girl was a bundle of nervous energy. At group, she couldn't keep still. And God, was she ugly—U-G-L-Y. Not plain, dour or nondescript, but flat-out repulsive. Like some blind man had put

78

her face together. Water-thin lips that stretched almost from ear to ear. A long nose that went on forever. Beady little eyes and, of course, thick glasses. She had the sallow complexion of one who didn't eat right, and acne scars that made her face resemble a sponge or barnacle you found at sea. All topped by frizzy, dirty-brown hair that reminded Shanicha of barbed wire. Who would want to run his fingers through that? she remembered thinking as she fought to stifle a laugh at group. And talking about hair—it grew like weeds over the rest of her body. She knew because Monique wore the most revealing of clothes; in theory so eyes wouldn't dawdle on her face. The intent was to appear sexy, but on a near-anorexic figure, the effect was the opposite. She appeared even more repulsive. With so much skin showing, Shanicha saw hair, like a bear, on her arms, legs, even her stomach, which was often bare due to the halter tops she wore. And as if God were playing particularly cruel joke, she was flat-chested to boot.

Monique, she recalled, always put herself down—her looks at least. "I'd bring a paper bag with me to parties," she cracked at group, "in case any guy wanted to fuck me without getting sick."

Her wild behavior and outlandish attire were her ways of compensating for her looks. At group, she admitted she was a sexual tease.

"I welcomed Roman hands and Russian fingers. I'd even given a few hand jobs, but that was as far as I went. Until I was raped, that is. This guy—no winner himself—wouldn't accept limits. He got violent and the whole time he was on top of me—and in me—he kept calling me a bitch, cunt and cock teaser. He raped me because he was pissed at me. This wasn't a horny guy that got carried away. I could feel his rage."

She talked of bringing it on herself. She was surprised it

hadn't happened sooner. After all, she had encouraged talk about her being loose—being easy.

The other girls felt she should bring criminal charges because he'd been so violent. This was no case of crossed signals.

"I couldn't face the humiliation of my life being dragged through the mud," she'd answered. "It's bad enough I'm a joke now, with my looks, behavior and all. I couldn't bear to have everyone talking behind my back about how someone would get close enough to fuck me."

At the same time she craved revenge.

"It was all so devoid of passion. I was just another notch on his cock. And when he was done, he got dressed and left me. People like him should be castrated—*in public*."

Monique was fucked up, Shanicha knew, but she was too much of a loose cannon to try to manipulate; too unpredictable. That she'd committed suicide wasn't itself so surprising. She was impulsive enough to do it on a whim, but Shanicha didn't think she could be easily controlled. Just what had pushed her over the edge? Shanicha wondered, then decided it wasn't worth her time speculating.

Well, Monique, she thought to herself, you wanted to be the center of attention. Enjoy the limelight.

Shanicha searched the near-silent faces in the crowd. Who would be next? The feeling of electricity shot through her again. Like a snowball that turns into an avalanche, she wondered what she had started, and how many it would consume.

Step right up, she thought. Who will be next? No tickets necessary. Don't be shy.

Step right up.

Who'll be next?

Don't be bashful.

Step right up . . .

Chapter Fourteen

She had finally done it and now she could bask in the aftermath. She ambled through the crowd as they talked about
Monique Dysart; talked of their fear and apprehension; talked
about *her*.

She looked at Shanicha, who looked befuddled, and smiled
to herself. Shell-shocked might be a better word. Envious.
Yeah, Shanicha was jealous, she thought. Monique *hadn't*
been her doing and she couldn't handle it.

She wanted to go up to Shanicha and whisper in her ear,
"It was *me*. Remember me? Dismissed me like all the rest,
but it was *me*. Me. Me. *Me!*"

The seduction of Monique Dysart, as she called it, had
begun the night Jocelyn Rhea hung herself, a week earlier.

She had chosen Monique because the girl was so unstable.
She tried to put herself in Shanicha's place to decide who to
target. She knew all the girls in the acquaintance-rape counseling group. . . .

—The *ever-thinning* acquaintance-rape counseling group,
she thought, and laughed to herself.

Who would Shanicha choose? Who was the most likely
candidate to pull her own plug?

She remembered an incident involving Monique a few
weeks before, in one of the lounges that housed a television.
A dozen girls were in the midst of watching *Melrose Place*

when Monique charged in. There was something else she just *had* to see. The other girls told her to fuck off and Monique flipped out. She threw her shoe at the screen, barely missing it, as she raged at them in a nonstop expletive-filled tirade.

Angela Colon, a streetwise Hispanic, finally had enough and went toe-to-toe with the much smaller Monique. No fisticuffs, just verbal brickbats were flung at one another, with the much slower Monique getting the worst of it.

Abruptly Monique surrendered, and within minutes was as deeply immersed in the nighttime soap opera as the rest of the group. Angela, she could see, was still seething. After the show, Angela left, giving Monique a look that could kill. Monique, though, was totally oblivious, talking about the show with the others, as if nothing had occurred.

Unstable. Just like Sharon and Jocelyn, she'd thought. *The* girl Shanicha would select.

The night Jocelyn hung herself, she chanced being seen with Monique. At four in the morning, even though everyone was awake, they were also groggy. She struck up a conversation with Monique and later went with her to her room. The two talked the rest of the night; Monique about her rape; she about made-up problems with her parents.

And just like Shanicha, over the next few evenings she brought up past-life experiences and how there could be a new start for both of them. Monique had scoffed at the notion, but she persisted in hopes of wearing the girl down.

She wasn't about to string Monique along for a month, though. Shanicha, she thought, was a bit too subtle. Even plodding. She knew *she* could do better. Had to, for it was painful being with Monique. Looking at her was bad enough, but up close she noted the girl had a bad case of body odor. Strange, since she knew Monique showered regularly.

Monique would sit in a robe on her bed, having *just* showered, and reek. The room itself had the pungent odor of a girls' locker room. It literally brought tears to her eyes. But Monique seemed unaware.

She also couldn't take Monique's whining. The outgoing, bubbly personality she presented on the outside was a sham; a charade. She bitched and moaned and complained about everything in private. She found fault with everyone and everything.

Tonight, a week after Jocelyn's death, she decided Monique must go. It was either that or *she* herself might jump to preserve her sanity. This talking someone into killing themselves was killing *her*. It was work. She wondered how Shanicha had gone through this twice already.

Monique was bitching, as usual. She listened for a while, then decided she could take no more.

"Life is a bitch," she told Monique, trying to get her back on the subject of suicide. "There's gotta be something better for people like us. If we only have the strength."

"The strength to do what?" Monique asked, though she'd answered the question for the girl dozens of times. She wanted to pummel her then and there. She'd brought a weapon, though she didn't plan on using it. She had an old-fashioned calendar; one of those that displayed the day of the week and date. Each day you had to manually change the setting. It was screwed to a heavy six-inch slab of marble, which served as its base. Before coming, she'd unscrewed the calendar and had the marble plate in her back jeans pocket, covered by a U. of P. athletic shirt.

"The strength to begin our next life, Monique,"

"Oh, yeah." She laughed. "You're really into that crap, aren't you?"

"What do you mean crap?" she asked, anger welling within. "Just yesterday, you were telling me about living in the South during the Civil War. *Your* past life."

Monique scrunched her face. *"Gone With the Wind."*

"What?"

"I made it up. Told you the story of *Gone With the Wind,* with me being Scarlet."

"No. No. No. You were telling me about *your* past life, not some made-up shit."

"Don't get into a lather about it," Monique said. "I want to be friends, and it seemed important to you. So, I kind of went along. *Gone With the Wind* seemed more believable than the *Wizard of Oz.* Both are my favorites."

"*Gone With the Wind? The Wizard of Oz?* Tell me you're pulling my chain. Tell me I haven't been wasting my time."

"Wasting your time?" Monique said, looking perplexed.

She could have left. Could have started fresh with someone else. But she refused to admit defeat. Shanicha would have this girl eating out of the palm of her hand by now. Shanicha would have her clawing to get to the window. If Shanicha could do it, she could, too. Maybe with a little help, but she could do it.

"Forget it," she said, putting on her best smile. "Look at the moon, out there," she said, pointing to the window. "I sometimes think I can see the face of a man," she said, and laughed. "Come, I'll show you."

Monique came to the window.

She pointed to the moon with one hand, while with the other she slipped the marble slab out of her back pocket.

"I don't see any man," Monique said. "I don't see anything. You've got some imagination." She laughed.

She hit her, then. Not too hard. Just enough to stun her, then quickly lifted the window and pushed Monique out head first.

Now, as she looked at Shanicha, her exhilaration was tinged with relief. Not with getting away with what she'd done, but being rid of Monique. She wanted to share her triumph. Not just with Shanicha. With the world. Shanicha was also so damn secretive; keeping it all to herself. An idea began to crystallize. A letter to the police. Not just about

Monique. About all three. Linking them all together.

Shanicha would be pissing in her pants. She'd know someone knew, but not who. Just one letter and she'd fade back
into the shadows. Yes, Shanicha, she thought. I'll do you one
better. Commit murder *and* tell the world. Top that, bitch.

Chapter Fifteen

Ariel wasn't surprised to find Russ McGowan had all the
relevant facts about this latest suicide when she and her partner returned to the station. When he met with his two detectives, there was no question in his mind what had occurred.
Of significance was how to put the best spin on what he
called an "unfortunate incident."

"We got ourselves a public relations nightmare. No crime,
but a hell of a lot of victims—and I'm not talking about the
three suicides."

Ariel wanted to query her superior on the second suicide—
the one hidden from them, but now was not the time, she
decided. Not when he didn't even consider the three dead
girls victims.

"As soon as the shit hits the fan in the media, panicked
parents will be banging on the doors of the University de-
manding to take their precious jewels home. Just like at Har-
vard, last year, when one girl stabbed another something like
twenty-six times, then hung herself."

He shook his head in exasperation. "The University's got
one hell of a problem. We can help by wrapping our end up
ASAP. Do we understand one another?"

Before Doug could speak for them, Ariel raised an objection, her eyes fixed on her Sergeant. "I question rushing to judgment on this one, sir."

From the corner of her eye, she saw Doug close his eyes and shake his head in resignation. She had briefed him on her talk with Lucius on the way back. True, he'd agreed, there was no suicide note, but there was also no sign of foul play. *He* had spoken to a number of students who knew the deceased, and they'd all concurred she was suicidal; holed up in her room lately, when she wasn't in class; irritable and combative, where earlier she had been carefree; far different than the self-deprecating party animal they'd known. Add to that, there was no sign of a struggle, of forced entry into her room, and no witnesses. An open-and-shut case, as far as he was concerned.

He'd almost begged Ariel not to go fishing on this one, but all to no avail. She couldn't remain silent.

"You're referring, I assume, to the fact there was no suicide note," McGowan said, clearly annoyed.

Ariel wondered where he'd gotten his information. Maybe a superior had debriefed Lucius. What was Lucius to do? Lie? She hadn't asked him to hold back anything. Didn't want him to.

"Doug found journals filled with poetry in her room," she answered. "Doesn't add up that someone with so much on her mind would kill herself without leaving something behind to explain her actions."

"You know, Dampier, I didn't know there was an instruction manual on suicides. Chapter three—notes required, with samples enclosed," he said, his voice dripping with sarcasm.

He'd abandoned his "we're-in-this-together, let's-figure-out-what-to-do" approach, and seemed to want to browbeat Ariel to drop her objections.

She simply ignored his condescension.

"There's also the contusion on the back of her head."

McGowan was nonplussed. This, too, had gotten back to
him. Lucius had most definitely been brought on the carpet
to tell all he knew and suspected.

"You're stretching, Dampier," he said, a bit more calmly.
"Look, a girl takes a header and ends up with a bump on her
noggin."

He closed his eyes and massaged his forehead with his
right hand, as if the problem—in this case *she*—would magically disappear.

"There could be a dozen explanations, none of them in-
dications of foul play. Anything else you want to put on the
table?"

"No, sir," she said with resignation. "I never said it *wasn't*
a suicide. I just cautioned against undue haste."

"Your caution is noted . . . and appreciated," he added as
an afterthought. He turned to Doug.

"What's your read?"

"With all due respect to Ariel, I concur with you. Suicide."

"Then suicide it is," he said, slamming his hand on the
desk. "Now we can let the University deal with their head-
aches."

If it would have done any good, Ariel would have given
her partner another tongue-lashing. But, aside from his obvious ass-kissing-demeanor, she knew her protests rang hollow. Maybe Lucius's gut feeling that something wasn't
kosher *had* swayed her common sense. No, chewing off her
partner's head would accomplish nothing. He hadn't gone
behind her back, after all. That they hadn't come to a meeting
of the minds was acceptable to her.

The least she could do, though, was check with the Medical Examiner. She knew Monique Dysart had gone to the
head of the class, as far as priorities were concerned. And
she had made sure, at the crime scene, that the contusion
McGowan thought so little of was noted.

Chapter Sixteen

Whenever Ariel saw Ed Cawley, she thought she was in a funeral home, not the morgue. Cawley was a six-foot-seven splinter of a man who wore a black suit to work each day. He had been the Chief Medical Examiner since Ariel had been at the Academy, fourteen years earlier, and rumor had it he'd been with the office since the turn of the century. He was actually sixty-one, going on eighty. What intrigued her most were his long delicate fingers, better suited to a violin or scalpel than a saw. He was crusty in a good-mannered fashion, and Ariel had gotten along famously with him once she'd transferred to homicide. He had a penchant for Whoppers—chocolate milk balls—and for Christmas and his birthday he'd find a dozen packages, each individually wrapped, on his desk. That she'd noticed his fondness for the chocolate had been duly noted by his respectful manner to her.

Having performed his autopsy on Monique Dysart, he'd excused himself to change, and returned in his black funeral attire.

Ariel had called Chanda, only slightly surprised to find she had woken her up, and after apologizing, told her she might be several more hours.

"I'll be waiting with baited breath," Chanda had deadpanned, and Ariel had had her first laugh of the night.

Now Ariel stood like an expectant schoolgirl, waiting to see if she got the part in the school play she so coveted. Cawley quickly doused her hopes. Nothing suspicious. A suicide.

"What about the contusion on the back of her head?" Ariel asked plaintively.

"What do you want me to tell you, kid?" he said. "That the girl was murdered? Would that make your day? Sorry, but I can't."

He referred to all cops as *kid*—*if* he liked you; asshole, if you got on his bad side.

"What caused the contusion?" she asked.

"You got a bug up your ass about that head wound, don't you?"

Cawley could be wonderfully crass, but if he liked you, whatever he said came out sounding charming, no matter how vulgar.

"All I can tell you is it didn't cause her death. It coincided with her fall. It didn't break the skin. I'd hazard a guess it was incidental contact related to the plunge."

He scrutinized her.

"You must be hard up for a homicide. This, kid, is what it appears—a tragic suicide." He turned to go, then stopped. "By the way, she was pregnant. Six weeks, I'd say. She may not even have been aware herself. If she was, maybe you have her motive."

Chapter Seventeen

Ariel thought she'd be bone tired by the time she got home. Almost five in the morning. But she was still on edge, probably from all the coffee she'd had waiting for the autopsy to be completed. Rather than toss and turn in bed, she went into her clutter room, stuck a Marvin Gaye CD into her player for background and let her mind wander. Soon, she knew, she'd wind down and be able to go to her room and fall asleep within minutes.

Tonight, her mind wandered to Phil Donato, her first Sergeant in homicide. She had only been in Phil Donato's unit for six months when he retired. It seemed the time had sped by. The six months with McGowan, by contrast, seemed an eternity with no relief in sight.

She was getting beaten down by the constant knocking of heads with her superior, which was precisely what he wanted. Make conditions unbearable for her and she'd ask for a transfer. She had to give the man credit. He was subtle. He was crafty. He knew just how far he could go; lines he couldn't cross. He'd never get caught with his pants down on a harassment grievance.

How she longed for the days of Phil Donato, when she'd been treated respectfully—at least by him.

Phil Donato had taken her under his wing—though she received no favored treatment—and had he still been around, she could bounce ideas off him, no matter how farfetched. She'd receive advice, a lecture, often support, but never ridicule. She was made to feel a valued member of a team, as opposed to McGowan ostracizing her all but out of the unit.

The day she'd walked into homicide, a year earlier, her welcome wagon had been Wayne Chompsky, a beefy bigot. He gave her the once-over and shook his head with approval.

"We were expecting a nigger."

Now she gave him the once-over, pinched his cheek and smiled before answering. "Well, honey, you got one."

He flushed. "I didn't mean . . ."

"Bullshit. If you're a bigot, I can live with that. But don't go apologizing when you don't mean it," she snapped at him, purposely coming on like a street-tough black bitch he best not mess with.

Chompsky now shot her a look of contempt, turned and left, mumbling under his breath.

So much for good first impressions, she thought. She caught the eye of what must have been her new Sergeant. He was standing in the partially open door of the only office in the squad room. He beckoned her over with his forefinger.

As she crossed the room, she took his measure. He was a compact, powerfully built man in his late forties, with close-cropped salt-and-pepper hair. On closer inspection, though, he looked far less robust. His face was pasty and deeply lined. Some would call it character. She thought hard living; and possibly hard drinking.

He pointed to a seat, told her to sit down and introduced himself.

"Nice scene out there," he began. "Here all of two minutes and already you've made an enemy—made a fool of him in front of the squad, no less."

"He deserved it," she said tartly.

"If he was a perp, you would have let the slur slide. But Chompsky, you had to bite his head off."

"He's a coworker. He should have shown some respect."

"He's an asshole. You'd have learned to ignore him soon enough. Now you've got to watch your back. Look, we could debate this all day, but it'd be a waste of both our time. Why were you so pissed is the question."

She said nothing, unsure of how to deal with her new superior.

"Two possibilities," he went on. "Because he called you a nigger *or* didn't recognize you were black."

Before she could respond, he held up a manila folder.

"I've got your jacket and you don't look black to me. Chompsky's not the first to mistake you for white. Won't be the last."

He looked at her, as if daring her to correct him. He took out a cigarette, but didn't light it.

91

"Let me lay it on the line for you. You come in here with a chip on your shoulder—justifiably so. The men resent you because you're female. Whites see a political hand in this, too; another black bumped ahead of a more competent white officer."

He again held up his hand before she could interrupt. It was infuriating, she'd thought; to be accused and not allowed to defend yourself.

"It's my dime," he said. "You'll have your chance, I promise. Okay, so they killed two birds with one stone. Black *and* female. Meanwhile, blacks resent you . . . well, for the same reason they've always resented you all your life. No one could tell you were black without a scorecard. Feel you probably kissed up to the man to get the promotion. Feel free to correct me if I'm out in left field."

She couldn't. She knew his views of their perception was correct. As the saying went—been there, done that. She'd seen it with each transfer and promotion. So she remained silent.

He paused, took a lighter off his desk and lit it, then shut the cover. Lit it and again did the same.

"So," he went on, "you can be bitter and not give a shit how you're perceived. Remember, though, you've got to work with these guys—even Chompsky."

He crushed the unlit cigarette out, as if he'd smoked it down to the nub. Ariel was dying of curiosity, and imagined he knew so. Who'd be the first to blink? she wondered.

"My advice, for what it's worth, is to suck up a little now until you've proven yourself to be a good cop on your merits. Not to me. To *them*. This ain't the friggin' NAACP or NOW. They may never like you, never accept you as one of the guys. You gotta live with that. I'm sure you already have. But you can earn their respect."

He now took out a piece of gum and popped it in his mouth, making a face as if it were stale.

"While you're at it, why not purchase a sense of humor. Crack a smile once in a while. Laugh at their crude jokes. Guaranteed it'll fly a lot better than the I'm-the-baddest-black-bitch-in-town attitude you're sporting."

He took the gum out of his mouth, looked at it distastefully and flung it in the trash.

"The floor is yours," he concluded.

"Why the friendly advice?" Ariel asked suspiciously. "It'd be a hell of a lot easier for you if I were gone. You've got to find me a partner, then another when the first doesn't work out. I'd think you'd want me out of your hair."

"Agreed, *if* I hadn't seen your file. *If* this were just departmental politics. Bottom line is you'll make a fine homicide detective, and I don't have many good ones. Most of my men are capable; some a bit better; some worse. There are no superstars here, except in their dreams."

He took another cigarette out, put it in his mouth, but still didn't light it.

"It's no secret I'm not long for the department. Emphysema. Only the department doesn't know, yet."

He took the cigarette out of his mouth and held it up.

"These have been part of my whole life. Killing me, but habits are hard to break. I keep 'em close, just don't light up. Look, Ariel—may I call you Ariel?" he asked.

"Ariel or Dampier. Just so it's no different than the rest of the squad."

"Fair enough. It's Ariel when I'm in a good mood. Dampier when I'm pissed. I'm Phil or Sarge, whatever suits you. Anyway, soon as I take my next physical, I'm history. I don't exactly get the cream of the crop when it comes to new detectives as it is. Another story for another time."

This time he tried a breath mint instead of gum.

"Need something in my mouth." He smiled, as if embarrassed. "Powers that be," he continued, "feel I lack ambition. Lack ability. Whatever, I'm not given priority on hotshots up for promotion. Wouldn't play their game, anyway. I got you because you're a pariah; a woman who's neither black nor white, pardon my being blunt. *But* maybe you're good. Maybe they got blinders over their eyes and they only see a pain-in-the-ass female—white chocolate at that. Maybe, then, I got a budding star, only no one knows it. And maybe you're my last chance to make a difference."

He was silent now. Then: "So welcome aboard."

She had proven herself before Donato left, and with his wealth of experience, he'd taught her more than all the rest of her superiors combined.

The ice had been broken with the rest of the squad, in the locker room, after what could have been a combustive incident.

Ariel had attempted to blend in with the seven other detectives of Donato's squad. She made compromises, held her tongue and kept a relatively low profile while going about her job in as efficient manner as possible. She wouldn't, however, give up her locker room privileges. Here the men adjusted; albeit reluctantly. They stole glances—especially Chompsky—at her in her bra and panties, but guys looked at her at the beach and she didn't tear their heads off. She wouldn't do so here.

One day she opened her locker and found a training bra. She hadn't thought about it before, but all the other detectives were present when she opened her locker; an oddity. It was like it had been planted, then word spread to see her reaction.

The woman in her wanted to disappear. It was difficult enough coping with her racial identity. Yet, even as a woman, she had been cheated with the breasts of a young teen. She likened herself to a tree that had begun to bloom, only to be hit by a drought. It didn't wither and die, but never fully blossomed. Television and magazines made her even more self-conscious, with guys hungering over full-breasted females; as if sexuality and passion could be measured by your bra size. Intellectually, she knew it was garbage, but she certainly wasn't bereft of emotions.

Now these goons had pressed her *other* button. *Dampier has no tits.* Let it get to her—make her explode—and they'd pounce on the weakness like piranhas.

Controlling her churning emotions, she held the bra out and, with her eyes fixed on Chompsky, said, "Sorry guys, this is too big for me," and tossed it at him.

The tension, though not dissolved, was lessened. They had got her and she had accepted it graciously.

But revenge was in order. She'd long ago learned that when these sophomoric pranks were pulled, you earned respect—points, she recalled being told—by doing them one better. Ignore the incident and you were the butt of further shenanigans.

After her shift, she went shopping; then called up a friend in the front office of the Philadelphia Eagles, who promptly filled the rest of her order.

The next day her seven "brothers" were greeted by the sight of jock straps attached to their lockers; each of varying sizes. And, in each was a further surprise; each had two lemons, or two nectarines. Covington had two grapes, Winston two marbles and Chompsky two raisins.

Each of the detectives—some more reluctantly than others—displayed their prize to the others. Sandoval proudly hoisted two apples with: "Some set of balls, huh!" And everyone had a good laugh when one of the raisins fell out of Chompsky's jock. "Too big for you, Chomp?" Covington yelled.

Ariel took it all in without a word. As several of the guys left—many to spread the word around—they made sure to pass her.

"Fucking-A good response, Dampier," from Sandoval.

"Didn't know you had it in you. Congrats," from Carter.

"Ranks with the best, Dampier. With the *very* best," from Covington.

That, more than cracking a tough case, got her entrance into the Boy's Club at homicide. Whenever a new detective came aboard, he'd soon find a jock in his locker filled with raisins. As the new guy shook his head at being humiliated, he was given the word Ariel had pulled the original.

Those were heady days—only eleven months ago. Ariel had played by *their* rules and won acceptance; done her job and then some and with that earned Donato's admiration. Now Donato was gone, along with all the other homicide detectives she'd started out with. She missed them; even Chompsky and his bigoted self. At least he was genuine; you knew where you stood. McGowan's crew, with the exception of her partner, could all have come from the same mold.

Thinking of Phil Donato and the "good old days" brought tears to Ariel's eyes. She normally wasn't the crying kind, but she realized work lately had become a *job*. Maybe McGowan was succeeding by making her miserable.

She yawned and was about to go her room. So tired, though. Why bother? She closed her eyes and fell asleep in the chair of her clutter room.

Chapter Eighteen

Shanicha had taken her shower after the hubbub of Monique's suicide died down. She'd been brushing her hair when word spread that classes had been canceled for the following day. Instead, Crisis Intervention Teams would provide counseling at The Quad, and in various campus buildings. The entire freshman class was also invited to Irvine Auditorium for a group encounter session. That was not what it was billed, but Shanicha knew that was how it would end. A lot of tears and hugging, the spilling of emotion; then a bonding of all those in attendance.

Bullshit, Shanicha thought. She had better things to do.

She fell asleep without a problem, but awoke to the sound of something crawling under her bed at five in the morning. A spider. A huge hairy spider intent on laying its eggs in Shanicha's womb.

She bolted out of her bed and was down two flights of stairs before waking up. Panting, she sat down on the staircase. Sleepwalking again. Two, three, sometimes four times a year, the same nightmare. Usually when she'd been overly stimulated . . .

—Like after a kill.

She trudged back to her room, sweat dripping like rainwater, as if she'd been caught in a sudden squall. Even though she knew it was only a dream, she had to be sure. She knew no spider hid under her bed, in her bedding, anywhere in the room. Yet, she tore the room apart, the exertion making her sweat all the more . . .

—A foul sweat.
—Pungent.
—With the odor of fear.

Her roommate slept through this all, once again, dead to the world once her head touched the pillow.

Satisfied there was no spider in her room, and exhausted by her efforts, she *should* have gone right to sleep. She knew she couldn't, though. Not without a shower. The odor of fear had attracted the despicable creatures before, and would do so again. No, she had to wash it away. Another shower, taking special care to lather every orifice, to cleanse her body of its dread.

When she was done, she had to choose the proper deodorant. Her arsenal of deodorants was akin to Imelda Marcos's shoe collection. Shanicha chose different deodorants, like perfume, for different occasions. She had sprays and roll-ons, scented and unscented; deodorants specifically for women and brands favored by men. Without a thought she chose Ban roll-on. Always did after her spider dream. With Ban, she'd protect herself from the encroaching arachnid. She then sprayed the room with another brand, as if it were a bug repellent.

Then, brushing her hair, she recalled the day the spiders had *really* attacked her.

She was the last of six adoptive children; the third crack baby. Her adoptive mother had been unable to conceive, and her parents were particularly interested in hard-to-place infants. Being black and born addicted to crack, Shanicha fit the bill.

Unexpectedly, two months after her adoption, her mother found herself with child. It was such a blessing, her adoptive parents tried again, soon after her stepsister was born. And again, they were blessed. And again. And again—seven natural children in all, no more than a year apart to add the brood of six they had adopted.

Being the last of the adopted children, and her mother coping with a not-so-pleasant pregnancy, Shanicha received scant attention. Many of the day-to-day responsibilities were turned over to one of her older sisters, Tanya. To say her sister wasn't thrilled was an understatement. She was boy-crazy at nine, pregnant herself at thirteen.

Shanicha was raised in New Canaan, a small town of three thousands souls, in the Poconos; in the mountains of Pennsylvania known primarily for their skiing resorts. Unlike her

inner-city brethren, woods, streams and caves made for wondrous adventures as she grew.

When Tanya was twelve and Shanicha seven, her older
sister took her to a cave one day, along with her latest
squeeze, Roger. They went deep into the cave where no one
could hear. Shanicha led the way, ignoring the laughter of
her sister and her friend, until her sister ran up to her. She
was breathing heavily and was flushed. Shanicha saw the top
three buttons of her sister's blouse were undone. She could
see her bra.

"Have you and Roger been making out?" she'd asked, not
knowing exactly what it meant.

Tanya seemed taken aback, then laughed. "Since when did
you learn about making out?" she asked.

"It's in the movies you take me to see, silly," Shanicha
had said with a pout. "Smushy kissing and hugging . . . and
other things." She looked down at the ground, embarrassed.
"You're spending all your time with Roger. You said we'd
explore the cave. Just the two of us. Now you're making out
with Roger."

"We're not making out," Tanya said, and again laughed.
"But we're tired. Tell you what. You stay here for a while—
just ten minutes. Then the two of us will explore the cave. I
promise."

Shanicha was silent. Tanya was full of promises. Made
many more than she kept.

Tanya found a crystalline rock and gave it to Shanicha.
"You can draw on the walls with this. Just a ten-minute rest,
and we'll explore the cave."

"Promise?" Shanicha asked.

"Word of honor."

And she was gone. Shanicha drew on the walls for a while,
hearing her sister laughing around the bend. She heard some
moaning, too, just like in the movies when people made out.

Bored, Shanicha went exploring on her own.

Later, much later, she heard Tanya calling for her in the distance. She tried to retrace her steps, but the cave was full of passageways. Sometimes her sister sounded close; then her voice would fade and disappear completely, only to re-emerge in a different direction a few minutes later. Sometimes, the sound would echo, coming from more than one place at the same time. Shanicha tried to follow the voice. When it began to fade again, she ran to catch it.

Ran into a tangle of spiderwebs that blocked her way. The gooey web stuck to her like cotton candy, as she tried to brush it off. She was sure the web was moving; pulsating. The web was alive, she thought. Only it wasn't the web. It was spiders; hundreds of them of all shapes and sizes, making a beeline for her.

Some got into her hair, and when she screamed, one plopped in her mouth for an instant. Some tickled her ears as they danced down toward her face. Others crawled up her legs. She batted them away frantically, but they seemed everywhere. When she felt them on her privates, she stopped swatting at them and just screamed.

—Screamed.
—Screamed.
—Then screamed some more.

Screamed when she was pulled free. Screamed as other hands batted the creatures off her. Screamed when a voice told her to stop. Stopped only when a hand slapped her face, then covered her mouth. The scream she now heard was Tanya telling her, "Shut the fuck up."

Her sister was crying now as she cradled Shanicha in her arms. She held her tightly, as Shanicha's body shook spastically.

"I'm so sorry, Shanicha. Please forgive me. Don't tell Mama. Forgive me, Shanicha. Don't tell Mama."

Only then did Shanicha begin to calm. She looked at her sister, tears streaming down her face. *Don't tell Mama what?* she wondered. Don't tell Mama she'd gotten lost? Don't tell Mama about the spiders? Then she understood. *Don't tell Mama that Tanya was making out with Roger.*

She wasn't scared anymore. She was angry. Furious that Tanya was thinking only of herself. Only fearful that she'd tell their mother she'd been making out with Roger. She said nothing, though. Nothing to Tanya. Nothing to Mama.

Tanya spent a lot more time with her for a while after that. Treated her good. But Shanicha saw the fear in her sister's face. *Fear she'd tell Mama.*

A year later, Tanya was pregnant, and it no longer made any difference. If you were having a baby, Shanicha now knew, you were doing a lot more than just making out.

Shanicha's nightmares started just a week after the incident. At first, she was back in the cave. The spiders were bigger. She couldn't brush them off.

After she had her period, at eleven, and was far more knowledgeable about what the changes in her body meant, there was a subtle change in the nightmares. Spiders still danced over her, but one—a big hairy female—always went for her genitals; inched her way in, laid her eggs, and covered them with a fine down web. Shanicha would awake, clawing at her privates, sure that thousands of baby spiders were ready to hatch any moment in her womb.

It was then she began her ritualistic showers. Wash the hideous creatures from inside her after the nightmares. Wash to keep them from returning. They came to her—especially the pregnant female—because of her smell; the odor of her fear.

Her body became a temple, and she became obsessive in her personal grooming. She'd meticulously clean her nails daily; slowly and with excruciating pain she would rid all traces of dirt from beneath her cuticles.

She refused to wear jewelry—even a watch—after a bracelet gave her a rash. . . .

—A rash that festered with the odor of her dread.

She wouldn't pierce her ears, though she was fashionable in every other way. They were a haven for dirt and germs; a trail easily followed by her tormentors.

She brushed her teeth a half dozen times daily. The mouth, after all, she heard on television, was a breeding ground for germs whose smell would give her away. Brush, floss, gargle. Then do it again.

She wore no makeup. Every pore of her body must be unclogged to release the odor of fear, so she could later wash it away. If it remained, buried under lipstick or mascara, she could be under attack at a moment's notice.

Deodorant, though, could mask the smell until she could shower. She thought perfume might help as well, but she was allergic. A rash. Crawling with germs. Heavenly allure for the spiders.

As she got older, she came to terms with her dreams; knew on an intellectual level why the nightmares persisted. But a deeper, more primal part of her being insisted on her taking precautions, lest the pregnant spider locate her and lay its eggs.

It was past seven when she finally felt clean.

This time she slept dreamlessly until three in the afternoon.

Chapter Nineteen

Two days later, when Ariel reported for her 4 p.m. shift, the squad room was abuzz. Doug, who always got there early, lest he miss anything, lassoed her as soon as she entered.

"Lieutenant's been holed up with McGowan for more than an hour, from what I hear. Looks like the shit's hit the fan," he recounted excitedly.

"I like it when you talk dirty, Doug. Really, it turns me on," she said, and blew him a kiss.

He flushed.

Ariel knew she was a tease, but it came naturally working in a hostile environment. Doug hardly ever used profanity, even with his fellow male officers. Ariel could count on one hand, with several fingers left over, the number of times he'd cursed in front of her. He made a conscious effort to be civil. Ariel was a woman, after all.

That the Lieutenant might be busting McGowan's chops meant little to her. Whatever it was, it wouldn't have anything to do with a case she'd be assigned. If it was choice, one of McGowan's clones would handle it.

She was taken aback, then, twenty minutes later when a disgruntled-looking McGowan summoned her and Doug to his office. They both stood, as Lieutenant Daniel Schumacher was sitting morosely in the only other chair in the office.

"The suicides at Penn," McGowan began. "We've got a problem."

McGowan handed a note to Doug, who read it and gave

it to Ariel. Before Ariel had a chance to read it, McGowan
asked her to read it aloud.

She shrugged, but did as he asked. It was written as a
poem, she thought to herself, then began to read.

Suicides at the University of Pennsylvania
Or murder most foul?
Pick your poison with care
For seek and ye shall find a hand behind the crimes.
That hand is mine.
A clue you ask?
For this must surely be a prank.
The bitches knew one another
Far better than you think.

"Signed, Without Scruples," Ariel added, though she
thought to herself that wasn't quite accurate. The letter, and
closing, had been typed. Most likely on a computer with a
laser-jet printer.

"A poem, sort of. Free verse. Someone who's read a lot
of Agatha Christie. You know, a bit over the top," she finished.

"Thank you for the literary interpretation," McGowan said
tartly, his eyes on his Lieutenant. "It came in today's mail.
Addressed to homicide."

He showed them the envelope.

"No prints on the letter or the envelope," he said, antici-
pating their question.

He looked at Ariel for the first time. "Seems to lend credence to your suspicions. Did these girls know one another?"
he now asked.

Ariel knew he was referring to the cryptic clue mentioned
in the poem.

"Casually at best," she answered. "All freshmen. All living
in the same dorm—same complex, that is. They didn't live

in the same building is what I'm saying. Those we interviewed said they weren't friends, not even acquaintances. Yet, this person infers the three had more than incidental contact. The note *does* add a new wrinkle, if it's authentic."

McGowan seemed to be digesting what she said, saying nothing at first and avoiding eye contact with Ariel. That Ariel's initial misgivings might have been justified must have been hard for McGowan to swallow, Ariel thought. She didn't know what to think herself. That the suicides were murders now seemed outlandish. After Monique Dysart's autopsy, even she agreed there seemed nothing to investigate.

"Our problem is this," McGowan said finally. "If we sit on this and whoever wrote it goes public, we'll be accused of a cover-up; in league with the University to protect its image."

He kept his hands clasped tightly as he spoke. It reminded Ariel of someone with constipation. McGowan was at one of two extremes. Some people spoke as much with their hands as their words. She hated to generalize, but she noticed it with Italians especially. On the other end of the spectrum was McGowan, who checked his emotions at the door. His hands *never* moved when he spoke, as if he'd bottled his emotions. Constipated, she thought, described it well. Especially since he was so full of himself. He began talking again, and Ariel put the image of him on the can—unable to take a dump—aside.

"On the other hand, until we learn otherwise, we can't have word leak we're investigating a possible serial killing."

He closed his eyes, momentarily, as if the thought made him ill.

Ariel said nothing. Even if she had initially been proven wrong, she *had* urged caution. She now looked prophetic. It would earn her no points with her superior to bail him out, so she let him squirm. Doug was silent, she knew, because all of a sudden simple suicides were becoming complicated.

"We have to take the note seriously," McGowan said after clearing his throat. "At the same time, we want a low-profile investigation. What's in this note is on a need-to-know basis only. This is your case, Dampier. You seem to have a contact with the campus police. Brief him, but except for the University of Pennsylvania Police Commissioner, whom I'll contact, it goes no further. You'll work with Doug, of course, but it's your baby. Do you understand?"

Perfectly, she thought. If it blew up in her face and knowledge of the letter became public, it was her ass on the line. He'd exonerated himself in front of *his* superior.

"Yes, sir," was all she said, however. "Is the second suicide ours now?" she asked.

McGowan held up a manilla folder. "It's *all* yours, Dampier." The way he said it made it sound like a disease he wanted no part of.

"I want to be kept informed every step of the way, of course. This is a *team effort*. We sink or swim together."

Bullshit, she thought. If it turns sour, her "teammates" would abandon ship—except for Doug. She'd be left to fend for herself.

She should have been pissed. Instead, she was elated. She *knew,* given his druthers, McGowan would have assigned the case to one of *his* men. But, due to the quirks of rotation, she and Doug had gotten the initial call. And this was the type of case she lived for. She had a mystery to unravel; possibly a felon to apprehend. She'd been out of the loop on such cases since Donato's retirement. Now, the case was hers, and she grasped it with relish.

Her first order of business was to rid herself of her partner. She wanted to speak to Lucius, and in this case three would be a crowd.

When they were back in the squad room, Ariel asked Doug to try to track down the letter. She didn't think it possible, but it would keep him out of her hair.

106

"If we can find out where this note originated," she told him, "it'll narrow our list of suspects. I have no idea how the U. of P. computer systems operate. You know, if you use a computer in one of the labs do you have to sign in or something? Can we pinpoint the printer? Why don't you start with that while I talk to the campus cop from the first and third suicides."

Ariel looked at her watch. Just after five. "It's too late now," she told Doug. "Our shift starts just as the University begins to shut down. I'll speak to McGowan to get him to authorize us some overtime. For now, let's both go over what we have with a fine-tooth comb, and see if anything out of the ordinary jumps out at us."

Doug acquiesced. He wanted marching orders. Needed direction. She couldn't have been more pleased.

Ariel then called Lucius, told him there was a new development and she needed to talk to him privately the next day.

"Why not meet at Houston Hall? We can get a bite at Skolniks," he said.

They agreed to meet at eleven.

Hanging up, she felt the adrenaline flowing. It was the case . . .

—And seeing Lucius again.

Definitely the case, she corrected herself . . .

—But Lucius was still on her mind.

Chapter Twenty

Houston Hall, Lucius told her the next morning, was the oldest student union in the country. Skolniks and the adjacent Burger King didn't mesh with that image.

Skolniks sold everything on its menu on a bagel, which was now as American as apple pie. That ten years earlier bagels were eaten primarily by Jews seemed ironic to Ariel. Ten years ago, Lucius wouldn't have touched a bagel. It represented the side of Ariel he'd wanted her to abandon.

And a fast-food restaurant like Burger King in the oldest student union in the country was equally incongruous.

As bagels went, Skolniks' were pretty lame, she thought as she slathered hers with cream cheese. Gentile bagels, she thought to herself, and almost laughed aloud. Too small, too squat and with a soft crust. Not the bagels her father brought home. Lucius didn't seem to mind as he gobbled down his grilled cheese on a bagel.

As student unions went, she had seen far better. This was too . . . *spacious*; dozens of tables with more than adequate lighting for students who came to study. Lucius told her there was additional seating upstairs; an area designated for smokers.

She had been to student unions that were a lot more intimate. Definitely not places for studying, but discussion and often heated debates. Dim, poorly lit, with music for those who came alone just to get away from it all. Houston Hall wasn't that at all, and Ariel, for one, was disappointed.

"So," Lucius said after polishing off his bagel. "You mentioned a new development."

She smiled. He said it so matter-of-factly, but he couldn't keep the curiosity out of his voice.

"Not here," she said. "It's not really private. Too many people coming in and out."

He nodded in agreement. "What do you say we stroll the campus. I know a perfect place, as a matter of fact."

Walking out, Ariel noted Lucius looked much better than two nights earlier. Whatever feelings of inadequacy had haunted him before seemed to have lost their grip.

They emerged onto the Campus Green, with its spacious lawns, crowded with students reading, studying, sunbathing and socializing. It was the heart of the campus, he told her.

To Ariel, it was wondrous. Just one block north, on Walnut Street, reality intruded. Here, though, was an idyllic campus setting far removed from the predators of the inner city.

They walked past the Button, a sculpture carved from rock in the shape of a button, replete with a rope that crisscrossed four central holes, much like a real button sewn on a shirt.

Just beyond, Ariel saw a knot of naked students—*butt naked,* without a stitch of clothing.

"What the fuck is that?" she asked.

"The Naturist Society," Lucius said without a trace of scorn. "First time I saw one of their rallies, I thought I'd have to arrest them," he said with a laugh. "But it's legal."

"You gotta be kidding," she said in awe.

"As long as they're not lewd or lascivious, nudity in itself is not illegal; at least in Philly. Their group is registered on campus; one of over a hundred student groups. They have meetings, and each spring a rally to extol the virtues of the naked body.

"Actually, there's nothing remotely sexual—hell, even erotic—about it. That's my *only* objection." And he laughed again.

109

Ariel looked at Lucius and laughed. But he was right. The only touching she saw was a man painting a rose on the back of a woman.

"This isn't spontaneous," he went on. "Highly organized. They get their permit and post signs so those who might be offended can steer clear. All three television stations cover it each year. Could use file footage and no one would know the difference."

Lucius, Ariel thought, seemed so at ease; so much in his element here. Students would pass and say hello. Others seeing him would wave. It was as if he were a professor taking a stroll.

Looking at the Naturists, Ariel saw an overweight man with a small pecker that seemed to be withdrawing into the man, like a turtle into its shell.

"Check out the hunk at two o'clock. He's hung like you, Boo."

He looked at her. "No one's called me that, well, since we split up."

She had given him the nickname when he'd banged his shin and gotten a bruise, when they'd been moving furniture into their apartment shortly after their marriage.

"Let me kiss your boo-boo," she'd said.

"Don't make fun of me." He'd laughed. "It hurts."

Soon they were making love. Ariel was kissing his penis. "You got a boo-boo here?" she'd asked.

"Will you kiss it and make it better?" he'd responded.

"Anytime," she'd said, and began administering first aid.

The name had stuck, shortened to Boo.

Now he was checking out the guy she'd compared him to.

"Like fuck he's hung like me," he said.

Ariel laughed. "I forgot, you're hung like a stud. At least that fits the black stereotype, Mr. Macho," she said, staring at his crotch.

"God, you're crass, woman. I'd forgotten. And stop looking at me like that . . . *there*," he blubbered.

Ariel burst out in laughter. "Sorry." Then she laughed again. "I can't help it."

"What?" he asked. "Laughing or staring?" And they both laughed.

When they'd recovered, Lucius looked at Ariel long and hard. She almost said something, but he beat her to it.

"I must admit the sex was good. Haven't had any better."

Now she blushed, but recovered quickly. "See any pussy over there that compares to me," she said, looking at the Naturists.

"*Ariel!*" he fumed.

"Just jerking your chain, Boo. Just jerking your chain."

"Liked jerking my chain, didn't you." And they both laughed again, at the sexual innuendo.

Lucius finally maneuvered Ariel just past Van Pelt Library to a clump of trees that all but hid the sculpture of a peace sign.

"This is one of my favorite places," he told her after suggesting they sit under a tree. "Usually, plenty of privacy. Political groups often rally here, with harangues on the cause of the day. Otherwise, it's almost like a sanctuary; out in the open, yet secluded."

Ariel couldn't imagine the area littered with angry students. It seemed so peaceful.

"A few years ago a group called SWAC met here," Lucius continued.

"That's one I haven't heard of," Ariel said. "A new right-wing group?"

"Hardly." Lucius laughed. "Students Without A Cause. Tired of all the political diatribes. They came with blank banners, handed out a blank list of demands, and shouted, 'We want nothing.' They submitted their blank list of demands to the President of the school, who got into the spirit and agreed to them all."

They both laughed.

"SWAC," Ariel said. "Students Without A Cause. God, to be young and foolish. It's a shame we're so full of ourselves at that age that we can't enjoy those moments at the time. We look back on them fondly when our life's lost much of its meaning."

"Maybe that's why I like this job so much," Lucius said. "Life does have a meaning."

They sat quietly for a good five minutes looking at the Naturists' group demonstration, TV crews shooting footage, making sure not to show too much of the bare essentials for family viewing. They sat in comfortable silence, Ariel thought, much as they had before they'd married. There was a lot of silence after, but it was silence born of tension, marred by hostility.

Lucius finally broke the mood. "So, you've got something to tell me, or are you trying to seduce me?"

"Boo!" she said, and punched him lightly on the shoulder. Then she turned serious, and took a copy of the note out of a pocket in her jeans. Before meeting Lucius, she had changed to casual attire—jeans and a 76ers T-shirt, so she wouldn't be conspicuous on campus. She watched him as he read the note, looked at Ariel, then read it again.

"Fucking-A," he said finally. "Someone might have killed those girls?" he asked in wonder.

"*Might* is the operative word here. Could be a sick joke, but it's gotta be taken seriously."

She told him of McGowan's marching orders. "A low-profile investigation. You can have in, if you want."

"If I *want*! I want, all right. No reason for those girls to die, whether it was suicide or murder. I've listened to this cluster-suicide shit until I'm blue in the face, but I still don't

112

buy it. There's too many support mechanisms on campus for this to happen."

"What do you mean?"

"At home these kids can brood, and their parents see it as a phase of adolescence. Many times there's also no one to turn to. Here there's people like me, residence hall assistants in the dorms, hundreds of student groups, roommates, faculty members and psychological counseling galore. And there's anonymity. What you say won't be spread around, like at high school."

Ariel noticed that Lucius talked with his hands.

—Hands that used to caress your body, a voice from within intruded.

"Let me give you an example," he went on. "Say you have a problem with . . . your sexual identity. You're a girl and all of a sudden you're finding yourself attracted to other women. At home you keep it bottled in, and like an ulcer it burns a hole and spreads. You're a freak, you think. There's no one else like you—at least that's your perception. Here, there's the Woman's Center. And there are gay/lesbian support groups for blacks, Hispanics, Asians, even gay atheists. You understand?"

"Someone to talk it out with," Ariel said, nodding her head.

"With no threat of disclosure, and without making value judgments," Lucius added. "If they can't help, they'll refer you to someone who can. Your parents, your friends—they're all kept out of the loop, if you wish."

"But there are suicides on college campuses," Ariel countered.

"Less than in the general population," Lucius shot back, then smiled. "I checked it out when this shit began. It happens, *but three in five weeks*? That's hard to swallow. With

113

Crisis Intervention, there's been more support than usual."

"So you think the note's genuine?" Ariel asked. "You think it's murder?"

"I hate to sound like your boss, but I think it's got to be considered."

He paused, and frowned, as if unable to phrase what he wanted to say. Finally, he just let it out.

"Look, Ariel, don't get me wrong when I say this, but I need your emotional detachment to help me out on this."

She looked him a question.

"I might get too caught up in this murder theory. I knew the kids involved, after all, and if there is a murderer I probably know her, too."

"Why not a him? Or was it just a figure of speech?"

"If it was murder, it had to be someone who could get close to the three girls, without anyone else noticing. A guy in the girl's dorm would stick out like a sore thumb with three separate cases." He paused. "Where was I?"

"My lack of emotions," she said with irritation.

He raised his hands in despair. "I knew you'd take it the wrong way."

"Oh, suddenly you know me," she bristled.

"I know parts of you," he said with a smile. "What I meant is, as an outsider, you can distance yourself, keep me from going off half-cocked. You're not part of this campus, is what I'm saying. And this campus is a community. My community. My extended family. It wasn't a putdown."

"Okay," she said, a bit mollified. "And you're right. I've seen how emotionally involved you get. It's not healthy. I'll keep an eye on you," she said with a wink.

"Now, down to business," she went on, turning serious. "Let's take this one step at a time. Tell me about Jocelyn Rhea."

"Jocelyn Rhea," he said dejectedly. "What bugs me about this murder theory is she *was* a candidate for suicide. If there is a murderer, the victims were not chosen at random. Of that I'm certain."

Ariel was taking notes, then looked at Lucius. "It hadn't occurred to me. For the sake of argument, let's say it is murder. You're saying the victims all had something in common. Something that could make their deaths appear to be self-inflicted. So the murderer had to be close to them. Close enough to really know they were walking time bombs; all capable of suicide."

"And Jocelyn fills the bill," Lucius added. "She was from Long Island. Father had money. Jocelyn did well in high school, but through hard work. She wasn't nearly as bright as a lot of her peers here. Once here, no matter how hard she worked, she got too many *B*'s for her father."

Lucius took out a toothpick and stuck it in his mouth.

"Her father was always on her case. He was paying the freight, so she didn't have to get a job. Her *only* job was to study. Why the poor grades? he'd ask, as if she was flunking out. He'd also call her several times a week, and if she wasn't in, he demanded an accounting of her time. He was still pulling the strings; exerting control. There was always that threat hanging over her head that he'd pull her out; have her go to a local school where she would live at home."

"How do you know so much about her?" Ariel asked suddenly. "A lot more than the others."

"She told me after she was raped."

"Raped?"

"A date rape. I *wasn't* there," he said with a tight smile. "I can only tell you what she related to me."

He paused, then went on.

"Her father frowned on her dating in high school—even on weekends. Here, she dated a lot. A way to get back at her old man, I guess, or maybe just catching up."

"Maybe a combination of the two," Ariel countered.

Lucius agreed. "Anyway, word was she was sexually active. Very active. Had a key chain filled with condoms instead of keys. I never saw it, but that's what I heard, after her suicide."

"At least she believed in safe sex," Ariel said.

"Yeah. Well, one night a call comes in while I'm on patrol. Jocelyn claims she was raped. Procedure is to take her to Support Services and a female officer takes her to Jefferson Hospital for an exam. Only Jocelyn insisted I take her. We'd talked. She'd told me about her father. She didn't want any stranger with her after the rape."

"I can empathize with her," Ariel said. "A stranger, even a woman, wouldn't necessarily be sympathetic toward her."

"That's how I read it, and Support Services agreed. On the way she told me the guy she was with got aroused so fast, he didn't use a condom. She was certain she was pregnant. Said she could feel a child growing within her. I chalked it up to shock."

He paused, as if thinking where to go from there.

"Here's where it gets hairy. Support Services is part of the campus police; manned by regular officers. There's a rotation. It's not a promotion, but on-the-job training. You're part of the unit for two years and then back on patrol. Or you apply for another special assignment. It's not permanent, is what I'm saying. But, like with the regular police, they're territorial. Want it or not, Jocelyn was assigned a female officer, after her hospital visit, and I was told to go about my job."

Lucius broke the toothpick in half and tossed it.

"A week later Jocelyn comes up to me in tears. She had her period. She's not pregnant. Why the tears? I ask. Seems it was her ticket out of school, she tells me. Pregnant, she'd have to drop out."

He shook his head in exasperation.

"What some of these kids will do," he said. "It boggles the mind."

116

He paused, as if pondering the point.

"Like the other two girls," he went on, "she went downhill from there. She had been an organization freak. When she read a book she'd highlight the important passages in blue. The second time she'd highlight in yellow. Third time orange. Showed me a book. Over half of it was blue, half of that covered in yellow and half of that in orange. For tests, she'd study only the orange."

Out of the blue he changed course.

"Do you still have a roomful of albums?"

"CDs now, but yeah, I have quite a collection."

"How do you organize them?"

Ariel laughed. "I don't. I've tried, but they're all just stuck in those wooden racks. It's a bitch, sometimes, finding what I want."

"Well, Jocelyn had hers organized. Alphabetically and by category. I found out later from her roommate she'd organize her clothes by color as well.

"Just after the rape, her roommate came down with mono. Spent some time in the hospital. Since she was from Philly, when she was discharged, she stayed at home and commuted. This way her parents could mother her. Never saw Jocelyn alive again. But after she died, I talked to her roommate. Jocelyn wore a different-color underwear each day of the week. Everything stored orderly, so she wouldn't have to dig through her drawers."

"You're going to tell me this changed after the rape, right?"

"You got it. I checked out her room after her roommate filled me in. CDs were haphazard. Clothes just tossed in her closet. On the floor of her closet, I mean. And no organization to the underwear. She'd also begun cutting a few classes. And we found brooze in her room. A lot of empty bottles of vodka in her trash. Trash she didn't trash. Seemed about as open-and-shut as you can get."

117

"Did she leave a note?"

"Handwritten." He took out his notebook and rifled through the pages.

Ariel smiled. "Still write everything down, I see."

"Still have a lousy memory. And it's a form of organization. You know, 'From the Files of Lucius Jackson.' And a kind of journal. I add notes and random thoughts. Got a desk full of them in my apartment."

Finally he located the page.

"Here it is," he said, and began reading, aloud, the suicide note:

I've made a mess of things. I'd like a second chance. You did your best, so don't blame yourself. We'll meet again, someday.

"What happened to the support mechanisms?" Ariel asked with a trace of sarcasm.

"You know how to hurt a guy, don't you?" he answered. He thought for a moment.

"Her roommate getting sick factored in. They were pretty close. She would have noticed the changes. I'm pretty sure Jocelyn was still in counseling for the rape. She should have gotten help there. My gut feeling—the rape short-circuited her emotionally. She stopped trusting people. Never came to me after she found out she wasn't pregnant. That's about it," Lucius said, and grew quiet. Then he perked up.

"If she was murdered, the support mechanisms *didn't* fail. She wasn't happy. Pretty screwed up, I'll grant you, but maybe she didn't hang herself." He shrugged. "A thought, anyway."

"Monique was pregnant when she died," Ariel said. Mention of Jocelyn's wanting to be pregnant had triggered her memory.

"Get out," Lucius said. "She kept it a secret."

118

"May not have known herself. She was only in her sixth week."

"Four murders then, if in fact it was murder," Lucius said.

"I hadn't thought of that, but you're right."

"What now? How do we begin?" he asked.

"You're deferring to me? How quaint."

"You're the hotshot homicide detective. I'm Tonto here; the loyal sidekick." He laughed, and Ariel joined him.

"We have to find some commonality," she said finally. "Narrow the search, if we're to give the clue in the note any credence. They were all freshmen, all lived in the same dorm, but they weren't friends. Hell, according to everyone we interviewed, they had no more than casual contact with one another."

Ariel paused, and when Lucius said nothing, she went on. "So were they in the same classes? Active in the same clubs? Attend the same church? Their lives touched in some way so someone could target them. The question, Tonto, is how do we get this information?"

"Computers," he said after giving it some thought. "If we can convince the campus Police Commissioner to cooperate, then ask the right questions, we'll find a link."

"Then how's about we go see your boss," she said.

"I thought you might want to take part in the rally first," he said teasingly, looking down at the Naturists.

"Only if you join me."

"Wouldn't do much for my image," he said.

"Your image as a cop or as a stud?" she asked with a smirk.

"You're bad, Ariel. You're so bad."

Chapter Twenty-one

Shanicha saw the white bitch cop with the campus fuzz from Locust Walk, outside the Steinbergh-Dietrich Building. It wasn't by happenstance. The campus cop, Jackson, reminded her of cops that used to come to class in elementary school talking about bicycle safety, what to do with Halloween candy and shit like that. Officer Friendly, he was called. Cops who weren't good enough, she figured, to be out where they belonged; guys with big guts and plastic smiles.

Officer Jackson couldn't cut it as a real cop, so here he was trying to endear himself to students on campus. While she had little respect for him, she had long ago learned not to underestimate even such a simpleton. That got you caught. He might be a toy policeman, but he was still the fuzz. And she didn't like the way he'd looked at her—almost into her head—at the scenes of the suicides.

Unlike many of her classmates, she steered clear of *this* Officer Friendly. Hell, she'd made it a practice to keep her distance from all cops. Unlike freshmen she knew, she didn't want to *confide* in Officer Friendly. She didn't want to cry on his shoulder when things got tough. And she certainly didn't want to get into his pants like Jocelyn. The fool girl thought he was cute, and so damn sexy with his bald head.

"I could get down on him," Jocelyn had said.

It was enough to make her gag, but she'd held her tongue.

She'd kept an eye on him after Monique died, and again today. The day before, she'd seen him talking to some girls

who knew Monique. And today, the *real* cop, bitch that she
was, was back on campus.

What did she want? Monique's death was old news. And
the two of them laughing like . . . like *lovers*

Shanicha took out a match, lit it and was absorbed by the
flame, until it just about touched her finger, then dropped it.
She didn't smoke. Germs . . .

—Which would attract the spiders.

But she had a dozen packs of matches in her purse. She
had always been fascinated by fire. Now she wanted to go
over to Officer Friendly and the white bitch cop, and set them
aflame.

Just like when she was eleven, in New Canaan. With seven
younger brothers and sisters, she was pretty much left to her
own devices. Since first grade, she had learned to control her
emotions. Blend in. At home, it was as if she hardly existed.
She could be gone for hours, pop in and no one was the
wiser. It gnawed at her sometimes. She wanted to be noticed.
Wanted attention.

After supper she went outside.

She watched the fireflies dancing on the gentle breeze.
Bringing the barest trace of light one moment, smothering
darkness the next.

"Firefly, burning bright, make me visible tonight," she
sang in hushed reverence, as if to a deity. "Firefly . . . burning
bright . . . burning bright . . . burning . . . bright."

She walked a mile to the DeLoatch barn; abandoned as
many other farms, when the soil failed to produce enough to
satisfy the bank. She ignored the musty odor. She sat in the
center of the barn, on the earthen floor, and lit match after
match.

They looked just like the fireflies.

She'd hold them in her fingers till the dimming flame

seared her flesh, then let loose. Then lit another, and another and still more. Mesmerized, she was barely aware of a wisp of smoke. Wood chips smoldered, then burst into flame. Within seconds, she was surrounded by a deafening conflagration.

She stood transfixed as the fire began to spread. Finally, fear, then self-preservation kicked in and awakened her to action. She'd fled, only to be drawn back to her creation when the crowd had gathered.

Except on holidays, she couldn't remember seeing so many people together at one time. She remembered watching the old barn burn. The flames frightened her, yet attracted her; filled her with dread, yet beckoned. She was brushed aside by those bigger, stronger, older—drawn by the beauty of destruction. She wormed her way back through to get a better view, only to be elbowed out just as quickly.

Frustration gave way to jealousy, then rage.

It's mine. Mine. MINE! she wanted to shout, but held her tongue. She listened, and found others who shared both the joy and trepidation that coursed through her body. Their hushed conversation strangely aroused her almost as much as the fire itself; maybe more.

"Look at that baby burn," Sam McGreedy said. He was so gripped by the inferno, the earth could have swallowed him up and he wouldn't have noticed.

"See how the blackness of the sky tries to smother it? Only to be swatted away by an even greater force." Sarah Turner, New Canaan's librarian and resident poet, waxed eloquent. "The gods in their full fury. Yet, the fire shall consume itself and succumb to the ravages of the night."

"You're full of yourself tonight, Sarah," Seth Rush said playfully.

"You're an old fart," Sarah responded. "Don't you—"

"Don't be startin' in on me," he interrupted. "Was only

teasing you and your highfalutin words. You're right, though. Sure a power to behold."

Shanicha wove her way through the crowd, quenched by the awe . . . awe *her* act inspired.

"Isn't it beautiful?"

"Beautiful until *your* house burns down." Laughter.

"Like a big campfire. Feels like we should be roasting marshmallows and telling ghost stories." From another.

"I'm afraid, Mommy. Let's go home. Pleeeease!" A child younger than she.

"Soon, baby." The mother never took her eyes off the fire.

Power, Shanicha thought. Power to destroy. No, it was more than that. Power to draw others. Command attention. Yes, command *their* attention. Shanicha bathed in the warmth of this new power. She'd had a taste—what her mother called forbidden fruit—and hungered for more.

There was a second fire a week later; this time no accident. It was still a curiosity.

By the third, after a three-day interval, the crowd seemed a bit uneasy.

All were abandoned buildings, they said to one another. All at night. The word came unbidden to their tongues.

Arson!

With the fourth, all pretense disappeared.

"There's an arsonist among us," Seth Rush said as the Mansfield place burned to the ground. Shanicha had snaked through the crowd, soaking it all in. The rush nearly bowled her over.

"Hush, Seth," Sarah, the librarian said, and Seth looked at her strangely.

She looked ill, Shanicha thought. She wondered why.

"No, Sarah," Seth said. "One of us, for God's sake. Maybe even you."

She looked at him in shock at the accusation.

123

"Maybe me," he added quickly. "No stranger could target a house so recently abandoned."

"It wasn't abandoned," Sarah corrected him. "The Mansfields went to visit relatives two days ago."

"Stop with your word games. You know what I mean, even if you won't admit it. Somebody is setting fire to our town. Someone who knows the comings and goings of folks. *Someone among us!*" he said, clearly agitated.

All were listening to Seth now. He spoke what they felt. Feared. Dreaded.

"Yes, one of us," a voice chimed in.

"Maybe you."

"Maybe me."

"Yes, one of us."

"Someone here now."

"Who will be next?"

"What if he's tired of vacant buildings?"

"Yes, what if he wants to taste death."

". . . of you."

". . . of me."

". . . of *all* of us; one by one like dominoes."

"I feel so violated," Sarah added. "*Raped*. A part of me has died. Trust. My eternal optimism in human nature. Gone. Forever."

They huddled together, safe in the comfort of family and friends. But Shanicha could sense that suspicions gnawed at them; the way they secretly stole glances at one another, without saying a word:

Maybe you.

We could be next.

Trust no one.

Shanicha took it all in like a tonic. They were afraid of *her* and didn't know it. Invisible, she had demanded attention. Now, she commanded attention. And awe. Fear. And terror. She could see it in their faces. They would be dreaming of her that night.

She hid a smile.

She set two more fires and then stopped.

She'd sensed danger. Security had been beefed up. Families closeted themselves in their homes. Vacations were postponed. Business trips outside of town rescheduled. Husbands sat watch on porches.

Yes, danger was lurking for Shanicha. She prized her newfound power too much to jeopardize it by impatience. She was extra careful. She planned. Listened. Moved among them unnoticed. She would strike when the time was right. There was even power in this, she realized. They were watching, waiting for *her*.

With no fires in close to three weeks, tensions lessened. The town let its guard down, just as she knew they would. Shanicha heard them talk while she sat among them on the porch of the general store; a kid, she was ignored.

"Maybe it was a stranger after all."

"Someone who hid in the woods."

"Gone now that we're aware of his presence."

"Thank goodness it wasn't one of *us*."

With each passing day, Shanicha longed to rekindle the interest of the town. She fantasized in school; was so absorbed, she hadn't heard Miss McAfee, her fifth grade teacher, speaking to her.

"I asked you a question, young lady," she said sternly.

"I'm sorry. I didn't hear."

"No, Shanicha, you *weren't* listening. Detention after school for you."

Shanicha hated Miss McAfee. Twice, the teacher had caught her with spiders; tormenting them, as they had her.

Ever since her encounter in the cave, she had sought out spiders . . .

—Looking for the female who would lay its eggs in her. Looking to destroy it, before she was devoured.

. . . out in the open where she couldn't be trapped. Once they were found, she tortured them for tormenting her. Pulled off their legs one at a time, then set them down and watched them squirm before squashing them under her shoe.

Once, she was so enthralled, she was unaware of her teacher standing over her. She looked up to see a look of disgust on the woman's face.

She got a lecture. And detention.

Several months later, Shanicha had a new toy. Flypaper. She'd lay it down when she saw a spider and watch as the creature crept onto *her* web. She was fascinated as one by one its legs became entangled, as it tried to free itself. These she wouldn't squash, but watched them wither and die, like frogs out of water too long.

Miss McAfee caught her at this, too. There was a lecture. And detention.

Shanicha didn't mind either. What did disturb her was the threat. If there was a next time, her teacher told her, she'd be sent to the principal *and* her parents would be contacted.

No, she thought. That *mustn't* happen. She'd spent five years blending in. Adjusted wonderfully. No tantrums. No emotional outbursts. No antisocial behavior. Nothing associated with *crack babies*. No way she would let that bitch of a teacher ruin it all.

And now she had been caught with her pants down, again—daydreaming. Soon, she thought, Miss McAfee, you'll regret getting in my face.

Shanicha and her classmates had all been at their teacher's house for a Christmas party, several months earlier. Things like that were common in New Canaan—before the fires. Shanicha had taken a spare key. Didn't know why at the time, but it was in her nature to be one step ahead of the opposition.

Two days after her detention, with everyone asleep, she slipped out of her house to Miss McAfee's. She unlocked the door and crept in; went to her teacher's room, matches in hand. Watched the woman's fitful sleep.

The old bitch, Shanicha thought, visited by her own demons. Gently, she closed the door. Locked it with a key that hung in the kitchen; a skeleton key that looked all the doors in the old house. Set fire to the curtains downstairs and darted into the woods.

Waited.

Waited for the crowd to arrive.

They did.

Shanicha joined them unnoticed. Listened.

"Do you think it's him?"

"He's never set fire to a house with someone in it."

"It's him, all right." It was Seth. "Played us for a fool. Lulled us to sleep the past three weeks. No one's safe. That's his message. It can happen to any of us."

". . . to any of us." And Shanicha saw the terror in his eyes. In others', too.

"Did they get her out?"

"They're trying."

"If I get my hands on the bastard . . ."

"Maybe it's you."

That started a fight.

Shanicha felt the power return like a shot of adrenaline. Stronger than before.

She watched as the two men pummeled one another, and could taste the blood. Her tongue darted through her parted lips. So good, she thought. So good.

All was silent, later, as they brought her teacher's body out. In the silence she heard one voice.

"Who'll be next?" A shrill voice that spoke for everyone.

You'll see, Shanicha thought.

The next night she hit the Tuttles' barn. A spiteful family, they shunned the rest of the townspeople. They carved out a meager existence and ignored the fires. None of their concern. Took no precautions. Heeded no warnings. Never had. Never would. Shanicha made them pay attention.

Six days later the offices of the *Weekly Clarion* went down in flames; the first building in the town itself. An editorial had upset Shanicha. Moaning over the distrust that tore the town apart, it ended with: "May the perverted mind perpetrating this horror on God-fearing folk be trapped in one of his infernos. May he then roast in hell!"

Shanicha responded with a letter to the editor; a letter in fire, if not brimstone.

It drew the largest crowd yet.

"We're all hostages," Sarah said. She was pale and wasted. Her complexion was pasty. Beads of sweat dotted her forehead though the night was crisp. Her brown hair, with just a trace of gray months before, had turned deathly white. Its luster gone, it had begun falling out like the leaves of autumn. She leaned on Seth, like a tree blown over by the wind.

"There'll be no deliverance," she rasped in a near whisper, yet all heard.

Shanicha listened.

"I've had it. I'm packing it in. Got some family in Vermont who'll put me up." From one.

"I can't sleep at night. I listen for the sirens. Doze off a bit and awaken with a start." From another.

"We got our valuables packed in a suitcase right by the door in case it's us he strikes. Whole family sleeps in the living room . . . in our clothes." From a third.

His wife finished for him. "How do you figure what's irreplaceable? Every day, I take something out and put something else in. It preys on me. All day. All night."

"I welcome the fire," Seth Rush said, and all eyes focused on him.

Was he the one? they all thought.

"I know it's coming. As each day passes, I get more wound up. You know, like one of those jack-in-the-boxes; tight, ready to spring. I'm irritable. My stomach tightens. I can't hold down food. The fire releases me."

He paused, and seemed to grope for words to make himself understood.

"I mean, with the fire there's relief. Understand? Probably won't be another tomorrow. I can relax a bit. A couple of days, though, and the pressure builds up again."

He's not the one, they realized; the tension easing just a bit.

"Yeah. Me, too," from someone in the back. "The waiting's the worst. The damned waiting."

Shanicha slipped in and out among them. A flea. A gnat. She preyed on their fear. Fed on their frustration. Drank of their sorrow.

Four days later she torched the library. Sarah had taken to her bed earlier that week. It was if she knew the town was being consumed from within.

Shanicha was angry. She liked Sarah Turner. She'd listen to her poetry at the library; marvel how she brought words to life. Sarah had power. She was visible. Shanicha was unaware that each fire that so fed *her* further upset the librarian until she grew ill.

The assistant librarian was too busy for poetry recitals. It made Shanicha angry, at the assistant librarian. At Sarah. So, she burned the library down.

Two days later, Sarah died. She had slipped into a coma before the fire at the library. She hadn't awakened.

A crowd gathered outside her house. Sarah had represented all that was good in New Canaan. If she gave up, maybe they should, too. Shanicha mingled among them, listening.

"I'm leaving. I couldn't bear the memories even if the fires stopped."

"Me, too," said another. "I can't look anyone in the face without suspicion."

"The town's dead. Sarah knew it and it killed her," Seth said. He had the same pasty, feverish look Sarah had. "It's one thing to mourn the dead, but another to walk among them. I'm leaving right after the funeral."

Over the next few days Shanicha watched them leave. Not everyone. Not even a majority. But enough. A trickle had become a steady stream. Could become a full stampede. No, she thought. Too many had no place to go. This comforted her. She watched them leave; a ragtag army in retreat. All their belongings stuffed into cars and vans. Drained. Weary. Defeated. Let them go, she thought. They offered nothing. *She* had their power.

Soon her family left, too. There was little to pack. She'd never been a collector. Never gotten many toys. Most of her birthday and Christmas presents were commonsense items like new shoes, a coat or a heavy winter blanket.

They were off to Philadelphia. A city. A *real* city. They'd stay with relatives until her father found a job.

She'd set only one fire in Philadelphia, and that wasn't until several years later. It had been time to blend in again. She'd relive what she had done in New Canaan. Done *to* New Canaan. It was enough, until she found something even better.

"Be careful, you'll burn yourself."

"What?" She looked up, her thoughts no longer in the past. A student. Someone she didn't know.

"Sorry to startle you but, well, you could have gotten hurt."

"Thanks," she muttered. She hoped he wouldn't stay long.

Worse, try to pick her up. A light-skinned, good-looking black, he probably thought with so few blacks on campus she would be easy pickings.

"Well, I've got a class. Careful, now," he said, and left.

Shanicha looked down and saw she had burned two full books of matches. Foolish girl, she thought, to draw attention to yourself. It's them, she thought. Officer Friendly and the white bitch cop. Playing with her mind. Putting her at risk.

She looked at them, but they were gone. How long had she been here? Without a watch, she couldn't be sure. The Naturists were gone as well, she noted. Must have been an hour. Maybe more.

She walked back to The Quad, her mind on the two interlopers. She'd keep an eye out for them. Like when she was eleven, she'd make herself invisible.

Chapter Twenty-two

The headquarters of the University of Pennsylvania Police looked anything but. Thirty-nine-fourteen Locust Walk had been home to the clergy of St. Mary's Church. The bedraggled whitewashed building reminded Ariel of a campus built *around* a recalcitrant homeowner who refused to sell out.

The first floor only reinforced her view. Three quarters of the classroom-sized first floor was the radio room. All that remained was a narrow corridor that passed for a waiting room: a table with a coffeepot and huge stain under it, on the Formica floor, and three small desks that might have been taken from a classroom—the kind with an armrest that's too tiny for students to take notes.

There they waited to see Frank Desjardins, the Commissioner of the Police.

At least the radio room looked familiar to Ariel: several computers manned by nonuniformed personnel, while two uniformed officers kibitzed, monitoring radio calls.

One of the men, a medium-sized, thin dark-skinned black with graying hair, greeted Lucius, who introduced him to Ariel.

"One of Philadelphia's finest," the man said sarcastically with a smile. "Myself, I've been here going on twenty years now, and I don't regret it for a minute."

He took out his wallet and showed Ariel a picture of his daughter.

"Not only doesn't the family have to worry if I'll get home alive, but this young thing is coming to Penn on a *full* scholarship. Something like twenty-eight thousand a year. One of the perks of the job. Something you might want to look into, if you have any children."

Ariel was spared having to tell him she was currently single, and without any children, when they were summoned to the Commissioner's office.

Frank Desjardins's office, as befitting a Chief of Police, was spacious and elegant. Plush carpeting, a mammoth desk, a small conference table and bookshelves bulging with books. On the wall a poster of a University of Pennsylvania basketball player dunking the ball. At the top it read, "Penn for a Safe City. Join the Team." To the right of the photo, "Slam Dunk Crime."

A nice touch, Ariel thought.

Frank Desjardins met them at the door of his office, and beckoned them to a squat table surrounded by four comfortable chairs. He was a shade shorter than Ariel, a once-physically fit man whose supervisory position didn't allow him to work out as much as he would have liked. He was by no means fat, but he was going soft. He had a wide, open, friendly face and ruddy complexion, topped off by the bristle-cut haircut of a drill Sergeant. His brown hair was graying. She pegged him to be leaning on fifty.

"I was on the phone with your Sergeant just a while ago," he said by means of introduction. "I've met Russ McGowan at a few conferences."

I'll bet you have, Ariel thought. McGowan attended every conference he could, and would make it his business to schmooze with officers of superior rank.

"The Sarge gets around," Ariel said in response, and she saw a cloud cross the Commissioner's face.

"Let's take a seat here," he said, referring to the table in the middle of the room. "I feel too much like a bureaucrat behind my desk with people in the office."

Lucius looked ill at ease, almost like a third wheel. Desjardins had all but ignored him. And why not, Ariel thought. His job was to get Ariel off his back—the *University*'s back, to be more precise. Lucius didn't factor into the equation.

"I was told you received a note. Could I see it?" Desjardins asked with a smile.

Ariel produced the letter, which Desjardins scrutinized, as if deep in thought.

"You can't honestly believe this gibberish," he finally said, waving the note dismissively. "Someone seeking publicity at the University's expense. Have you uncovered *any* evidence of foul play?"

If he had spoken to McGowan, Ariel knew, he knew there was no such evidence; at least not yet. He was putting Ariel on the defensive, and she had no intention of following *his* game plan. She ignored his last question and addressed his initial comment.

"It doesn't matter, Commissioner, if the letter is legitimate or not. We *both* have to treat it as authentic. For the sake of argument, let's say the girls *were* killed. We sit on the letter. The University sits on the letter and another girl dies. Whoever sent the letter to us then decides to go public. We—the police department—have egg on our face, granted, but it's far worse for you, you being the University."

She saw him looking at her intently, so unlike McGowan, who avoided her gaze.

She went on. "If the writer goes public and you've quashed the note, parents will go ballistic. The University will look for a scapegoat. I don't have to draw you a picture."

"No you don't," he said with a tight smile. "Your Sergeant promised you'd keep your investigation low-profile. You're not suggesting we release the note to the press, I hope."

"Not at all. Panic is the *last* thing we want. It could be just so much nonsense, but we have to investigate. Then, if the letter becomes public, the University and the police department issue a joint statement detailing the steps taken after the note was received. We add the investigation is ongoing; not just beginning. That the University didn't sweep it under the rug looks good. Better, *you* look good."

He sat back in his chair, visibly relaxed. She could imagine him going back to his desk and taking out a cigar after they left. Puffing on it until the tension within him had dissipated with the smoke. She could smell the odor of cigar smoke, and noted an ashtray on his desk; to the left of the sign that said, "Please Refrain from Smoking."

"So what can I do for you?" he said after a moment.

"First," Ariel said, getting down to brass tacks, "I'd like you to assign Patrolman Jackson to be my liaison on campus."

"Done," Desjardins said.

"My partner, Doug Thiery, will also be on and off campus. He'll be on his own. I'll make sure he drops by to introduce himself, though."

"I'd appreciate that."

Ariel couldn't quite place his accent, but Desjardins wasn't from the Northeast. Nor was he from the South. Possibly

Texas or some state in the Southwest. His voice had a sooth-
ing quality, though at times he laid it on thick to lull irritants
like her.

"Lastly, we'd like access to your computer files. Strictly
under the supervision of Patrolman Jackson," she added hastily.

"For what reason?" He was leaning forward again; agitated
without appearing to be outwardly.

"Again, assuming the letter's authentic, there must be
some link between these three girls. Whoever targeted them
didn't do so randomly. They *all* had experienced adjustment
problems to University life. All three were deeply troubled.
All three had become withdrawn recently, and exhibited
symptoms of depression. In short, all three were prime can-
didates for suicide.

"Were it not for the note, I wouldn't be here now. These
girls were *chosen*," Ariel said, leaning forward herself.

Then she paused.

"*If* the letter is authentic," she added with a shrug, and sat
back.

"And with our computers," Desjardins went on for her,
"you can possibly link them together."

"It narrows the field. The alternative is to bring a dozen
uniforms on campus to question the freshman class."

Desjardins laughed. "I suspect you and your Sergeant
don't get along."

His comment had come out of left field.

Ariel said nothing. She had no idea where he was going.
Silence seemed the best strategy.

"He led me to believe you were a lightweight. And he
wouldn't try to con me. I know his type; one reason I left
the public sector.

"Here, I've got seventy-five officers under my supervision,
and I know each and every one personally," he said, looking
at Lucius for the first time.

"I know Patrolman Jackson is one of my proactive officers; one who takes our outreach philosophy seriously. Someone the students trust. Someone who listens," he said, pointing towards his ear.

"Your Sergeant, on the other hand, has . . . what, eight detectives under his command." It wasn't a question. "Yet he doesn't know you very well. He's a fool. You can tell him so, though I doubt you will."

They both smiled.

"It will be our secret," Ariel said.

The Commissioner laughed heartily.

"Well, we certainly don't want a dozen uniforms questioning the freshman class. Might as well call the media if we do that, and show them the note. No, I think it best if you and Patrolman Jackson do your computer search, and then ask your questions discreetly. Are we in agreement?"

She nodded affirmatively.

Ariel wondered who had done the manipulating. Desjardins was one smart cookie, she thought. She mustn't underestimate him because of her disdain for upper-management superiors.

"I'd appreciate it," he said, standing, to signal the meeting was at an end, "if you'd allow Patrolman Jackson to keep me up to speed. He would anyway," he said with a wink. "But I don't want him going behind your back."

"There's no need to be secretive," Ariel said. "I fully expect Patrolman Jackson to keep you briefed."

At the door she turned. "Oh, and I'll tell my Sergeant you asked about him." And now she winked.

Desjardins laughed again. "You do that."

The Commissioner's secretary found a computer terminal where they could have privacy. Once alone, Lucius shook his head in exasperation.

"Felt like a house nigger," he said. "Nothing racial," he

136

added quickly, "but it was like I wasn't there except that one time he looked at me. Made sure *I knew* he knew all about me. Except for that, I didn't exist."

"Don't take it personally," Ariel said. "He was working me. Sizing me up, and then deciding how to handle *me*."

"Tell you, Ariel, I'm a bit disillusioned; not just by today. They preach being up front here. We know their agenda, supposedly. Make sure the students follow rules, teach them to be accountable for their actions and get them to voluntarily comply with the standards of the institution."

He laughed. "I sound like a walking advertisement, but that's how often they instill their philosophy in us. We're told there's no organizational red tape, like with your department. No one working at cross-purposes, like when you weren't informed about the second suicide. No need to worry about being stabbed in the back by someone looking for a promotion. One big happy family," he said, shaking his head.

Ariel looked at him as he was booting the computer. She didn't understand where he was going.

"I've known all along," he continued, "that the name of the game was protecting the University and its reputation. I can accept that. But Desjardins is no different than *any* supervisor. He's the main man and he made damn sure I was fully aware of it in there. There comes a time, though, when you have to weigh the reputation of the University against lives being lost. I'd err on the side of caution. Fuck the school and protect the kids at all costs."

Lucius's hands were in constant motion on the computer keyboard. Command after command, most of it Greek to Ariel. She was the first to admit she knew little about computers. Fortunately, Doug knew enough, so she was spared— once again—having to learn.

"Do you think Desjardins knows we were married?" Lucius asked without taking his eyes off the computer screen.

"Even he has his limitations," Ariel answered. "He's a

bureaucrat—a very good one, I suspect, but what does he *really* know about you? Precious little, I'd say, but enough to make you think he knows more. I dropped your name after the divorce. No way he knows. Doesn't even know my father's a professor on campus."

Sam Solomon was a political science professor at the University. Knowing his biracial children would have a hard enough time fighting racial bigotry, he and his wife didn't want them to carry the further stigma of his religion when they were growing up. Ariel and her brother carried their mother's surname.

"You're right," Lucius said. "He's a fucking bureaucrat, nevertheless, no matter what he says. Protect the University really means *protect his job*; watch his ass." He went silent, working the computer.

"Boo, he's not so different than most of us. *I* take a lot of shit to keep my job in homicide. I even gave up a part of myself to marry you."

He looked at her, then nodded.

"We all make concessions," she went on. "The difference is each of us has a limit as to how far we'll go. The McGowans of the world have precious few. Desjardins, on the other hand, is no beast. He won't protect a murderer at the University."

"I'd like to think so," Lucius said.

Finally, he had the computer where he could access the files they'd want, and the two of them went to work trying to link the three suicide victims. The problem, as Lucius had said earlier, was asking the computer the right questions.

"When people get bills that are fucked up, when a dog gets sent a driver's license or a person who is alive is told he's dead, it's all blamed on a computer glitch," Lucius told her as he typed Sharon Ingster's name into the computer and her records popped onto the screen.

"It's CYA—cover your ass. *People* program computers.

People input information. Those computer errors that drive us up the wall are *human* errors. If we don't get the answers we want, there can be just two reasons. Either we're not asking the right questions—human error—or there is no link between the three girls."

"Not everything is in the computer, Lucius," Ariel corrected him. "There are ways they could be connected that aren't stored in there," she said, tapping the monitor.

"Let's hope that's not the case here," he said.

An hour later they were staring at a blank screen, wondering what other questions to ask. Printouts lay scattered on the floor. Data, Ariel said, she would give to Doug to tie a third girl to where two others had crossed paths.

"It'll keep him busy, and out of our hair," she'd told Lucius.

Lucius had smiled. "You *are* bad. The poor bastard."

"You try working with him and see how long you can take him. On his own, with a specific assignment, he might find something. Other than that he's a royal pain in the ass."

They tried everything they could think of. And, while two of the girls would sometimes fit one category, never would all three.

Classes: Even freshman had a phenomenal menu to choose from at Penn. All three took WATU classes—Writing Across the University—but none the same class. Monique and Jocelyn took biology; Sharon chemistry. Jocelyn took Spanish, Sharon French, but Monique took no foreign language.

Clubs and organizations drew a blank: Jocelyn had joined Students Against Acquaintance Rape, which made sense to Lucius. The others had not. Sharon worked with the homeless. Monique wasn't a joiner.

Sports proved no better: Sharon, an athlete, was involved in field hockey and volleyball. Jocelyn belonged to a jogging club. Monique, nothing.

Religion: Sharon and Jocelyn attended different churches. Monique, nothing.

Dining plans at the University, jobs, sorority pledging; the list went on.

Nothing.

Nothing.

Nothing.

"We're not asking the right question," Lucius finally said, exasperated.

"The linkage won't be found on the computer," countered Ariel.

"Whatever, we're burned out," Lucius said, looking at his watch. "It's seven o'clock. I don't know about you, but I'm starving. What you say we give this a rest and get something to eat?"

"Sounds good, but *not* Houston Hall. You want a bagel, I'll bring you a *real* bagel. And Burger King . . ."

"I was thinking of some home-cooked food. I cook a mean burger. Thick and rare, like you like it. The kind you can't get anymore at restaurants."

"You cook? Get out," Ariel said.

"The basics. Had to after Dyann died. Either that or eat out every night and turn into a blimp."

"You really want me up to your place, Boo? The apartment you and your wife shared? I don't think so."

"C'mon, Ariel. It's dinner. Nothing more. We could go to Smokey Joe's, but it's a cop hangout."

"No," Ariel said quickly. "That's out of the question. This is a low-profile investigation. I shouldn't be seen around campus with you in a bar your buds frequent at night. Maybe I should just go home."

"I don't bite, Ariel. I can deal with you seeing the apartment Dyann and I shared. A day doesn't go by when I don't think of her. But you were part of my life, too. Let me cook you some dinner. Then go home and we can let our minds wander to the question we *should* be asking."

"You got mustard? You used to hate the stuff. Made me brush my teeth before you'd kiss me."

"Dyann liked mustard, too," he said with a weak smile. "I adapted. Have it, just don't go near it myself."

"Beer? Not the light shit. *Real* beer."

"Got it." He smiled.

"I do the dishes, without you hovering over me."

"No problem."

"How can I say no to an offer like that," she said with a smile of her own.

Ariel hoped she was doing the right thing. Not the *right* thing. The *smart* thing. She still had strong feelings for Lucius, and she expected he might feel the same way about her. She hadn't felt so relaxed—well, since she and Lucius had fallen in love. Throw caution to the wind, she thought. A good dinner with good company. Then home. Not to think about the fool question to ask the computer, but to plan a new strategy.

As they walked to Lucius's apartment, her mind drifted to what lay immediately ahead.

Just dinner. *With Lucius.* Dinner and good company. *With Lucius.* Dinner. *With Lucius.* Then home?

Chapter Twenty-three

While Lucius fussed over dinner, Ariel absorbed the feeling of his seven-year marriage. Dyann Jackson, Ariel knew, had managed an antique store on 7th and South Street, catering to blacks. It was the recently rejuvenated South Street, not the South Street cut off from the University of Pennsylvania by the Schuylkill River; the western end of South Street with its boarded storefronts, mom-and-pop stores not favored by the stylish-hip, and poor black folk who sat on their stoops in the summer heat. The South Street not on any tourist's itinerary. Dyann Jackson's store, on the other hand, was in the heart of the South Street that drew tourists like flies to shit.

The Jacksons' living room—Ariel couldn't think of it solely as Lucius's—had an Afro-centric, though understated, look. There were prints of African origin, and artifacts bespoke of the Jacksons' African heritage.

Ariel noticed a shelf with a number of framed photos, and chanced a look. She had never met Dyann, but she immediately saw her allure to Lucius. Aside from being extremely attractive, and almost as tall as Ariel, Dyann Jackson was as black as, if not blacker than, Lucius; with full lips and an engaging smile. Her hair was in braids, a style currently in vogue, and while she was slender, one could see her full breasts in all the photos. She possessed, Ariel thought, a regal bearing; someone most definitely comfortable with herself.

Over dinner, Lucius spoke about Dyann, as if he'd kept her bottled within the six months since her death.

At one point, he shook his head, as if angry with himself.

"What am I doing? You didn't come her to hear about your competition."

Ariel laughed. "She's not . . . she's *not* my competition. Our marriage was doomed because of the way I am and your needs. I'm happy you found someone who could fulfill your needs. And just as you're a part of my life, I am curious about Dyann." Ariel paused. "She was your Nubian Princess."

Lucius blushed at the mention. Their marriage, Ariel knew, hadn't ended due to irreconcilable differences, but because Ariel couldn't live up to what Lucius wanted her to be: his

142

Nubian Princess. Even if she didn't look the part, Lucius *might,* just might have been able to live with Ariel had she acted the part.

"She was just about everything I'd ever wanted," he said.

"*Just* about. There were imperfections," she said teasingly.

"Nothing to speak of," he backtracked.

"So, why no kids, if you don't mind me asking?"

"She couldn't. Something about a cyst when she was a teen. We'd considered adoption and kept putting it off. We'd gotten serious about it, again, just as she was diagnosed with cancer. The cyst, while benign, was a warning in a sense. The doctors were optimistic, early on. Caught it early. Since she was young, they could attack the cancer aggressively. The first chemo seemed to have worked. Then she started feeling bloated." He paused, as if recalling the past.

"We referred to the cancer as *it*. Not *the cancer*. But always *it*. The insidious *it*. With each subsequent treatment, the doctors told us up front, chances of success decreased. They'd given it their best and everything that followed was a shot in the dark. Fortunately, for both of us, the end came quickly. At some point she decided to go out with dignity. She didn't want to live sick to her stomach due to the battle between the cancer cells and the drugs."

He paused in reflection, then shook his head.

"Once the doctors told us it was terminal," he went on, "she stopped the chemo. We had a month where she felt, well, *almost* normal. Then the cancer mounted its final assault. It took her in three weeks." He fell silent.

"You loved her very much," Ariel said. "I envy you."

"You never found anyone?"

"You were a tough act to follow," Ariel said defensively.

"Bullshit. I was an insensitive lout. Charmingly insensitive," he added with a laugh.

"True, but you had your endearing qualities." She laughed, then got serious. "You know my problem. I had to come to

143

terms with myself. When we married, I hadn't. After the divorce, I was mad at the world. But also furious with my parents for thinking I could exist without an identity. *They* made a conscious decision to marry. That they'd face ridicule was something they considered long and hard before marrying, then accepted."

She nibbled at some homemade chocolate-chip cookies Lucius had brought out to the living room.

"I had no choice," she continued. "And, to be totally honest, I was neither black nor white. I'm just coming to terms with who I am. I like that person. But finding someone to share my life has been no easy task. Everyone wants me to be something I'm not. Just like you," she finished.

"My Nubian Princess," he said, shaking his head. "That's what I'd wanted. God, we were young and foolish."

"Speak for yourself," she shot back, but was smiling.

Ariel cleaned the dishes, and Lucius kept his promise by keeping his distance. Then they talked some more; about everything, about nothing. She had to admit, she felt more at ease with this man who had so infuriated her than with *anyone* she'd met since they'd divorced.

"What say we have a dance? Just for old time's sake?" he asked.

"I don't know."

But he was up, checking through his CDs until he found the one he wanted. Tina Turner's first comeback album, *Private Dancer*. He put on what had been *their* song, "Let's Stay Together," held out his hand, and she reluctantly joined him.

Like slipping into an old pair of slippers, she thought. Broken in and, oh, so comfortable. She put her head on his shoulder and let the music sweep them away.

As if the song were written for them. About breaking up and making up—*always* making up. But they had broken up, without making up. He had found someone new. His new love was gone, though, and she felt so comfortable with her body next to his.

He kissed her tentatively, and she didn't resist. Kissed her again, this time with more confidence.

Ten minutes later, they were in bed together, and it was as if the past eight years had been nothing more than a blur. He knew where to touch her to make her body sing. Even with Lucius, she'd made fun of her small breasts; a defensive response, she knew, so the disappointment would be less. But Lucius hadn't been disappointed. As he did now, he had doted on her breasts, which, while small, were incredibly sensitive. He took her nipple in his mouth and let his tongue massage it. And, as before, she climaxed.

Selfish as he could be, when it came to lovemaking, his greatest desire had been to please her. Over time he'd learned all her erogenous zones. Foreplay with most of her partners could be calculated by a stopwatch. With Lucius, foreplay was a part of the main event. And when he finally entered her, as he did now, she was liked a caged animal given its freedom. She gave herself totally to him, and as she reached orgasm—for the third time—so did he, as if they were one.

And, as before, when they were done, she lay on his bare chest; both totally exhausted. Both knowing, though, chances were good they'd soon begin anew, and the wave of fatigue would dissipate.

As she relaxed on him now, her beeper went off. She looked at her watch. Nine-thirty. Technically, she thought, she was still on duty. Having come in early, however, she felt no guilt at knocking off early. She giggled at the thought. She'd be screwed if McGowan ever found out what she was doing. That thought brought another giggle. She'd *been* screwed, and God, did it ever feel good.

"What's so funny?" Lucius asked.

"Tell you later. I gotta call in now. I'm still on duty, you know," she laughed again.

Barry Hoffman

It was Doug. She sat on Lucius's bed naked, his hands rubbing her shoulders; every so often brushing against her breast—literally driving her to distraction. But she wasn't about to push him away.

Doug told her he'd had no luck tracing the letter. He began to go into detail, but Lucius's hand was cupping her left breast, and the last thing she wanted to hear were the frustrations Doug had met.

"You can fill me in tomorrow," she said, biting her tongue, to stifle a sigh, as Lucius's fingers kneaded her nipple.

"There's something else."

"What, Doug?" she asked, trying to keep the irritation out of her voice. Lucius had switched to her other breast.

"McGowan wants me to investigate the campus cop; the one you're working with. Doesn't want you involved. Doesn't want him to be suspicious."

Lucius was pinching her nipple. Hard, but not so hard as to make it hurt. She was having trouble concentrating.

"Why this interest all of a sudden?" Ariel asked. She should have felt guilty talking about Lucius while he was driving her mad, but she wasn't about to ask him to stop.

"McGowan thinks it's more than mere coincidence this same cop responded to each call. And he knew so much about the girls. It wasn't my idea . . . ," he said, without finishing.

She knew it wasn't his idea. In cases like this, Doug had *no* ideas. He just did as he was told.

Lucius's hand was now creeping down Ariel's stomach. She didn't have long to consider its destination. His every move was slow. He was patient, wanting *her* to feel every sensation.

"Do what you're told, Doug. Just keep it low-key."

"Right. Just what McGowan said."

"And Doug, when you're done, I've got something for you."

146

She was about to tell him about the data dealing with linkage, but Lucius's hand was on her pubic hair; his fingers making temporary little braids, then pulling it every so slightly. Fuck, she thought, Doug could wait until the next day.

"One last thing," he went on.

God, Doug, she thought, why not come over and join us. By the time you're done, he'll be done.

"To cut overtime, we're to work the eight-to-four shift. Overtime only if something comes up. And anything happens during the day, McGowan wants to be called immediately. We still report only to him."

"I can live with that," she said as Lucius's fingers now played with the lips of her vulva. She was about to hang up.

"Oh," Doug said. "I almost forgot. You coming in tonight? McGowan wants to know what's up."

Looking for a minute at Lucius's penis, she knew very well what was up, and had to stifle another laugh.

"It's been a long day, Doug," she said as Lucius's fingers slid ever so slowly between her lips. "Tell him I met with Desjardins, the Police Commissioner on campus, and he pledged his total cooperation. Tell McGowan he said hi. Look, I gotta go pee. Anything else?"

"No!" he almost shouted. "You . . . I'll see you tomorrow." And he hung up.

Finally!

Ariel thought of telling Lucius about the call, but her recent conversation was the farthest thing from her mind.

"You're bad, Lucius," she whispered, and let out a long-suppressed sigh. "So bad, you're good." And for the next thirty minutes she was clay and he the sculptor. She gave herself completely to him, and when he was through she was not in the least disappointed. Not once did he call her his Nubian Princess, as he always had. Maybe, she thought, he was coming to terms with her.

147

They lay quietly a while after. "We gotta talk," she finally said.

"Yeah, we gotta talk." And he laughed.

"Not about *that*," she said, referring to ending up in bed together, though at some point, it was something to be discussed.

"McGowan wants you investigated." She gave him the rationale.

"Why tell me? He may have a point," he said, his hand massaging her belly button, another of her erogenous zones. Her whole body, she thought, tonight was an erogenous zone.

"Don't even say that in jest," she said, chastising him, though not pushing his hand away.

"But why tell me? You're too good a cop . . ."

"It's not because of tonight," she interrupted. "I would have told you anyway. Told you because you didn't kill those three girls."

"You have proof, or is it your feminine intuition?" he asked, trying to sound casual. His hand rested on her pubic hair.

"My gut tells me you didn't do it, but I can back up my instincts. We talked about this before. A male in the girls' dorm. No way you could have killed three girls and not be spotted. You don't throw someone out of a window and hang someone in a girl's shower and *not* be seen."

"But don't I blend in? Aren't I likely to be overlooked?"

"Not well enough. Look, Doug's no Sherlock Holmes, but he's a stickler for detail, and a good interrogator. He spoke to *everyone* on the floor of the two suicides we covered. When he asked if they saw anyone, he would make sure they understood *anyone*. Even you."

Ariel paused and met his eyes.

"Lastly, I saw the look of despair on your face after Monique Dysart's death. I know you, Boo. You're not a good enough actor to put on a mask like that. You were physically and emotionally devastated. You blamed yourself. You were shaken, and it was no con job. You didn't kill those girls, so why shouldn't I tell you you're being investigated?"

Lucius looked her a question.

"Boo, you'd find out anyway. You think no matter how circumspect my partner is, word won't get back to you? Better you learn it from me than get it secondhand. I'm a good enough cop to know that."

She smiled. "Bet you another home-cooked dinner you'll have heard something by tomorrow afternoon."

Lucius laughed. "You're on, though it's one bet I hope I lose."

"Now it's your turn. Something you wanted to tell me."

Lucius looked Ariel up and down as she lay in bed. She didn't mind. When Lucius looked at her she felt sexy. Her tits were too small, and she was too damn skinny for her own good; no, too thin for the men she bedded. She always felt they wished there were more of her. It was irrational, she knew, because men enjoyed sex with her. But Lucius had always looked at her like she was special. Even toward the end, when they fought, sex with Lucius made their differences seem trite; at least for a little while. So, he could look at her all he wanted.

Finally, he spoke. "This isn't easy for me, Ariel. I mean, what I have to say. You know how much I loved Dyann. I couldn't have constructed a more perfect spouse for me. We had sex—often, and it was good. But, God forgive me, there were times I was making love to her and you'd intrude."

Ariel said nothing. She didn't know *what* to say.

"We made love, but there was no passion. I feel so alive when I make love to you. Some kind of chemistry."

He laughed, to cover his discomfort.

"I can't find the words to express it, but you felt it, too. I know. That's what I meant when I said Dyann was *just* about everything I ever wanted. I won't lie and say I'd trade the

149

life she and I had together for ours. But, I can't deny the intimacy I felt when we made love—then and now. Something I never had with Dyann. I guess I never stopped loving you, is what I'm trying to say."

"But love doesn't necessarily make a good marriage. We found that out," Ariel said.

"We could give it another try. *Not marriage,*" he said quickly, then laughed. "Least not yet. But seeing each other?" He shrugged.

"We'd end up hurting . . . ," she began, then started over again. "No, *you'd* end up hurting me, like before. See, our problems were *your* hang-ups."

"I think I've changed. Matured in eight years," he countered.

"No, you haven't. Intellectually, you can accept me, but when your friends talk and stare, and I refuse to toss off the white part of me, your emotions would take over. Some people aren't intended for interracial marriage, and you're one of them."

"You're wrong, Ariel. I can be supportive." As he spoke now, his hand danced gently over her pubic hair. She didn't push him away.

"I can be good for you," he said. He massaged the outside of her lips, and she sighed.

"I'm not asking for a commitment." He inserted his finger, ever so slightly, then withdrew it. Did it over and over, like a rabbit wanting to come out of its hole, but fearful of a predator awaiting.

"Just consider the possibility." As his fingers probed more deeply, he kissed her on her forehead, eyes and nose.

"Just don't toss me out of your life," he said.

They made love a third time.

When they were done, Ariel looked at him. "You're bad, Boo. You just seduced me. Sexual harassment." She laughed, then turned serious.

"I can't make any promises. *Won't*. I still have unresolved conflicts of my own to work out. I'm no poster child for the biracial offspring of an interracial marriage. I've flitted from one short-term relationship to another, trying to find myself; and my soulmate. All were self-destructive. I thought I needed someone to validate that I could be loved for who I was. I don't want us to get together for the wrong reasons."

"What can be so wrong, when it feels so right?" he asked.

"Bull, Boo. It was so right the first time, and look what happened. Tell you what. *After* this case, we'll see just how much each of us has changed. We'll go slow. Give whatever we feel now a chance to blow up in our faces. Okay?"

"I can live with that," he said, and kissed her. "Will you stay the night?"

"No. If I do I might never leave."

"Can't blame a guy for trying," he said with a smile.

She pointed at him. "You're pure bad, Boo. Pure bad."

Chapter Twenty-four

Alone, after Ariel had left, Lucius wondered what the hell he was getting himself into. He didn't regret his feelings toward Ariel. They'd always been there; rekindled now that Dyann was dead and she had reappeared in his life.

He didn't regret admitting to Ariel he'd thought of her while making love to his wife.

He wanted her, but was he setting himself up for another fall? As lovers, no two people were more compatible. But the bigger question was, could they coexist out of bed? He needed time, but he felt he could reconcile himself to accept her being biracial; live with the identity she had carved out for herself. But could he take the heat from others?

Eight years ago, he couldn't. He'd felt uncomfortable taking her to parties. Hell, he'd felt uneasy walking the streets with her. Whites seeing them together cursed him out; a black man with a gorgeous white woman. Only his intimidating size had prevented a physical confrontation more than once. He could live with that sort of finger-pointing.

But he remembered being seen with her at parties. He recalled feeble attempts to assure those in attendance he was with a black woman.

And then Ariel had changed the rules. From identifying herself as a black woman, early in their marriage, all of a sudden she'd discovered her white side. Rediscovered it, she'd said, but it had been galling nevertheless.

If he was serious about Ariel, he would have to accept her as she was, regardless of how she defined herself. At parties, he'd have to take pride in her identity. He would have to stare down those who felt he was betraying his race. Could he take the heat?

She had been right. This was not something to rush into, especially as he knew he was still feeling the aftereffects of Dyann's death. Vulnerable, he could make a fateful error that would come back to haunt the both of them.

As if the evening hadn't been full of enough surprises, he had hit on the computer question that had eluded them both. Watching Ariel dress had only aroused him further. He was so relaxed, so at one with himself as he watched her, that the question had come unbidden to his mind.

Human error.

It had been there all the time for him to see, but he hadn't asked the computer. He'd been about to tell her, but on a whim decided to check it out on his own. He could be wrong, and didn't want to raise her hopes. And selfishly, when she left, he wanted her mind entirely on him.

You're bad, Boo. Pure bad. Her words echoed in his mind.

Chapter Twenty-five

When Ariel got home, she found Chanda on the couch reading. She had called Chanda earlier to tell her she was having dinner with Lucius. She saw Chanda eye her with anticipation, then return to the book.

"What you reading?" Ariel asked, coming over to the couch.

Chanda showed her the book. It was a book of interviews with children of biracial marriages.

"Thought I'd get to know what makes you tick," she said.

"What have you gleaned so far?"

"You people got serious problems. It's like bi's."

"Bi's?" Ariel asked.

"Bisexuals. I met some on the street. Talk about being fucked up. First these guys get urges for other guys. It's not something to take lightly, and it can be difficult to handle, what with all the bias against gays. He finally comes to grips with his homosexuality, and *bam,* a few years later he's turned on by a woman."

"I'd say that could lead to confusion," Ariel said with a laugh.

"Are you any different? I mean, some days do you feel black and other days white?"

Ariel considered her comment for a moment. "It's more like phases. I went through my black phase with Lucius. Then I explored the Jew in me, at a time when blacks were becoming hostile toward Jews. It did get confusing. Personally, I think I'm reaching an equilibrium, coming to grips with the real me, but I may be deluding myself."

She thought for a moment, frowning in concentration.

"Yeah, we got problems. Well, I'm going to hit the sack. Starting tomorrow, my shift starts at 8 a.m."

"No, you don't," Chanda said, jumping up. "You called *hours* ago, telling me you were having dinner with Lucius. Some dinner, I'd say. *Five hours*. Did he have you for dessert?" she asked excitedly.

"Chanda!" she said, flushing.

"He did! The two of you did it! On your first date, no less."

"It wasn't our first date, young lady," she said defensively, but she was smiling. "We were married, for God's sake."

"Don't keep me in suspense. I want all the details."

You're damn well not going to get *all* the details, Ariel thought, feeling herself blush again. But she had some serious shit to think about, and Chanda had helped her before. So, she'd give the PG-13 version.

She went to her clutter room and came back with a CD she had recently purchased by Diana King. Music had helped Lucius get her into the sack tonight. Music could help her explain the evening to Chanda.

"This song says it all; at least it's a good introduction." It was the first cut, "Love Me Through the Night," a soulful ballad tinged with King's reggae roots.

Ariel pressed the pause button, during the chorus when the singer belted out the song's title, as Chanda broke in with her interpretation.

"He wanted you to stay the night," Chanda said.

"Yeah, but I had to get back to you."

"Bad move."

"Listen to this part coming up," Ariel said, smiling, as they listened to King singing about lovers giving one another what they wanted, what each needed. Ariel didn't have to spell it out for Chanda. The girl could use her imagination.

154

This time Ariel let the music play as Chanda commented.

"Get down, Ariel," Chanda said. "Giving you what *you* need."

Ariel laughed again. She felt so relaxed. She could almost feel Lucius's touch as she listened to the song.

After it ended, Ariel gave an abbreviated version of the evening. Dinner. Talking about Dyann. Dancing. Ending up in bed. Doug's call. More time in bed with Lucius.

"Gonna leave the rest to my imagination, aren't you?" Chanda said when she'd finished.

"I don't kiss and tell. I've got *some* pride."

"So, are you two getting back together?"

This time Ariel noticed no fear in the youth's voice. Good. She knows she's not threatened.

"He'd like to. I'd like to, but . . ." She felt like Doug, starting something, but not having the nerve the finish the thought.

"But what?"

Ariel shook her head in exasperation. Chanda wasn't about to let her off the hook.

"We have a lot of baggage that needs to be dealt with," Ariel finally said. "At some point I'll have to bring up the abortion. He'll have to come to grips with his real feelings. If I marry, I want children. That will be a big hurdle. And like I told him, good loving doesn't make a good marriage. He has to love me for what I am, not what he wants me to be."

"Do you know what you are?"

Ariel looked at her. "Subtlety isn't one of your virtues, you know that?"

"You said just a while ago you'd reached a balance, but—"

"But maybe I was deluding myself," she finished. "Yeah, I'm still working on myself, I guess. Always will be, to be perfectly honest. He'll have to accept that, if he wants me."

She'd begun pacing the room again. Now she stopped, and looked at Chanda.

"I'm going to level with you. I don't know if I'm capable of a relationship. My greatest fear is I'm emotionally stunted. Crippled. Not adept at the give-and-take that makes or breaks a relationship."

Tears were forming in her eyes. She wiped them away.

"On my way here, I was asking myself—is Lucius my soulmate? That's not the right question. Am I capable of making a life with *anyone*? I'm afraid of letting Lucius down."

"You're certainly full of yourself, aren't you?"

"I'm trying to have a serious—"

"No," Chanda interrupted. "You're putting yourself down again. Putting all the responsibility on yourself. I'm not one to talk, but seems to me a relationship is a two-way street. I see only two questions you have to answer."

"Pray tell, oh-wise-one," Ariel said with a wan smile.

"First, can you love one another? Assuming it's yes, then, can he accept you as you are? Can he accept the white or Jewish you? *And* can you accept his blackness?"

"Come again?"

"Can you accept that this dude is a black man living in a white world where he's been kicked, spat upon and treated like a piece of shit," she said, her knees resting on the couch. "For a moment, put yourself in his place. A black man who can't pass for white. Do you know what *he's* been through?"

"You know, we hardly ever talked about *his* past," Ariel admitted.

"See, the black Ariel thought she could identify with the black Lucius. Just because I'm white, doesn't mean I've lived like all other whites. You've experienced some of what he has, but not all. You gotta learn more about him. And he's got to learn what you've been through, living in two

worlds—at times rejected by both. Then, you'll know if the
·two of you can make a go of it."

Ariel came to the couch and gave Chanda a hug.

"You're amazing, you know that? It's been me, me, *me*.
Him adjusting to me. All right. Time I start learning about
him."

"Why not invite him over for dinner tomorrow," Chanda
suggested.

"So you can psychoanalyze him?"

"Maybe," she said coyly. "And, maybe I'm just curious.
If he *is* the man for you, and if I stick around for a while . . ."

"You want to see if he meets with your approval," Ariel
finished for her.

"That's not exactly what I was going to say. . . ." she
trailed off.

"But it's how you feel."

Ariel pondered for a moment.

"All right. I'll call him tomorrow. See what he says."

"I'll go to a movie after dinner."

"Chanda!"

"Well, you don't want me eavesdropping, do you, and
three's a crowd."

"You are infuriating. But if you insist . . ." And they both
burst out laughing.

Ariel wasn't thinking about the case as she went to bed.
The Diana King song wove its way through her body.

Lucius gave her what she wanted tonight, and then some.
And despite all her misgivings she wanted more.

Chapter Twenty-six

For one of the few times since coming to stay with Ariel, Chanda had trouble falling asleep.

Love and sex.

She'd never really linked the two. Probably because, like Ariel, she was emotionally crippled.

Chanda had never known love. Certainly not from her family. And not from the street. It had struck her as Ariel was saying loving someone doesn't necessarily make a good marriage.

Chanda would even admit she was sexually stunted. Having sex with someone and making love were two very different concepts. The sex she'd had involved no love.

With all she'd been through, she wondered if she could ever find love. And with the life she had led, could she find passion in sex?

Young as she was, she feared she might be emotionally maimed for life. She felt happy for Ariel, but a bit envious, too. She and Lucius might never get together again. Or, if they did, it could end in disaster. But they had loved. Might love again. And sex for them was part of being in love. She hoped Ariel wouldn't throw it away frivolously. She agreed with Ariel that, if she rejected Lucius, another man might never come her way.

One day, it would be *her* turn to open up to Ariel. She had her own insecurities. Sure, she was old beyond her years because of all she'd been through, but there was so much she was uncertain about. She wanted so much to find *her*

Lucius; someone who could make her feel alive with his touch, his very presence. She just hoped it wasn't a pipe dream.

She was sure of one thing, though it would be quite some time before she'd confide it to Ariel: She was finished with the streets. If Ariel would have her, she would stay, get her degree and make a life for herself. Then, and only then, could she search for those deeper emotions that so eluded her.

Chapter Twenty-seven

Cleaning her nails in her dorm room, Shanicha cursed the two cops who kept intruding in her mind, intent on pinning the three suicides on her. Even as she'd planned Sharon Ingster's death, she had wondered how many would follow—*by her hand*. It wasn't like she was going to do this her entire four years in college. Half the fun was doing evil without *anyone* knowing.

She enjoyed the challenge, relished the anticipation and reveled in the aftermath of her two projects. But it was *work*. Draining at times. And there was the slim chance of choosing the wrong victim; someone whom she couldn't convince life was intolerable. If that occurred, that person would be a threat to her.

As the deaths mounted, the risk became greater. She had planned on stopping at three. There were so many other opportunities on a college campus. So much mayhem she could cause.

Monique Dysart's suicide—*a real suicide*—was the fly in the ointment now. Should she go for one more or put it to rest? She recalled the day she had found the button to encourage Jocelyn Rhea to cross over. Jocelyn, who had been so eager to please her father. Who needed to work harder to get the better grades he demanded. His phone calls becoming more and more strident. His calls were not all that much different from the letters Sharon Ingster received from her mother, Shanicha had thought at the time. Not vindictive and spiteful, like the letters, but equally insulting and deflating. There was no love, no real concern in her father's conversations, just disappointment and thinly veiled threats.

With each call, Jocelyn became more and more distracted, to the point she was averaging a *C* in Spanish. She *had* to pull it up to a *B,* or she'd be home at a local college the following year. Maybe deservedly so, she'd told Shanicha.

Oddly, she was not overly shaken by Sharon's suicide. She wouldn't talk about it in group, but she did confide in Shanicha.

"I was more intrigued than horrified. I felt like I was on the outside looking in, you know. I watched the reactions of the others, and thought this girl's got more friends in death than when she was alive. And that was kinda neat."

So Shanicha had bided her time, talking about past-life experiences without making a big thing of it. It was only a matter of time before she would have the necessary leverage.

At group, Jocelyn finally exposed that raw nerve.

"I hate being so dependent on my father," she told them one day. "He sends me a check every two weeks; almost as if he's counted what I'll need to the last penny. I'd get a job, but I'd be packing the moment he found out. Anyway, it's like the check validates he still has faith in me, so I look forward to those Thursdays like a child waiting to open presents Christmas Day."

Really, Shanicha thought. Sealed your doom, honey. *You're history*.

The next day Shanicha volunteered to help sort out dorm mail. No one objected. Volunteers were always welcome. And she pocketed two of Jocelyn's father's letters. He only wrote when he sent a check, Jocelyn had told her.

Jocelyn was upset when the first didn't arrive; hysterical two weeks later when her mailbox yawned at her with nothing to show.

"My father must be really pissed. I'm so afraid he'll show up at any moment to whisk me away."

She had stopped answering her phone, fearful to confront the man. It would ring insistently, literally driving her out of her room.

She'd told Shanicha the residence hall advisor had come by one day to make sure she was all right. Her father had called, concerned. Jocelyn told the RA she was fine. She just didn't want to speak to him right now.

"God, I wish I'd been pregnant," she'd told Shanicha. "I can't hack it here, but I don't know if I could bear his disapproval if he came to get me because I wasn't capable."

Shanicha had pushed and pushed some more.

Jocelyn had surprised her by showing her a rope she had purchased a few days earlier. It wasn't actually a rope. A clothesline, but Jocelyn had knotted it and put the noose around her neck.

"This is how I'd go," she'd said, "if I wanted to start fresh. I don't want to be splattered on the sidewalk like Sharon, for all to gawk at."

Shanicha had said *nothing* to dissuade her.

And with a little more prodding, Jocelyn had hung herself. Jocelyn knew another two weeks wouldn't pass without her father coming to get her. He'd sent no check, so she knew he'd given up on her. She was ducking his calls, and he couldn't abide her defiance.

Shanicha was in her room when she'd heard the first screams. She had planted the seed. Nourished it. Watched it blossom, and couldn't be placed anywhere near the scene of the crime.

One more or rest on her laurels? The question still tugged at her. Only two had died by her hand. She owed herself another. But was Monique's death a sign others would follow; the cluster effect the shrinks feared? And there were the two cops snooping around; especially Officer Friendly, who looked at her as if she was hiding something.

For now, she decided, she would let events dictate her course of action. She would continue to go to group; possibly to locate her next victim, and also to keep up pretenses. But there was no rush. She'd see if others followed Monique of their own volition. Even that anticipation excited her. Just how far did her tentacles reach? Everyone seemed to be showing the strain; almost as if it were finals week. *Some* must be thinking of following their classmates' lead. Others were worried about friends. Still others were being pestered by parents; their being overprotective could backfire as well. There was little talk now, but she could see it was on their minds. That in itself made her day.

She'd also keep an eye on the two cops.

Most definitely, an eye on the two cops.

There was so much more she had to do. Wouldn't be prudent to be impulsive with them around. Patience; a virtue that had always rewarded her.

Chapter Twenty-eight

It had been staring him in the face all along. Ask the right fucking questions, he reminded himself. Sometimes, though, even asking the right question wasn't enough, as Ariel had cautioned; especially to a computer programmed by University personnel intent on protecting the University's image.

Lucius had gotten up at eight that morning, feeling exhilarated and exhausted. He hadn't had sex with anyone since Dyann's death, and here he and Ariel had gone at it three times in one night.

It had been more than just sex with Ariel. It had been intense, invigorating, passionate lovemaking. But he felt like a basketball player just off the disabled list. Adrenaline had kept him going at first, but like a player just returned, if you weren't in game shape it caught up with you fast.

Sex with Dyann had been generally of the wham-bam-thank-you-ma'am variety, though it was her desire, not his. She wasn't into foreplay, got aroused quickly, and Lucius went along for the ride. Dyann was like Disneyland. You stay in line for an hour for a two-minute thrill. Dyann was a sprinter, Lucius thought. Ariel, on the other hand, was a marathon runner when it came to sex; long, slow and torturously delicious.

Lucius felt guilty as hell comparing the two; worse still, as a sexual partner Dyann paled in comparison to Ariel.

Regardless, he had what he labeled an erotic hangover when he awoke.

At the campus police headquarters, his first attempt to es-

Barry Hoffman

tablish a connection between the three girls proved futile. He punched up computer statistics of campus crime. Rape on campus, according to figures the University had provided the State and Federal government, was nearly nonexistent. One case in 1992, one in 1993, none in 1994. Current-year stats weren't available, but the pattern was clear. He knew why the stats didn't jibe with what he knew of campus life. He blamed the cobwebs in his head on Ariel. He was still feeling jet lag from their night together.

While acquaintance rapes occurred on campus, only those in which a criminal complaint was filed would be statistically noted. Acquaintance rape, he knew, rarely ended up in court. Instead, just as with Jocelyn Rhea, it was funneled through the Special Services Unit, formerly the Victims Support Unit.

Lucius remembered Desjardins telling them the reason for the politically more correct euphemism.

"We do much more than help victims. The unit provides self-defense clinics, walking escorts, courses to prevent crimes like theft and harassment, a Town Watch program, as well as outreach programs to help the homeless. Victims Support is too restrictive a term."

Lucius understood the new kinder, gentler nomenclature was more accurate, but it was also good public relations. The word "victims" had such a negative connotation, and the University looked to put a positive spin on all it did. While part of the campus police department, manned by regular officers, the unit was more interested in helping victims overcome their ordeal than in punishing the culprits. He couldn't argue with their rationale, but as a cop, there was a fine line he was often forced to straddle. And having grown up on the mean streets of North Philly, he knew, too, that students at the University were accorded much more latitude and leniency than anyone in his old neighborhood. Some of the more militant black students were quite bitter at the double standard. He couldn't argue with them.

164

Lucius also knew date rape was often a subjective matter. Was Jocelyn Rhea raped or was she pissed she hadn't been in control? She was sexually active, after all. He knew this didn't mean squat as to her culpability. Prostitutes were raped, though many cops were loath to put in the time to catch the rapist of a whore. Date rape, though, was often as murky as the Schuylkill River. For this reason, he had no problem with the University's policy in this area, even if it was self-serving.

First and foremost help the victim. That meant accompanying her to Jefferson Hospital, specially trained to handle rape cases. Then Special Services would intercede on behalf of the victim. The case wouldn't be closed until the victim herself made her intentions known.

Odd, though, he thought, that not *one* case ended with a criminal complaint. The skeptic in him considered the tarnished image a number of acquaintance rapes—referred to *only* as rapes in the stats—would give the University in the minds of parents who didn't want to even think their precious daughter might have intercourse, much less be *raped* while on campus.

But Jocelyn Rhea claimed she had been raped. *That* he knew for a fact. The question he'd considered the night before was could Sharon Ingster and Monique Dysart also be victims of date rape; hence the elusive link?

Unfortunately, records kept by Support Services were strictly confidential. He couldn't just go down there. . . . Or could he? A plan was percolating his mind.

Lucius and Dyann had had Asha Reynolds—a fellow campus police officer—over to their place a number of times; both when she was married and later, when her husband had been fatally injured in a car accident. He'd hung on for three days on life support before succumbing to massive internal injuries.

And Asha had bent over backward to comfort Lucius during Dyann's illness. She had been there as well after Dyann had died; someone to talk to. She had subtly inferred more than once that conversation was not the only solace she could provide. Lucius hadn't been ready. She was nice enough, and a good looker . . .

—But no Ariel.

Asha had been with Special Services for eight months. Had taken over the Jocelyn Rhea case after Lucius escorted the young woman to Jefferson Hospital.

What the hell, he thought. He'd give Asha a try.

This he needed to do alone. He called Ariel, who was about to beep him. She made it easy.

"Monique Dysart's parents are in town to pick up her body," she said. "I've got some questions to ask. I also want to call the other parents to see if I can establish a link. Then I'll have to brief my Sarge—"

"No need to go on," he interrupted. "I'll talk to some students and see what I can get."

"By the way," Ariel said, "how about dinner over *here* tonight? Chanda is dying to meet you."

Ariel had told him about Chanda the night before. He agreed, and yes, seven would be fine.

After he hung up, it struck him that neither of them had alluded to the events of the evening before. For his part, it was excitement over the lead he wanted to pursue. Or so he rationalized. But what about Ariel? "After the case . . ." he remembered her saying. All right, he thought, we'll keep it on a strictly professional level for now, but it didn't make it any easier keeping her from intruding into his thoughts.

Free, he went over to Special Services and asked Asha to lunch. Nothing fancy, he told her, just one of the many stands—trucks, actually, that sold a variety of edibles. You could get pizza, a hot dog, a fruit salad, or for the more

166

adventurous, Korean, Japanese, Chinese or Thai.

They settled on a fruit salad, Asha being a health nut.

She was a light-skinned black; the color of chocolate mousse. Lucius had wondered if like Ariel, she was biracial, and earlier she'd seemed to read his mind. Without even asking, she'd shown him a picture of her parents; both light-skinned blacks.

He'd wondered if he was that transparent, or if she was so insecure she had to prove her blackness to all the "brothers" she met? Had he wanted to make an issue of it, he could have commented that one or both of her parents looked biracial also. But he'd let it pass.

She was trim but full-figured, medium height but long-legged. A fine-looking woman, he thought, with a sardonic wit. Some other time he might have been attracted. But he'd had Dyann, and Asha had been married as well. When he'd lost Dyann, he would think about her at times; she and her thinly veiled invitations. At some point he would have to get on with his life. He could feel comfortable with Asha; not as a mate, but a friend. Maybe even a lover.

With Ariel back in his life, even temporarily, his only thought now was to pump Asha for information. He'd charm her, give her hope and string her along.

You're a bastard, he thought to himself, but he needed to establish the connection, if one existed, and he could think of no other way.

He took her to the Peace Sign, where they'd have privacy.

"It's been a while," she said tentatively. "Thought you might have found yourself another woman."

"No." He laughed. "I've been in my own little cocoon. Only now do I feel it's time to venture out. One can't grieve forever. You got a man in your life?"

"No one special. Been waiting for the right guy, if you know what I mean?" She looked down, as if not wanting to meet his eyes.

Barry Hoffman

He got her meaning and though he hated himself, he flirted with her a bit. Talking, laughing, establishing a rapport. Eventually, he steered the conversation to the recent suicides.

"Terrible thing about Jocelyn Rhea. That was your case, wasn't it?" he asked.

"Yeah. Poor kid. She'd had individual counseling, then group sessions. I thought she was getting better. Didn't seem so bitter. She'd pretty much decided against pressing charges."

Lucius was going to ask if the other two girls had been raped, but he decided to change tactics and take a chance.

"Odd how the other two suicides were victims of acquaintance rape," he said, as if the information were common knowledge.

"I thought so too, until we were briefed on the clustering. All *three* were in the same group; you know, group counseling."

She looked around to make sure no one was in earshot.

"Monique was my case, but not Sharon Ingster," she confided. "I peeked at her file, though. She was in group with Jocelyn and Monique."

"Some group," Lucius said. "All of them killing themselves. Must have had an intern leading their sessions."

Asha laughed. "Not at all. Isaacs himself led their group. Acquaintance rape is of particular interest to him. I talked to him a number of times about the fine line between passions leading to intercourse and rape. I don't buy this 'no means no' bull."

"I know some feminists who would argue with that," Lucius said. He was glad he'd gotten her talking. All he intended now was to intersperse a comment here, a question there, and let her provide further information.

"Yeah," she said, "feminists who are married and pencil in sex with their husbands on their calendar; once or twice a month. Really, Lucius, especially among young adults,

168

there's a time when two people are in bed, naked, both turned on. There's been more than a little foreplay. Now all of a sudden, he's ready and the girl changes her mind. Could you blame the guy for misinterpreting the word 'no'? The guy's dick is at work, not his brain."

"Did Isaacs share your views?" Lucius asked. Stanley Isaacs was the head of Psych Services on campus. If Lucius played his cards right, he might be able to find out the names of the other girls in his acquaintance-rape group. One of them just might be a murderer; or someone with a deep-seated problem who had sent a letter to the police.

"He didn't agree *or* disagree," Asha said. "He felt both men and women had to become more sensitive to what he termed the 'mating ritual.' He understood the passions aroused in the male, and women had to be educated not to tease—intentionally or inadvertently. But men had to be taught that 'no does mean no.' He straddled the issue, as far as I was concerned."

"How many other girls are in his group?" Lucius asked, trying not to sound overly interested. Just keeping the conversation going.

"Two who filed complaints with us, and a third girl who must have been referred by the Women's Center. They meet Tuesday and Thursday at 5 p.m., after classes."

Lucius knew that not all victims of date rape filed a complaint with Special Services. Some, feeling the need for guidance, turned to the Women's Center or other campus groups. These groups were *supposed* to liaison with Special Services, but it didn't always occur.

A committee was studying the problem and would issue guidelines. Lucius knew they wouldn't all be followed, which would lead to the formation of yet another committee.

They had finished their lunch and begun strolling along Locust Walk. A beautiful spring day had brought out what seemed like every group on campus with a cause. Tables lined the Walk with students hawking leaflets. A three-piece band was playing what Lucius guessed was alternative music. Not heavy enough to be metal, but not folk either. When Lucius couldn't categorize such music, he consigned it to the alternative niche, whatever the hell that meant.

Asha was getting ready to return to work. Lucius decided it was now or never. One more question. She'd know she had been used when he asked it, but hoped he had the charm—the wiles—to get her to acquiesce.

"I need a favor, Asha."

"Name it," she said.

"I can't go into details, but I have more than a passing interest in the acquaintance-rape counseling group. I need to know the names of the other three girls."

She looked at him, and he could see confusion, then hurt and disappointment.

"Fuck it, Lucius, have you been playing me? Ask me to lunch to pump me for information, knowing how I . . . knowing I have feelings for you."

"No, I swear, Asha. I admit, I am working with the Philadelphia police, but I didn't ask you to lunch with any ulterior motive. It's just that it's been on my mind—an obsession, I guess. All of a sudden we were talking about it, and I couldn't say stop."

"So if I don't tell you, you won't be pissed." It was a statement.

"I'm not going to beat it out of you," he said with a smile.

"I could get into a lot of trouble. What you're asking is held in the strictest confidence."

"I know, and I don't want to sound melodramatic, but the information could save one of those girl's lives." He held up a hand. "Don't go pumping me now. I've *already* told you too much." He paused, then made eye contact with her. "Look, all I want is their names. When this is over, I'll tell you all about it over dinner."

Asha bit her lip, deep in thought. Lucius had dangled the carrot of a possible relationship. It was mean-spirited of him, because he knew there was no possibility for the two of them. But the information was essential. He'd debate the ethics of his tactics later.

Finally, grudgingly, she told him two of the names.

"Those are the ones who filed complaints with us. I never found out the other girl's name."

"Thank you, Asha. It's important."

"I hope you weren't fucking with me, Lucius. You're good people. A good friend. I was hoping . . ." She paused. "Just don't be a stranger. I'll know then that I was just your whore."

They had been on Walnut Street, across from where she worked. She darted across, through oncoming traffic, so Lucius couldn't follow. Once across the street, she turned and looked at him, hurt evident in her face. Then she turned her back on him and went into the Special Services building.

You're a shit, Lucius told himself. It was why he'd joined the campus police force while Ariel was in homicide. She would have played the hand the same way, without feeling remorse. Not because she was without feelings, but as was the case now, the ends did justify the means. It didn't make him feel any better, however.

Chapter Twenty-nine

Lucius called Stanley Isaacs and set up an appointment for 6 p.m. According to Asha, the acquaintance-rape group met today. He wanted to speak with Isaacs *after* the session for a number of reasons. He knew he'd have to cancel dinner with Ariel. The disappointment he felt was genuine.

When he reached Ariel, a part of him was glad she sounded as disconsolate as he felt. He was evasive. No, nothing dealing with the case, he told her. He promised to fill her in the next day. They'd compare notes on the investigation in the early afternoon. They also rescheduled dinner for the next evening.

At 4:30, Lucius sat in a squad car across from the Mellon Bank Building at 37th and Walnut, which also housed Isaacs's office. A foot patrolman, he'd told the Commissioner's secretary he was following up a lead. Desjardins, she told him, agreed he could have use of a squad car, but he wanted to be fully briefed the next morning.

Lucius positioned the car so he could see the only point of entry into the building; the one on 37th Street that led directly to various University offices. The other, on Walnut Street through the bank, was closed for the day.

He knew in passing the two girls Asha mentioned would be going to the group session, though neither one particularly well. It was the third girl he wanted to get a look at.

Three girls entered the building between 4:45 and 4:55. The two he already knew arrived almost surreptitiously. The third came last, nonchalantly.

Lucius was glad he was in the car, because he couldn't hide his surprise. No way, he thought, *she* had been raped. On the other hand, he hadn't thought Sharon or Monique had been raped. There was a difference, though. *This* girl exhibited none of the signs of depression he'd seen in the other two. Then again, maybe therapy was working for her. He stayed in the car until ten after five just to make sure he wasn't mistaken. No one else entered. He added her name to those of the other girls in his notebook, and circled it. Why, he thought, hadn't she reported her rape to Special Services?

His plan, formulated over the course of the afternoon, was to arrive early, find out who the third girl was and be up in

Isaacs's waiting room when they left. Phase one had been successful. He would wait half an hour before going up to Psych Services.

Psych Services was on the third floor. There was a generous waiting area to the left after you entered, and a large reception kiosk on the right, with room for two secretaries. Like Desjardins's office, Psych Services was housed in an eroding shell whose interior had recently been refurbished. Chic and state-of-the-art came to mind as Lucius entered.

He was surprised to see a freshman manning the reception desk; one he'd noticed in the crowd at all the suicides. A small world, he thought. A small world.

"Haven't dropped out, I hope," he said, trying to hide his surprise.

She blushed. "It's for my work/study; you know, part of my financial-aid grant."

He informed her he had a 6 P.M. appointment with Dr. Isaacs.

"Not having problems, I hope," she said teasingly.

"Purely professional," he responded. Then. "How are you coping? The suicides at The Quad, I mean."

"Seems to be the question on everybody's mind," she said. "See a freshman—a *female* freshman—and wonder if the next time you see her she'll be laying face-down on the concrete. Is that what you're here about?"

"It's a confidential matter. And you didn't answer my question."

"I've got my head screwed on straight," she said. "Anyway, I'm the glue that holds this place together. I don't know what Dr. Isaacs would do without me, so even if I were depressed, I wouldn't leave him in the lurch," she added with a smile.

Just then the intercom buzzed. After a short conversation, she turned to Lucius.

"Dr. Isaacs said he'll be with you in just a few minutes.

173

He asked you to wait in his office." She pointed down the hallway. "Second door on the left."

Ensconced in the psychologist's office a minute later, he cursed the doctor's efficiency. Isaacs didn't want Lucius seeing who came out of the group session. He would be a tougher nut to crack than Asha, but Lucius had additional ammunition.

Isaacs entered his office at six-oh-one. Lucius, as always, was taken aback by the man. On first glance one would think he was a twenty-one-year-old; a student, not quite old enough to be a graduate assistant. When he sat down in his cushy leather chair, it all but swallowed him up. Lucius was reminded of the Lily Tomlin character Edith Ann, who was supposed to be a child sitting in a chair meant for an adult.

Isaacs's first order of business, the first time he met you, was to assure you he was no escaped mental patient masquerading as a psychologist.

"I have a condition," he remembered the man telling him, in a deep husky voice that was at total odds with his appearance, the first time they'd met; a condition with a name long enough to wrap around your head, which Lucius had forgotten once it was out of the shrink's mouth.

"At twelve, the aging process slowed, and it didn't look like I'd aged a day when I turned eighteen. When I turned thirty, I looked sixteen, and now at forty-one, I look legal—twenty-one. I seldom get carded now when I order a beer. A hell of an accomplishment, I can assure you.

"It's hell on my patients until they get to know me. No matter what I say, it's tough not thinking they're pouring out their troubles to a guy just out of college. It's one reason I abandoned private practice for the University."

He'd paused to clean his glasses, before going on.

"On the other hand, I've since found it has its advantages working with youngsters and college-age students. They

174

seem to think I can relate to them. Now, let's move on, shall we."

Lucius remembered thinking it was not just the face that looked young, but the entire package. The man's whole body seemed somehow stunted. He was no midget, but he was short—five-foot-nothing with shoes. He was small-boned, even brittle-looking, with a lean, almost cadaverous appearance. Sneeze and you might bowl him over.

His eyes, though, were penetrating—even predatory, Lucius had thought; not the eyes of a child, even a suspicious one. While you spoke, he was taking stock of you. More than that, Lucius thought, he was dismantling you psychologically. After one conversation he knew a great deal about what made you tick, your insecurities, fears and eccentricities. Lucius felt laid bare, his secrets exposed without having spoken them. It was discomforting, to say the least, especially for a cop who was supposed to have the upper hand.

"What can I do for you, Officer Jackson?" Isaacs asked now. He wore old-fashioned horn-rimmed glasses he kept taking off and cleaning, like an absentminded professor.

"Sharon Ingster. Jocelyn Rhea. Monique Dysart," Lucius said. "Ring a bell?"

"Let's not play games, Officer," Isaacs said, sounding pompous, obviously to compensate for his lack of physical stature. "The suicides. Of course they ring a bell."

"All three part of your acquaintance-rape counseling group, Doctor, is what *I* was thinking."

If Isaacs was surprised, he hid it well. He took off his glasses, and blew on them, wiped them with a cloth and put them back on.

"I'm well aware of that. It's most unfortunate, but a coincidence, I can assure you."

"Would you feel differently if they weren't suicides, but murders?" Lucius asked, his eyes focused squarely on Isaacs.

The doctor stood now, clearly angry.

"Come now, Officer Jackson. Are you trying to concoct some sort of conspiracy to mesh with your somehow learning the three girls were part of the same counseling group?" he asked derisively.

Lucius held out a copy of the letter the police had received. Isaacs took it, read it once, sat down and read it a second time. He took off his glasses and massaged his eyes, deep in thought.

"Are the police involved?" He had gone ashen.

"Yes, but they're not aware *yet* of the link the three girls shared." He paused to let the implied threat sink in.

"Let me be totally up-front with you," Lucius said, meaning nothing of the kind. "This"—pointing to the letter—"along with the coincidence of the three girls being in your counseling group could be devastating for the University in the wrong hands. Like you, I'm looking to protect the school. I'm also trying to make sure Monique Dysart's apparent suicide is the last. If you cooperate, we may be able to nip this in the bud—*in house*. I'm sure you're aware of the alternatives."

Isaacs looked at the note again. He really did look like a frightened child, Lucius thought.

"Within the parameters of confidentiality, I'm more than willing to cooperate. That murder is a possibility is most disconcerting."

The man sure loved big words, Lucius thought. He was positive it was just a facade to hide Isaacs's insecurities. Knowing this made Isaacs far less intimidating. Lucius knew he would get what he wanted; could make the shrink sweat at the same time if he wished.

"There are three girls left in your group," Lucius said, naming them. "Correct?"

"Correct."

Lucius had decided a frontal assault best. Lay his cards on

176

Here's how it works:

Each package will carry a FREE 10-DAY EXAMINATION privilege. At the end of that time, if you decide to keep your books, simply pay the low invoice price of $11.25, no shipping or handling charges added. HOME DELIVERY IS ALWAYS FREE!
There's no minimum number of books to buy, and you may cancel at any time.

AND AS A CHARTER MEMBER, YOUR FIRST THREE-BOOK SHIPMENT IS TOTALLY FREE! IT'S A BARGAIN YOU CAN'T BEAT!

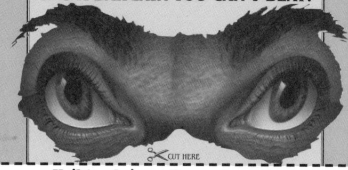

✂ CUT HERE

- -

Mail to: Leisure Horror Book Club, P.O. Box 6613, Edison, NJ 08818-6613

YES! I want to subscribe to the Leisure Horror Book Club. Please send my 3 FREE BOOKS. Then, every other month I'll receive the three newest Leisure Horror Selections to preview FREE for 10 days. If I decide to keep them, I will pay the Special Members Only discounted price of just $3.75 each, a total of $11.25. This saves me between $3.72 and $6.72 off the bookstore price. There are no shipping, handling or other charges. There is no minimum number of books I must buy and I may cancel the program at any time. In any case, the 3 FREE BOOKS are mine to keep—at a value of between $14.97 and $17.97. Offer valid only in the USA.

NAME:_____

ADDRESS:_____

CITY:_____ STATE:_____

ZIP:_____ PHONE:_____

◼ **LEISURE BOOKS**, A Division of Dorchester Publishing Co., Inc.

the table at the outset to unnerve the doctor and possibly make him assume Lucius knew even more.

"Are any of these girls capable of murder?"

"Not in my professional opinion," he said haughtily, then talked to Lucius as an equal.

"These girls are angry at what happened to them, but not one of them has ever broached the idea of physically harming their assailants. So, I don't see them capable of murdering someone with whom they can identify."

"Any of them dysfunctional enough to write a crank letter?" Lucius said, purposely using a word Isaacs could identify with rather than say the word *ill*.

"All three are progressing, so my first inclination would be to say no. But on the other hand, to be brutally frank, I never thought any of the other three were suicidal. They were depressed, to be sure, but we were making wonderful progress. Their deaths have devastated me."

"You haven't answered my question, Doctor."

"With the trauma they faced, yes, any of the three are capable of writing such a note. But murderers? No, no, a thousand times *no!*"

"Two of the remaining girls in your group were referred from Special Services," Lucius said, naming them. "What of the third?"

"She was a walk-in."

Isaacs took out a handkerchief and wiped his forehead, which had begun to sweat profusely. "This is most distressing. These girls are confronting their demons, based solely on the fact that what they say will be held in confidence. You want me to betray that confidence."

"I'm not asking for their case histories, Doctor, but chances are one of these girls is either a murderer or, for some perverted reason, informed the police she is. Maybe a cry for attention, but I'm no expert, am I?"

Lucius paused to let Isaacs compose himself, then continued.

"You say she was a walk-in. Who referred her?"

"She said the Women's Center."

"Did you contact them for verification?"

"Certainly not. She wasn't here for a job interview. It doesn't matter how they get here. Once a young lady seeks help, she gets it."

"Did she go to Jefferson or any other hospital for an exam?"

Isaacs closed his eyes. He was clearly agitated.

"No," he finally said. "The rape occurred several days before she sought guidance. She showered thoroughly as soon as she got back to her dorm. A normal response, let me add. She brooded for two days, and when she felt overwhelmed she went to the Women's Center."

"Do you find her story credible?"

"Most definitely," he said with increasing confidence. "Most rape victims don't come forth immediately. You must know many—maybe more than half—never come forward at all; and I'm not talking about acquaintance rape. I am certain there are dozens of girls on campus now who feel they have been violated, but believe they are at least partially responsible and let it rest. They want to get past the encounter, not relive it. So, there's nothing unnatural for a young woman to try to put such an incident behind her. In this case she did, but two days later she was still unable to come to grips with the rape."

"Who suggests group therapy?" Lucius asked, changing the subject.

"I often recommend it. I always lay it out as an option, after individual counseling. Some never want it. Others need a good deal of individual therapy before they can bare themselves before others."

"What about the three who are left in your group?"

178

Isaacs bit down on his lip, again looking very young.

"Only Shanicha specifically requested group therapy. The others all followed my recommendations after numerous individual sessions. Shanicha came for two individual sessions and then requested group. She said she felt uncomfortable talking to me. She wanted to hear and speak with peers who had gone through what she had."

"Has she responded?" Lucius asked, knowing he was pushing his luck.

"She's been mostly an observer," Isaacs said, "but that's not unusual. She'll participate when she's ready."

"Could she be faking?"

"I don't believe she's that good an actress," Isaacs said. "I'm not going to divulge the specifics that transpired in our initial sessions, but I can assure you she went through a traumatic experience. I pride myself on being able to read my patients, Officer. I've had my share of charlatans. Shanicha is no sham. In her mind, she was forced to have intercourse without her consent . . . and worse."

"Just a few more questions, Doctor, and I'll be out of your hair," Lucius said with a smile.

"Whatever," Isaacs said, sounding tired and defeated.

"I noticed a student at the reception area when I came in. Do many students work here?"

"A few as part of their work/study grants."

"Do they have access to patients' files?"

"Absolutely not. Only my personal secretary has access to mine. No student touches any patient's file."

"But they do see who comes for appointments." It wasn't a question.

Isaacs shrugged, indicating yes, so what?

Lucius decided it wasn't worth the hassle of further antagonizing the man by asking him about work schedules. If he wanted to find out if work/study students manned the reception area when the girls came for group, he could do so easily.

He stood up and extended his hand.

"I want to thank you, Doctor. You've been most cooperative."

"What will you do next?" The doctor sounded more anxious than he wanted, which pleased Lucius. He could very well need to speak to the man again, and he'd pressed all the right buttons.

"That's not my call," he answered. "Chief Desjardins will make that decision. We do want to keep this in-house, after all. Especially if the letter is a hoax."

"I appreciate that."

"And you will keep our chat confidential, I hope. The more people who learn of this letter, the better the chances of a leak."

"I understand completely."

Isaacs walked Lucius to the door. They shook hands. Isaacs's palms were damp, and again Lucius was pleased.

As Lucius returned the squad car to police headquarters, he had to decide what he would *really* do next. He was certainly not going to talk to Desjardins first. Keeping what he'd learned in-house was just what the Chief would want to do.

Lucius didn't know if Isaacs had grasped the ramifications of the three suicides all connected by date rape and common group-therapy sessions. If it was made public, there'd be hell to pay and scapegoats to finger. Because of his initial silence, Isaacs's head would be one of the first to roll.

Right now, though, there were only two questions, as far as Lucius was concerned. Was Shanicha Wilkins a murderer or had she sent the letter either for attention or because she was far more disturbed than Dr. Isaacs suspected?

Tomorrow morning, he decided, he would tell Ariel. For reasons that had nothing to do with preserving the University's reputation, he felt it best that as few people became aware of his findings as possible. Shanicha might spook if word got out; even if she wasn't considered a prime suspect.

He and Ariel would have to devise a strategy to expose the girl. Then he'd go to Desjardins and Ariel to McGowan.

Personally, he felt the letter a hoax; a desperate cry for attention. Shanicha's name hadn't been mentioned by any students he'd spoken to until today. No way she could have pushed two girls out their windows and hung Jocelyn Rhea without anyone seeing her.

—But have you asked the right questions? his mind retorted.

He'd brainstorm tonight. Tomorrow he wouldn't be alone. He was certain he and Ariel working together could bring Shanicha to ground, whether her crime was murder or sending the letter for some other reason entirely.

He and Ariel working together. He liked that. Liked that a lot.

Chapter Thirty

Shanicha sat in Houston Hall with three other girls shooting the breeze. One of the white girls was braiding Shanicha's hair. It was something she now took for granted; girls styled her hair like she was a Barbie doll. She had long coal-black hair that had the feel of cotton. Her mother and sisters changed her hair style several times a week; sometimes daily. It was one of the few times she commanded attention at home.

At times she could hardly recognize herself after they were

done. She felt like a different person, took on an entirely different persona. Knowing she had hair that some would kill for, she gladly reciprocated, styling classmates' hair in a way that would pass muster as having been done professionally.

She would have rather been by herself, but she knew she had to keep up pretenses. She was a popular, well-liked girl, with a lot of friends but no close confidant. She'd gossip, but pick up far more than she gave. She'd crack on others, and accept their teasing in return.

But only one portion of her was interacting with the other girls. She had the ability to socialize on autopilot, while thinking about far more serious concerns at the same time. This was her *other self*; for all intents and purposes her best friend—her *only* real friend.

She had seen Officer Friendly in the squad car across from Psych Services when she came in for group. He thought he was so clever, she thought, but to her he stuck out like a fox in a chicken coop. It did bother her, though, that he was *waiting* for her, for she instinctively knew he wasn't there by chance. He was watching her. Stalking her.

This was reinforced at six, when she exited the building and saw the vacant squad car across the street. He must be upstairs, she thought, with that little twerp Isaacs.

Talking about her.

She decided to wait at a partially enclosed bus stop. Sure enough, he came out of the building forty-five minutes later.

She wondered what he knew that had brought him to Isaacs.

She wondered what the shrink had divulged.

She wasn't afraid. Had never been . . .

—Except for the spiders.

Just as the crack had robbed her of a conscience, long practice had drained her of fear of capture.

Rather, she felt anticipation. She, Officer Friendly and that white bitch cop were involved in a stare-off. *She* certainly wouldn't blink first. They couldn't have much, she thought, or they would have brought her in for questioning. Or maybe just a chat to size her up. What did they have, though? she wondered. She'd been so careful.

Since fourth grade she had shunned the limelight. Not seeking notoriety, she was able to do so much more. In fourth grade, though, she had almost gotten caught, and in the process learned a valuable lesson.

She had accused Mr. Randolph of molesting her. The idea had hit her when she'd come to class early one day to drop off a volcano she had made for a science project.

Her teacher was tutoring another girl. They were both all smiles, and a number of times he touched her shoulder or arm. The idea that followed came naturally. It would be so much more fun than her instigating fights between classmates, which she'd been doing for years. In passing, she'd say this to one girl or that to another, and soon they were at one another's throats.

It was a lot more fun watching the girls fight than the boys. Boys postured and ended up in a wrestling match. Girls, on the other hand, went for the kill, figuratively speaking. Scratching, clawing, biting, hair-pulling. It was vicious; primal. And teachers had a much tougher time breaking up fights between girls. Male teachers, in particular, had to be careful where they grabbed a girl. Heaven forbid they touched a breast inadvertently. It made them tentative, and the girls were allowed to pummel one another far longer than boys.

Even that was getting old real fast, though.

Mr. Randolph was known for being friendly. He was a big cuddly man with a thick red beard that he constantly kneaded with his fingers. New Canaan being a small town, no one thought it odd that he'd voluntarily come over to his student's houses and tutor them in the evening or weekends.

No one thought it out of the ordinary that he routinely took five or six students on picnics one Sunday a month. No one thought it peculiar that he encouraged students to come to class early if they'd had problems with their homework. He was a dedicated teacher and parents climbed over one another to get their offspring assigned to his class.

What Shanicha noticed was that his attentions were directed almost solely to girls. The picnics—girl-only affairs. Girls received most of his tutoring. In class, girls sat on his lap. In the hall, they held his hand. He was a touchy-feely person; his hands on the shoulders or arms of girls, like now, as Shanicha observed without being seen.

It was all very innocent.

Shanicha was a bit envious, she'd be the first to admit, because she was never invited to the picnics, though she certainly was popular. Mr. Randolph never volunteered to tutor her at home even though her grades were mediocre. And he didn't dote on her like he did with his favorites. Maybe he sensed she wouldn't welcome his attention. Maybe some inner antenna warned him she was malevolent. But it pissed her off nevertheless that she was invisible to him. Pissing Shanicha Wilkins off was just asking for trouble.

The next day she came in early, saying she'd had problems with her homework. He quickly helped her, all the time keeping his distance. She came again two days later and three days after that. He seemed no more comfortable. He had the beady eyes of a deer who sensed danger.

Then she told her sister Tanya, who told her parents, who stormed into the principal's office with Shanicha in tow.

"Tell Mr. Lowry what Mr. Randolph did to you," her mother prodded gently.

She hesitated, letting a tear fall.

The principal came around his desk and knelt down to her. She retreated, as if afraid *he* might touch her.

184

"Honey, please," her mother beseeched. "Spit it out and be done with it."

She told.

"Mr. Randolph. He . . . he asked me to come early, so I could get better grades," she began.

"He . . . he made me sit on his lap. He rubbed my shoulder, then touched me here," she said, pointing to her breasts. She stopped and looked down.

"Go on, Shanicha," her mother prompted. "Tell what happened next."

"He put his hand up my dress and touched my privates," she blurted out, and began to cry.

Her mother held her, patting her back, saying everything would be all right.

When she'd cried herself out, she told the rest of the story. How her teacher said it was their secret. How no one would believe her if she told anybody. And how he made her come early twice again, the last time making her touch his penis.

It was all a lie, of course, but from the look on Mr. Lowry's face, she knew she'd been convincing. She had interspersed fact with fiction. It was known students came in early for help. It was common knowledge he was touchy-feely, but it had always seemed so innocent. The lie built upon known truths made what she said seem entirely credible.

What surprised Shanicha was how other girls came forward with similar stories, *after* Mr. Randolph had been removed from class and word spread. First, it was the girl who had been there when she'd brought her volcano. Then, two others. Six in all. They were lying, Shanicha knew, but they seemed to want to share the spotlight.

Mr. Randolph had adamantly protested his innocence when Shanicha's charges were relayed to him. The girl just craved attention, he said. His record was spotless. He had nothing to hide.

But with six others soon corroborating Shanicha's story, with their own tales of molestation, the humiliation must have been too much to bear. Unmarried, living alone, one night he stuck a gun in his mouth and blew his brains out.

It had been her first taste of blood and she craved more, like a lion having killed its first human; no longer fearful of the two legged-creatures.

Shanicha also felt relieved. She had been the center of attention for a short time, until the other girls came forward. She didn't like it one bit. She had to tell her story over a dozen or more times, despite her mother's promise to spit it out and be done with it. Some, she knew, would come to her teacher's defense. If the other girls hadn't come forward *she* would be scrutinized. It was, after all, her word against a popular, beloved teacher.

It would only be a matter of time before others would recall incidents that would expose her as the manipulator she was. She had been an idiot not to have realized the danger she had placed herself in.

Fortunately, not only did others come forward, but the fool ate his gun before the incident could snowball into a full-fledged investigation.

He was guilty so he killed himself to avoid further embarrassment; even incarceration. That was the prevailing reaction to his suicide. And with him gone, the episode was buried. Shanicha was too young to know at the time, but that was what happened in small towns. A blot on their good name had been erased before it had become state, even national, news. The early investigation had been low-key and circumspect. And with Randolph gone, *no one* talked about it. Not the other six girls, and certainly not Shanicha. Soon it was as if he had never existed.

Shanicha had learned to shun the spotlight ever since. She had acted impulsively. She had been a fool. Yet, she had escaped.

Now, she again felt trapped by Officer Friendly. Following her, checking her out, keeping tabs on her. Would he start talking to her friends next?

She could kill the fucker. She really could, she thought, as she laughed at the crass joke one of her friends told.

She could kill the fucker, and that white bitch cop, too.

Chapter Thirty-one

Lucius was tired as he arrived home, but jazzed all the same. He'd accomplished so much. There was now a viable suspect. He was tempted to call Ariel but decided against it, as he tried unsuccessfully to stifle a yawn. What he needed, he told himself, was a shower and a good night's sleep. He knew, as he lay in bed . . .

—Thinking of Ariel
—Thinking of him and Ariel the night before.

. . . he'd organize and get a better handle on what he'd discovered.

He opened his door, and the smell of hamburger cooking assaulted his nose. He took out his gun and carefully ventured into the kitchen.

A female, her back to Lucius, asked—mumbled actually— "You want your burger rare, medium or well?"

She turned, and was chewing on a hamburger; the cause of her garbled speech. "You might want to put that away," she added, pointing to the gun. "If I wanted to rob your place, I'd be long gone."

"Who are you? How did you get in here? And what the fuck are you doing here?" he asked incredulously. She was a girl, he thought, in her mid-to-late teens.

"Chanda. Picked your lock," she said, answering his first two questions. "You got some valuable shit here. I'd suggest a deadbolt, at the very least. What about that burger?"

"Ariel's Chanda," Lucius said, making the connection. He holstered his gun.

"The one you stiffed tonight. You look like a medium-rare, since you won't tell me." She put a hamburger in the frying pan, and put it on the stove.

Lucius was dumbstruck. Ariel had told him about Chanda, but hadn't done her justice. Her face was long and lean, her lips full and covered with a garish shade of lipstick. Her sky-blue eyes were fixed on him, as his were on hers. She had long, thick, wheat-colored hair that many a boy must have wanted to run his hands through.

She wore a tight pair of jeans and an equally revealing "Kurt Cobain Lives" T-shirt. Both looked painted on. Through the T-shirt, Lucius could see she wore no bra. He could see her nipples as if the shirt were transparent. It was obvious she had worn the clothes as a test for Lucius. Would he chastise her, act like a father? Would he jump her bones? Or just keep gawking at her, as he did now?

To keep from staring, he went to the fridge and got a beer. "Rare, if you don't mind," he said as he took a swallow. "You here to make sure I'm not cheating on Ariel," he said tartly.

"Don't go ballistic. If half of what Ariel tells me is true, you wouldn't cheat on her." She shrugged. "Or anyone else for that matter."

"Ariel told you about *me*?" he asked, unable to hide his surprise.

"Of course she has. Why do you think you were invited to dinner?"

"To get your approval?"

"Not exactly," she said coyly. She turned the burger over and looked at him.

"Look, the two of you *might*—and I emphasize the word *might*—get back together—"

"And you think you'll be the odd man out, so to speak," he said, finally understanding.

She shook her head. "You grownups think you know it all. You know squat." She turned the burger over once more. "I wanted to size *you* up," she continued. "I might reject *you*. Wouldn't tell Ariel. She's free, half-white and twenty-one. She has to make her own choice. Whether I stay or not is my decision."

"You're something," Lucius said, taking another swallow of beer. "You break into my home, and now we're going to play twenty questions to see if *I* pass muster. You gotta be putting me on."

"No different than I did with Ariel."

She took the hamburger from the pan, put it on a bun she'd heated in his microwave and handed it to him on a plate.

"Why don't we sit down," she said, taking her half-eaten burger and sitting at the kitchen table.

Lucius followed suit. He'd just about gotten over the shock of her being in his kitchen when he'd gotten home. Maybe he should get to know her. After all, he and Ariel might . . . No, he stopped himself. He didn't want to think of long-term possibilities, yet.

"Look, Chanda," he said after tasting the burger and telling her it was just right, "let me put you at ease from the get-go. First, neither Ariel or I have even begun to think of a future together. But, for the sake of argument, let's say we decided to try again. You're Ariel's responsibility. I'd abide by the rules the two of you set. No way I'm about to impose my value system on you. From the way you're dressed, I know you wanted to see my reaction. It's no different than

189

if one of Ariel's friends came over dressed to the nines. None of my business. None of my concern."

They went on for half an hour; Chanda baiting him, Lucius refusing to let the girl rile him. Personally, he didn't approve of the way she dressed. It had to do with her safety, not her taste or lack thereof. A female walking around with just about everything showing was asking for trouble. He might express his concern as a friend, if they made it that far, but he wasn't going to father or bully a seventeen-year-old street-wise kid into submission; a runaway, whose first response might be to flee.

Lucius had made coffee for the two of them and they'd split his last cheese danish.

"Do I get your stamp of approval?" he asked finally. Oddly, he wanted very much to be accepted.

She didn't answer the question. Instead she surprised him.

"You and Ariel won't make it if you haven't come to terms with yourself as a black man in a white society. I'm not going to tell you how it feels to be black. I haven't the foggiest. But I do know how it looks when a black man and a white woman are seen walking down the street. Are you man enough to deal with that?"

"I dealt with it, if you'll recall."

"Rather badly, from what I hear."

He was about to respond, but she ignored him and went on.

"Do you have enough self-respect to stand up to blacks who will look at you as a traitor to your race for marrying a white woman?"

"She's not . . ."

"She's *white* to anyone who doesn't know her. Forget how she sees herself. She walks in a room, she's a white woman to everyone there. You're with a white woman. Can you take the heat this time?" She raised a hand, again, before he could respond.

"Don't tell me. Just think about it before you commit to Ariel. It would be a shame to see her hurt a second time."

Lucius laughed. "You do speak your mind, don't you? Just as Ariel said." He took a sip from a second beer he'd opened.

"Tell you something, just between the two of us," he went on. "You're pretty damn fond of Ariel, though you won't admit it. You care for her. *You* don't want to see her hurt."

Chanda blushed, but said nothing.

"I like you, Chanda," he added. "*If* we do get together, you with your painted-on clothes and I will get along just fine. And, if we agree not to commit, I hope you'll still be willing to put me in my place when I act the fool. Because, understand this, Ariel and I are going to remain friends regardless. Our parting wasn't amicable, but we were both fools not to reconcile, *as friends,* for eight years. It's not going to happen again, that I promise."

The phone rang before Chanda could respond.

"Hold that thought," he said, and took the call in the living room.

When he returned he felt distracted, and could see Chanda was aware.

"Look, I best be going," she said. "Other homes to break into and that sort of thing."

Lucius walked her to the door. She opened it, turned and smiled.

"It's been," she said.

"Interesting? Informative? Revealing? Disappointing?" Lucius asked.

"It's been," she repeated. Then she looked at him. "The clothes were a bit much, huh?"

Lucius laughed. "A bit much."

"See you tomorrow for dinner?" she asked.

"Count on it."

"Like your steak rare, too?"

"Almost walking. But I like my fries well done." He

shrugged, knowing his tastes were a bit eccentric.

"*If* I was scouting you, you'd have passed," she said, turned and was gone.

What a kid, Lucius thought, wondering what he might be getting himself into.

Then his thoughts turned back to the phone call. A female, obviously masking her voice.

"Officer Jackson?"

"Speaking."

"There's something you should know about them three girls that got killed on campus."

Even the words didn't sound right to Lucius. She was trying to sound uneducated.

"Go ahead," he said.

"Not on the phone," she responded. "Can we meet tonight?"

"I guess so. How about—"

"Go to The Button at eleven," she interrupted. "Walk west on Locust Walk. I'll signal with a flashlight. Go as far as the Compass, then start over again. I want to make sure you're not followed. I'm really afraid, so come alone."

He began to ask a question, but she'd hung up, and he was listening to a dial tone.

Who could it be? he wondered. One of the girls from group? Asha? It was someone on campus. Not only was she familiar with its landmarks, but she sounded like it was part of her everyday vocabulary. When students were to meet, it was often at *The Button*. And the Compass was often overlooked by strangers. It had been sculpted in the ground. Campus lore had it if you crossed the Compass before final exams, you'd fail.

And once she started giving directions, her entire vocabulary had changed. She no longer sounded uneducated. Still, she'd managed to sound like any one of a hundred girls on campus.

192

He looked at his watch. Just after nine. Time for a shower, jot down some notes in his pad, then meet his Deep Throat. He checked his gun to make sure it was loaded. Force of habit. He hadn't fired it except at a target range in his fourteen years as a cop. Nevertheless, he checked to see if it was loaded daily. And when under stress or excited, he sometimes did it twice; even three times.

Chapter Thirty-two

She had left Psych Services before the policeman, but not before he had asked about her. She had been working at Psych Services to help pay for school since the beginning of second semester; just a few weeks after Shanicha Wilkins had gone to see Dr. Isaacs.

The first semester was to get acclimated to campus life and routine. Work/study kicked in the second semester for freshmen. She'd started as a volunteer at Psych Services, complying with her work/study requirement by being a tour guide for prospective students and their parents. She had become familiar with all that was required, then sabotaged the sophomore who had just started the job for her work/study prerequisite. The girl had been let go, and rather than train someone new, she'd been asked if she wanted the job.

That had been the easy part. More difficult had been getting access to conversations in Dr. Isaacs's office and the group therapy conference room.

Actually, it had not been all that hard. Surfing the Internet they all had access to at the University, she'd come across information on a wide range of topics she'd thought illegal:

explosives, breaking and entering, how to create a new identity and surveillance techniques. From the last, she'd learned how to bug Isaacs's office and conference room.

While she sat at the reception desk, it was assumed she was transposing dictation, but she was, in fact, eavesdropping.

She'd listened to the cop's discussion with Dr. Isaacs, surprised first that he'd targeted Shanicha, and later that he had asked about *her*. *If* he matched her hours at Psych Services and those of the acquaintance-rape group, the correlation would be obvious. *She* could become a suspect.

She had to do something before he told anyone else. The City police would suspect nothing, if the campus cop was out of the way. She could also make it more difficult afterwards by varying her hours. There was no real need to keep track of Isaacs's rape therapy group anymore. She already knew enough about each girl.

The only threat, then, was the campus cop. He had to go, and it had to look like Shanicha could be responsible if Isaacs blabbed to the City cops.

For the next hour she scouted the campus for a suitable location to ambush the patrolman. She found the perfect spot, not far from Steinberg-Deitrich Hall. On the right were a number of buildings with narrow alleys. One that led to the Delta Psi Fraternity house was best. It was long and particularly narrow. At the end and to the right, completely out of eyesight, was a metal staircase; a twelve-to-fifteen-foot drop. On the ground, she found a twelve-inch pipe.

Perfect.

She'd called Officer Jackson. Made it short and sweet. Just enough to ensure he would come. She'd stopped back at The Quad at 9:45 and found Shanicha in one of the lounges, shooting the breeze with a bunch of girls.

Perfect. Just perfect.

At a phone booth, at 10:30, she'd called the Resident Advisor on Shanicha's floor and told her Dr. Isaacs wanted to see Shanicha at eleven. It was important and confidential. Make sure she got the message, she had told the RA.

At 10:45, wearing dark clothes and gloves, she was at the alley, keeping an eye out for her prey. She was pumped and, oddly enough, not a bit nervous. Was this the way Shanicha felt just before putting one of her many plans into action? she wondered. The anticipation was like foreplay in sex. You wanted it to continue forever, yet you also wanted it to end and get to the main event. Penetration—liftoff, she called it— was almost anticlimactic, as she rarely achieved orgasm before her partner. Once he'd done his business, he could care less about her needs.

She was in the foreplay mode now, and this time she'd be in control.

She saw him just before eleven, at The Button. He looked at his watch and began advancing toward her at eleven sharp. No one else was around. She moved toward the rear of the alley when he passed Steinberg-Deitrich. She had a nondescript flashlight she'd brought to school with her but had never used; the type you could buy at KMart or a hundred other places.

She turned it on and off three times. Waited and repeated it fifteen seconds later. She saw him at the mouth of the alley. Slowly he walked toward her. She moved to the right, turned the light on and put it at the top of the stairs. She moved farther back where she wouldn't be seen.

She watched as he approached stealthily. She wondered what was going through his mind.

—Foreplay.
—The anticipation.
—*Nothing was better.*

Was he afraid? Did a part of him want to turn tail and run?
She felt her breath quickening; the adrenaline flowing. Control; she loved being in control. He went right for the flashlight. Stared at it on the ground and bent down to retrieve it, like a pencil he'd dropped.

She slipped behind him then, and hit him with the pipe with all her might squarely on the back of his head. He didn't yell. Didn't scream. Grunted maybe, but it was all but inaudible. And like a Slinky, he pitched headlong down the stairs, his head thumping two, three, then four times on the stairs before he came to a rest at the bottom.

She dashed down, careful to avoid the pool of blood that was forming where he rested. His eyes were open, looking at her, yet seeing nothing. She wasn't about to feel for a pulse, but stood transfixed, watching for any sign of movement.

He was at peace.

With God.

Dead as a doorknob.

She gently placed the metal pipe in the pool of blood, picked up the flashlight, turned it off and came to the mouth of the alley. Still all clear.

Farther down, toward The Button, was another alley where she had left a gym bag. She quickly took off the dark clothes and replaced them with a nondescript jogging suit.

—As nondescript as she.

Ten minutes later, at 11:22, she was in Houston Hall, studying with some other girls from The Quad. At ten to twelve, they went back to their dorm; four girls together who would draw scant attention.

Her roommate was gone. She'd been blessed. The girl had a boyfriend with an apartment off campus. At the beginning of the semester she'd finally gone to bed with him and began staying over one or two nights a week. Now she stayed over just about every night. Over a period of weeks, she'd brought many of her clothes, books and other belongings over to his place. Now, she stopped by once every so often, for something she needed. For all intents and purposes, she had no roommate.

She lay in bed naked. She'd put on a nightgown when she'd returned, but the adrenaline was still pumping and within minutes the gown was covered with perspiration. She took it off, took a quick look at her unspectacular body, then turned the light off and lay in bed.

Slowly she began to unwind. The stalking and killing had been exhilarating, but the escape and ensuing time before she had gotten back to The Quad had been unbearably unnerving. Had she been seen? Did anyone suspect? Would cops walk into Houston Hall and search her gym bag? Was she acting normal? Something would go wrong because, in the past, her best-laid plans had always gone awry: the fire that went out before it had a chance to spread; the teacher who had offed himself; Monique, who'd refused to jump.

She'd been a nervous wreck. But she was safe now, in the womb of her bed, and as the tension melted away, she replayed the night like a tape on a VCR.

Again. And again. And again.

Chapter Thirty-three

Ariel and Chanda sat on the living room couch both lost in their own thoughts. Actually, Ariel wasn't thinking. She was physically and emotionally drained, and one look at Chanda told her the youth was as well.

Barry Hoffman

She'd been called by McGowan at three-thirty in the morning.

"The campus cop you were working with at Penn has been attacked," he told her, as if he were reading a weather report.

Ariel was dumbstruck. *Lucius attacked.* For a moment she said nothing.

"You there, Dampier?" her Sergeant asked tartly.

Ariel figured he was pissed that he had been awakened early in the morning.

He then filled her in as best he could. Told her Lucius was at HUP, the Hospital of the University of Pennsylvania.

"If this is connected to the suicides, it's a whole new ball game," he said without elaboration. "We have a six A.M. meeting with Commissioner Desjardins. Get some answers for me before then. I want to know if there's a connection."

She hung up, her mind still in a fog. As she jumped into a pair of jeans and sweater, questions came at her like a swarm of bees. What did McGowan mean by *a whole new ball game*? She thought of the obvious and the ominous. Attempted murder was far more tangible than tracing a letter that in all probability was a hoax. With the recent suicides on the Penn campus, the media would have more than a casual interest. McGowan, she knew, would want *his* men on the case, given his druthers.

That the attack was directly related to their investigation was without question, in Ariel's mind. What had Lucius found out that had caused him to cancel dinner? She cursed him—and promptly regretted it—for going off on his own. Was he trying to impress her? Show her he could be as good a detective as she? What nerve had he touched that someone would add validity to a note taken only half seriously? And, most important, how was Lucius? McGowan had only told her he'd sustained a head injury and was in surgery.

Ariel was going to leave Chanda a note, but decided to wake her and see if she wanted to accompany her to the

198

hospital. Chanda had told Ariel of her visit with Lucius, while being evasive about what had transpired.

—Like the two of them had shared a secret, she thought.

Chanda had immediately asked to come.

"I may not be able to stay with you at the hospital—" Ariel began.

"Don't worry about me," Chandra had said. "Do what you have to do. I want to be with him. And be there for you when you need me."

Ariel had looked at the girl. Chanda read people quickly and remarkably accurately. If she disapproved of Lucius or was neutral, she wouldn't be holding in tears Ariel saw her wipe away. She and Lucius had come to some kind of meeting of the minds. And now Lucius was in surgery. A head wound. Tough enough for *her* to bear; so much more so for a youth, even a toughened one like Chanda.

At the hospital, while waiting for Lucius to come out of surgery, Ariel spoke to a campus patrolman who had been the first called to the scene.

Patrolman Mark Danforth was young—twenty-four, twenty-five max—Ariel's height, with short-cropped black hair. He was white, but like many campus patrolman she'd seen, tanned, so he looked darker than she. He was most definitely nervous, being the center of a police inquiry.

Ariel sat him down and apologized for having him repeat his story.

"If it means anything, I was working with Lucius . . . Officer Jackson. We weren't strangers is what I'm trying to say," Ariel told him.

"Lucius was . . . *is,*" he corrected himself, and looked down for a moment. "He's a good cop and a hell of a nice guy. We weren't tight, but we all know one another pretty well."

Barry Hoffman

"So, who made the call?" Ariel asked, wanting to get down to business, to keep her mind off Lucius's condition.

"A Delta Psi frat member was trying to sneak his girlfriend into the house for . . . well . . ." Danforth stammered and blushed.

"A study date," Ariel said to break the tension. "He wanted to study her up close and personal."

"Yeah, a study date," the young officer said, and laughed. "He told me otherwise initially. Had sent the girl away soon as he discovered the body. But the mention of perjury freaked him and he came clean."

Danforth had an engaging smile, Ariel thought. She wondered just how friendly he'd been to the frat member, though, to make him tell the truth.

Danforth took out his notebook, looked at something, then went on. "The call came in at 3:05 a.m. I was on patrol and got to Delta Psi at 3:10. An ambulance had already been sent for. Neither the boy nor his girlfriend had seen anyone. From the dried blood, I think Lucius had been there for several hours."

"Was he on duty?" Ariel asked to confirm what she already knew.

"No. He was on special assignment."

"Working with me," Ariel said.

Danforth started to tell Ariel about the alley, then paused and drew a diagram on a blank page of his notebook.

"He must have seen or heard something in the alley, pursued and been hit from behind. He fell or was pushed down the stairs. There was a metal pipe next to him. The weapon, I believe."

Ariel wondered what Lucius had been doing out *after* his encounter with Chanda. She had told her Lucius had received a call just before she left, and seemed preoccupied after he'd taken it. So, Ariel thought to herself, he gets a call around nine, and if Danforth is correct, was assaulted a few hours later; say between midnight and 1 a.m. No, she thought, he hadn't been out for a stroll and seen something suspicious. He'd been lured. The attack was premeditated.

Danforth's notebook also reminded Ariel that Lucius took copious notes. She wondered if his notebook was at the hospital.

"Anything else?" Danforth asked when the silence had stretched on for several moments.

"His personal effects. Where would they be?" she asked.

"I can check for you ma'am, uh . . . Officer, uh . . . Detective. Sorry, no offense."

She smiled at him. "No offense taken. Track them down for me, please."

When he'd left, Ariel had gone to the ladies' room. Looking in the mirror, she saw a woman barely in control of her emotions. There was no color in her face, she thought, and laughed. Talking about looking white. She looked like Casper the fucking ghost; a name she'd been called derisively in high school by black kids when she associated with whites.

Her hands shook as she cupped them to gather water to splash on her face. Get a grip on yourself, Dampier, she told herself. Things are likely to get a lot worse before they get better.

There was a knock at the door. She came out. Patrolman Danforth was holding a plastic bag. "His personal effects," he said when Ariel stared.

She took the bag. "That will be all for now. Thanks for your help."

"I'll be praying for Lucius," he said, and turned to leave.

"You do that," she said bitterly. Ariel didn't believe in prayer. No God was going to help Lucius. He was in the hands of a surgeon.

Danforth turned and looked at her, confusion etched on his face.

"I'm sorry," she said, understanding her lack of faith was

evident in her tone. "It's been a long night for all of us."

After he'd left, Ariel turned to the contents of the bag. Lucius's notebook was there. She took it, went over to the uniformed officer in charge and signed the notebook out.

She sat down with Chanda, who knew better than to pester her with questions, and read the last few entries. When she was done, she had a good sense of what Lucius had accomplished and felt a glow of pride at his resourcefulness.

He'd found a link, pursued it and had a suspect in mind. McGowan wanted answers. She had some, but she would play her hand carefully. This was *her* case, and she was not about to give it up without a fight. Not about to have one of McGowan's clones with a horde of uniforms spook Lucius's suspect.

At just after five, a doctor came out to speak to her, with Chanda behind her, taking in every word.

She told him she was investigating the attack on his patient, but she was also a close friend.

"I was married to him, at one time. The closest to a relative he has, I guess. How is he?"

"He's alive," the doctor began.

He went on to tell her his name was Kaplan. Dr. Sidney Kaplan. And the first thing Ariel thought was *he's old*. Really old. Elderly. Geriatric.

He was short, slightly stooped, and shuffled more than walked.

—Old.
—Really, *really* old.

He held his arms crossed in front of his chest, his hands hidden in his underarms. Ariel wondered if he did so intentionally because his hands shook.

—Hands that operated on Lucius.

—Old hands.

—Arthritic hands.

He wore thick wire-rimmed glasses on a face that had wrinkles on top of wrinkles. His eyebrows billowed, thick as a beard, atop his eyes. Behind those glasses, though, there was a twinkle in the old man's eyes; eyes that still held youth and vigor. Eyes that were kind, yet sad at the same time, as if he'd seen death more times than he'd care to admit.

Ariel wondered if it had been a good idea to bring Lucius to HUP rather than Jefferson.

"You operated on him," Ariel said skeptically.

Kaplan smiled. Then laughed. "Young lady, one day God willing, you'll reach my age and see that wisdom and patience are virtues that can overcome physical failings."

He held his hands out. They weren't palsied and misshapen. They were rock steady. He smiled again; an infectious smile; a comforting smile.

"As I said, he's alive, but in a coma. There was internal bleeding from the trauma to his head. We had to relieve the swelling. We were successful."

"Then he'll be all right." Ariel said it as a statement.

"If you're asking if he'll live"—he shrugged—"I'd say I'm cautiously optimistic. As for being *all right*, if you mean the man he was before the attack, that I can't promise."

"What do you mean?"

"There may be brain damage. Just how extensive, we won't know until he awakens. Just when he'll come out of the coma he's in, I can't predict. I'm sorry, young lady, I wish I could be more optimistic. We've done all we can. It's in his own hands."

"God's hands," Ariel said tartly, thinking back to Officer Danforth.

"I don't mix religion and medicine. The ACLU would

frown on that," he said with a smile. "We've done what *we*— as doctors can. It's up to *him*—the patient—to respond. He's young, relatively speaking," he said with another smile. "And he's strong."

"Can you tell what happened to him?"

"From the injuries, it appears he was hit on the back of the head with a blunt instrument. When he fell down the stairs he hit his head several times. I would hazard a guess that he was left for dead."

"Any idea when the attack took place?"

"No disrespect, but if he died, with an autopsy we could be precise. His living complicates matters."

Ariel looked at him crossly.

"I'm sorry, but you are asking me as a police officer, not as a friend of the patient. A relative, I'd use a better bedside manner. A policewoman, I'll be blunt."

"*I'm sorry*, Doctor. I'm obviously upset," Ariel said. "You're right. You're talking to a homicide detective now, not a relative of the patient. Go on."

"With his injuries and without an autopsy, I'd say the attack occurred no more than four, four and a half hours before he was brought in," Kaplan said.

"That was just before three-thirty," Ariel said. "So the attack was between eleven and eleven-thirty."

Kaplan shrugged. "I said no more than four, four and a half hours. Not before eleven and not after one. More, I cannot give you."

"Can we see him, Dr. Kaplan?" Ariel asked.

"And who would this pretty young lady be?" he asked Ariel, but was looking at Chanda.

"My daughter," Ariel answered hurriedly.

"Trying to put something past an old man," he said, but then shrugged. "Who am I to argue at five in the morning with a homicide detective? You can both see him for a few minutes. I must warn you, though, he suffered other injuries aside from the head."

Ariel closed her eyes. She thought she'd heard the worst.

"Nothing life-threatening, mind you, but I want you prepared. He had a broken jaw, fractured cheekbone and broken nose. His collarbone and one arm are also broken. His face will heal, as will the other injuries. It's up to him as to if he lives. The next forty-eight hours are the most crucial."

He turned. "Come. Now that I've told you the worst, see your friend."

Ariel had left the hospital fifteen minutes later. Chanda wanted to stay.

"All right," Ariel said. She was too emotionally hungover to argue. And why shouldn't Chanda stay if she desired? Chanda and Lucius seemed to have bonded. Ariel didn't like the idea of a death watch, but at least Chanda cared. When Ariel had first met the youth, Chanda's compassion had been robbed. *Her* healing had begun, and for that Ariel was thankful.

"I meet with the brass," Ariel said derisively, "in half an hour. I'll come by after."

"Are you going to be all right?" Chanda asked.

Ariel smiled wanly. "I'm on autopilot. I have a hunch I've got to convince the powers that be that I'm up to handling this investigation. Right now, that's all that's on my mind. I owe it to Lucius. Later, I'll need a good cry. Then, if I'm still on the case, I'll go after the bitch who did this to Lucius. Go after her with a passion."

Chanda smiled in return. "Go for the balls."

Half an hour later, Ariel was surrounded by a handful of men who would dictate the course of the investigation. They were in Commissioner Desjardins's office, at his request. Besides Desjardins and McGowan, Lieutenant Schumacher was present, as well as her partner, good old Doug.

"At least we know Jackson's innocent," McGowan began, as if to relieve the tension.

"What the hell's that supposed to mean, *Sergeant*?" Desjardins demanded, with the emphasis on the other man's lower rank. "You telling me he was a suspect? You were investigating one of my men behind *my* back?"

Ariel had to hold back a smile. She could see McGowan begin to squirm. Desjardins wouldn't take kindly to one of his officers being investigated, and now McGowan had to face the music.

As McGowan told why he had Doug checking up on Lucius, Ariel thought she might have a possible ally in the Commissioner. As in McGowan's office, the Lieutenant said nothing. He was an observer. Later, he'd orchestrate damage control with the media. Now it was McGowan versus Desjardins, and *she* knew who had more on the ball. Knew, too, the same man had more at stake. For McGowan, this was just another case. For Penn, its reputation as a safe haven for academic excellence was on the line.

Ariel, for her part, had to decide just how much of what she knew she should divulge. She had to hold back; keep enough in reserve should it look like she was losing the case. From McGowan's thumbnail sketch of what Doug had found out about Lucius, she knew he wasn't aware of their marriage. So, she couldn't mention Chanda's meeting with him, and the phone call that led to his attack. She decided to wait until McGowan showed his hand. Then she'd play her trump card; Lucius's notebook.

"We seem to have gotten off on the wrong foot, Commissioner," McGowan said to appease Desjardins. "I sincerely apologize for what must seem like going behind your back. I can assure you, that was not *my* intention."

He looked squarely at Doug as he said the last words, as if to shift the blame to him. Good soldier that he was, Doug remained silent.

"The question," McGowan said, as if now dismissing the incident, "is was this attack a result of Officer Jackson's investigation, or a mere coincidence? Dampier, can you shed any light for us?"

Ariel looked at Desjardins as she spoke, which she thought, ironically, must have pleased her Sergeant. No staredown for the moment. She'd arrived just before the meeting, so whatever she said would come as a surprise to McGowan. From his tone, he probably thought she'd come up blank. She was going to enjoy this.

"Officer Jackson spoke to me this afternoon. As you know, Commissioner, with your permission we've been attempting to establish a link between the three girls who committed suicide. Officer Jackson thought he'd found a connection, but wanted to check further. Whatever he found out must have panicked someone."

"It confirms, then," McGowan said, adding his two cents, "that the suicides were actually murders."

"Not necessarily," Ariel said, enjoying the look of irritation on McGowan's face for contradicting him. She'd read Lucius's notes, and there could be a second explanation. She was still focused on the Commissioner.

"The note could have been a hoax, and Officer Jackson was close to exposing the perpetrator."

"I agree," Desjardins said, breaking his silence. "We have two scenarios. How do we proceed now?" he said, looking at Ariel, but McGowan answered.

"With all due respect to Detectives Dampier and Thiery," he began, a speech Ariel was sure he'd rehearsed a number of times before this meeting, "this has turned into a much more sensitive case than any of us had suspected. It's one thing to perpetrate a hoax, quite another to attempt murder to keep it a secret. I'd like to assign two of my more experienced men to handle the case."

He sat back, as if waiting for Desjardins to agree.

Barry Hoffman

Desjardins looked at the Lieutenant.

"With all respect to Sergeant McGowan," Desjardins said with just a trace of sarcasm, "I strenuously object. What we *don't* need are more cops on campus. It's tough as it is to keep a lid on it with Detectives Dampier and Thiery poking around, but they've been here since the first suicide."

He paused and then looked at Ariel.

"Moreover, Detective Dampier and Officer Jackson have established a rapport. Anyone new has to start from scratch, and without Officer Jackson's perspective, until he recovers. What are your thoughts, Detective Dampier?" he concluded.

You're sly, she thought, looking at the Commissioner. She wondered just how much he knew. Was he aware she and Lucius had been married? Regardless, he'd put the ball in her court. She could make it near impossible for McGowan to wrest the case from her if she played her hand right. Chanda said to go for the balls. Why not? She'd hit McGowan with her best shot, right off the bat.

"I know how Officer Jackson's mind works better than anyone, Commissioner. We were married for three years."

She paused to let it sink in. Desjardins looked nonplussed; McGowan dumbstruck. McGowan looked at Doug like he wanted to bite his head off.

"I know how he operates. And," she said, removing Lucius's notebook from her purse, "I can decipher his notes, like no one else, to learn just what he discovered and how."

"His notes are that explicit?" McGowan asked, and held out his hand for the notebook.

"No. He uses a lot of shorthand he created that would take experts to decipher. Having been married to him, I have intimate knowledge of how his mind works and what his words mean." She said the last with a smile.

McGowan seemed absorbed by the notebook, then utterly confused. "You can make heads or tails of this?" he asked.

"Yes, sir," she said, making eye contact with him for the first time.

"It's settled then, wouldn't you agree, Sergeant?" Dejardins said, rising. "We proceed as before." He now looked at McGowan's superior. "The Lieutenant and I can draft a statement concerning the attack on Patrolman Jackson; one which in no way connects the two incidents."

The Lieutenant gave a slight nod, and Desjardins smiled in return.

Outside the office, a red-faced McGowan glowered at Ariel.

"You're on the hot seat now, Detective. You want this hot potato—*you've got it*. Have something for me by this afternoon. I don't want that SOB calling me, asking about our progress. I want to tell him how his Sherlock Holmes fucked up and almost got himself killed."

Without waiting for a reply, he stormed off.

"Fuck you, too," Ariel said, low enough so McGowan couldn't hear, but Doug could.

Doug, for his part, looked hurt. "Why didn't you tell me? You know, about the marriage?"

"Because it had nothing to do with whether Lucius should be considered a suspect."

"But I looked like an ass."

"You'll get over it."

"Where do we begin?" he asked, resignation in his voice.

"I'm going to track down Lucius's movements yesterday. *Alone.*"

She waited for an objection, but none was forthcoming. Good, she thought. As always, with no clear-cut avenues of investigation, Doug just wanted to be told what to do.

"I want you checking all campus dormitories for anyone who was out of their dorm between 10 p.m and 1 a.m. Females, in particular, but get a list of everyone. Then, starting with the women, let's get some answers for our Sergeant.

Which were alone? Who may have seen anything, no matter how inconsequential? Who was acting strangely?"

"This could take days," Doug said in exasperation.

I hope it does, Ariel thought. I want to keep you at arm's length. She had to throw him a bone, though.

"I'm sure Commissioner Desjardins can spare you a couple of men. But *only* to compile your list. I want you and only you to do the questioning."

He looked at her, mystified.

"I want to know their reaction, not just their statements. I know and trust your instincts," she said truthfully. This was something *he* was good at. "Who's holding back? Who's lying? Later I'll want to know who we can lean on. Do you understand?"

Now he smiled. "For a minute, I thought you were trying to get rid of me."

"Perish the thought, Doug. Perish the thought."

And now, at 8 A.M., she and Chanda were sitting at home on the living room couch, each coming to grips with the enormity of the night's events.

There had been no change in Lucius's condition when Ariel came by the hospital to get Chanda. The youth came home without argument, but spoke only in monosyllables in response to Ariel's telling her how she had seized the investigation from McGowan. She couldn't worry about the girl now, though. She knew, to be at her best, she had to unwind. An hour's nap, shower and breakfast. Then she'd speak to this Asha Lucius had started with at Special Services.

When she got up, Chanda finally spoke.

"I want to help catch the fucker who did this."

"You want to hang with me, Chanda? That wouldn't be helping one bit."

"I want to do something. *Must* do something," she shouted,

then calmed down. "No, I don't want to *hang* with you," she said sarcastically.

A thought had been drifting in and out of Ariel's subconscious since the confrontation between McGowan and Dejardins. Everyone still considered the note a hoax. But, what if it *was* murder. Three murders carried out by a college freshman to look like suicide. *If*—and it was a big if—that was the case, Ariel knew they'd been carefully planned and executed. And there just might have been trial runs earlier. Like previewing a show in Boston or Philly before its Broadway debut. Maybe Chanda could help. Even if nothing came of it, she'd at least feel useful.

"You say you want to help. Let me bounce this off you." And she told the youth her theory.

"Make sense to you?" she asked when she'd finished. She had seen Chanda's eyes light up as she had explained herself. Maybe it had merit after all, Ariel thought. Saying it out loud seemed to lend it credence.

"If it was murder, yes," Chanda said, as if trying to rein in her enthusiasm. "But what can I do?"

"Grunge work, but important grunge work."

"Go ahead, spell it out."

"I'd want a list of all teen suicides the past three years—when our murderer was in high school. I can get the department to download that for you. But I need to know the circumstances. For that you'd have to go to the library and bury yourself in newspaper accounts. Interested?"

"I said I wanted to help," she answered. "I don't care how boring you make it sound; if we're talking murder, someone will have to do it sooner or later. Right?"

Ariel agreed, and spent ten minutes explaining how she wanted the suicides prioritized. When she was done, she yawned.

"I don't know about you, but us old folks aren't used to

all-nighters. I'm catching some zzz's before I follow Lucius's path." She got up to go her room.

"Can you download the list of suicides?" Chanda asked, with a pleading look in her eyes.

"You're hopeless. *And* sadistic." Ariel called Doug and told him what she needed. She hung up, looked at Chanda and smiled. The girl's eyelids were at half-mast.

"You can go to my clutter room and turn on the computer. Doug will download the names and dates in a bit. Now, *I'm* off."

As Ariel walked to her room, Chanda called from behind. "Thanks, Ariel. It's been a long time since anyone considered *my* feelings, and went out of their way to make me feel useful. Feel wanted."

"Whatever," Ariel said, yawning, but she was smiling.

Chapter Thirty-four

Someone's fucking with me, Shanicha thought as she watched the morning news on Channel Six, in a lounge filled with other students. Word had already spread about the attack on Officer Friendly the night before, but it was rife with rumor.

Depending on who you listened to, the cop had been knifed, clubbed, shot or garotted. His assailant was a strung-out junkie, a white racist pig, a Peeping Tom caught in the act or a disgruntled student on campus.

The last was what bothered Shanicha. Why one of them?

The news clarified a lot. A Lieutenant Somebody—Shanicha didn't catch the name—read a prepared statement. The cop had been hit on the head, and had fallen down a stairway in the alley next to Delta Psi. He was in critical, but stable condition. In a coma. The next forty-eight hours were critical to his recovery.

Hit on the head with what? Shanicha thought. A metal pipe? Piece of wood? Baseball bat?

Yes, a baseball bat. That's what Peter Lyle had been beaten with; a baseball bat. The boy had died. Shanicha had been responsible. She hadn't known the kid, but it was her doing.

Her mind drifted back to one of her crowning achievements.

She had gone to high school at Southern, in South Philadelphia. It wasn't much of a school anymore, but there was an annex for those who wanted to take college prep courses. Most of Southern was black, as was the Annex. But there were some whites.

Having grown up around whites until her family had moved from New Canaan, she didn't shun them like most of the black kids. She hung with everyone. Hung with no one. She was part of half a dozen cliques, but she didn't consider herself part of any. She had kept a low profile, stirring up a fight here and there; nothing special. Patience. Wait until the opportunity presents itself, she told herself. It *would*.

It did.

When one of the white girls came to school, her face a mass of bruises, she saw her chance for mischief. She'd followed her to the girls' room. They'd known one another, but the girl was a loner. Not a geek or dork, but someone who just didn't fit in.

"What happened to you?" Shanicha had asked. "Get beat up by your old man or your boyfriend?"

"I wish. At least, I'd have a story to tell. Truth is, my baby sister left a doll on the stairs, and I took a tumble. Cushioned the fall with my face." She made an attempt at a laugh, then grimaced.

Barry Hoffman

By lunch, rumor had it the girl had gone out with one of the black boys, who'd forced her to do the nasty, then beaten her black and blue when she threatened to tell her parents.

Shanicha had spread the story. Or at least one version. It had been blown all out of proportion by the time it reached the schoolyard. A couple of black boys who'd been seen with the girl had been targeted, and all hell broke loose. A nice free-for-all, with a dozen kids sent to the hospital, and two dozen more given suspensions or detention.

Shanicha had enjoyed the sight, but had expected more. Some stitches, a couple of casts and all would be forgotten. Unless, she thought . . .

By the end of the day word had it that a bunch of white boys were going to waylay a brother after school. Shanicha knew Calvin Freeman was going to visit his grandparents in New York for the weekend. He'd found out at the last moment, and told Shanicha to let his homeboys know he couldn't hang with them.

By nightfall, a story circulated that Calvin was in the hospital, beaten to a pulp by a gang of white boys; white boys who just happened to be at 24th and Oregon at the moment.

Shanicha went home and didn't come out until she heard the sirens.

Folks were on the corner talking . . .

". . . white boy got himself killed."

". . . killed by some brothers."

". . . police gonna have themselves a field day."

". . . all because of that white girl that got raped."

". . . the one Calvin was seeing?"

". . . Calvin's at the hospital, too."

". . . leastways, he ain't got himself killed."

It got even worse as the story spread.

—*Better,* as far as Shanicha was concerned.

214

Born Bad

The truth came out the next day. Six black teens, with baseball bats, had chased a group of whites near 24th and Oregon. One boy—an honor's student—had fallen across from a church. He'd been surrounded, kicked and smacked in the head with baseball bats until he was unrecognizable.

The youths had bolted.

The police had been slow to arrive.

Fights, especially on a Friday night, were all too common in Philly, and had low priority when received by 911 operators. When the police arrived, Peter Lyle lay dead.

Shanicha basked in the city-wide attention the story attracted. There was a 911 scandal and a promised shake-up.

—Because of her.

One of the assailants had dimed on his buds in exchange for immunity. The five others had been arrested and would be tried as adults.

—Because of her.

Racial confrontations occurred Saturday and Sunday night, even with police out in full force. No one was killed, but there were numerous injuries and the situation was volatile.

—Because of her.

School was shut Monday while District officials, parents and the police determined how to diffuse tensions.

—Because of her.
—All because of her.

If Shanicha had kept a scrapbook, it would have been bulging. She had to pat herself on the back. There was no better

215

feeling, she thought, even if it couldn't be shared.

Now, though, Shanicha shouldn't be thinking what was used to knock Officer Friendly upside his fool head. What bugged her was the message she'd received, to meet Dr. Isaacs. She had waited at the locked entrance on 37th Street for forty-five minutes to no avail. She'd been out of The Quad, alone, *without an alibi,* when police said the cop was attacked.

Shanicha didn't believe in coincidences. She wondered who the hell had called. It was too early to check with Dr. Isaacs, but she *knew* it was a crank. Or worse, someone had lured her out of The Quad—*when Officer Friendly was assaulted.*

The police spokesman theorized the attacker had been someone from off campus; a drug dealer or burglar. Shanicha didn't buy that crap for a minute.

For the first time, she wondered if Monique's death was a suicide. The girl was capable of suicide, but . . .

She was beginning to feel like a caged animal. First Monique. Then Officer Friendly and that white bitch cop looking at her. Now the mugging of the cop.

She was sweating profusely. She could smell herself; a foul rancid odor that nauseated her. A smell that could attract the spiders. She had to keep from bolting out of the lounge. She left slowly.

She needed a shower.

—Before the spider came.

—Before she laid her eggs.

—Laid eggs to hatch in her womb.

216

Chapter Thirty-five

Ariel decided to confront Asha Reynolds with an all-out frontal assault. Ariel was pretty sure she knew what Lucius had found, but needed confirmation.

When she identified herself, she could see the woman wasn't pleased to see her. Her nails were bitten to the quick, and her face was drawn and pallid. Was it guilt at having exposed Lucius to danger? Or simply fear that she herself might face dismissal for betraying confidentiality?

Ariel wanted to heighten the tension the woman felt. She suggested they go to Locust Walk.

"I don't think you want this conversation to be overheard," Ariel said, looking at her with recrimination.

Ariel also wanted to keep her moving; moving toward Desjardins's office, at 39th and Locust. Three blocks from the campus police station, Ariel took out Lucius's notebook.

"Officer Jackson spoke with you yesterday," she began.

Asha Reynolds said nothing.

Ariel told her how Lucius had linked the three suicides to acquaintance rape. Told her he needed confirmation and came to Asha. Told her she knew Lucius had manipulated her. Both were free of their mates, Ariel told her, and Asha was interested in Lucius.

"So, you told him what he wanted," Ariel finished.

"That's bullshit," Asha said without conviction. She was biting one of her nails, though there seemed nothing left to bite.

"This is his notebook. Lucius didn't just make notations. His notebook was a journal; a diary of sorts with personal asides, feelings, even recriminations. He purposely manipulated you into giving him information that was confidential by leading you on. He felt like a heel, but lives were at stake. Still are, including his own."

"And how do you know all of this?" Asha asked, her voice shaking.

"I was Lucius's first wife. We'd become lovers recently. You never had a chance with him. He knew it, deplored what he had to do to get your cooperation, but never regretted doing his job."

"It's all conjecture on your part," she said. "I told him nothing."

Ariel opened the notebook and read the names of two of the other girls in Dr. Isaacs's acquaintance-rape counseling group. Showed her Lucius's notations.

"See, he has an appointment. 'AR at Special Services.' Here are the names of two girls, and 'corroborated by AR.' "

Asha remained silent.

"I'll make your decision easy. We can go to Commissioner Desjardins right now. You'll tell him what you know. Then, you'll be terminated for giving out confidential information. Or . . ." She paused.

"I answer your questions, and you'll spare me," Asha finished, as Ariel had anticipated. "How do I know it won't go further?"

"You don't, but you're an insignificant cog in this investigation. You led Lucius to Dr. Isaacs. He's the one I'll lean on. No one cares how I get to Isaacs. Look at it this way, I'm offering you immunity, so to speak, for your cooperation. Isaacs becomes the University's fall guy. He's important enough so if he's hung out to dry, the media, parents, alumni—*everyone* will be appeased."

Asha sighed, shrugged in resignation, confirmed that she

had given Lucius the names of the two girls, then asked Ariel what more she wanted.

"What about the third girl? Lucius's notes said you only knew two."

"I only knew two. The other didn't file a complaint with Special Services, so I had no idea who she was."

"No clue at all?" Ariel asked skeptically.

"None," she answered tartly, then glared at Ariel.

"I want you to know I don't appreciate how Lucius used me to get what he wanted," she told Ariel, her anger mounting. "I was his whore. I'm sorry he was attacked, but maybe he got what he deserved," she said bitterly, with her head held high.

Ariel could have let it go.

Should have.

Didn't.

"Men are often accused of letting their dicks do their thinking," Ariel said. "Before you violate a trust again, before you put your job on the line, make sure your pussy doesn't get in the way of your brains."

With that Ariel turned and left.

Ariel now had what she needed to bring Dr. Isaacs to his knees. More, she now knew why Lucius had circled Shanicha's name in his notebook. There was scant mention of her in his notebook, only that he'd seen her enter Psych Services. But she hadn't filed a complaint with Special Services, and that tipped Lucius off that she was a fraud; was using the counseling group to get access to students who might be suicidal.

If Asha thought Ariel had played hardball with her, it was nothing compared to what she had in store for the good doctor. She had called earlier, as a perspective patient, and was told the doctor was booked for the day.

Ariel purposely arrived at 11:25, when Isaacs *should* have

been with a patient. She showed her shield to the receptionist and asked to see Dr. Isaacs.

"You'll have to wait until his session is over," the middle-aged woman replied politely, but firmly. "Dr. Isaacs is adamant about not being disturbed when he's with a patient."

"I don't think so," Ariel shot back. "This is official police business."

The receptionist looked flummoxed, but did nothing.

"Tell you what," Ariel said. "I don't want to put you in an awkward position. Call Dr. Isaacs and tell him there's an obnoxious cop who insists on speaking to him about a meeting he had at six P.M. yesterday. He'll see me, I assure you."

The woman smiled wanly, but made the call. She held the phone away from her ear for a moment, but once she repeated Ariel's demand, she visibly relaxed. She hung up and looked at Ariel.

"He'll be with you in a moment," she said warily.

Isaacs came out to greet Ariel, and she could see at once that he felt more than a little awkward that she towered over him.

"What is this, Detective . . ." He paused, after they were in his office, apparently having forgotten her name.

"Dampier," she said, taking in the man who looked like a slightly older Doogie Howser of TV fame.

"What is this meeting you're referring to, Detective Dampier?" he said evasively.

"Don't be coy, Doctor. You met with Patrolman Jackson last night to discuss your acquaintance-rape counseling group. Officer Jackson was the University liaison with *me* on the investigation. He showed you a note indicating the suicides were murders. You provided him with information that very probably is the reason he is in a coma now. Remember *that* meeting, Doctor?"

Isaacs removed his glasses, and began wiping them. He

was playing for time, Ariel knew, deciding just what he could divulge to be rid of her.

"We met, Detective," he finally admitted. "But, as I told him, there's a question of confidentiality. I could only answer some very general questions."

"So you didn't speak to him about Shanicha Wilkins?" Ariel asked.

Isaacs nodded. "My hands were tied."

Ariel stood. "Two can play this game, Doctor. I'm going to haul your ass downtown, and book you for obstruction of justice. *Three* girls who were part of your counseling group committed suicide, Doctor. Somehow you didn't feel this was of relevance to the police. The charges won't hold water. We both know that. But, *after* you're booked, my Lieutenant will hold a press conference and let the public decide your culpability."

"You wouldn't."

"I'm a real SOB when a fellow officer is lying in a coma, and you have information I need. Should I read you your rights, *Doctor*?"

He had his glasses off again; wiping off imaginary dust.

"Sit down, Detective," he finally said.

"I want to know everything you told Patrolman Jackson," she said after taking a seat. She took out Lucius's notebook and waved it at him.

"Skip anything to protect yourself, and I'll know it. Then it's your ass."

He blanched at the obscenity, then produced a tape. "You don't have to worry about my leaving anything out. It's all on tape." He put it in a recorder on his desk, pushed play and sat back as Ariel heard Lucius question the psychologist.

"I'll even throw in a bonus," he said when the tape ended. "Miss Wilkins called earlier today, asking if I had left a message for her to meet me last night at 11 p.m."

"Had you?"

221

"Of course not. Apparently someone did, and she waited outside until 11:45."

"You're her therapist. What do you make of it?" Ariel asked.

"She could be establishing an alibi," he said.

"But you don't think she's capable of violence. You said so on tape."

"Detective, these girls are in therapy because they're troubled. I told Officer Jackson I didn't think them capable of violence. But corner someone who is clinically depressed— one symptom of which is irrationality—and I couldn't rule out violence."

"Did any of the girls in your session see Patrolman Jackson before you met him?"

"No. Patient confidentiality. Patrolman Jackson was in this office before the girls from group left."

"Then why would Shanicha Wilkins feel she was cornered?"

"You have a point. She shouldn't have felt threatened, *unless* Patrolman Jackson confronted her after our discussion."

Ariel wasn't about to tell him he hadn't. Any meeting would have been in the notebook. And Lucius had had only enough time to leave and return to his apartment, to be greeted by Chanda at the time she said he'd arrived.

She made a mental note to herself. *Everything* else fit. Shanicha Wilkins was Lucius's suspect; now *her* suspect. At some point, though, she had to confront the question of how this girl got wind she'd been under suspicion.

She thanked the doctor and got up to leave.

"I trust our discussion will be held in confidence," he said warily.

"I'm not a campus cop, Doctor. I'm not concerned with the University's reputation. My Sergeant will be made aware of our conversation. At the moment, though, I don't see that you have anything to be worried about. While I personally find withholding evidence reprehensible, no one has a desire to persecute you. You will, I am sure, contact me if something comes up at your group sessions. No matter how inconsequential," she added. "And you will keep *our* conversation confidential."

"You have my word I'll be forthcoming and discreet," he said, clearly deflated.

It was how Ariel wanted to leave him. A threat of disclosure hanging over his head to assure future cooperation.

"Then we understand one another," she said.

Without waiting for a response, she left.

Chapter Thirty-six

At 3:30, Ariel met with McGowan. Half an hour earlier, without his knowledge, she had briefed Commissioner Dejardins. She knew McGowan's confidence in her was tenuous, at best. Because of his indifference and hostility, she didn't feel she owed him her loyalty. Desjardins, on the other hand, like Phil Donato, wasn't blind to her ability. She would cover her ass, in case McGowan tried to sabotage her.

"Does your Sergeant know you're briefing me?" he'd asked after Ariel had sat down.

"I think you're aware, Commissioner, we've been butting heads for some time. To be quite honest, he'd have me off this case in a New York minute, given the opportunity. I'm not too proud to ask for support, should that occur."

"It's a dangerous path you're traveling, Detective," he responded. "Playing both sides against the middle."

"Hardly," Ariel responded, then frowned. "I've got a job to do with someone who disrespects me looking over my shoulder. I know my Sarge's agenda, and he doesn't want me along for the ride. I want Lucius's attacker. You have a vested interest in my success, which is why I'm here. I think I know who did it. I just don't want her spooked before I can box and wrap her."

"You've got my attention." He sat back as she told what she'd found out.

"Do you think the three girls were murdered, or is the Wilkins girl perpetrating a hoax for some perverted reason?" he asked when Ariel had finished.

"I honestly don't know, *yet*. But in my opinion she did attack Lucius, which is reason enough to go after her."

"You have a plan, I assume," he said.

"I need two, maybe three days to dig into her past. She's no novice, if she's a murderer. I don't want to lean on her until I know what makes her tick. Then I'll pounce."

"So, you're asking for time." He mulled it over for a few seconds. "What if she kills again in the interim? It's my ass if I go to bat for you."

"Common sense dictates she maintain a low profile. My partner and your officers are combing the campus for suspects and witnesses to the attack on Lucius. She won't risk anything now."

"I tend to agree with you, but . . . let me spell out what bothers me. One, why the note to the police? If she is a murderer who's kept a low profile, why expose herself?

"Two, the last suicide was only a week after the second. What prompted her to move so quickly?

"And three, why the attack on Patrolman Jackson? What did he really have? All the attack did was lend credence to our suspicions the suicides were murders."

He sat back in his chair, mulling his questions over.

"I'll tell you, something doesn't wash," he finally said.

"Could she be going off the deep end? Is she so totally ir-rational now, she's a time bomb who doesn't know herself when she'll go off?"

He shook his head, as if not liking the sound of what he'd just said.

"My question is, what's the alternative?" Ariel answered. "Bring her in and hope she'll crack? Talk about thin ice. One misstep now, and she knows we're onto her, and if she says nothing she's home free. I say it's safer to dig first, and if I'm right, we can shake her up when we bring her in."

He sat back in his chair, weighing his options.

"All right. Three days, max. I'll have my men stretch out their canvassing to maintain a presence at The Quad while you're hunting. If you come up empty, then it's your boss's call. Agreed?"

"Agreed."

Ariel got up to leave, then looked at Desjardins.

"Commissioner, how did you know Lucius and I had been married?"

"I told you I know my men," he said with a smile.

"You're good. But not that good."

He laughed. "Got me. Look, I do know my men, but not *that* well. I was a detective once myself, many moons ago. After our first meeting, I looked in Patrolman Jackson's folder. He may have forgotten, but you're mentioned as his first wife. 'First wife, Ariel. Job—law enforcement.' In marches Ariel, a homicide detective. Too much of a coinci-dence."

"But you held it back from my Sergeant."

"I know his type. And I'm a quick read. I figured you for a good detective the first time we met. I wanted you on the case, so I gave you some slack. You played your hand well, so your Sergeant had to defer to my wishes." He smiled.

"I appreciate your faith in me," she said, not knowing how she felt about Desjardins being so quick a study.

"Just don't let me look like an ass. Come back with enough to hang this girl."

"Make a bet on it," she said. For you. For the girls she killed. For Lucius, she thought to herself. Mostly for Lucius.

And now she was briefing McGowan, who, oddly enough, seemed all but indifferent to the investigation. Their Lieutenant had earlier successfully brushed off any connection between the suicides and the attack on the campus police officer, and there was no great interest in one of all too many muggings in the city. Had it not involved a police officer, it would have been relegated to page 2B of the Metro Section of the *Inquirer*, "Metropolitan Area News in Brief"—mostly crime-related stories.

McGowan told Ariel the story would die if the officer lived. If he died, it would be news for a few days, but it certainly wasn't a high priority.

Ariel was initially befuddled by his reaction. She had rehearsed her rationale why she should be allowed to pursue Shanicha Wilkins, as opposed to bringing her in for interrogation immediately. McGowan, though, didn't want the girl brought in at all.

"The Lieutenant and I have been mulling this over, Ariel," he said, one of his paste-on smiles on his face.

Ariel didn't like it when he called her by her first name. It indicated he wanted her to be his buddy; part of the team. It always meant she was being relegated to the back of the bus again.

"We think," he continued, "Commissioner Desjardins is so intent on looking out for the University's reputation that he's gotten overly caught up in linking the suicides to the mugging of one of his cops."

Ariel had purposely avoided his gaze at the outset, to make him feel more at ease, but now she made eye contact.

"The note is obviously a hoax," he continued, "perpetrated

very possibly by your suspect. And, while I understand and sympathize with your concern about the assault on your ex-husband, the Lieutenant believes it to be a mugging. No conspiracy. There are just too many holes."

Ariel reined in her anger. The man was so transparent. The constant mention of the Lieutenant was his way of saying *he'd* been given orders and *his* hands were tied. She couldn't very well argue with *him* because *his* boss had decided this and that. Bullshit, she thought. McGowan was using his superior to justify burying the case.

"I think it's time to put you and Doug back on the wheel," he said, meaning the regular homicide rotation. "You can pursue your line of inquiry as time warrants."

She was prepared to argue, but McGowan cut her off. "I've got to contact Commissioner Desjardins. I'll tell him of your suspicions, but I think he'll be happy to see the investigation disappear."

Ariel left McGowan's office stewing. Should she call Desjardins? No, McGowan was already on the phone. She could only hope the Commissioner couldn't be sweet-talked by her Sergeant.

In the meantime, Ariel didn't want to sit by idly. Even if Desjardins prevailed, she knew she'd be on a short leash. She wouldn't get the three days the Commissioner had allowed, unless she got results. She decided to page Chanda. Ariel had given her a beeper that morning, in case either had to contact the other. The irony didn't escape her that Chanda's research might be pivotal to the case.

Before leaving Commissioner Desjardins's office, she had gotten a copy of Shanicha Wilkins's admissions application. When Chanda responded to Ariel's page, she told her to start on a new line of inquiry.

"I've found some interesting material already," Chanda began, full of enthusiasm.

"We can talk about that tonight. My problem now is my

asshole boss wants to put the case on the back burner. Bury it, basically."

Chanda was silent. Ariel could palpably feel her deflation over the phone.

"I need ammunition, which only you can provide. Are you game?"

Ariel wanted some response from Chanda. Anything but silence.

"Of course," Chanda said without much enthusiasm.

"I have a suspect. I won't even mention her name. Not because I don't trust you," she added hurriedly, "but I don't want you looking for *her*. Looking for her, specifically, will cause tunnel vision, and you may miss something else of equal importance. Understand my rationale?"

"Yes," Chanda said. "Go in blind, and hope to prove your theory. I can live with that."

"Okay. Go back in the *Inquirer* to 1987, and look for crimes or incidents that occurred in New Canaan." Ariel spelled the town out for her, and told her the location.

"Look for anything in 1987, then 1986 and 1985. Call right away if you get anything. If I don't answer, tell whoever does it's a family emergency."

Twenty minutes later, Lieutenant Schumacher was back in McGowan's office. Desjardins apparently hadn't caved in. She stared at her phone praying Chanda would call before she was again summoned by her superiors.

She was so absorbed, she literally jumped when the phone rang. It was Chanda. She was excited.

"I found something. Eight years ago, just like you said. There may be more, but . . ."

"You can check later," Ariel interrupted. "I need something *now*," she said, glancing at McGowan's office.

"Okay. Over a three-month period, there were a series of fires in New Canaan. Clearly arson. At first it was thought a stranger was involved, but a second story suggests it was someone in the town. A teacher died in the fire. In the last—most recent story—it seems there was a mass exodus from the town after the library burned down. One third of the town up and left. The fires must have stopped. There were no additional follow-ups."

Maybe there was a God after all, Ariel thought. She had a concrete lead.

"Great job, Chanda. You know what I want now." It was a statement, not a question.

"Keep going back and see if there's anything else."

"You got it, kiddo. Call, but don't page me. I have enough for McGowan."

Just then McGowan opened his door and beckoned her. She said good-bye, took a deep breath and reined in her enthusiasm. Let them do the talking, she told herself. Play it by ear.

McGowan had lost his paste-on smile and sunny disposition. He was pissed, but not at her.

"That bastard Desjardins went over our heads," he said, looking at the Lieutenant, who, as usual, remained silent and noncommittal.

"He wants us to vigorously follow up the Shanicha Wilkins lead. God forbid we abandon the investigation and she strikes again, and all that shit. The bottom line is I can give you a day to come up with something tangible. If we draw a blank, we've done our best. Do you have a game plan?"

Ariel often had to keep from laughing at McGowan's sports analogies. "Team players." "Getting with the program." "A game plan." What next? she thought. "Win one for the Gipper"?

She told him she had a lead and explained the New Canaan fires. She wanted to visit the local sheriff the next day.

"Putting all your eggs in one basket, aren't you?" he asked, but before she could answer, he agreed. "Take Doug with you, though. These small towns may not be too hospitable to a female detective poking into affairs they'd like to keep buried."

Ariel wanted to object. Aside from a four-hour drive round-trip with her partner that conjured up thoughts of her own suicide, she wanted him to check out the other information Chanda had said she'd located.

Discretion being the better part of valor, however, she decided not to antagonize her superior any further. *If* she came back with what she hoped, she would have more than her one precious day.

Back at her desk, she spoke with the sheriff in New Canaan, and explained how a case she was working on might have roots in the arson in his town. He was guardedly cordial, agreeing to meet with her at 11 a.m. the next day.

She contacted Doug with their itinerary for the following day, then called Chanda, saying she'd meet her at the library.

She *was* putting all her eggs in one basket, she thought to herself. She couldn't—*wouldn't*—come back empty.

Chapter Thirty-seven

Shanicha had been on edge all day. Already, she'd taken three showers and it was just past 4 p.m. The white bitch cop hadn't returned, but another cop she had seen at two of the suicides was still on campus; a nerdy-looking guy who looked like he'd have trouble fighting his way out of a paper bag.

Word quickly spread that campus cops were compiling a list of anyone who had been out of the dorm between 11

P.M. and 1 A.M. She knew she was on the list and needed an alibi. Knew hers was lame.

She'd called Dr. Isaacs and confirmed her worst fears. No, he hadn't asked to meet her the night before.

Who, then, had put her at risk? A prank was one thing, but if it wasn't—and deep down she knew a prank was too coincidental—someone intentionally wanted her to be a suspect in Officer Friendly's mugging.

She'd been questioned by Officer Nerdy at noon. He hadn't impressed her at all. He seemed content merely going through the motions to collect his paycheck. She told her story, said her RA could verify the call, and told him she had called Dr. Isaacs that morning and found out it was a hoax; "a sophomoric prank," she told him. "Goes on all the time here."

He took her statement, gave her his card, in case she thought of anything else, thanked her and sent her on her way.

No sweat, she thought, though she *had* been sweating, and wondered if he could detect her pungent odor. A shower— her second of the day—was definitely in order.

Now, at four, she sat on the lawn of The Quad, mesmerized by dozens of small fires erupting from grills brought outside. The dorm was sponsoring a barbecue. Fascinated, she watched as lighter fluid was doused on charcoal, which then erupted into flames when a match was tossed in. It reminded her of the only other fire she had set after she left New Canaan.

To Shanicha, there was nothing worse than a friend who turned on you. You invested a lot of time and emotion with friendships, sharing secrets, hopes, fears and dreams that formed a sacred bond. Friends might drift apart, but certain confidences were never meant to see the light of day.

Shanicha had shunned close ties with *anyone*. The decision had been made for her at birth. She had no conscience, no scruples, no compassion; all necessary for those special ties that bind friends together.

Her earliest memories of school were her attempts to control her emotional outbursts; to blend in. It drained her of the energy necessary to pursue even casual camaraderie with others. And how could you make friends when you were seeking out weaknesses in others to exploit—to create havoc in the schoolyard?

A confidence shared with Shanicha was akin to a secret shared with a spy. Any possibility of a close friendship ended with her charges of molestation against her fourth-grade teacher. She had become an island unto herself; no way anyone could know what she harbored.

She had always been popular, though, with lots of so-called friends. But she was tight with no one . . . until Tia.

Shanicha soaked in gossip, passed it along and watched the results. She talked about everything with kids she hung with, but said nothing of consequence herself. With her self-deprecating sense of humor, there were few parties or sleepovers she didn't attend. Always, though, she had a hidden agenda; probing for the frailties in others for the inevitable backstabbing.

Why she let her guard down with Tia Hughes, she couldn't say. Tia was a gypsy; an army brat who'd been all over the country, as well as Germany, moving to a new school each time her father was transferred.

But her parents had separated just after they'd moved to Philly. Tia, who had had few close friends, because she knew she or they would invariably be separated by military transfers, was now particularly vulnerable.

Normally, Shanicha would have feasted on that vulnerability and fed the girl to the wolves. As a matter of fact, she immediately gravitated to the girl when she appeared in the middle of her junior year of high school.

Tia was the color of iced tea, with large oval-shaped brown

eyes that, Shanicha thought, hid some terrible sadness. Her face was perfect except for a long thin scar that coursed its way from the corner of her lip to just under her chin. With makeup, it could hardly be seen.

She had a figure that had boys bumping into one another as she glided through the hallway between classes.

Yet, she kept her distance; socializing without joining any of the many cliques.

Somehow, this girl was able to gut Shanicha's defenses. They began spending a lot of time together. Tia spent most afternoons at Shanicha's house, always finding some excuse not to have Shanicha over to hers. Shanicha found it odd, for there was precious little privacy at her house, with her younger brothers and sisters and their friends parading through a house that was meant to accommodate half their number. This wasn't New Canaan, where she'd had a room of her own. With Tanya now having three kids, no husband and no inclination to leave the family nest, Shanicha shared her room with two of her younger sisters.

Yet Tia would rather spend time at Shanicha's than at her own house, where, with only one sister, she had her own room.

She finally told Shanicha the reason, when she came to school with a cast on her wrist. She'd fallen down the stairs, she told her teachers. Shanicha didn't believe it for a moment. Her eyes told otherwise.

"If I tell you, promise it goes no further," Tia had said after school, at Shanicha's house.

Oddly, when Shanicha vowed to keep *this* secret, she knew she would.

"My mother's an alcoholic. When she has too much to drink, she gets abusive. At my father. And with him gone, now me." She touched the scar on her face.

"Three years ago, when I was fourteen, we had a terrible fight. I'd poured at least half a dozen bottles of liquor down the drain. See, when my father was on maneuvers, my mother seemed to drink all day, cursing the boredom of most of the small-town army bases where we were stationed. Cursing my father. Cursing me. She'd have been long gone, she told me when she was really soused, if it weren't for me. Like it was my fault she was staying with my father."

Janice, Shanicha's nine-year old sister, came in and sat down on the bed next to Shanicha, as if she belonged.

"Girl, get your ass out of here!" Shanicha jumped at her, and raised her hand as if she was going to strike the child. Janice let out a yelp and bolted out of the room.

"It was the booze talking, I knew," Tia went on after they'd both had a good laugh, "but it still stung. So, I got rid of the problem. When she found out, she hit me two, three, four times, and without thinking I slapped her back. She came at me with the end of a broken bottle. That's how I got the scar. The blood seemed to snap her out of . . . I don't know, her insanity, I guess, and she rushed me to the hospital."

With her sleeve, she wiped tears from her eyes, then without thinking touched the scar, which Shanicha recalled was something Tia did when she was nervous or upset.

"She'd get better for a while, then go on a binge. My father finally had enough and split. Yesterday, she got skunked before she went to work. I tried to snap her out of it; coffee and a lot of yelling. I knew she was close to getting fired. I was just trying to help and she went ballistic. Swung a frying pan at my face. I stopped it with my wrist," she said, holding up the cast.

"I don't know how much more I can take." And she began crying uncontrollably.

Shanicha found herself telling her friend secrets she'd never told anyone before. Not the *big* secrets, which shaped the core of her existence. Those were forever buried within. But she told Tia about the spiders and her fear one would plant its eggs within her womb. Told her about going all the way with Jamal Walton the summer before. It felt good to share, she thought. Maybe everyone needed someone to confide in.

Shanicha wouldn't have minded if they had just drifted apart, which is what they did. There was only so much she could share with Tia. And she didn't want any one person monopolizing her time. There was mischief to be done and no way could Tia be included.

Meanwhile, Tia's mother had begun going to AA meetings, and her father was considering returning home. Slowly, Tia came out of her womb and started making other friends.

Shanicha didn't want to be part of any group, so she and Tia saw less and less of one another.

She was alone again; by choice.

It was another invaluable life lesson for Shanicha. When all is said and done, you have only yourself. She didn't blame Tia, or bear her any ill will. All would have been forgotten had Tia not told others Shanicha's secrets.

She heard girls talking about her and Jamal. She found a rubber spider hanging from her locker.

She never knew why she never confronted Tia. She suspected it was done without malice. Just girl talk, and when Shanicha's name came up, Tia forgot her vow of secrecy.

Regardless, Shanicha had never been so furious. Anger, she knew, was counterproductive. Getting even was so much sweeter.

Before their friendship had fizzled—they'd never argued or officially ended their relationship—Tia had finally brought her to her home. Having bared the secret of her mother's alcoholism, she had nothing to hide.

Now Shanicha bided her time; what she did best. Through the grapevine, she heard Tia's mother had fallen off the wagon—again. She and Tia were constantly at one another's throats. Her father had once again fled. Tia's mother spent more and more time in local bars and less time at home. Tia, then, was able to have her new friends over often, without any parent hovering over.

Every third Friday Tia hosted a party at her home. After the boys left, Tia and her friends would crash for the night.

Shanicha had learned this from both listening and keeping an eye on Tia's house, without being seen. The darkness shrouded her as she hid between two houses. She became one with the night.

Like clockwork, as soon as Tia's friends would arrive at 9:30 or 10, her mother would vacate the premises, often stumbling on her way out.

Shanicha got the idea how to get back at Tia while watching Tia's mother amble off. She saw a firefly, and it triggered memories long dormant.

With her experience in New Canaan, setting fire to Tia's house was a no-brainer.

She poured gas on the steps leading up to Tia's room, half an hour after the lights went off; after the boys had left . . .

—To make escape more difficult.

. . . then more gas on the inside front door. She dropped a bottle of Tia's mother's scotch outside a side window that bordered an alley, set two fires, then slipped out the window herself.

As the fire department wheeled the bodies of four teens out of the house several hours later, Shanicha felt herself back in New Canaan. She mingled with the crowd, just listening. It hadn't been much of a fire, but the neighbors were jazzed.

". . . police think it was arson."

"Look at her mother crying. Crocodile tears, if you ask me."

". . . fought *all* the time, them two."

At Tia's funeral, Shanicha felt nothing. She had no conscience. No compassion. No scruples. *No friends.*

Shanicha had to congratulate herself as the investigation pointed a finger at Tia's mother. The fire was not only arson, but there had been a deliberate attempt to prevent the escape of those inside. It made the tragedy that much more horrifying. It was an angle the media played up big time.

There was but one suspect: Tia's mother, who constantly bitched about her insolent daughter at neighborhood bars. She was arrested and found guilty. Her husband's testimony about his wife's uncontrollable outbursts helped seal her fate.

It was ironic, Shanicha thought. In a way justice had been served.

Shanicha could smell the burgers from the barbecue. In the dark recesses of her mind, she could also smell her friend's body lapped by flames.

Both smelled delicious.

Chapter Thirty-eight

She sat watching Shanicha mechanically chewing on a burger, as if unaware of what she was doing. She thought Shanicha looked concerned and unsure, and it gave her goose bumps. She was beginning to comprehend how Shanicha felt as she manipulated others without their knowledge.

I'm fucking with your mind, Shanicha. How does it feel?

To have gotten the best of Shanicha with the fake call from Isaacs the night before—well, it didn't get much better than that. It gave her great comfort, especially since her attack on the cop had not gone as planned.

Wasn't that always the case, she thought. *Her* fire extinguished before it really caught. Monique, whose suicide had to be assisted with a bump on her noggin and a push from behind. And now the cop she'd killed who hadn't died. It was maddening.

Fortunately, the cop was still in a coma. Even if he recovered, Shanicha was his prime suspect. But still, she'd botched the job. Fucking maddening.

That she had Shanicha thinking about her, though, made all the frustrations pale in comparison. She wondered just how far she could push Shanicha. She wanted to keep fucking with her mind to see how she would react.

She put a hand in her pocket and fiddled with a key. A master key. She had gotten it when room assignments were made for new students and those who couldn't bear their current roommates between first and second semester. She'd volunteered to help, and in the ensuing confusion had made an imprint of the master key.

She'd learned how to make a duplicate of a key from the Internet, just as she had learned to bug Dr. Isaacs's office. The world the Internet opened was truly awesome, she thought. She could have ordered a book from one of the mail-order companies mentioned on the Net, on how to bug someone's room, but it was chancy. She would have to open a post office box, send a money order and face exposure when she picked up the parcel. It could be traced back to her.

But surfing the Net brought the same results; without the risk and far quicker.

She'd been in Shanicha's room, without her knowledge, just once, several weeks before. As much as she had been tempted, more often would be too risky. What if she was seen coming out of the room? She was not about to give herself away. Not when she was having the time of her life.

She didn't know what she'd thought she would find in Shanicha's room, but she'd been sorely disappointed. She'd hoped to locate a diary or a scrapbook, but Shanicha was too smart. The only oddity was an array of a dozen or more deodorants on Shanicha's desk. It struck her as peculiar, but she couldn't fathom any significance. She did note, however, that Shanicha's roommate had a computer.

She made her way to Shanicha's room now with that computer in mind. Just about everyone was at the barbecue, so she didn't fear being spotted. What she had to do would only take a moment, anyway.

Inside Shanicha's room, she went to her roommate's computer and typed a message: "Who had you meet Dr. Isaacs last night?"

Looked good, she thought to herself. Nice bold letters. Would freak Shanicha out. Fuck with her mind, she thought.

As she made her way outside, her only worry was that Shanicha's roommate would see it first. Then again, she thought, what if she did? It would just create another headache for Shanicha. It was perfect, regardless of who saw it first.

She would be on Shanicha's mind for a change, without her knowing who. She felt so . . . so—*in control!* And it felt exhilarating.

Now, she thought, what for an encore? She wasn't finished with Shanicha by a long shot. Yes, Shanicha, she thought, I'm gonna fuck with your mind. Show you how it feels, then fuck with it some more.

Chapter Thirty-nine

Ariel shivered, involuntarily, as she checked the Chevy Cavalier out for the day's trek to New Canaan. No, the thought of failure didn't faze her. She was confident, if not cocky. But four hours with Doug Thiery was another matter. She had never been cooped up with him, alone, for more than twenty minutes, and even those times he'd been insufferable. Two hours each way. If McGowan had a sense of humor, he would have considered this one of his crowning achievements.

The night before had brought a mixed bag of news. She had called Dr. Kaplan, and he'd sounded down.

"My lady detective who's also a friend of the patient," he had greeted her when she identified herself. "You know the old cliché. An attorney who represents himself has a fool for a client. Does it apply to pretty detectives investigating an attack on a friend?"

"Doctor, in this case, it's just additional incentive."

"Not tunnel vision?" he asked.

She laughed. "I'll consider your critique."

"And I'll win the lottery tonight," he shot back.

"So, how's our patient?" she asked, wanting desperately to change the subject. She wouldn't allow others to second-guess her judgments because it was Lucius who had been assaulted. She felt she was putting *more* into the case because Lucius was involved. But more didn't necessarily translate into better. Best not to dwell on it. It would only be counterproductive.

She'd called, after all, to find out if Lucius's condition had improved; she never outwardly considered the possibility it might have deteriorated.

"No change," he said, without elaboration and sounding weary.

"Is that good or bad?" she asked, concerned.

"Good and bad. Don't quote me, but as far as survival, I'd say he's out of the woods."

"But . . . ?"

"The protracted coma bothers me. He had a smack to the head you wouldn't wish on your worst enemy, pardon my bluntness. And *then* he fell down a flight of stairs to boot."

He was silent for a moment. These pregnant pauses drove Ariel up a wall, especially when she spoke to him over the phone.

"You think it might be permanent, then?" she finally asked.

"Don't you be putting words in my mouth, my pretty detective," he said, followed by another pause.

"What then?" she asked, her concern turning to exasperation.

"Forgive me," he said, seeming to read her unease. "I'm an optimist by nature, which I must temper with a dose of pessimism for balance. I've been wrong in the past—once or twice," he added, and this time Ariel laughed.

"To see the hurt in someone's eyes when you've built up their hopes is a terrible sight. But," he said with a sigh, "that's *my* problem. As to your friend, it may not be today or tomorrow or even next week, but he *should* come out of his coma. That said, I just hope he's not . . ." He paused, and Ariel could picture him searching for the proper words.

"A vegetable," she said for him.

"I wouldn't go that far, but I am concerned whether he'll be able to make a complete recovery."

"So we both wait," Ariel said.

"The most difficult part for both families and doctors," he said, and again she could hear the weariness in his voice.

This morning she had called and, again, there'd been no change.

Chanda, on the other hand, had struck pay dirt. Ariel had had to literally drag her from the library, she was so immersed in her research.

"I've so much to tell you, Ariel," she'd said, "and so much more to do."

"You can finish up tomorrow, when I'm off to New Canaan."

Ariel hated for Chanda to miss school, but she'd promised to call a friend to find out assignments she'd missed. And it wasn't as if she were sitting home or holding vigil at the hospital. Learning, Ariel knew, came in many forms. Chanda was learning more than she ever could at school, and her success was its own reward. And she was so enthusiastic that Ariel didn't have it in her to rebuke her for missing a couple of days of classes.

At home, Chanda took out a notebook. "Where do you want me to begin?"

"New Canaan. I'll be there tomorrow. Anything besides the fires?"

Chanda smiled. "A teacher committed suicide in . . ." She checked her notes. "In 1986, a year before the fires. He'd been accused by a number of girls in his class of molesting them. The children being minors, no names were mentioned."

"I'll ask the sheriff there about that tomorrow," Ariel said. "*Maybe* another piece to the puzzle. What about the list of suicides?"

"That was a bitch," she said, rolling her eyes. "I never knew there were so many. I mean life sucks, but suicide is so . . . so final. Where to start," she said, as much to herself as to Ariel, paging through her notes.

"Try students who attended Southern High School."

Chanda looked at Ariel. "You haven't told me your suspect yet."

"Lucius found her. I just followed his lead." She told Chanda how Asha had led her to Isaacs and the acquaintance-rape counseling group; how Lucius suspected one of the remaining girls in the group of being either a murderer or perpetrating a hoax with the note. Finally, she held up the admissions papers Desjardins had given her. "This would have helped you today. Will help. I didn't get it until late this afternoon."

"Who is she?"

"I don't want to tell you yet."

Chanda looked at her irritably, almost pouting.

"It's not what you think. I'm not holding back. I *do* need your help. But giving you her name would make you close your eyes to other possibilities. Lucius's doctor made me come to grips with that possibility last night. I'm so close to the situation, I might be looking for something that's not there. I haven't told the sheriff in New Canaan whom I suspect either. I want *him* to tell *me*. Otherwise, it's like putting a square peg in a round hole. We see her presence when it's not really there."

Chanda still didn't look mollified.

"Take the teacher's suicide, for example. If she wasn't in his class or associated with the molestation charges in some way, it's got to be discarded. Tomorrow we'll look at what both of us have, and see what fits. *Then* I'll give her to you. Now, any students from Southern?"

Chanda flipped through her notes again, then brightened. "Two. Both last year. Both girls," she said excitedly, and read their names. "Two months apart."

Without Ariel asking, she was back rifling through her notes.

"Only two other high school students took their lives last year. One at Central and one at Northeast High."

"You did great," Ariel said, not trying to hide the pride she felt.

"And tomorrow?"

"You are a glutton for punishment. It's back to the fires. And back to Southern. First, fires in South Philadelphia, the past . . ." Ariel paused to think. "The past three or four years. Maybe a pattern of fires. You know, three or four in a span of a few months. But don't overlook isolated instances."

"Right," Chanda said. "Square pegs in round holes."

Ariel took out a city map and drew a circle where Chanda should concentrate.

"She's black?" Chanda asked.

"You're a quick study," Ariel said. "Yes, and moved to a black neighborhood from New Canaan. Any fires she set would have been in a black neighborhood—"

"Where her presence wouldn't have stood out," Chanda finished for her. "And she went to Southern, so you want me to check what?"

"Anything unusual. You'll see it if it's there."

"And what will you do with all of this information?" Chanda asked.

"I'm going to get into her mind. Start thinking like she does. Problem is, right now I don't have enough raw data. So, we start from afar and hone in. She went to Southern. There were two suicides there last year. What else happened at Southern? We take what I learn at New Canaan and match it to the incidents at Southern. Hopefully, patterns will emerge. Right now, time is our enemy."

Chanda looked her a question.

"First," Ariel said, lifting one finger, "McGowan is giving me one day. It's New Canaan or bust. Two," she said, now raising two fingers, "Commissioner Desjardins has his own deadline—three days. He's afraid the girl may strike again. I doubt it, but I can't blame him. And three," she said, raising a third finger, "finals are two weeks off, and then the semester ends. If she murdered those girls on campus, the evidence that will entrap her is there. With the end of the semester, and the girls from The Quad scattered like pollen by the wind, no way I can reconstruct what happened."

Ariel was now pacing the room.

"Not only is time the enemy, but no way McGowan's going to give me anyone other than Doug to check out leads. To become one with this girl, I've got to interview her friends, enemies, neighbors, classmates. It . . . all . . . takes . . . time," she said, pausing briefly to punctuate each word. "So, I need you to provide some focus."

Ariel saw Chanda staring at her.

"What?"

"I've never seen you so animated. It's like a narcotic. You're high as a kite; the high that drugs give you for a short time."

Ariel looked at her.

"I've experimented, okay. Only a couple of times. I didn't like not being in control. But the high . . . I can relate to it."

Ariel decided not to press the point, and instead knelt down in front of Chanda.

"It's what homicide—any detective work, actually—is all about. McGowan's kept me at arm's length from these type of cases. Understand something. Ninety-five percent of the work any cop does is routine. Some of us live for cases like these. The highs *are* like a narcotic, and the lows depressing as hell."

She was up and pacing the room again, though her eyes were focused on Chanda.

"But these cases," she went on, "make all the other shit acceptable. I've been on autopilot, just going through the motions, for a good while. These past few days, though, have been like a transfusion."

Ariel shook her head, as if she couldn't put it into words.

"I think I understand," Chanda said. "I had a friend who

245

wrote music for this band of his. Most of what he cranked out was mediocre, and he knew it. Twice, though, he came up with a tune that was like nothing he'd done before. You could see the change in him; a change in the whole band, when they played those songs. I'd never seen him happier.

"Problem was, a week later he was trying to top what he'd done, and it didn't happen. He'd go into a funk; a deep dark pit where no one could reach him. Then it would be back to writing the same old shit he'd turned out before."

Ariel smiled. This girl was perceptive, she thought to herself. She hadn't lived the highs yet, but she understood.

"I'll tell you, Chanda, the highs are worth it. You go through your life like my partner; wanting everything mapped out for you. No forks in the road where you make the wrong turn and you're fucked. He seems happy, though, but one day he's got to have regrets. For me, I hunger for the challenge. I've had cases like this that led nowhere. It's damn depressing when you hit that final dead end in the road. But even those, the trip was worth it. I need that to exist—at least professionally."

Ariel paused and met Chanda's eyes. "You know what's best about a case like this?"

Chanda shook her head no.

"Knowing there's someone there for you when things fall apart. Too often they do. When I sink into my funk, you'll be there to kick me in the ass, give me a hug and make the depression bearable."

Chanda said nothing, but the look in her eyes spoke volumes. Ariel knew she'd made her day.

As Doug got into the car, on the passenger's side, Ariel wished Chanda was with her now. Two hours. *Each way.* She could almost see him salivate. He'd chew her ear off with . . . with drivel.

He was silent for the first twenty-five minutes, as Ariel

maneuvered around, between—almost through—cars on the Schuylkill Expressway. She drove like a New York City taxi driver; narrowly missing the tail of one car, cutting in on another, just avoiding his front fender. Doug grasped the door grip, his knuckles white. Ariel could imagine him in silent prayer.

It gave her time to think of this man of many contradictions. The man had money, but you couldn't tell from looking at him. His wife was a teacher in the suburbs, so between the two of them they pulled in over $100,000 a year.

While they had two young children, his mother had set up trust funds for their college education. As a tenth anniversary present, she'd paid off their mortgage. Then a year ago, she'd passed away. An only child, Doug got close to half a million in stocks and his mother's home, worth at least that much, maybe more. A family home for seven generations, and he refused to sell the property. It was a retreat of sorts, he said, occupied by the Thiery clan no more than two to three weeks a year.

Yet, from what he'd told Ariel, he made it sound like he lived from paycheck to paycheck. He literally bought clothes from thrift shops, clothes that were on sale or from designer boutiques like KMart and Value City. Athletic equipment for his children was purchased at Play It Again Sports, a store that bought and sold used sporting goods.

He appeared to wear the same blue suit each day, complete with stains and frayed sleeves and elbows. Ariel had been wrong, though. One day he told her he had *three* suits; all identical.

He borrowed newspapers from other detectives in the squad, to the point where one detective would bring his paper from home and hand it to Doug, then borrow one to read from someone else in the squad at the end of the day.

Doug read voraciously, but owned only a handful of books. He was a library man and made damn sure he returned his books on time. Others he bought at yard sales and flea markets.

And his car, a real piece of work; literally hung together with bandaids and shoestrings. Well, at least with shoestrings. The wiper blade on the driver's side worked sporadically, so he'd affixed a shoestring to it. One of the other detectives had razzed him for weeks after seeing him in a driving rainstorm, one hand out the window, manually using the shoestring to pull the blade.

"How can you pass State inspection with that windshield wiper?" she'd asked him once.

"I'll get around to fixing it a week before my inspection."

And he did. He'd tinker with his car. And if it was something major, he'd call his father-in-law, who more often than not could take care of the problem, if only to pass inspection. And he charged for parts only.

They'd talked vacations once. Ariel had treated herself to a trip to the Bahamas. He'd been thoughtful, then shook his head.

"Couldn't go. Can't get there by car."

"You afraid of planes or something?" she had asked.

"Do you know the cost of plane tickets?" he'd asked in response. "We'd get there and have no money for a hotel."

So his vacations revolved around how far they could get by car. Atlantic City. Beaches in Delaware. Beaches in North Jersey. *Maybe* a trip to Washington, D.C. Virginia was nice. Good beaches. Sometimes, the family would just get in the car and drive, with no destination in mind. Other times he'd visit flea markets. A lot of good buys there, he'd told Ariel.

Once and only once, he'd convinced her go to out socially, on their day off. It was her birthday and, being between men, she was alone. They ended up going to an off-track-betting parlor on Market Street. Always aggressive, she'd bet exactas and trifectas; cashing in on a trifecta for $65. He would invariably bet on the favorite—bet $2 for it to show; come in third place. After losing three races, he'd finally won. For his $2 bet he'd proudly brought back $2.10.

She'd want to strangle him. Two salaries, a house paid for, college taken care of, a hefty inheritance and *he bragged about good buys at flea markets.*

A man of many contradictions.

Once they were on the Northeast Extension of the Pennsylvania Turnpike, which would lead to New Canaan, Doug slowly unwound. He pried his hand off the door grip. Only a few times did he steal a glance at the speedometer, which crept near seventy-five. Ariel would glare at him, and he'd scrunch deeper in his seat. When he was fully comfortable, the danger arose.

Doug spoke.

"You gonna drop it on the sheriff that you're black?"

"Half black," she corrected him.

"You gonna tell him?" he persisted.

She didn't know if he was curious or intentionally baiting her. They'd had this conversation before.

There were times she'd hailed a cab, knowing that if the cabbie knew she was black, he would have sped by. She knew when she rented one apartment in particular that the landlord was a bigot. If he knew she was black, no way would she have gotten it. And the apartment was sweet. While browsing for jewelry or clothing in a department store, she drew no special attention. But if they knew she was black, someone would have had their eyes on her.

She passed. Not intentionally, but she knew she passed because she didn't broadcast her blackness. When she was married to Lucius, she would feel guilty for passing—felt like a goddamn fraud.

But she'd come to grips with it after her divorce, when she had a better understanding of just who she was. What was she supposed to do, anyway—wear a sign: "Hey, I'm black"? It was ludicrous to feel remorse when she was spared the indignities of blacks who looked black. She *never* denied her blackness; never wore makeup so she could pass; never wore her hair in a style that made her appear white.

To be honest, though, in her work she played the race card—but as a strategy.

With a black in an interrogation, she'd gotten the looks of disdain and disgust all white cops got. "I'm not gonna tell you nothing, you white bitch motherfucker." Dissed because she was white *and* female.

When it suited her, during the interrogation, she'd drop it on the perp she was black. He'd immediately look to Doug, who'd nod his head in acknowledgment.

"What the fuck happened to your *black*?" the befuddled man would ask.

"Camouflage, shithead," she'd answer.

Then she'd tell him how she was mistreated and abused by white cops because she was black. She'd play on his sympathies.

"You know how hard it is being black," she'd confide. "Every fucking case I get, I'm judged not on my skill, but my color."

It was a complete lie, which made it all the more plausible.

To a white perp, she'd let him think she was white if it helped. Especially if the dude was a novice.

"You're not like the niggers we get in here," she'd start.

"What you mean?"

"Soon as they get here, they're trying to cop a plea, because they know the system. You know, 'Been there, done that,' " she'd say, using the popular Mountain Dew slogan.

"Been through here so many times, we're on a first-name basis with some. They ask about my family. God's honest truth. They know they're going to serve time, so it's like we're a damn used-car lot. They begin haggling for the best sentence. *You,* you'll ask for a lawyer and get screwed."

She'd go on, his confidant. Often it worked.

Sometimes, though, when a white was particularly abusive, agreeing niggers were the scum of the earth and got away with whatever they wanted *because* of their race, she'd play the game until the end. With a signed confession, she'd lay it on him. *She* was black. He'd blanch. It was bad, but it felt so good.

Now Doug had asked the magic question again. Would she tell the New Canaan sheriff she was black?

"I doubt it, Doug. I won't deny I'm black if he asks. I won't act *white*. But this is a small-town cop who'll piss on me because I'm a woman. He'd shit on me if I walk in waving an 'I'm black and I'm proud' sign."

"Aren't you being a hypocrite?" he asked.

"You don't get it, Doug. The name of the game is getting what we need. What purpose is served by announcing I'm black? If he's a bigot, it'll just antagonize him and we'll get squat."

"What about after?" he asked. "You know, like after your interrogations, sometimes."

Doug enjoyed her interrogations. Stone-faced, he'd wait for the other shoe to drop, and crack up once outside.

"If only I could bring a Polaroid in to capture their expressions. Dampier's Wall." And he'd go into another laughing jag.

"What if I have to make a follow-up call?" she asked him. "I need this sucker's cooperation, for God's sake. I won't hide what I am, but I'm not going to broadcast it either."

She shook her head and pressed a bit harder on the gas.

"Why all this black shit, Doug? In a small town like New Canaan, my being Jewish might antagonize him as much as my color. You never ask me why I don't march in and say, 'Hi. I'm Detective Ariel Dampier and I'm Jewish.' Why is that, Doug?"

"Well . . . because . . ." he said, leaving the sentence unfinished.

"Because it's an asinine question," she finished for him. "So why should I march in and announce I'm black?"

"I'm sorry," he said. "I didn't mean any harm. I was just . . . you know . . ."

"Wondering," she finished for him. "We've had this discussion before. You waiting for me to change my answer?"

Doug shut up for ten minutes. Enough time to remind her of her childhood; especially adolescence, when she couldn't win for losing.

She had gone to an integrated elementary school in Center City. She associated with both blacks and whites. In second grade, color was irrelevant until she brought two white friends home. Her mother was there and gave them milk and cookies.

"You got a maid!" Robin had said, sounding impressed. "You must be rich."

"That's my mother," she'd answered.

"But she's *black*. You're *white*."

"My mother's black and my father's white," she'd said, not knowing then what she was, or what the big deal was.

It was the first time she'd been labeled by society. She was no longer just Ariel. She was one of the *black* kids in class.

There were times she'd come home from school crying because of the taunts of whites *and* blacks. To whites, she was black, plain and simple. To blacks she was "Casper" or "Oreo" or "bleached yourself again, bitch." She was a target because she talked proper English spoken at home, not the language of the streets. Her parents being well off, she dressed better than many of the black kids, which incensed them even more.

She had friends, both black and white, but it was a delicate balancing act. If she hung with white kids, even her black friends would turn their back on her.

"You're too good for us," they'd say, if only to save face

with the other blacks in class who persecuted her. When she stuck with her black friends, she was "going back to her kind."

There were ramifications in all she did. Where she sat in the cafeteria offended someone. Whom she sat with on bus trips pissed someone off. Whom she spoke to in the goddamn girls' room could have someone on her case the rest of the day.

It was all so transient. In fifth grade, she remembered a heated argument with a teacher about the Emancipation Proclamation.

"Lincoln freed the slaves," her teacher parroted from an erroneous textbook. Ariel had raised her hand.

"That's not true, Miss Decker."

They'd read the Emancipation Proclamation in class, and the teacher read a portion again, for Ariel's benefit.

She shook her head. "He only freed the slaves from the states that seceded," Ariel persisted. "Which meant nothing. The slaves in the border states that remained loyal to the North were still slaves."

Her teacher had argued that Lincoln was a humanitarian; Ariel that it was all politics. She'd read as much in books her mother gave her. Books by people with credentials. Books most eleven-year-olds avoided like the plague. She didn't win over her teacher, but the other black kids were impressed. Even those who hassled her.

Their admiration and acceptance lasted all of two days. Soon as she began hanging with some of the white kids, her "Lincoln had no intention of freeing the slaves" was promptly forgotten.

It got worse—got physical—when she began dating. She was that "black bitch" who dated cute white boys. "Bitch puts out—that's the only reason he dates her."

That it wasn't true meant nothing. She'd lose her temper and being a string bean, more often than not came away the worse for wear after the inevitable catfight. She'd been goaded into it, she knew, but there was only so much one could take.

Not only had she lost the fights, she'd been suspended for fighting. More than once. A model of behavior she was not.

Her father had come into her room when she was fourteen, while she sat on her bed with a bag of ice beneath a swollen eye. He looked at her, and given a sad smile.

"You're supposed to hit with your fists, not your eye," he'd joked.

She'd pouted, but felt a smile fight to escape.

Her father had been a mysterious presence in her life. It wasn't that she was ignored or unloved. He taught her to play cards: twenty-one, gin and poker. Then he taught her to count cards and other "tricks" that had earned him extra spending money when he was young.

He took her on trips every Saturday he was in town: to museums, to parks, to kite-flying festivals. She rode her first hot-air balloon with him, and almost upchucked her breakfast. He took her to baseball and basketball games, though he wasn't much into sports.

And he taught her how to shoot a gun. He was a good shot, she remembered. And a good teacher. He was deadly serious when he taught her how to shoot. It was the only time he shared something so intensely personal with her; something to do with his sudden disappearances.

He never told her why he'd go on trips, ostensibly to Israel, for months at a time. Why, thin as he already was, he returned sometimes truly emaciated. In appearance, she reminded him of James Coburn; tall, white-haired, with a short-cropped white beard and regal bearing. He was a man of few words, remaining silent when a nod or look could convey his thoughts or feelings.

So when he came into her room after that particularly bad beating, she didn't expect a pep talk. She didn't get one.

Born Bad

"Your mother and I have been unfair to you. Selfish. You suffer because we fell in love. Come, I want you to meet somebody."

He took her to a kosher butcher shop on Haverford Avenue to Murray Rubin; "Uncle Murray," he told her to call him. She'd learned later that wasn't his real name. She suspected this because at times she'd call his name and he wouldn't respond. Yet "Uncle Murray" he remained to this day.

He was a short barrel-chested man of about fifty, with muscular arms, he told her, from carrying carcasses and cutting meat. He always seemed to need a shave. There were scars on his arms that she'd learn later were from bullets and shrapnel.

She never learned his real name, but later found out he'd been a Mossad agent. And while her father wouldn't admit it, she suspected he too worked for the Mossad or a similar intelligence group. Those trips to Israel were not speaking engagements or exchange programs.

Uncle Murray was as garrulous as her father was reserved. He taught her how to defend herself, and from him she learned about her Jewish heritage. He was her rabbi, in all things secular. He never talked religion nor mentioned God.

There were no philosophical underpinnings to his teaching of self-defense, like with most of the martial arts. He told her winning a fight was based on a controlled state of mind.

"When you can, avoid a fight. Even if you win, you make an enemy."

But if a fight was inevitable, there was no such thing as a good sport or playing by the rules.

"With your classmates, you defend yourself. If necessary, you hurt them. You only maim when your life is in peril. You are attacked by a rapist, you maim, then get the hell away. Go for the balls, his throat, his eyes."

Then he showed her.

She was a good student; a quick study, she overheard him telling her father. He helped her rein in her temper and channel her aggression.

"You are an angry child," he'd tell her. "And with just cause. In a fight, however, you must never let your emotions rule your actions."

Even more important, in accepting her dual racial identity, he taught her what it meant to be a Jew.

"Being Jewish is like being black, only we've been persecuted far longer. You're shunned because of what you are, not who you are or what you do."

He told her of the ghetto mentality of Jews. "Often they were isolated and ostracized. But just as often, they wanted to be apart from others, just as many blacks today no longer espouse integration, but racial pride."

He didn't sugarcoat anything for her. With thinly veiled contempt, he told her how the passivity of Jews in Russia, Poland and Germany nearly led to their extermination.

"When we were given our own country, we were forced to be aggressive or we'd literally be wiped out. The Arabs' desire to drive us into the sea was no idle threat. We fought. We prevailed. There were no rules. No boundaries. Only survival. When the life of you and your family is at stake, the game changes. You do what you must. You may not be proud later, but you're alive."

She knew he was talking from experience. There was a haunted look in Uncle Murray's eyes when he spoke about Israel and the War for Independence. He had done things that sickened him. But he and his country had survived.

He talked cryptically at times, but Ariel intuitively understood. She didn't need the gory details.

In high school, she had few fights. She only had to fight once (and face the inevitable suspension) before word got around it wasn't worth the scars to mess with her.

Uncle Murray's lessons also served her well at the Police

Academy. She easily held her own against far larger and stronger men. If it meant fighting dirty, so be it. No instructor ever chastised her for winning, no matter what her tactics.

Thinking back, she would never recall childhood or adolescence with fondness. She'd been hassled from that day in second grade when she discovered what it meant to be black in White America. She'd battled the enmity of both blacks and whites through high school and beyond. She didn't know it then, but it all led up to coming to terms with herself.

After her divorce from Lucius, she had become an island onto herself for a long while. Simon and Garfunkel's "I Am A Rock" became her personal anthem.

She'd learned, though, that self-imposed isolation didn't bring contentment, much less happiness. Over the course of several years and fragile relationships with men she didn't love, she'd finally decided no one was ever going to be satisfied with her. Thus, she would no longer let others shape who she would be.

I must be satisfied with myself. I'm black. I'm Jewish. I'm Ariel Dampier. What I am is what you get. If you don't like it, tough shit. I must be able to live with me.

With that rationalization came inner peace for the first time in her life.

". . . before McGowan moves on."

It was Doug, talking and looking at her strangely when she remained silent. She laughed to herself; wondered how long he had been talking. She looked at the odometer and saw they were no more than ten miles from the exit that would take them to New Canaan.

"What?" she asked.

"How long before McGowan gets his promotion?"

"The sooner the better," she answered.

"I don't know what you got against him. We're a hell of a lot more efficient with McGowan than we ever were with Donato."

"Bullshit, Doug," she said, trying to control the rage within her. "It appears more efficient, but check the stats. Our clearance rate isn't much better. Any improvement is not McGowan's doing, but the better detectives assigned to the squad. Look, I don't want to talk about it now. I want my mind focused on the sheriff in New Canaan, not Phil Donato."

"Don't go biting my head off. Just trying to make conversation."

Don't get me started, Ariel thought, but said nothing. Now was not the time to be thinking of her former Sergeant. If he were alive, he'd tell her as much.

Keep your focus, he'd say.

She would.

Chapter Forty

Shanicha felt like a bungee jumper in free fall. Once you stepped into the breach, your fate was no longer in your hands. At the moment, someone else was pulling the strings, and *she* was the puppet. She had to regain control. And while her stomach churned with apprehension, in the darkness of her mind she knew she would. And that someone who was yanking her chain would pay dearly for the anguish she'd caused.

First, it had been the message on her roommate's computer screen, which confirmed the call the night before had been no prank.

"Who had you meet Dr. Isaacs?"

She'd erased it immediately, fearful her roommate might

walk in at any moment, but the words burned in her mind. She could feel the spider closing in, and ran to shower. She was drenched in water before she realized she was still fully clothed. What if someone walked in? *Snap out of it,* she chided herself. *You're becoming unhinged.*

She undressed, then soaped and rinsed. Lathered herself again, then let the water cleanse her. Cloaked herself in suds once more, then let the water soak her every pore.

She returned to her room dripping wet, as she hadn't taken a towel or robe. In her room, she remained naked, allowing the air to dry her body. She caressed her breasts and squeezed her nipples as she paced.

Only *she* could love herself. Her birth mother hadn't; her adoptive parents had been too wrapped up in their unexpected natural children; her sister Tanya too into her own sexual needs.

She'd had sex with boys, but they never made love to her; were neither adept at the art, nor cared to satisfy her needs. She'd found she was incapable of loving another. It had been stolen at birth, along with her conscience and compassion.

Only she could supply the adoration she sought. Not only did she love herself, she made love to herself—often. It was akin to an out-of-body experience. She could see a part of her slip away, turn and lavish her with love in a way no boy could.

Ever so slowly her other self would touch those pleasure spots only she was aware of, until she could barely contain herself. Her other self had no sense of time. No need to rush, be done, then depart. Her other self was there only for her enjoyment, could bring her within a breath of climax, then withdraw and begin anew. Hours could pass before her other self knew she could take no more. Then, and only then, did her other self satisfy her completely and selflessly. And afterward, her other self would merge and snuggle within her until she needed more loving.

Shanicha found herself in bed, dripping with sweat after her lovemaking. This perspiration, though, wouldn't attract the predator she feared. It was sweat tinged with her sex; a natural repellent to that other female who searched her out, with its webs and eggs.

Now calm, she could logically analyze the message that had been on the computer screen. Somebody knew *something*. Somebody wanted her to have no alibi for when Officer Friendly was assaulted. Just what did this person know? More important, who the fuck was it?

She fell asleep having made no headway in answering either question. She woke up at 6 a.m. to WXTU, the city's country/western station. Several minutes later, her roommate stood over her, her eyes closed so she couldn't see Shanicha's nude body. Her outstretched hand held something.

"There was a letter under the door with your name on it."

Shanicha was instantly awake. She sat up and plucked the envelope from her roommie's hand.

"Is it from that special someone?" her roommate asked.

"What special someone?" Shanicha asked, hardly paying attention.

"Some guy you met who makes your heart throb. Who—"

"Stop, please, before I gag," she interrupted. "You watch entirely too many soap operas."

"So don't tell me," she fumed, and stormed out of the room.

Shanicha opened the envelope and read the typed message:

"When are you going to tell group about *your* rape?"

"Fuck," she said out loud as she read, reread, then read the message again. "Fuck, fuck, fuck," she said, then got out of bed and burned the note, the contents imprinted on her mind.

And unbidden, a third question popped into her mind. What did she know? Who the fuck was it? And why? Why? Why? Why?

Why was someone playing with her mind? Intuitively, she knew it was a *she*. She knew the bitch was female . . .

—Like the spider attracted to the warmth of her womb.

. . . but nothing else. *Yet.*

This time she didn't panic, but began to slowly unwind. "Keep it up, bitch," she said aloud. Each message was a clue that would lead her to the who, which would answer the other questions.

She knew more would follow. Right now someone *else* was pulling the strings, and she didn't like it one bit. Now *she* stood at the precipice. She had to hold on. She had to be patient. She refused to become that bungee jumper. Refused to relinquish control. No one, but no one, would get the best of her. For if they did, all was lost, and she'd be unable to fend off the spider.

With its webs.

With its eggs.

Chapter Forty-one

When Ariel reached New Canaan, she surprised Doug by driving past the police station.

"I'm afraid to ask," he said, rolling his eyes, as she slowly drove around town.

"Then don't," Ariel said, not making it any easier for her partner.

"Okay," he sighed. "Why did we pass the Sheriff's office?"

"Did we?" Ariel replied, barely holding back a smile.

"It was back there about—"

"I'm funning you, Doug," she said. "I know we passed it. I want to get a feel for this town before I see Conover. Show him us city cops ain't got shit for brains," she said in her best street-ghetto accent, which wasn't particularly good.

"Seriously," she went on, "something's not right about this place. It's almost . . . oppressive. Did you see the three or four stores boarded up on their main street? And coming into town, a number of homes were abandoned and in disrepair. Something more, but I can't put my finger on it, yet."

They drove, and she could see Doug looking, too. While no free thinker, if given direction, he proved no fool. So, she wasn't taken aback when he told her to stop by the park.

"Look at the playground," he said.

She did. It was empty. "So?" she asked.

"What *don't* you see?" he responded to her question excitedly.

She got it then. "Kids! There are no kids."

"And not just at this playground," he added. "We passed others and they weren't just empty. They looked abandoned; the grass not cut, swings and seesaws broken. That's commonplace in Philly, but not in these towns."

They continued to drive, and Ariel pointed out that not only didn't she see any kids, but no one pushing strollers.

"Most of the people are old. Elderly. Pushing fifty and sixty. I can count on one hand those under forty," Doug said.

"Maybe they're at work," Ariel said, but didn't believe it herself. New Canaan was *old*. More, New Canaan seemed to be dying.

They pulled up to the Sheriff's Office. The shingled building was in need of a fresh paint job. There were two policemen inside, both closing in on fifty.

Sheriff Tyler Conover—"My friends call me Ty"—looked

to be the same age as he ushered the two detectives into his office. He was medium height, with a Marine's haircut; not shaved bald, like Lucius, but cropped to the scalp with an electric razor. He reminded her of the stereotype of a drill Sergeant.

He had an open face, with an engaging smile, but there was an aura of sadness about him, as if he'd seen his share of suffering.

"So, tell me about this investigation that's connected to our town," he said after asking if they wanted coffee or a soft drink.

On their way up, Ariel had suggested Doug take the lead.

"Mano to mano," she'd said. "I don't want him to feel threatened by a pushy female detective from the big city."

Doug told him there had been several suspicious suicides on the University of Pennsylvania campus, followed by an attack on a campus police officer.

Conover looked them over closely. "Read about the ruckus at the University. But the attack on the cops and the suicides weren't related; leastways, that's the story your people put out. Someone trying to pull the wool over the eyes of the public?" he asked with a wink.

"The media, actually . . . and parents of students at Penn," Doug answered honestly. "We didn't want them connecting the two, since we're uncertain the suicides were in fact suicides. Reporters swarming all over the campus, we don't need."

"And a suspect from New Canaan goes to the University," Conover said, as a fact, not a question. "Why the interest in the fires back in eighty-seven?"

"From what we read they were arson and no one was ever charged," Doug answered.

"No one ever caught," Conover corrected. "Three months of hell and then it ended. Killed this town," he said sadly.

"Anything unusual strike you about New Canaan when you drove in?"

"The boarded buildings. The abandoned houses just outside of town," Doug said. "And no children. No young people at all."

"Very perceptive. I'm impressed," Conover said, and sat back. "I came here in sixty-five, fresh out of Vietnam. Didn't want to see no more killing. Wood mill was the lifeblood of the town. Still is, for them that stayed."

He took a sip from the cup of coffee he'd gotten for himself.

"Drunks Friday and Saturday night were our biggest problem, and it wasn't tough to handle. I became Sheriff in seventy-three when my predecessor had a heart attack at a high school football game."

He now took out a pipe and began packing it with tobacco.

"Mind?" he asked, holding out the pipe.

Ariel and Doug shook their heads.

"Where was I?" he asked himself. "The fires. When they started in the spring of eighty-seven, and when we were certain it was arson, everyone thought it a stranger. But the homes targeted at first were either abandoned, or the families had gone away for a short period of time. Pretty soon suspicion arose it was someone from town."

He paused and lit the pipe.

"Terrible thing when you begin to suspect your neighbors. Your coworkers. Your friends. Even family members. Then the fires got closer to town, and finally one was set with someone home. Our only fatality directly related to the fire. A teacher. Nice young woman. Young people in particular took it hard. Hell, everyone took it hard."

Ariel looked at Conover curiously, and he picked up on it.

"We had another death. Sarah Turner, our librarian and the soul, I guess you'd say, of New Canaan. She took it all personal, got sick and finally took to bed. Died the night the library was torched. Wasn't seen by the town as a coincidence. The fire—all of them, actually—killed her just as surely as if she'd been in the midst of the inferno.

"That's when folks began packing up and moving out. First, families with young children. Then young folks who had skills and were able to get jobs. About one third of the town, but those that left were our future."

He sat back, puffing his pipe, deep in thought.

"You know, I used to think no matter what the tragedy, with time the wound heals. Never totally goes away, mind you, but you move on. Happened to me with Vietnam. Not here, though," he said, shaking his head.

"You can see it on the faces of the old-timers. They're waiting for the next fire. The arsonist is long gone, but they're still waiting."

"There are *no* children left?" Doug asked.

"Didn't say that. Used to be two classes of each grade, with twelve per class. Now we combine grades. We have six total in grades one through three. Town's dying. Young people move away, now, because they see no future here."

"You stayed around," Ariel said, talking for the first time.

"Captain doesn't abandon ship," he said. "I had to set an example for the others. I leave and it's a stampede."

"That the only reason?" she persisted.

He looked at her more closely, then looked at Doug.

"Set me up, didn't you? Had him asking all the questions, but this is *your* investigation," he said with a smile. "Afraid I wouldn't show a woman the same respect I'd show a man." It wasn't a question.

"Something like that," Ariel said. "No disrespect intended. Now, why did you stay?" she said, leaning forward in her chair.

"Not going to find anyplace safer, leastways, not these days. There are rapists and child molesters in Allentown, not too far from here. Drugs are everywhere, even here. And murders in small towns. The Devil left New Canaan and it's been quiet ever since. Like we paid our dues. No crime to speak of. Hell, it's even pretty quiet on the weekends. No reason for me to leave. I'll be long dead before the town finally is put to rest. Now, ma'am, let's cut to the chase and tell me who you suspect."

"Did you know the Wilkins family?"

"The Negro family?" he asked.

Ariel nodded.

"Knew everyone. It's a small town. They were one of three colored families in New Canaan. Can't say nothing bad about them. Not like the heathens you got where you come from. Hardworking and law-abiding. Left town when the others did."

"After the last fire?"

"We had one fire after most people left, but it put itself out before it really caught. Some say it doesn't count," Conover said.

"Was Shanicha Wilkins in the class of the teacher that died?"

Conover was looking hard at her now.

"Girl would be college age now, I'd reckon. She your suspect?"

Ariel nodded.

Conover picked up the phone and made a call. Asked if Shanicha was in Audrey McAfee's class in eighty-seven. Listened, asked a few questions, then hung up.

"She was in her class," Conover said, "but from what the principal says, there was never any trouble between the two of them. Said Shanicha never was a discipline problem after kindergarten."

"What happened in kindergarten?"

"Don't rightly know, but might be able to steer you to someone who does." He began to stand up.

"What about the teacher who committed suicide the year before the fires?" Ariel asked.

"Son of a bitch. Pardon my French," he said, sitting down and looking at Ariel with renewed respect. "I'd forgotten about that. You did come prepared."

"Something about being accused of molesting children in his class," Ariel volunteered.

"Bunch of hogwash, if you ask me. I knew Tom Randolph. Knew him well. A good man. No way he'd molest any kids. But," he said, and his face clouded over, "if he was innocent, why would he kill himself? Asked myself that question a lot when it happened."

"Are you sure he did?" Doug asked.

"This may be a small town, Detective, but we don't do shoddy work. Powder residue on his hand. Note in his own handwriting. Door and windows locked from the inside."

"Sorry," Doug backtracked. "No offense."

"Who accused him?" Ariel asked.

"They were minors. I could say it's confidential. Would, except it was Shanicha Wilkins. After she came forward, a bunch of other girls did, too. Two of them recanted, after Randolph killed himself, but by then it didn't matter, did it? Everyone wanted the whole episode put behind us. Out of sight, out of mind."

"Any other incidents before the fire out of the ordinary?" Ariel asked.

"That be it," Conover said. "This was a quiet town, as I said. Look, if you want to speak to someone who knew Shanicha in kindergarten, we should go now."

He talked as he led them out of his office.

"Mabel Dawson's retired now. Only sixty, and volunteers at the school. But only when her health allows. Takes a nap between two and three most days. Not the woman she used to be."

As Conover led them in his police car to Mabel Dawson's

house, Ariel knew they'd hit pay dirt. McGowan would say suspecting Shanicha of being an arsonist was stretching things, but that she *had* accused her teacher of molesting her, and her teacher had ended up committing suicide—*that* was, she hoped, enough to get his attention.

Another thought struck her. Intentionally or otherwise, Shanicha had caused a man to kill himself without her actually being there. Could she have done the same with the three girls at Penn? Intriguing, she thought, but decided to tuck it in the back of her mind for the time being.

Mabel Dawson lived one block from school, which was at the end of the main street, aptly called Main Street. Ariel noticed, for the first time, the house reminded her of a small bungalow, but the property was well cared for. She couldn't spot a weed in the meticulously manicured lawn, and flowers of every sort surrounded the house with a multitude of colors.

Conover went into the house first, and came out shortly, beckoning them in.

"Don't tax her," Conover warned. "She had a heart attack four years ago, and two minor strokes since. She's alert now, but if you tucker her out, she'll confuse one student with another."

As he left he told them he'd be in his office if they had anything further to ask.

Mabel Dawson did look the worse for wear, though she tried to cover it. Ariel thought her to be a prim and proper tyrant of a teacher, at first glance. The do-it-my-way-or-the-highway type. One who considered fun and school as contradictions.

She was short, made more so by a slight stoop. She was thin and brittle-looking; like a pile of match sticks that could be blown over by a modest breeze. Her face was covered with liver spots and too much makeup to mask them. A simple gray dress was buttoned to the neck. She wore her limp gray hair in a tight bun.

Ariel was drawn to her hands, though; palsied from arthritis. Her fingers were bent and twisted every which way, like branches of a tree.

But her voice was strong, and when she talked about her students, her hazel eyes became focused and animated. Ariel knew she'd been wrong. Mabel Dawson had been a model teacher for young children: patient, energetic and compassionate. It made her appearance now all the more depressing.

Seated with tea and homemade chocolate-chip cookies, Ariel got right to the point.

"What can you tell me about Shanicha Wilkins, a student of yours in—"

"Nineteen-eighty-two; kindergarten," the woman finished for her. "Gotten herself into trouble, has she?"

She slowly raised her cup of tea with both hands, grimacing as she took a swallow.

"Why do you say that? Was she trouble in school?"

"She was a crack baby. Bet you didn't know that," she said with a wink. "Back in eighty-two, it was thought crack babies were permanently brain-damaged. Couldn't learn. Balderdash. Her parents had six, no, seven, no six—well, it doesn't really matter—*a lot* of adopted children, and three were crack babies. Shanicha was the youngest; a stick of dynamite ready to explode."

She put the teacup down, yet held onto the cup; so they wouldn't notice her hands twitching, Ariel thought.

"I was a lot spryer then, but she drained you dry. Always challenging, at the beginning. She'd color, then begin to break the crayons, then throw them at the other children. Once or twice she'd have spasms; tiny seizures, her arms flopping at her sides. I'd hold onto her for dear life, trying to hug the demons from her, but she pushed back as if fearful of . . ." She stopped and shook her head, then finished. "Of love. Oh dear," she said to no one in particular, and went through the slow-motion ritual of taking another sip of tea.

Barry Hoffman

Ariel could tell she was upset. Her hands shook even more than before.

"Anyway," she said when she was finished, and had composed herself, "it continued for about half the school year, and then she became a model student. All her demons exorcised."

She laughed, but it was joyless.

"Thought she had me fooled," she went on. "Had everybody fooled, but I knew. Her eyes never changed. Her demons were under control, but still there. Those eyes followed my every move, making sure I wasn't spying on her. They were always ablaze, ready to erupt. I was sure she would explode many a time, but she had mastered her emotions. She learned to rein in her need to destroy, to hurt others. But sometimes I wondered. A frightening child, Shanicha."

On a whim, Ariel decided to ask her about the molestation charges.

"Do you remember when Shanicha accused a teacher of molesting her?"

"Lies. All lies," Mabel Dawson said, clearly agitated. "She and the rest of them. I sought her out at recess, the day she made those reprehensible accusations. Didn't speak to her. Didn't get too close, but I saw her eyes. The same eyes I'd seen in kindergarten. But now there was triumph in them as well. She'd outfoxed them. Yes, a truly frightening child."

Ariel and Doug thanked her, and she walked them to the door. They had urged her to finish her tea, but she'd muttered, "Nonsense," and had slowly and painfully risen. Her face in a grimace, step by tiny step she accompanied them to the door.

"I love to look at my flowers." She winked. "Thought I was being polite, but wanted to see my flowers. Can't tend to them like I used to. Some of my former students take care of them now. Them that's left. So many gone. Shanicha's gone, too. Good riddance, I say."

270

They left her at the door looking at her flowers. Looking back at her as they walked to their car, Ariel saw how age and infirmity had sapped a once-vibrant woman. How could there be a God, she thought to herself, who would allow such suffering?

Doug wanted to drive right back to Philly, but Ariel insisted they stop by Sheriff Conover's office.

"We may need his help again. No harm in massaging his ego. We'll tell him what Mabel Dawson had to say, and he won't feel excluded."

On the drive back, to Philly, Doug started in on Ariel right away.

"Is Conover a bigot?" he asked, not caring to discuss what they'd learned.

"You seem to care more than I do," she answered.

"But is he?"

"We all have our prejudices, Doug. I'll be honest with you. I don't mind working with gays, but I find their lifestyle abhorrent. Unnatural. Doesn't make sense, does it, as someone discriminated against because of my race—my races, actually."

"What does that have to do with Conover?"

"He has two perceptions of blacks. Those he knew he accepted because they conformed to New Canaan's norms. They were good, hardworking folks, he said. He has the typical small-town stereotype of inner-city blacks. He views those of us who live in the inner city as drug addicts, pushers, unemployed, on welfare, jive-talking and prone to crime.

"Doesn't make him a bigot. Makes him uninformed. If he knew I was black, he wouldn't think less of me. He doesn't hate the entire black race, is what I'm saying."

Doug changed subjects, and Ariel tuned him out. He could talk nonstop; carry on a monologue with her and wasn't aware—or didn't care—that she had drifted off.

Talking about Conover got her thinking about the Sheriff,

271

Commissioner Desjardins, McGowan and ultimately Phil Donato. Conover and Desjardins were like her former Sarge in many ways. Decent people in bureaucratic positions. They could be manipulative; it was the nature of administration, but unlike McGowan, they wouldn't step on others to get what they wanted. She couldn't let her bitterness toward McGowan blind her to the decency of others. It made her miss her mentor even more.

She had wondered why Donato was shown such little respect by his superiors. Wondered, too, why he hadn't advanced up the command ladder. *She* knew he was capable, even if his superiors didn't.

At a barbecue at his home, after he retired, she'd finally asked why he'd been passed over for promotion. He was in bad shape. He walked like Mabel Dawson, but for a different reason. He could hardly breathe, the emphysema in its final stages. An oxygen tank on wheels trailed him like a dog who'd been his constant companion. He called it his jaws of life.

"I wasn't passed over. Becoming a Sergeant was my worst career move. I'm the first to admit I'm little more than a adequate Sergeant, because I'm no administrator. Maybe I was hoping—even trying—to fail, so I'd end up back on the street."

Ariel looked at him in confusion.

He smiled. "My father was a fireman. A hero in his neighborhood. Put out fires and went into blazing buildings to save lives. He was looked up to, admired, respected—revered."

He paused, closing his eyes. It was obviously an effort to speak, but there seemed a desperation within him to make her understand.

"I became a cop for the same reason: to make a difference. My first years I was a beat cop, at a time when we walked the streets alone. I knew most everyone, and they knew me. The one-to-one relationship between a cop and the neighborhood he patrols can only be accomplished by walking the beat. At least that's my opinion. I may not have been loved, but I was respected. I was a presence. I was needed."

He put on the oxygen mask and breathed deeply, like a man smoking a fine cigar.

"It changed with patrol cars. They insulated us from the community. Maybe neighborhoods were changing as well. But once in a car, I sensed a change in how we were perceived. We were depersonalized. Viewed as interlopers."

He stopped talking for a while as he tended to the grill. He turned a thick porterhouse steak over, while letting two others cook a bit more. He ate his rare. Restaurants would call it blue. He kidded others, saying he wanted his meat still moving when he ate it.

Then, as if he hadn't stopped, he continued.

"Without a home, like a lot of cops, I bounced from one special unit to another: fraud, vice, narcotics and finally homicide. I was making a difference, even if it wasn't on my own terms. Unfortunately, I also had a family to feed, so I went for a promotion and was soon making my way up the ladder of success," he said bitterly.

He took another whiff of oxygen.

"And what had I become? A fucking bureaucrat; yet another step removed from the streets. I don't know if I could have been an effective administrator, but as I had no appetite for the job, I began to go through the motions. No way was I going to work my way up. The money wasn't worth the politics and ass-kissing."

"So you muddled along," Ariel said.

"Yeah, muddled along. A career Sergeant. I'm sure I lost the respect of those above me in the chain of command. Where was my ambition? My drive? So, any good detectives assigned to me eventually transferred, and a conscious effort was made to give me malcontents, or worse, mediocre offi-

cers; those who should never have been in homicide in the
first place.

"I also got some of the first blacks, Hispanics and women;
many who turned out to be far superior to their white or male
counterparts. So despite myself and the department's best
efforts, our clearance rate never plunged to the point my job
was in jeopardy. Ironic, isn't it?"

He was silent, and Ariel thought he'd talked himself out.
But he gathered himself one last time.

"It not that I don't have drive. It's that I'm off the street
and out of my element. If it weren't for the pay, I'd be back
in uniform in a heartbeat. Domestic squabbles, delivering babies, hassling pushers. I gave up being in touch with people
for a few extra bucks, and I've been miserable ever since."

He turned over the two other steaks, and grew quiet, then
added:

"I'm no happy camper, Ariel, because I lost sight of why
I became a cop. Something you should keep in mind when
that day comes you're offered career advancement. Consider
that my final lesson."

Two weeks later he was dead.

"Sometimes I think I'm talking to myself," Doug said, and
Ariel was back in the present.

"Nonsense," Ariel said. "I just didn't want to interrupt."

She saw they were making better time than she thought.
They'd be on the Blue Route soon; longer in miles, but far
less traffic than the Expressway. It was time to see where
Doug stood. If they put up a united front, it might be enough
to convince McGowan that Shanicha was a danger and the
investigation should continue.

"Doug, I know you don't want to go out on a limb, but
what's your take on Shanicha as our perp?"

"Everything is circumstantial. . . ." he began, and wound
down before completing the thought.

"Did you think we'd find a smoking gun in New Canaan?"

she asked irritably. "She's a crack baby prone to emotional outbursts. She accused a teacher of molesting her; a man who later committed suicide. And one of the fires killed another of her teachers. Even if the campus suicides are just that, someone attacked Lucius. It's Shanicha. We can't let her go."

"I agree," he said, surprising her. "What about this for a game plan. *I* present McGowan with our findings. *I* suggest we continue to dig before we bring her in for questioning. You concur with me, but it's my recommendation."

"You'd do that for me?" Ariel asked, wondering why the sudden support.

"McGowan's out to get you. And to be perfectly blunt, it's your own damn fault. You fight him tooth and nail—sometimes just to irritate him—and then expect him to back you up on what is at best flimsy evidence. You've backed yourself into a corner, one of your own making.

"But we have too much on Shanicha to let go now, so let him have my head in a noose if he wants. I'm a team player. I'll survive if we're wrong."

"I could kiss you, Doug Thiery," she said.

"Pleeease!" he almost shouted in horror.

"Could, not would. Wouldn't try to seduce a married man. You should know that."

He visibly relaxed.

"Just get us downtown in one piece," he said, glancing at the speedometer. "By the way, what do I tell McGowan is our next move?"

Ariel told him she'd done some checking, and would continue later that day. There had been two suicides at the high school Shanicha attended the year before. They'd start there.

As they got back onto the Expressway, off of I-95, Ariel tried to step into Shanicha Wilkins's mind, as she'd told Chanda she would the night before.

A crack baby, prone to outbursts of rage until the middle of kindergarten. Adopted. Probably never knew her birth mother. An emotional cripple, just as *she* was a social pariah because of her mixed race.

You're full of anger, Shanicha, Ariel said to herself, but have spent years blending in to hide your fury from the outside world. You refuse to get close to anyone, for you've got secrets that can't be divulged.

Did you start the fires, Shanicha? Did you revel in the power of striking fear into an entire community? Forcing them to flee, to escape your wrath? Did you intentionally kill your teacher in the blaze? Do you hate that much?

Yes, she was certain was the answer to all her questions. You're so full of venom, Shanicha, that it's poisoned your soul.

But what of the molestation charge? It didn't quite fit. You want to blend in, but you were the instigator. Were you molested, or was being in the forefront an aberration? Perhaps an experiment? Regardless, imagine how you felt when he killed himself. A perfect crime to manipulate someone to take their life from afar. You're clever, Shanicha, and you prey on others' weaknesses.

I'm getting into your mind, girl. Not quite there, yet, but worming my way in, peeling your psyche back layer by layer by layer.

Chapter Forty-two

It was a little before noon when Chanda finished her research for Ariel. There had been several racial confrontations involving students from Southern; one in particular stood out.

And, in the area Ariel had circled, there had, likewise,

been a number of fires. One piqued Chanda's interest immediately. Four girls from Southern had perished in a blaze. Not only was it clearly arson, what made it even more reprehensible was the arsonist had purposely set two fires so escape down the stairs was impossible. The girl's mother had been found guilty, despite her repeated denials.

Chanda should have felt a sense of accomplishment. She did, but there was also a void.

—It's over.
   —Done.
      —Finished.

She'd report her findings to Ariel, and that would be the end.

—Over.
   —Done.
      — Finished.

Ariel would investigate, interview, interrogate. She would put the pieces together. She'd bring Shanicha down. Or would she? Would she have enough to crack such a tough nut?

She should go home, she thought. She'd done her part.

—Over.
   —Done.
      —Finished.

But it wasn't. Chanda decided to try to tie up one of the loose ends herself. She took a bus to Southern, entered without anyone giving her so much as a second glance and went to the library. There, she found a yearbook from the previous year. She found Denise Hughes, Tia's younger sister. She had been mentioned in a number of the many articles that followed the tragedy. She had been over at a friend's house the night of the fire.

In the yearbook was also the name of the sponsor of the school newspaper—Mr. Hitchcock.

A bell rang, and Chanda could hear the halls filling up. She had five minutes, she knew, to locate Denise Hughes. She mingled with students in the hallway, asking several if they knew where she might be. The third girl she asked, a dark-skinned black with a weave, looked her up and down, shrugged as if passing judgment . . .

—Finding her harmless.

. . . and told her she was probably in the cafeteria.

Even in a large cafeteria, Denise Hughes wasn't hard to spot. She must have had a different father than her sister, Chanda thought, because she looked nothing like the picture of Tia she'd seen in the newspaper.

She wasn't ugly, but she wouldn't be entering any beauty pageants soon. She wasn't fat, but she would be as she got older. She was big-boned and shapeless. Unlike many of the other girls who might have been poor, but made hand-me-downs or thrift-store clothes appear fashionable, Denise didn't seem to give a damn about her appearance.

She was sitting with another girl, who could have been her twin—in appearance—if Chanda didn't know better.

Chanda sat down and introduced herself.

"I'm Lorna Parker. Are you Denise Hughes?"

"What's it to you?" the girl said, trying to come off tough, Chanda thought, but unable to pull it off. Maybe, she thought, it was the slight lisp that made her tough-girl act sound so pathetic.

"Mr. Hitchcock assigned me to write an article about your sister for the school paper. Like it's something I want to do, right," Chanda said, feigning indifference, "but I got him for

English and my grades suck. It's kiss his ass or flunk the course. Tell me to get lost and I'll just make something up," she said, and shrugged.

Chanda stood up, as if to leave. She had a feeling about this girl; knew how to handle her. This was her territory, she thought; the thought itself a bit surprising. But, yes, black, white or whatever, she could relate to these kids who were her age.

"Yo!" Denise called. "No one told you to get lost. Look, my sister and I didn't hang in the same circles, and we weren't tight," she said, and shrugged. "But I don't want you making up stuff about her. What you want me to tell you?"

Chanda asked some neutral questions to which she already knew the answers, making believe she was writing down every word, when she was actually scribbling gibberish. Before Denise got bored and told her she'd had enough, Chanda got to the point.

"So all her best friends died in the fire?"

"Yeah, the girls she hung with."

"No one she'd been tight with was spared?" Chanda asked, a throwaway question to set up a more direct approach.

"She'd been tight with Shanicha Wilkins when we first got here, but they had some kind of falling out. Don't know what it was about, but once Tia became Miss Popularity, the two of them didn't see much of each other."

Chanda got the impression Denise was envious of her older sister's popularity. Not only hadn't they been close, Chanda didn't think Denise was too broken up by her sister's death. Probably hadn't mourned her long.

"Where could I find this Shanicha?" Chanda asked. "She graduate?"

"Won't find her around here," Denise answered. "Lucked out and got a scholarship to the University of Pennsylvania. It's a black thing," she said, laughing.

"No offense," she added, between giggles. "Being black

has its advantages sometimes. Quotas and that kind of shit. Got a scholarship because she was black. University needed to add some color," she said, and she and her friend cracked up again.

Chanda had what she wanted, and thought it best to split before she aroused Denise's suspicions with questions about Shanicha.

Outside, she reveled in confirming her suspicions, but in the back of her mind a voice echoed:

—It's over.
 —Done.
  —Finished.

Again she resisted the urge to admit she'd accomplished all she could. What struck her about her trip to Southern was how she'd been able to get close with her peers without arousing suspicion or stirring up distrust. Ariel might get the same answers, but she would have to do so in an adversarial confrontation. These kids despised cops. No way they'd give Shanicha up on their own volition. It would be a battle for Ariel every step of the way.

Chanda was sure Shanicha Wilkins was Ariel's suspect. The fire that killed a former friend; now a student at Penn. Ariel hadn't given her the name, but Chånda knew she'd found the girl Ariel suspected.

But, even if Ariel got students here to talk, what would she do then? Chanda thought. Confront Shanicha and try to break her? What if Shanicha toughed it out? Ariel had nothing on her, as long as Lucius remained in a coma. Even if he recovered, he might not have seen his assailant. A germ of an idea had been fermenting in Chanda's mind. To get to Shanicha, someone had to breach her defenses.

Ariel would be pissed. As a matter of fact, Ariel couldn't find out until it was too late, but Chanda thought *she* could get close to Shanicha, in a way Ariel never could. Close enough to get the girl to give herself away.

She went with her gut and took the subway to Central, first stopping at home to pick up something she'd need. And she confirmed her suspicions by looking through Lucius's notebook, which Ariel had also left in her clutter room.

She felt a twinge of guilt, going through Ariel's belongings, like a mother checking up on her errant daughter. Ariel respected *her* privacy, and she felt like a hypocrite. Yet the temptation—the need for confirmation—was too strong, and when Shanicha's name leaped out at her—*not only there, but circled*—there was no second-guessing the ethics of her behavior.

Once at Central, she went immediately to the guidance counselor's office, having rubbed her eyes to make it appear she'd been crying.

Miss Bankston looked at her crossly when she entered.

"You missed school yesterday, and come in today twenty minutes today before dismissal," she said, looking at the daily attendance sheet sent to her.

Frances Bankston was an obese woman with triple chins who had long ago come to terms with her weight problem, Chanda thought. She wore a button saying, "I'm fat. Call me portly, plump or horizontally challenged and I'll sit on you." It was a large button, for a large woman with a lot to say. When she sat, she *sat*, for getting up was a chore. But she took it in stride; even used it to her advantage when confronting teens with problems they thought insurmountable.

"Look, honey," she'd told a friend of Chanda's, "want to be in my dress for a week; hell, for an hour? You think life sucks. I've had this body for forty-two years, so don't tell me you've got problems."

Then she'd go about making you feel you were worth something; that the world couldn't get along without you.

Chanda had met with her a few times since Ariel had enrolled her at Central. Chanda had told the woman little about herself, and the counselor hadn't pressed. She was there, though, she said, when needed.

Chanda needed her now; had to convince her she needed help desperately.

The counselor stopped haranguing about Chanda's attendance when she looked up and saw Chanda's reddened eyes. She was instantly supportive, almost, but not quite, getting out of her seat to console her.

Slowly Chanda told the counselor her problem.

"I've been seeing this boy for a while now. Don't try to make me tell you his name. If you do I'm outta here."

"I'm not going to force anything out of you, child. Go on, what happened?"

"I think he . . . he raped me."

She looked confused, just as Chanda wanted.

"You think? You mean you don't know if you had intercourse?"

Chanda bit her lip—bit it *hard,* to keep from laughing.

"No. He fucked me," Chanda said, purposely using profanity to make her point. "I just don't know if it was rape."

"Did he force himself on you?" she asked.

Chanda shrugged, and looked down before answering. "We were into some heavy necking. At his house, with no one home. He wanted me to . . . you know. And his hand was. . . . My clothes were . . . Then he . . ." She burst out crying. She purposely left each sentence fragment dangling, inferring much, but actually saying very little.

"I told him to stop, I think," she said between sobs. She wanted to sound confused and make no sense whatsoever. From the look on the counselor's face, she was succeeding.

"Why don't you start at the beginning," the woman suggested.

"I can't. I feel so dirty. It was my fault. I deserved it. No one can help me. I'm sorry, I shouldn't have come here."

She got up to leave.

Miss Bankston laid a heavy hand on Chanda's arm to stop her.

"Look, Chanda, I can't let you go like this. You came to me for help. Please let me help you."

Chanda shook her head. "No matter what you say, you know me. It can never be truly confidential. Anytime I see you, it will all come rushing back. I need to talk to . . . a stranger."

"I won't betray your confidence, Chanda. You have my word."

"No!" And again, Chanda made to leave.

"Okay," Miss Bankston blurted out. "What if I can get you some professional help, away from school?"

"Well," Chanda said tentatively. She opened her purse and gave a card to the counselor. Before coming to Central, when she'd stopped off at home, she had taken the card from Ariel's clutter room. She'd seen it when Ariel had let her use her computer.

"A friend told me he helps people who've been . . . *maybe* raped."

The counselor examined the card. "He's at the University of Pennsylvania. I don't know if he'll see a high school student."

"Then I won't see anyone," she said with a pout.

The counselor rolled her eyes. "No harm trying." She placed a call, explained the situation first to a receptionist, then to the doctor himself. She made it sound like a matter of life and death. Then there were the inevitable "Uh-huhs" and "Yes, I sees," and other coded phrases when two people were speaking about a third who was present. She hung up and looked at Chanda sternly.

"I had to do some fancy talking, Chanda, but Dr. Isaacs agreed to see you on the condition you'll be totally frank with him. No beating around the bush, young lady. It's up to you. Do you really want to see him?"

Chanda nodded, then dabbed her eyes with a Kleenex.

"Okay, then." The counselor took out a card of her own, and wrote something on the back. She told Chanda where to go and said to give the card to the receptionist. "He'll see you in an hour, so you have plenty of time."

Chanda reached for the card, but the counselor withheld it.

"With your permission, I've asked Dr. Isaacs to call me so I know how you're doing."

She held up a hand as Chanda was going to speak.

"He won't divulge any specifics. I do need to know you're seeing him. I need to know you'll be able to cope with what happened. I'd be remiss if I just let you walk out the door and forgot you ever came in. Do you understand?"

"Yes, ma'am."

"Okay, then," she said with a smile. "Remember, I'm here if you need me. To talk. To cry. I'm here for you."

Chanda got out quickly, before the woman got up and hugged her.

An hour later, at three, she was in Dr. Isaacs's office. Chanda Dupree, she'd told the receptionist. She told Dr. Isaacs, between sobs, how she and her boyfriend had gone all the way. He'd wanted it. She'd thought she wanted it, but at the last minute had wanted to back out. He wouldn't listen to her, and she really didn't know if she'd wanted him to. She was confused. Felt guilty. Felt violated. But she'd enjoyed it, nevertheless.

"I feel like I'm all alone," she finally said. "I mean, I know other girls have been raped on dates, but they put up a fight. I told him no, then yes, then no again. You've probably never met anyone like me before."

"On the contrary," the diminutive doctor said. "Most of

the young women I see have had experiences very much like yours."

"I don't believe it," Chanda protested. "I'm not calling you a liar," she added hastily. "You're just trying me make me feel better. I appreciate it, but it's a lie, nevertheless."

"I assure you, Chanda, it's no lie. When you're ready, you'll meet girls like yourself in group."

"Group?"

"Sessions with several young women who've had similar experiences."

"I'd like to meet with this group. I can't believe there are others like me."

"All in good time, Chanda," he said soothingly.

"You're putting me off. There isn't any group of people like me," she said, raising her voice.

"Let's calm down, Chanda. This group, which I assure you exists, meets Tuesdays and Thursdays. What if the two of us meet again tomorrow—Friday, and then again on Monday. Do that for me, and if you still desire, you can start group on Tuesday. You have my word."

Chanda agreed. He talked a bit more, with Chanda not really listening, and when he finally finished, Dr. Isaacs walked her to the door.

"Leslie will give you appointments for tomorrow and Monday," he said. "Remember what I said. Don't be so hard on yourself. You may not be blameless, but that doesn't give anyone the right to make you do something against your will."

Once outside, Chanda realized her biggest problem was what to tell Ariel. Say something now and it would be . . .

—Over.
  —Done.
    —Finished.

She decided to wait until after group on Tuesday. She'd meet Shanicha face to face. Surely, Ariel would be more willing to let her continue then.

The question why she wanted to continue intruded into her consciousness. Partially, it was because Lucius still lay in a coma. Then too, there was helping Ariel. But deep down, she knew she was deluding herself. Those *were* reasons, but not *the* reason. Like Ariel, she'd gotten caught up in the hunt. She had no doubt Shanicha was guilty, but she didn't think Ariel could bring her down with what she had. It wasn't that she wanted Ariel to fail, but she wanted to see this through; see if she could get past Shanicha's defenses and take her to ground. The chase was intoxicating, and she refused to give it up.

No, she thought to herself, as she walked home. It wasn't . . .

—Over.
  —Done.
    —Finished.

Not by a long shot.

Chapter Forty-three

Dr. Isaacs led Ariel out the rear door of his office. It was Tuesday and he was meeting with his group in a few minutes.

Five days had passed since Ariel had been to New Canaan. She had accomplished so much, but wondered if she were any closer to turning Shanicha Wilkins.

After they'd returned from New Canaan, Doug had convinced McGowan that Shanicha Wilkins was a viable suspect, but it was too soon to bring her in and turn up the heat.

"She's going to be tough to crack," he'd told their superior. "We've got to show her we know what she's done. We do it right or we won't get it done at all."

He'd been persuasive, Ariel thought. She had sat there playing second fiddle, little more than an ornament. McGowan liked that. Liked the fact that Doug had taken the lead and Ariel was deferring to him.

To impress them, McGowan had called up Commissioner Desjardins with them present, and put the conversation on speaker phone. He told Desjardins what his detectives had uncovered.

"It's clear to me the Wilkins girl is the one we want. The problem is proving it."

"Are you saying the suicides were murders?" Desjardins asked skeptically.

"I think she attacked one of your officers," he said, not willing to commit himself further, Ariel thought. "We need time to build a case. Time to dig up more on this girl to use when we bring her in."

"So you don't think she's a danger at the moment to anyone on campus?"

"I think you should maintain a presence at her dorm. There are a lot of girls to question who were out when your officer was assaulted. Question them, their friends and roommates," McGowan suggested.

"That's not exactly the role of my officers. We compiled a list and you had a man question them. I don't want my officers becoming the enemy. As I said, it goes against everything we stand for."

McGowan rolled his eyes in exasperation at his two detectives. Doug surprised Ariel by speaking out.

"If it's all right with Sergeant McGowan, I think we should

287

continue as we have. We can drag it out for three, four, five days. You can have your men be a buffer between the students and the City police. I'll push and prod, be somewhat disagreeable. Your men calm the kids' fears after I've spoken to them. This way, you maintain your integrity and your presence at the same time."

Ariel was impressed, and apparently so was McGowan. The two men quickly agreed. The three-day moratorium—now down to two—was lifted.

Best of all, McGowan thought he'd relegated Ariel to a secondary role in the investigation. It would allow her to pursue her leads without McGowan peering over her shoulder. Ariel wouldn't be surprised if her Sergeant bought Doug a drink, after work, and laughed at the turn the case had taken.

One of the problems being a woman in the Boys' Club of the Philadelphia Police Department was being on the outside of social gatherings at cop watering holes after work. The exclusion wasn't formal, but women had to earn their way into the Club. Men were automatically accepted on the basis of their gender.

With other units, Ariel had gained acceptance and joined in, though she found it odd how much time male cops spent away from home in their off hours. It was like they had no other life outside the Department. Or maybe they had problems at home they wanted to avoid.

Ariel, on the other hand, made a conscious effort to leave her work at the office. Socializing with the guys, at times, was part of the job, but she had no desire to become a regular, even when she was wanted.

In homicide, she'd slowly gained acceptance by Donato's squad. She had purchased that sense of humor he'd suggested, and was on the giving and receiving end of any number of sophomoric pranks. Again, part of her job description, she thought, though she wondered if the men would ever grow up.

With McGowan and his clones, she was strictly on the outside.

Early on, photography had been her key to breaking the ice. Her father had an interest in photography, which Ariel shared. He had wonderful shots of the people of Israel, which somehow made the country more accessible to her. While not loquacious, he'd tell her stories about those he'd photographed.

She became a people person with a camera as well. She'd bring her Nikon to work with her and snap black and white candids, which she'd print herself in a makeshift darkroom at home.

She always made enough copies to give to all the men in each shot. It cost a few bucks, but the investment paid off a hundredfold in good will. She'd take her camera to bars her fellow officers frequented, and give both the cops and bar owner candids that brought a smile, but never humiliated anyone. She had plenty of the more embarrassing shots, but those she kept for her private album. If she ever left the force and put together a book, she'd have hell to pay . . . and so would they.

She had gotten into the club through a back door, of sorts, but in this case, the ends justified the means and she never had to sacrifice her dignity.

Cops shared information, useful techniques, and told war stories after hours. It was invaluable and, too often, female officers were excluded.

Some women had groups of their own, but they weren't the same. A lot of bitching and sexist jokes at the expense of their male counterparts. Ariel could taste the bitterness. They would rather be with the men, but here they were— women's night out.

Ariel had been a homebody in recent months, as Donato's

detectives were transferred or retired. With Chanda, now it was by choice. Still, she resented the fact she had become the butt of McGowan's ridicule after hours. Word had gotten back to her; she still had friends in the Department. Subtly, he questioned her ability, judgment; even her work ethic. And tonight, Doug, who all too often was on the outside looking in, could probably revel being one of the guys.

Ariel thought she should brief Desjardins personally, but she was beat, and anxious to see what Chanda had found.

When she got home the house was empty. Chanda had left a message on the answering machine saying she was running late, but would fill her in over supper.

A pang of loneliness shot through Ariel as the message ended. She'd become accustomed to having Chanda there when she got home. Hell, she'd become plain accustomed to Chanda being part of her life. She was both a friend and a daughter to Ariel, though she'd never admit the latter to the girl.

A shower, she thought, and maybe a short nap was in order. She left a note on the fridge, telling Chanda to wake her up when she returned.

Ariel hadn't been asleep more than twenty minutes when she felt ants dancing on her toes. She opened her eyes to Chanda, who'd been playfully tickling her. It was a little after five.

"Where you been, kiddo?" Ariel asked, stifling a yawn.

"Out doing stuff," Chanda said, not meeting Ariel's eyes. "I brought some pizza home. I want to know about your day, and you'll want to know what I found out."

Over pizza, Ariel filled Chanda in on the New Canaan trip and how she'd been taken aback by her partner's support. Told Chanda Shanicha Wilkins was her suspect. Even had a picture from her admissions application.

"I've treated him like a jerk, but maybe I've been too harsh. He is insufferable, and has his limitations, but he was a real mensch today. Kind of like . . . a partner."

"So cut him some slack," Chanda suggested, garbling her words while still chewing a slice of pizza. "With that Sarge of yours, you need every ally you can get," she finished between bites.

After dinner, Chanda told Ariel about some of the racial confrontations at Southern.

"There's one in particular you probably remember—the Peter Lyle beating."

"The one where all the 911 operators became scapegoats," Ariel said, shaking her head. "Sure I remember."

Chanda showed Ariel copies of some of the articles. "Seems to fit Shanicha's pattern. Instigating something, then sitting back and watching the fireworks."

"It's a starting point. Anything else?" Ariel asked.

"Shanicha started a fire and killed a friend she'd had a falling-out with," Chanda said.

"You know this for a fact from reading some news articles," Ariel said with a smile.

"The articles were a start. I kind of did some digging on my own," she said, not making eye contact with Ariel.

"What kind of *digging*?" Ariel asked, very attentive now and feeling a twinge of foreboding.

Chanda told her about going to Southern and meeting Denise Hughes.

"Shanicha set the mother up to take the fall, I'm sure. She was the perfect patsy. And Shanicha wouldn't just have a falling-out with a friend. She didn't get mad. She got even. Dead even."

Ariel didn't know what to say. She was proud of Chanda's initiative and the results she'd achieved, but upset Chanda had gone off on her own, without consulting her.

"Don't get me wrong, Chanda, but I'm a bit concerned. You're not Nancy Drew solving crimes without an element of real danger. You could have gotten hurt. And you could have compromised the investigation."

She knew the last sounded selfish, but it was true, and had to be said.

"Pardon me for having a mind of my own," Chanda said testily. "You weren't around . . ."

"You could have waited," Ariel interrupted.

"And you would have shot me down if I had."

"That's my prerogative. It doesn't justify your going behind my back. How can I impress upon you both the danger and the delicate nature of an investigation? What if you'd been picked up as a trespasser? What if Denise Hughes had seen through you? McGowan would chew my ass out if he knew you were doing research for me. Imagine his reaction if he got a call from the principal at Southern."

"I'm sorry. I guess I went off half-cocked, without thinking it through," Chanda said, and became quiet.

"Consider it a lesson learned," Ariel said without rancor. "Look, you did wrong, *but* you did good."

"Really?" Chanda asked.

"Really. I'm going to talk to some of Tia Hughes's neighbors and to her father," she said, picking up one of the articles. "Maybe even Tia's mother. The same with the Peter Lyle incident, and the two suicides."

"Anything I can do?" Chanda asked.

"I wish there was, but . . ."

"I know," Chanda finished. "Time for the real cops to do their thing. I understand. I'm just glad I was able to help."

Ariel couldn't put her finger on it, but it was unlike Chanda to give up so easily without a fight.

She became even more concerned when Chanda began avoiding her over the next few days. Maybe she *was* pissed at being excluded, after being of so much help. Maybe she was having a delayed reaction to Lucius's attack. Over the weekend and into Tuesday, there'd been no change in his condition.

Chanda listened, over supper several days later, as Ariel was able to implicate Shanicha in the Peter Lyle beating, but she was strangely detached. Almost bored. Unfortunately, Ariel couldn't afford to dwell on the subject.

She needed the luxury of time her partner had bought. She had leads, but there were so many doors to enter, and many false corridors before she was able to pin the blame for the death of Peter Lyle on Shanicha.

It was nothing that would stand up in court, moreover. As so often with this strange girl, Shanicha manipulated others and got her pleasure from the devastation that ensued. She was like a man who paid two whores to make love to one another. He didn't take part, but got his kicks merely watching.

Ariel was getting to know Shanicha from the inside out. Shanicha was far worse than any killer she'd apprehended; even those who'd showed no remorse. Shanicha's machinations were carefully planned out and executed. She pressed buttons and cared little—not at all, Ariel corrected herself—who was hurt in the process. But she was so fucking clever. Much of what she did wasn't illegal, and pinning anything on her was nearly impossible.

Luther Woodson, for example, was proof to Ariel of Shanicha's complicity in Peter Lyle's death, but Shanicha couldn't be legally held accountable. Woodson, two months shy of his sixteenth birthday at the time of the beating, had been the first to crack under police pressure.

As was often the case when the perps—six in this case—were caught, the DA's office made a deal with one, then went after the others with a vengeance.

The media had feasted on Peter Lyle's death and the ramifications of the 911 operators' poor response to the many calls that poured in; witnesses who saw the youth running, falling, as his friends fled, alone facing the wrath of the angry black teens.

One of the many ironies of the incident was that Peter Lyle didn't attend Southern. An honors student at Cardinal Dougherty, he'd been at 24th and Oregon only to fetch his cousin, who was getting married the next day.

The police and the DA's office needed one of the assailants to turn quickly, in order to save face. A drawn-out investigation would only compound the perception of ineptitude by the police. If they had gotten there quickly in the first place, Peter Lyle would be alive. Or so the media said.

The police had their suspects in custody, but none of those who'd dialed 911 could positively identify them. It was dark; the assailants were black; how the hell were people boarded up in their homes supposed to identify the attackers?

Luther Woodson had been offered a deal, mainly because he'd been along for the ride and was the least culpable. According to a girlfriend of one of the others, Luther simply drove the stolen car used, and kept an eye out for the police. He could be given a break without the community screaming bloody murder.

When Ariel tracked him down, he told her about the deal.

"This cop told me I was as guilty as the dudes that hit the white boy upside his head with the bats. Whoever turned first would be given immunity, and cop to a lesser charge. All the others would be charged with murder and tried as adults."

He was fidgeting the whole time, his hands in perpetual motion, his eyes looking left and right as if expecting an attack at any moment.

"All I'd done was drive the fucking car. So I ratted on them to save my ass. If it weren't me, would have been one of them. That's the way it goes down here. Nobody dimes till the shit hits the fan. And the shit was flying."

He paused to light a cigarette, his hands shaking.

"Only thing I didn't know was none of them others had been offered a deal. But how the fuck was I to know? We was all in separate rooms with cops jerking us around."

Luther was charged as a juvenile and served six months of a two-year sentence for auto theft. The others got twenty-five to life.

Once out, Luther had moved in with some relatives in West Philly.

Ariel had found him at a playground, watching a pickup basketball game. There were no referees, and precious few rules. Games were hard fought, for the winning team played until they lost. Losers might wait hours to get another game.

Luther was by himself when Ariel showed him her shield. She could see from his eyes he was a user. He'd been reluctant to talk, at first.

"How's it going, Luther?" she'd asked.

He shrugged and said nothing.

"Guess not many of your homeboys want to hang with someone who's dimed on his friends."

"What you hassling me for? Ain't done nothing."

"You're using, Luther. Parole violation. Want me to take you downtown?"

"Ain't using," he said without conviction. "What you want, lady?"

"I have a few questions about the Peter Lyle beating, Luther. Be straight with me and I'm gone. Give me attitude and you'll be back in the slammer."

"Why you busting my chops? I gave the cops everything they wanted."

"Not everything, Luther. What caused the fight at Southern the day the Lyle boy was killed?"

He looked at Ariel and shrugged. "Shit, that's ancient history."

"Well, I'm interested."

295

"Word passed that this white bitch got balled by one of the brothers who then beat her pretty bad."

"Who started the rumor?" Ariel asked.

"Don't know." He shrugged indifferently. "You know how it is. Just gets passed around. I'd tell you if I knew."

Ariel decided not to press, at least for the time being. The boy might be telling the truth.

"Why'd you go looking for trouble *after* the fight in the schoolyard?"

"Word was that Calvin had been beat up by some white boys after school."

"Calvin who?"

"Calvin Freeman. Thing was, it was bogus. He'd gone visiting someone, but we heard he was in the hospital. Nothing would have gone down if that bitch Shanicha had passed along Calvin's message."

"Shanicha who?"

"Shanicha Wilkins. Calvin told her he was going to . . . New York, that's it. Was going to New York and to make sure we knew. Bitch didn't tell us nothing. Next thing we heard, Calvin was in the hospital."

"Who told you that?"

"That I don't know. Calvin was gone and all. Nobody knew where he was. Rumors started flying. God's honest truth."

Ariel believed him. She had her link, though. Like a leaky faucet, once he started talking he couldn't be turned off. He told Ariel about the beating and its aftermath with hardly any prompting.

For corroboration, she found Calvin Freeman, who told her, yes, Shanicha was supposed to let his friends know he'd gone to New York.

When she laid it all out for Chanda that night, she'd feigned interest, but Ariel knew it wasn't genuine.

Monday was far less rewarding, initially. Ariel spun her

wheels going nowhere most of the day, trying to confirm Denise Hughes's contention that Shanicha and Tia had had a falling-out.

The four girls who would know, unfortunately, had all died in the fire that killed Tia.

Neighbors were of no help.

"Tia didn't bring no friends around at first," one woman told her. "That good-for-nothing mother of hers was forever drunk, and making a fool of her damn self. *I* wouldn't have brought friends around if I was her neither."

Ariel finally went to Southern and spoke with Denise Hughes.

"What's this interest in Tia all of a sudden?" she asked. "She dead and buried. Let her be."

Ariel ignored the girl's bitching. "What kind of falling-out did your sister and Shanicha Wilkins have?" Ariel asked, getting right to the point.

"It was about some boy. Don't ask me who. Don't know. Don't care."

"Why weren't you home the night of the fire?"

Denise looked at her real surly, then seemed resigned to being pestered until she said something the cop wanted to hear.

"Tia and her friends would bring some boys over. They didn't want me around, if you know what I mean."

"Did Tia see any one boy in particular?"

"Tia didn't confide in me. For all I know, they took turns fucking each other."

"Give me a name, Denise, and I'm outta here," Ariel said, adding an edge to her voice.

"Alonzo Richardson. I know *he* had a thing for her."

It took another hour to track him down. He was pumping gas at a station on Point Breeze, in South Philly.

"You were at Tia Hughes's house the night she died," Ariel said after she'd flashed her shield. She couldn't believe

297

none of this had come out at the trial. Tia's mother must have had a wet-behind-the-ears public defender for an attorney. According to court records, it was an innocent slumber party. No boys involved.

"How did you find out?" Alonzo asked, looking scared.

"This is another matter entirely, Alonzo. Let's just say it was common knowledge those girls weren't alone all evening."

"We left—"

"I don't care when you left. You and Tia were close, right?"

"It was an on-and-off thing with her. She was fishing. Caught me and threw me back several times."

Ariel was impressed. Alonzo was no jive-talking punk. He was tall and dark-skinned, with hair cropped close to the scalp. She wondered why he was pumping gas and asked him.

"Only way I can learn to be a mechanic. I got my high school diploma, but I didn't learn nothing. My uncle's been taking care of me the last few years. Said if I ever decided to make something of myself he'd make me a first-rate mechanic. He was true to his word. I pump gas now, but soon I'll be making decent money and one day I'll have a station of my own," he said with pride.

"Why was Shanicha Wilkins pissed at Tia?" Ariel asked after she'd made him feel at ease.

"You know about them two?" he asked, surprised.

"Enough."

"Tia had a big mouth. Wanted to impress her new friends. So she told them Shanicha had done the nasty with Jamal Walton."

"How did Shanicha react when she found out?"

"Ignored it. Never confronted Tia. Man, was Tia relieved. Knew she'd been wrong, but she couldn't take it back. A

dozen times she told me she was going to apologize to Shanicha, but she never had the nerve."

"So there were no confrontations?"

"Shanicha steered clear of Tia."

When Ariel related her day to Chanda, the young girl was
unimpressed.

"Not much more than I got in half an hour."

"That's not the point, Chanda," Ariel said. "I'm building
a foundation. Without one, a house can't stand. When I confront Shanicha, I'll know why she had it in for Tia Hughes.
Use it to show the girl I know her inside and out."

"And that's going to make Shanicha fold her tent and con-
fess?" Chanda asked sarcastically.

"There's that and Peter Lyle, and having no alibi when
Lucius was attacked. Then there's everything we dug up in
New Canaan. And tomorrow, I try to learn whether she had
any part in the two suicides at Southern last year."

"But no smoking gun." A statement, not a question.

"No smoking gun," Ariel concurred.

"Right now I'd lay odds Shanicha walks. You don't have
squat, if she's as devious as you portray her."

"Why so pessimistic? A few days ago you were going
behind my back to speak to Denise Hughes."

"Reality set in, I guess. She's going to walk unless Lucius
wakes up and can identify her. Sorry, I don't mean to depress
you, but I'm just being realistic. Don't want my hopes
dashed." She shrugged.

Ariel was worried about Chanda's attitude, but couldn't
deny she was right. If Shanicha didn't crack during an interrogation, they had nothing.

Tuesday, Ariel looked into the two suicides.

She visited Simone Cox's mother first. Things didn't look
good when a tall willowy white woman answered the door.
Ariel apologized for the intrusion, but wondered if she'd
mind answering a few questions about Simone's death. It

might help an ongoing investigation, she told her.

"A year ago I'd have shut the door in your face." The woman smiled wanly. "But through family therapy, we've learned not to bottle things up."

Samantha Cox was in her midforties, but looked younger. She had a trim figure and warm open face. Her blues eyes, however, spoke of suffering the loss of a child. Bags underneath her eyes told Ariel she still spent sleepless nights agonizing over the suicide.

She told Ariel to come in, and showed her a picture of Simone. The resemblance was striking; even the sad eyes.

"I blamed Simone's suicide on myself for months," her mother began. "She got pregnant her senior year of high school. She had planned to go to college and didn't love the baby's father. I agreed to an abortion. I knew my husband would be dead set against it, so I gave my written authorization without telling Don. He found out, and it eventually led to our separating. At least, that's how Simone viewed it. Me, too, I guess—at the time."

She had been making tea when Ariel knocked, and asked if she wanted any. Ariel politely declined.

"Where was I?" she said out loud to herself when she returned. "Yes, the separation." She sighed. "I'd had a brief affair. Don sensed it. I wasn't very good at hiding things from him. Hiding the abortion was the last straw. I should have seen the change in Simone. She blamed the breakup on letting us down by getting pregnant. Her grades plummeted and she'd come home late school nights. We had terrible arguments. She swallowed a jar of sleeping pills. Left a note asking us to get back together, as if her death would solve all our problems."

She took a sip of her tea, and shook her head at some unspoken thought.

"Funny, but Don and I reconciled—with a lot of therapy, of course. In a way she did bring us closer."

Her eyes were watering, and she wiped them with a tissue.

"I'm sorry," she went on. "It's terrible to have to lose a child to find out you still love a man you thought you'd outgrown."

"Did Simone confide in any of her friends, Mrs. Cox?" Ariel asked. She could feel the woman slipping away. Guilt and self-recrimination. She wanted to get the woman to distance herself from her daughter.

"After the abortion she hardly saw her friends. Matter of fact, she began hanging out with black students at school. Maybe it was a form of rebellion. She'd never had any black friends before."

Ariel could see Mrs. Cox didn't approve of Simone's new friends. She could almost feel her partner spying over her shoulder, urging Ariel to tell the woman she was black. Or wondering if Ariel would tell her when she was done.

"Anyone in particular. Mrs. Cox?" Ariel didn't want to bring up Shanicha's name unless she had to.

"She never had any of them over here. She knew I'd be uncomfortable."

Exasperated, Ariel brought up Shanicha's name.

Mrs. Cox shook her head, then brightened. "Wait here a minute, will you?" Before Ariel could answer, she was gone.

She returned with a diary. She turned to a page near the front and read a passage about one of her friend's parents splitting up.

She showed Ariel the page.

"See, she mentions her friend's name."

She then thumbed midway through the book and stopped.

"Here, she's talking about her boyfriend. Mentions his name, too. See." Again, she showed a page to Ariel.

Finally, she went to the end.

"When she started hanging around with blacks, she must have been embarrassed, because there are no names, only one letter; a first or last name. Here," she said, and read.

"*S* and I talk about starting over. A new life with new parents. Learning from mistakes so we don't make them again. *S* can't have me over to her house. Her mother doesn't approve of whites. Parents can be so unfair."

Mrs. Cox showed Ariel the diary with an *S* enclosed in a diamond.

"There are a few other notations with just a letter, but she mentions this *S* girl most often. Could she be the girl you're referring to?"

"It's possible, Mrs. Cox. Did your daughter have any therapy before her death?" Ariel asked, hoping she might have confided to a psychologist.

"I misread her signs of depression," her mother answered in return. "I was so into myself and my problems. She killed herself on her first attempt. There was no time for counseling for her."

She closed the diary and clutched it to her bosom.

"May I have the diary for a few days?" Ariel asked. "I promise to return it. It could be helpful in our investigation."

Mrs. Cox looked pensive, then handed the book to Ariel.

"I guess if it will help. As long as I get it back. I read it and am surprised how little I knew my daughter. If I'd only known . . ."

She was no longer talking to Ariel.

"I'll take good care of it, Mrs. Cox," Ariel said, but the woman didn't seem to notice.

Ariel let herself out. Simone's mother remained seated, her mind far away.

Alexis Stewart's mother, Suzanne, wasn't as responsive or helpful. Ariel was struck, again, that the family was white. *If* Shanicha was involved, there was a reason. It was something to ponder later.

"Forgive me for being bitter, Detective, but when Alexis killed herself the police treated *us* as being culpable. We must have been awful parents to allow something like that

302

to happen. I'll never forget their look of derision. If you insist on dredging up the past, I'll have to call our attorney."

Ariel could feel the hostility, and for the moment decided against pursuing the matter.

Once in her car, she heard a tapping on her window.

"I'm Alexis's sister, Nina," a girl said, looking furtively behind her, when Shanicha opened the window. "Mind driving around the corner? I don't want my mom to see me taking to you."

Two minutes later, Nina was telling Ariel about her sister.

"Neither of my parents have come to grips with Alexis's death. They refuse to go to a shrink, yet insist *I* get counseling," she said, rolling her eyes.

She showed Ariel a picture of the two of them. Both were a bit chubby; Alexis with her hair cut short and styled; Nina as she was now, with straight, shoulder-length brown hair.

"Alexis got knocked up and couldn't tell my parents. It would have been bad enough to admit she was sexually active, but pregnant and wanting an abortion to boot . . ." She shook her head. "No way."

Nina took out a cigarette and lit it, sneaking a look at Ariel, as if waiting for disapproval. Ariel said nothing. She wasn't a social worker. This kid obviously was dealing with her own hang-ups and feelings of guilt. She just waited the youth out.

"Alexis wouldn't have told me if I hadn't caught her shooting up one day. Heroin. She was strung out and yelling at me not to follow in her footsteps. She hoped the drugs would cause a miscarriage, but all it did was zonk her out. She finally took an intentional overdose. Left a note saying the only way she could abort and live with herself was to die with her baby and start all over."

"Did your sister know Simone Cox?"

Nina nodded. "They'd been friends. Not real close, but friends. Simone killed herself two months earlier. Alexis thought it heroic—that was her word, *heroic*. Taking control, she said."

"Did she know Shanicha Wilkins?" Ariel asked.

Nina laughed. "If my parents knew she was hanging out with a nigger, Alexis wouldn't have had to kill herself. They would have done it for her. I got nothing against blacks myself, but Mom and Dad, they blamed the decline of the neighborhood, drugs, crime and everything on them. After Alexis got pregnant she didn't bring anyone home."

"Does that mean she might have had black friends she was afraid to have over?"

Nina shrugged indifferently. "Maybe. She didn't confide in me."

"Did she keep a diary?"

Again Nina laughed. "Writing her suicide note was the *only* thing she wrote she didn't have to. She was good in math and science, but hated English with a passion. Writing was a chore and a bore to her."

Ariel thanked the girl and let her out. She had a tenuous connection; Simone and Alexis *had* been friends. Simone had begun hanging with blacks, possibly including Shanicha. Alexis had stopped bringing friends home. There was nothing tangible, but Ariel saw the hand of Shanicha in Alexis's death. In any confrontation, however, Simone and her diary were what she'd use.

It was just after five when she finally got to Dr. Isaacs's office. She wanted to bounce something off him. It was a long shot, but worth pursuing.

"Making any progress, Detective?" Isaacs asked as he ushered Ariel in. Already, he was wiping his glasses. Ariel smiled to herself. She made the doctor nervous. She didn't have to worry about him hiding anything.

"Chances are good Shanicha was involved in a suicide of a high school student last year," Ariel said, deciding to further unnerve him. "And in fourth grade, she accused a teacher of molesting her. He killed himself shortly after."

"Are you pinning that one on her as well?" he asked sarcastically.

"It got me thinking," Ariel said, avoiding a direct answer. "Hypothetically speaking, could someone like Shanicha convince another person to kill themselves?"

Isaacs pondered the question for several minutes before answering.

"Hypothetically, one person could plant the seed in another."

Ariel leaned forward. "How?"

Isaacs seemed intrigued. "Well, if it were me—and remember, I'm a trained psychologist. I've studied the subject of clinical depression among adolescents for years. Shanicha, on the other hand, has no training or reference whatsoever. But, if it were me, I'd focus on the weaknesses in the other youth. I'd harp on her inadequacies. Make her feel she'd done something so reprehensible there was no one to turn to for solace. Make her feel there was no reason to live. I'd have to hammer at her constantly and isolate her from others who might comfort her."

He paused, as if thinking he might have missed something.

"I don't see, though, how it applies here. The three girls who committed suicide were getting positive reinforcement from myself and the other girls in group."

Ariel ignored his conclusion. It seemed to her no coincidence all three girls had been in Isaacs's acquaintance-rape group-therapy sessions.

"In such a case," she went on, "someone could commit suicide without the other person being present. Right?"

"In the scenario you've presented, yes. It's highly unlikely, but possible."

"One more question, Doctor. The semester's coming to an end. What happens to the girls in your group? I mean, they aren't magically healed with the end of the semester. Turn in a paper and get a passing grade."

Isaacs laughed, seemingly now at ease.

"Very perceptive of you," he said with a smile. Then he turned serious. "These girls are still troubled. The two girls from out of town, I've referred to psychologists in their hometowns. It will remain confidential and their health plans will cover the cost."

"And Shanicha?"

"I'll continue to see her. We'll have a smaller group. Just Shanicha and a new girl starting group tonight. A high school girl who thinks *maybe* she was raped."

"Business that bad, Doctor?" Ariel asked lightheartedly. "Recruiting from the high schools?"

"Hardly. With the end of the semester, I've got a book to work on, conferences to attend and speaking engagements. This is a favor to a counselor."

Ariel thanked him and exited through the back.

She was only mildly surprised when she found Chanda not at home.

"Out doing stuff," was scribbled on a wipe-off board on the fridge. Ariel was disturbed, however. Not that Chanda was out. That was part of their agreement. Her home mustn't become a prison. She couldn't stifle her need to come and go as she pleased, as long as she was home at the agreed time and let her know if she'd be out.

Still, Ariel had gotten so used to bouncing ideas off the youth she felt, well, cheated.

Showering, Ariel remembered what had been tugging at her mind since leaving Isaacs's office. The two suicides at Southern had been white. If Shanicha were responsible, was it significant? Chanda might have an idea . . .

—But she's *out doing stuff,* fool, she said to herself.

"Think for yourself, for a change," she said aloud. In a way, it made sense. Shanicha would target strangers. She could be too easily connected with blacks she hung around. Simone and Alexis had isolated themselves from their friends. Shanicha could sneak into their life and no one would be the wiser.

For better or worse, Ariel was at the end of her leash. No sense dragging this out any further. She had her ammunition. As important, she knew Shanicha; knew what drove her, how she got her kicks. She was a psychopath. She hurt others solely for her own pleasure and felt no remorse whatsoever. She liked playing God.

Ariel would bring her in for questioning. A little friendly banter. Then a full-fledged frontal assault.

Over supper of microwaved lasagna, Ariel wondered why she'd put the confrontation off for so long. She'd wormed her way into Shanicha's mind and had proof, of sorts, to back up her allegations.

She was looking forward to the battle of wills, she told herself. It wasn't fear of failure that gnawed at her. She knew the girl was capable of murder. She had killed in New Canaan, was in great part responsible for the death of Peter Lyle, had torched Tia Hughes's house and helped drive Simone Cox and possibly Alexis Stewart to suicide.

Oddly enough, while she knew Shanicha capable of contributing to the suicides of the Penn students and the attack on Lucius, something didn't *feel* right. She looked over her notes and saw the questions she'd highlighted in blue, then yellow and green, until they were almost illegible. They plagued her as much now as they had before.

First, how did Shanicha find out about the meeting between Lucius and Isaacs?

She had no answer.

And how did Shanicha know she was a suspect as a result of the meeting?

Barry Hoffman

She had no answer, and like acid it ate away at the foundation of her suspicion that Shanicha had in fact been Lucius's assailant.

Second, why so transparent an alibi? A call to meet Isaacs at 11 P.M. Shanicha was too adept to have such a flimsy alibi. It didn't wash.

She had no answer. Her foundation crumbled further.

Third, how did Shanicha convince the three girls at The Quad to kill themselves? This was not as disturbing. Not only had Isaacs admitted the possibility, but in New Canaan, a ten-year-old Shanicha had inadvertently accomplished just that with her molestation charge.

Fourth, why only one week between the second and third suicides? Shanicha was methodical. She analyzed, planned and had the patience of Job. Angry as she was at Tia Hughes for spreading rumors about her, six weeks passed before she incinerated the girl. Shanicha was no typical serial killer who accelerated her pace because she got fewer thrills from each stalking.

Shanicha's rampage had begun no later than age ten. She struck when the spirit moved her, yet had remained invisible until Lucius tracked her down. Her only mistake had been not filing a complaint with Special Services at Penn. Had she done so, she would have never become a suspect. So, why the rush all of a sudden?

She had no answer.

"Dammit, Shanicha," she said aloud, "talk to me. Why am I so full of questions when I know you're a killer?"

She had no answer.

Chapter Forty-four

Shanicha dreamed she was trapped within the spider's web. The more she fought, the more she became entangled and immobilized.

She lay naked on her bed, legs spread wide, ensnared in a silken fiber as unyielding as cement. The spider, its forelegs perched atop her pubic hair, glared at her in triumph. It had never been so close. Its eyes were merciless, unsparing and totally devoid of compassion.

Her eyes.

The spider had her eyes.

It wormed its way into her genitals, and despite herself, Shanicha felt herself become wet; making entrance that much easier. She moaned, and her breath quickened as its legs probed in its own perverted ritual of foreplay.

She awoke as its head entered her, and she vomited on her bed. Puked over and over until dry heaves wracked her body.

Shaking, she searched her genitals for any sign of the creature.

It was a dream, she said to herself over and over.

It was real, some inner voice answered.

She found nothing, but still was not satisfied. She rushed to the lavoratory and showered, lathering her genitals again and again. She had brought a razor, and carefully shaved her pubic hair. She could feel the gentle, persistent patter of the spider's legs on the hair as she did so. Almost like someone whose leg has been amputated still has feeling in the missing limb.

She'd thought of the hair as a sort of barbed wire that would impede the creature's progress, but now saw it as a hiding place where the creature could lay in wait to pounce when ready.

Back in her room, she put her soiled bedding in a plastic bag. Washing it was unthinkable. She must destroy it, or like radar, it would leave a trail.

She paced, shivering, but refused to put on clothing. The spider had never breached her defenses so easily. She had always known when it was under her bed, and made good her escape. But it had been on her—*in her*. Another moment . . . She shuddered at the thought, and felt her stomach roil anew. Once it was within her, she knew she was doomed.

This last nightmare had been by far the worst—the culmination of almost a week of torment—but the dreams themselves had become more frequent and intense ever since she'd found the first message on her roommate's computer screen five days earlier. Then there was the second message, slid under her door Thursday morning. She'd gone to a morning class, and returned to find another envelope. She'd opened it, her hands shaking.

"Three down. Two to go. Which of us is next?"

The words echoed in her mind as she put a lit match to the paper.

She sat on her bed, and calmed herself. All right, Shanicha, she said to herself. What do we know about this cunt? She took out a scratch pad and wrote.

(1) Someone who knows I'm in group therapy.

(2) Someone who knows what goes on in group.

(3) Someone who knows I'm not there legitimately.

She drew an arrow straight down and wrote the word "link." What was the link? "Isaacs," she wrote. Not Isaacs himself, she decided. She couldn't imagine him the culprit. No, he couldn't have gotten in the dorm three times to leave his messages, and he wouldn't have someone do it for him.

Who then? Someone who had access to Isaacs's files? Maybe he had someone transcribe his notes. But who? She was sure, however, that somehow everything revolved around the shrink.

She burned the paper. She'd never kept any written record of her activities. If she got hit by a car that day, no one would have the faintest idea of all she'd done. As always, the thought gave her pause and filled her with regret, but it was the price she'd long ago agreed to pay to assure her freedom. Only fools kept tokens and journals detailing their kills. She was much more like Jack the Ripper. He struck, then vanished. A hundred years later, there was still debate as to his identity.

She felt exhausted and took a nap. Almost immediately, she dreamed of the spider again. Under her bed, beginning to climb toward her.

She awoke and looked at the clock. Ten minutes. She'd been asleep all of ten fucking minutes. No way, though, was she going to sleep again that night. Not with the creature lurking about.

No way was she going to leave her room either. She wanted to be there when the bitch struck next.

At four, her roommate brought the mail.

Another letter. She'd forgotten there was more than one way to reach her.

Her hands felt numb, like she'd stuck them in a pail of ice, as she tried to open the envelope, and it dropped. She picked it up and dropped it again. Her roommate looked at her strangely.

"Are you all right? You look—"

"Stop spying on me, bitch," she shouted back. "If I want to know how I look, I've got a mirror."

"Sorry. I was just concerned."

"Go fuck yourself and your mother, too. Give me some privacy!" she screamed at the girl.

Her roommate turned red. Mumbling under her breath, she left the room, slamming the door behind her.

Stupid. Stupid. Stupid, Shanicha thought. She'll tell everyone I'm snappish and irritable.

She finally got the envelope open and gasped at the contents.

"I did the cop for you."

"Fuck," she said aloud. The attack on the cop *wasn't* random. Someone who knew a hell of a lot about her had mugged him . . .

—Tried to kill him.

Someone who knew too much about her had lured her out of the dorm so she'd be a suspect. Someone. Someone. *Someone*. But who? And why?

She decided to skip group that night. She knew she looked a wreck. She didn't want to be around anyone. Didn't want Isaacs's probing eyes taking her apart.

She lay down to rest for just a bit. Woke up to the spider almost touching the mattress. She had to stifle a scream. Looked at the clock.

She'd dozed for fifteen minutes.

Forty-five minutes later, the phone rang. It's her, Shanicha thought. "I'll know your voice, you bitch," she said aloud. "You stupid little bitch." And grabbed the receiver, only to be greeted by Dr. Isaacs.

"Shanicha?" he asked, and when she answered he went on. "You missed group today. I was concerned. Are you all right?"

His voice grated on her like sandpaper. *No you asshole. I'm not all right. Someone is trying to drive me insane,* she wanted to say.

"I'm okay. Just had bad stomach cramps. My period and all. A bit worse today than usual."

312

She'd long ago learned the mention of her period embarrassed males no end. In high school, she'd once had her period for an entire month. Or so she'd said to different people when it suited her needs.

Got out of a couple of tests she wasn't prepared to take. And that was when she was going with Jamal Fucking Walton. He'd begun to get more and more aggressive. Tired of playing with her tits, he'd gone South one night.

"Jamal, honey. I'm on my period."

His hand disappeared from her Southern region *real* fast. She almost laughed out loud. Much better, she thought, than claiming a headache. And much more effective.

". . . on Tuesday, then."

"What?" Shanicha asked. She hadn't been listening to Isaacs.

"I hope you feel better, I said. See you on Tuesday. Okay?"

"Sure. Tuesday. I'll be fine by then."

Friday, she'd finally fallen asleep at three in the morning. Felt triumph that she didn't have another nightmare until 5:30. Then slept until her roommate's clock had awakened her at six.

Feeling lethargic, she hadn't gone to class Friday. Went to lunch, but had no appetite. Had been bitchy with some of her so-called friends.

"You're depressed," she could imagine Isaacs's admonishing her. He'd told her both in private and at group the telltale signs, and she was exhibiting far too many.

It was her dreams, though, that upset her the most. The damned spider inching closer every time she fell asleep; depriving her of the rest she desperately needed.

There were no messages Friday, Saturday and Sunday. She should have felt more at ease, but knew intuitively the girl was toying with her. She almost wanted to receive a message, as each led her closer to her tormentor. And she'd had so little sleep, her fear of the arachnid so intense.

Monday morning, her roommate unceremoniously dropped an envelope on her after she awoke at six. They hadn't been speaking since Shanicha's outburst Thursday. Her roommate spent less and less time in the room. She'd come in just before it was time to go to bed, and leave soon after she awoke. Where she spent her day, Shanicha couldn't care less. It was good to have her out of her hair. Silence was best between them now, lest she bite the poor girl's head off for some innocuous remark.

Shanicha had spent most of the weekend in her room; studying, she told her friends who asked where she'd been the few times she ventured out. In truth, she spent hours in the sho.er, trying to rid herself of the odor of fear that permeated her. Worse, when she slept and was visited by the spider, she could sense a change in its mood. The spider was . . .

—Getting impatient.
—Getting pissed.

And she'd be back in the shower.

Now she was greeted with another envelope. She opened it, like it was a letter bomb, and saw the words.

"I'm Back!"

"You goddamn fucking bitch," she said aloud, now that her roommate had left. "I'm going to hurt you. Hurt you bad. Make you sorry you ever thought of fucking with me."

Nothing more until the next day. Then a letter in her mailbox. Two pieces of paper this time. On the first:

"The cop's out of the coma."

On the second, just one word. "Psych."

This girl was playing her, Shanicha thought. She almost felt jealous. She was good . . .

Born Bad

—As good as her.

Just to make certain, Shanicha called the hospital, pretending to be a reporter.

"No change," she was told curtly. "We've told you people, there would be no further statement until he's regained consciousness."

"Psych," the second page had said. She was supposed to get freaked out over the first page, and feel the fool after reading the second. *And she had.*

She'd gone to one class Tuesday, but felt herself dozing off and slipped out. It wouldn't do to wake up from a nightmare in the middle of class.

Back in her room, she had finally given into exhaustion and gone to sleep at noon, setting the alarm for four. She couldn't miss group. Had to keep up pretenses. Couldn't arouse suspicions.

She had awakened at three-thirty to the spider worming its way into her genitals for the first time. She'd showered and shaved her pubic hair, preparing herself for the creature's onslaught the next time she slept. Three and a half hours had been the most she had slept at one time since the dreams had begun. But with more sleep, the spider had finally reached her.

Getting dressed for group, she decided to tell the others about the spider. If she got a message relating to the spider that night or the next morning, she'd know it was one of the other girls in group. If the spider was mentioned after, she'd know it was probably someone with access to Isaacs's files.

It was time, she decided, to go on the offensive.

She was surprised to find a new girl in group. Isaacs introduced her and explained she was a high school student who'd been date-raped. The girl looked a bit awestruck, sitting there with a bunch of college students. As Isaacs began the session, Shanicha interrupted.

"I've been having a dream lately. I'd like to share, if it's all right?" she asked.

Isaacs looked dumbfounded. Shanicha, after all, had said very little in group. He appeared quite eager to hear her dream.

Shanicha started at the beginning, when she and her sister were in the cave. She felt both invigorated and sapped as the words poured out. Oddly, she held nothing back; except, of course, what had prompted the latest dreams. She described in detail its latest assault.

She was met with stunned silence. Because of what she said, and because it was cool-as-a-cucumber Shanicha who had said it. Finally, Dr. Isaacs asked a question.

"Have you been under any undue stress lately. Aside from the aftereffects of the rape, of course?"

Let me tell you about stress, Doctor, she thought to herself, but instead hesitated, as if concentrating.

"Well, finals are coming up, and that's always stressful," she said with a laugh, and the other girls joined her.

"And Sharon, Jocelyn and Monique have spooked me. Everyone seems so on edge at the dorms; like waiting to see who'll be next. So, yes, I guess I've been under more stress lately."

The other two college girls talked about stress they'd been feeling of late, and Shanicha withdrew into her shell.

She'd shown her hand and would wait to see how it played out. And, while she hated to admit it, she felt a lot better having purged the secret from her system. It was like a dash of Drano to her psyche. The spider was there. She hadn't flushed it from her mind, but she no longer felt at the edge of the precipice.

Soon she became absorbed in the new girl's story. Chanda told what happened to her, and the doubts and guilt that assaulted her daily as she tried to cope with what had occurred.

"I just don't know if I was raped, is what I've been telling Dr. Isaacs. I mean, while saying stop, a part of me wanted him to continue. Was I sending mixed signals? And if so, can I fairly accuse him of rape?"

She seemed both stunned and relieved when the other two girls said they, too, had felt the same ambivalence after their rapes. Shanicha joined in, if only to keep up pretenses. Again, she wondered why Isaacs refused to delve into the possibility that they might well have acquiesced, might have wanted to be screwed, and their protests had rung hollow; not only to the boy, but themselves.

Shanicha thought the new girl particularly brittle; someone she would feast on like a vampire if she were targeting another victim. When the session ended, Isaacs asked Shanicha and the new girl to remain for a moment.

He led Shanicha to his office, closed the door and smiled broadly.

"I think we've had a breakthrough, Shanicha. I'd like to discuss this with you in private, possibly tomorrow. If the dreams continue, I may want to prescribe medication temporarily. Sleep deprivation will only fuel your depression and strengthen the hold the nightmares have on you."

Shanicha reluctantly agreed. She needed a private session with Isaacs like she needed a third tit. But she knew she had to play the charade out. And who knows, maybe medication would banish the spider until she caught the bitch toying with her.

"Let's go out to reception and see when I have a free hour."

At the receptionist's desk, the student intern, Jessica, unsuccessfully attempted to locate Dr. Isaacs's calendar.

"I saw it a while ago . . . I think," she blurted out, haphazardly moving piles and causing further chaos.

"Dammit," he said to no one in particular, but Jessica acted as if she'd been slapped in the face.

317

"This place has gone to hell since Mia changed her hours," he said. "Breaking in someone new this late in the semester . . ." He stopped and shook his head sadly.

"Look, Jessica, I can see my presence is only making matters worse. Just find the calendar and bring it to me."

He turned to Shanicha.

"I'm sorry, Shanicha. It's a mess here, as you can see. Can you call the office tomorrow morning? I'm sure my calendar will have been found by then," he said, giving Jessica a look that could kill.

"Sure," Shanicha said, but her mind was elsewhere. On Mia. Good old Mia. That cunt Mia who was toying with her. Gotcha! she thought. An idea began to coalesce almost immediately. An idea involving the new girl. So fragile. So malleable.

She left, but waited outside . . .

—To pounce.

. . . to put her plan into motion. A few minutes later, the youth exited, almost colliding with Shanicha.

"What did the good doctor want?" Shanicha asked.

"To schedule an appointment to go over what was discussed in group. Only his receptionist can't find his calendar. He also wanted to get a quick read on my reaction to the group."

"Your reaction?" Shanicha asked.

"If I felt comfortable. If I wanted to continue."

"Do you?"

"Of course. I mean, I'd felt so alone before. Dr. Isaacs said others felt the same way I did, but they were only words. Actually meeting others who not only shared my experience, but my feelings was . . . I don't know—refreshing." She scrunched up her face. "That's not the right word."

"Comforting," Shanicha said.

"Yeah, that's it. Comforting."

"Look, Chanda, I know we just met, but would you like to talk some more? Not right now. I've got a prior obligation. But"—she checked her watch—"if you can come by at, say, eight, I could show you what a campus dorm is like and we could chat."

"Really? I wouldn't be intruding?" Chanda asked.

"Not at all."

"Cool. I can't stay out too late, but an hour or so . . . I'd really like that."

Shanicha told her where The Quad was located.

"I'll meet you out front. You can't get in without proper ID, unless someone escorts you. See you at eight, then."

That gave Shanicha an hour and a half to confront Mia.

Plenty of time.

It had been staring her right in the face all along. But, then, Mia was so . . . *forgettable*. She remembered Mia from New Canaan. Mia with Mr. Randolph had given her the idea that led to her first kill. She'd been surprised Mia, along with other girls, had echoed her charges of molestation with ones of their own. But it was so like Mia. Trying to belong, yet never quite pulling it off.

And then she'd bumped into her at Southern years later. Actually, Mia had come up to her.

"Remember me?"

Shanicha had looked at the white girl without recognition.

"New Canaan. Mr. Randolph."

Shanicha remembered the face then, but not the name.

Later, she had used Mia in what turned out to be one of her greatest triumphs: the beating of Peter Lyle. Mia had come into school bruised and Shanicha had started the rumor that Mia had had sex with, then been beaten by, a black boy. It was odd that Mia had never denied it. Thinking about it now, she guessed Mia liked being the focus of attention, even for something humiliating.

And Mia had been a student receptionist at Dr. Isaacs's office. Now that Shanicha thought about it, Mia had been there *every* time she went to group until Officer Friendly had been mugged. There, yet all but invisible. That was Mia, Shanicha thought. There, yet all but invisible.

For her plan to succeed, though, she'd have to act pissed, but hold back the fury that now threatened to overwhelm her. She wanted to gouge the cunt's eyes out and make her swallow them. Yet a part of her still admired the girl. Were it not for good old Dr. Isaacs, Mia might have eluded her for days. Shanicha doubted if she could have kept the spider at bay that long.

Fifteen minutes later, she knocked on Mia's door. When Mia opened it, her eyes widened.

Shanicha smiled. Confirmation. Caught you with your pants down, didn't I? she thought to herself.

"How's tricks, Mia?" Shanicha said, entering the room, Mia backing up with every step Shanicha took toward her. There was no one else in the room.

Mia remained silent, sweat beginning to glisten on her forehead.

"Any notes you want to give me *personally*?" Shanicha asked.

"I don't know what you mean," Mia finally said with effort.

Shanicha recited the notes from memory.

"Your mistake, Mia, was being too damn slick. The message on the computer was a nice touch, but committing yourself to paper . . ." Shanicha shook her head disapprovingly. "A bad move. 'I did the cop for you.' A confession, for God's sake. I've kept all your notes," Shanicha lied, "and they're incriminating."

"Who said I typed the notes?" Mia asked.

"Who said they were typed?" Shanicha responded. "But you're right; the notes incriminate someone, but not necessarily you. What fingers you are your work hours at Psych Services. *Always* there during our group sessions. Then, right after the cop is attacked, you change your schedule. Not smart at all. A call to that geek who's been questioning us is all that's needed and you're fucked."

Shanicha paused to let it sink in, then continued.

"So let's stop playing games. I was responsible for Sharon and Jocelyn's suicides. I admit it, just as I did in Mr. Randolph and Peter Lyle—with your help. Your turn."

Mia no longer looked petrified.

"Monique was mine," she said proudly. "And the campus cop."

"Why the cop?" Shanicha asked. It had gnawed at her.

"He was closing in on you, but if you were cleared, he would have come after me next."

"How do you know?"

"I bugged Isaacs's office and the conference room he used for group," Mia said with a smile.

"Son of a bitch," Shanicha said. "You're good. Did the campus cop get a look at you?"

"No. I'm home free," she said with a wide smile.

"Unless I bring them your notes and point them to your work schedule."

Mia's smile disappeared.

"Why were you toying with me? I don't understand that at all," Shanicha said.

"I was jealous, I guess. And angry. No one thinks I'm capable of what I've done, because I'm invisible. A nonentity. To even you. I remember the first time we met at Southern. You didn't have any idea who I was. Don't think I didn't know. It hurt. It was only six years and I no longer existed. Hell, my parents wouldn't know me except I'm their damned daughter. I wanted your respect. Taunting you seemed to be the only way. You know, turning the tables. Making you the prey."

She paused.

"Are you going to turn me in?" she asked, looking down, as if not wanting Shanicha to see her fear.

"And open myself up to scrutiny? I think not."

"But you're going to get revenge." It wasn't a question.

"Not necessarily," Shanicha said with a smile. "Look Mia, I admire what you did. You had me going a while. I underestimated you. *Everyone's* underestimated you. We're two peas in the same pod. Sometimes it's a bitch doing what I do and not being able to share it with anyone. We could be, I don't know—maybe partners."

"Partners?" Mia asked, aghast. "You and me?" she said, pointing to Shanicha, then herself.

"*If* you prove yourself worthy."

"What do you mean?" Mia asked warily.

"Well, I did catch you at your little game. Hmmm. We need a sort of initiation; something to prove your worth."

Mia was silent.

Shanicha outlined her proposition. She told her about Chanda.

"You convince her to take a plunge and we'll be like Thelma and Louise; only no one will know we've done anything, so we can't get caught. The girl's fragile. She already feels isolated. She has no one to turn to. You befriend her. You did it with Monique, and she was a tough cookie. Prove to me you can do it again."

"What if I say no?" Mia asked.

Shanicha shrugged. "We'd each go our separate ways. *But* you'd always be looking over your shoulder. Always wondering if I'd someday come after you. Imagine, ten years from now, we bump into one another and you're wondering if it's payback time."

She paused to let it sink in, then offered the carrot again.

"But, as partners, we'd each have too much to lose diming on the other. And the plans we could hatch—it would be so cool. Your choice. Chanda's coming over at eight, so make your decision now."

Mia visibly slumped. "All right," she said finally. "I've got nothing to lose, I guess. What do you want me to do?"

"Just stay put until about 8:20, then come to my room. I'll leave you alone after a while. I don't expect you to break her in one night, but I suggest you get her back tomorrow and every day until she cracks. Convince her, if you can, to stop going to see Isaacs. Not tonight, but plant the seed he'll dime on her to her parents or whoever referred her to him. You've worked for him. Tell her he's broken confidences before. He's even spoken to you about patients. Use me as an example. Tell her he told you my spider story. You went into work tomorrow, and he tells you one of his group patients thinks she's being stalked by a spider. She won't confide in him again."

Mia smiled. "We'll make a good team, won't we?"

"Classic, Mia. Classic."

Shanicha met Chanda outside The Quad at eight, took her to her room, and the two of them chatted a while. Chanda wanted to talk about how miserable she felt; how life sucked. She even mentioned ending it, once.

Shanicha, though, turned the conversation away from gloom and doom at every opportunity. She talked about campus life, being on her own, and the good friends she'd met. She saw Chanda appeared confused at her positive frame of mind. Shanicha assumed it was because she'd been raped so recently. Chanda probably thought her own rape should have been the only thing on Shanicha's mind.

Eight-twenty, on the dot, there was a knock on the door. Shanicha greeted Mia like a long-lost friend and introduced her to Chanda.

"Mia knows all about what happened to me. She's been a pillar of strength. A good listener."

"Are you a patient of Dr. Isaacs?" Mia asked.

Chanda looked at Shanicha.

"Go on, girl. Anything you say stays right here."

Chanda reluctantly told her story, speaking to Mia, but stealing glances at Shanicha, who was frankly bored and didn't try to hide it.

Three quarters through, Shanicha yawned. "I'm going to take a shower while you two get acquainted. It's been a bitch of a day," she said, looking at Mia, "and I'm bushed. I hope you don't mind, Chanda."

Shanicha thought Chanda looked distraught.

"Don't go pouting. We'll see a lot of each other, girl. Tomorrow, if you want. Mia can meet you outside The Quad. Okay?"

Chanda shrugged and Shanicha, again, thought she looked bewildered; like a fish out of water.

Poor girl, she thought to herself. Abandoned again. She almost pitied the kid. So fragile. So malleable. She almost regretted having given her to Mia. *She* could have had such fun with her. But now was not the time.

At nine, when she returned to her room, they were gone and her roommate had returned. Shanicha left, without saying a word, and went to Mia's room.

She was alone.

"So tell me, how did it go?"

Mia shrugged. "She seemed upset you left. We talked for fifteen, maybe twenty minutes, and then she had to go. She'll be back tomorrow, though."

"Bring her to your room after you meet her," Shanicha suggested. "Tell her I'm on my period and feeling like shit. Let her call me, if she wants, and I'll sound like death warmed over. Then spin your web."

"She seems like one troubled kid," Mia said.

"She is. That's why I chose her. Troubled. Isolated. Abandoned—even by me." Shanicha snapped her fingers. "Abandoned by even me. Tomorrow, it's my period. Thursday, it'll be another excuse. Wean her away from Isaacs with his betrayal, and with me losing interest in her, all she has is you. It's perfect."

"You're good," Mia said with obvious admiration.

"No, girl, I'm *bad*." And they both laughed.

In her room, Shanicha finally wound down. What a day, she thought. From the depths of depression—as close to breaking as she'd ever been—to being on top of the world again.

She thought of the spider. "You had your chance," she whispered, though she knew she could have yelled at the top of her lungs without her roommate stirring.

"You blew it. You'll never get that close again."

She caressed herself, and soon that part of her she loved so much was making love to her. Her other self had been buried deep within since the day Mia had left the message on the computer screen. Now she was hungry, and Shanicha gave herself over to her.

Afterward she slept.

Dreamlessly.

Chapter Forty-five

Ariel was pissed; seething, though she loathed herself for acting like a . . . a worried mother. She didn't know why, except a sixth sense told her something was amiss. More than once she stared at the note on the fridge, "Out doing stuff," and wondered just what the hell Chanda was doing.

Then at seven, Chanda had called and been evasive as hell;

out of character with the girl of recent days—all too reminiscent of the youth who'd fought her tooth and nail when she'd first arrived. Chanda promised to be in no later than 9:30 or ten, and Ariel bit her tongue, not wanting to nag that there was school the next day and Chanda shouldn't be out as late as she pleased.

Still, she worried. Chanda had been so detached lately. So . . . lost. And cynical. She as much as told Ariel that Shanicha was home free, and Ariel wondered how she should— *could*—respond when deep within she felt the youth was probably right.

If she guaranteed she'd break Shanicha and failed to deliver, her credibility would be shot. Chanda might well have to learn the hard lesson of life that good doesn't always prevail. The guilty too often got to walk. But, she thought, hadn't that been a lesson the girl had lived with much of her life? It didn't make sense she would be so upset by something she knew to be a fact of life.

Ariel hoped Chanda wasn't doing anything foolish. She had never thought Chanda used drugs, but maybe she'd been naive. Chanda had been on the street for God knows how long. The temptation had always been there. And she'd said she'd experimented. With life kicking Chanda in the ass once again, Ariel fervently hoped the youth wasn't looking for solace in coke, crack or heroin.

The two of them needed to talk. Maybe they both needed to get away for a day. Yes, Ariel decided. After her interrogation with Shanicha—regardless of what transpired— she'd take Chanda down to the Jersey shore. While it wasn't balmy, Ariel loved the beach this time of year. The wind sometimes chilled her, and going into the water was out of the question. But it was so peaceful. So open. So free.

At Ocean City, even Atlantic City, the beaches were nearly deserted. *Her* beach. *Their* beach, she corrected herself. No screaming kids, or teens kicking sand in their face. No senior citizens taking up their space. No tourists intruding.

A day at the shore. She needed to get away and clear her mind. And she was sure Chanda would respond as well.

Her thoughts were interrupted by the phone. Best not be Chanda, she thought, telling her she wouldn't be home till midnight. "Out doing stuff."

It was Commissioner Desjardins.

"Sorry to bother you at home, Detective," he said, "but it looks like Shanicha might be on the prowl again. The girl's not even from the University. We've got a picture of Shanicha accompanying her into The Quad. I thought you might—"

"I'll be right down," she interrupted. "Maybe we can use it tomorrow," she said, thanked him and hung up.

She had phoned him earlier and told him she was bringing Shanicha in for questioning the next day. He'd sounded more than a little relieved. Even if she wasn't charged, Desjardins's thinking probably was she would walk the straight and narrow the rest of the semester.

Ariel wrote a note for Chanda. She was sorely tempted to say, "Out doing stuff," but wouldn't stoop to such juvenile behavior. Halfway through, Chanda walked in.

"You and I have a lot to talk about, girl," she said, more harshly than she wished. "Not now, though. Looks like Shanicha may have a new target and Commissioner Desjardins has a photo."

"She does," Chanda said softly. "It's me."

She turned from Ariel.

"I'm sorry you had to find out this way. I was going to tell you everything tonight."

Ariel was rocked. "Back up a minute. What exactly do you mean 'It's me'?"

"I'm Shanicha's target. Then again, maybe not. But I sorta set myself up."

"Stop being so fucking cryptic," Ariel blurted out. "Start

Barry Hoffman

at the beginning and tell me what you've done."

Chanda did, omitting nothing.

"What were you thinking of?" Ariel asked when she'd finished. "After what you'd done at Southern, and our talk."

"I was thinking you were getting nowhere with Shanicha. I was thinking she had nothing at all to worry about. I was thinking of Lucius in a coma, dying or a vegetable, and Shanicha walking free. I was thinking someone had to do something. Someone who could get close to her."

"The girl's a murderer, Chanda."

"And that knowledge is my protection, can't you see? That and the fact I'm not depressed or suicidal."

"What about the position it puts me in?" Ariel asked with an edge to her voice. "Did you stop, even for a moment, to consider what my boss will do when he finds out the girl staying with me made herself a target without telling anyone? He might even think I put you up to it, for God's sake."

"It was my decision. How can he blame you?"

"He can blame me, all right. You're my responsibility and it looks like I'm letting you run roughshod. I opened the door by letting you do research. That's supposed to be *my* job, not that of a teenager. If I were in his place, I'd be perfectly justified in firing my ass. That's just what he'll do, too."

"But that's not fair."

"Chanda, *life isn't fair*. You're not some naive child. You've been kicked around and shit upon. You know McGowan is out to get me. Jesus, Chanda, what were you thinking?" she asked, totally exasperated.

"I'm sorry," Chanda said weakly.

"No, you're not," Ariel shot back. "You wanted Shanicha. You thought only you could drag her to her knees. Wind back the clock and you'd do it again. The worst thing is, you did it behind my back."

"Come off it," Chanda shot back, showing emotion for the first time. "If I told you, you would have gone along, right?"

Ariel was silent.

"See? I may have been wrong. No, *was* wrong, but I've gotten close to the girl. You've got her fear of spiders now that you can use against her. But no way I would have gotten near Dr. Isaacs's group if I'd confided in you. You just admitted as much. Your boss would never condone it."

"We're going in circles," Ariel said finally. "I've got to call Desjardins and tell him I'll be a while. No matter what, Chanda, I'm fucked. I'm sorry, but that's reality."

A few minutes later, Ariel was back.

"Let's see if we can salvage something; maybe a little damage control. You said you got close to Shanicha and then she left you with this girl Mia."

"It was like the two of them were close, but it felt . . . I don't know. Staged. Mia walks in and a few minutes later Shanicha is gone."

"Maybe you came on too strong to Shanicha? Aroused her suspicions. You're not trained in this, after all." Ariel couldn't help the parting shot, though she knew it counter-productive.

"Can we stop the recriminations, Ariel? I feel like shit already. Felt like I was betraying you since Thursday. Couldn't you sense it?"

"Damn right. You had me worried sick." She laughed. "I thought you might have been on drugs. But I never suspected . . ." She didn't finish, just shook her head.

"Could this Mia girl be involved? You know, an accomplice?" Chanda asked.

"No way," Ariel said emphatically. "Shanicha works alone. That's what makes her so dangerous. Always has. She's too smart to involve someone else. If she shares her secret with only herself, no one can rat on her. This is a new wrinkle. One I don't like."

"What are you going to do?"

"Commit suicide." She saw the look on Chanda's face,

Barry Hoffman

and immediately regretted her flip remark. "I was kidding."

"Funny," Chanda said. "*Not*."

"I'm going to level with Desjardins. Then we'll call McGowan and it'll be in his hands. While I'm gone, you might want to check the help-wanted ads for me."

Before Chanda could respond, Ariel added, "My droll sense of humor again. I may end up walking a beat, but I won't lose my job. Get some rest. It may be a long night."

Ariel had a feeling this investigation was getting away from her; propelled with a life of its own, rather than she controlling it.

Her meeting with Desjardins, and then with Desjardins and McGowan, only reinforced her perception. It hadn't turned out as expected; hadn't eased her misgivings one bit.

Desjardins had been noncommittal, but supportive, when she met with him alone. She didn't know if he'd go out on a limb for her; or if, in fact, it would make any difference. But he didn't blame her.

"You should feel proud, in a way," he'd said. "You reached this kid who hasn't had anyone care for her in years. She wasn't going behind your back to be sneaky. She defied you to help; help *you*."

McGowan, for his part, listened without expression. Ariel was surprised he didn't lay her out right then and there in front of Desjardins. It would be like him; showing a colleague who was in charge.

Finally, after asking a number of questions, McGowan asked Ariel to wait outside.

"We have some decisions to make. Don't go far," he told her.

Twenty minutes later she was summoned . . .

—To the principal's office, she thought to herself.

330

McGowan took the lead.

"While I can't condone what you've allowed to occur, we've decided Chanda has provided us with an opportunity we can't ignore. She's gotten close to the Wilkins girl. I know you want to bring her in now, but at best it's a long shot. Maybe, just maybe, Shanicha Wilkins will incriminate herself. Anyway, we've decided it's worth a try."

"You want to continue?" Ariel asked incredulously.

"In the best of worlds, we'd use a *trained* undercover officer," McGowan said. "But we don't have that luxury, do we?" he asked with a bitter edge to his voice.

"She'll be in danger," Ariel protested. She felt panic rising within her. This wasn't at all what she'd expected. She'd thought her job in homicide was in jeopardy. Never had she considered they might want Chanda to continue to see Shanicha. She felt overwhelmed; totally unprepared for this turn of events.

"I wish you'd reconsider," she told them.

"She'll be wired," Desjardins interjected, for the first time. "So the danger is minimal. I'll have officers in The Quad. At the first sign of trouble, they move in."

Ariel didn't know what to say.

"Bottom line," McGowan said, "it's up to Chanda. Sometimes you've got to seize the initiative. This is one of those times."

They spent the next fifteen minutes going over details, with Ariel's mind sluggishly following along. Then she was dismissed. She was told to bring Chanda in the next day for a briefing.

When Ariel got home, Chanda was asleep on the couch. Ariel decided against waking her up, but she must have only been dozing. She was fully awake before Ariel could put a blanket over her.

"Still have a job?" Chanda asked tentatively.

"We both do, if you insist."

331

Barry Hoffman

Ariel explained to the bewildered youth.

"They don't want me to stop?" Chanda asked, as if unable to comprehend what Ariel had told her.

"They see an opportunity," Ariel said bitterly. "See, I've put my ass in a sling. If something goes wrong, McGowan has me for a fall guy. As for Desjardins, my feeling is he didn't think we had enough to break Shanicha. I don't think he's thrilled, but he's letting McGowan make the call."

"Holy shit," Chanda said. "Holy shit."

"Look, Chanda," Ariel said, trying to keep emotion out of her voice. "It's your decision, but think it through. You won't be on your own. McGowan will set the agenda; call the shots. You're to entrap Shanicha; get her to say something that can hang her. What I'm saying is you'll be on a short leash. You'll do what you're told, knowing you're just a puppet on a string. There'll be no more freelancing."

"Ariel, if there's a chance I can help put her away, I've got to do it," Chanda said. "I'll play by the rules. No more going it alone. I know your job is on the line if I fuck up. It's my fault you're in this position, so no way I'm going to stab you in the back . . . again."

"You didn't stab me in the back. No one—least of all me—is confident we can take Shanicha down with an interrogation. We know she's guilty, but have nothing on her. You, Desjardins, McGowan all shared my doubts. Just happens you acted on them. It's your call. Just keep in mind, I don't like it. Not one bit. As much as I want Shanicha, your safety means much more to me. It's up to you."

"Then let's do it."

Ariel shook her head and smiled weakly. "No way I was going to convince you otherwise, was there?"

Chanda returned the smile. "No way."

"Then we'll do it my way. Tonight you learn self-preservation. I'm not leaving it up to Desjardins to protect you."

332

"I've been on the street. I can handle myself."

"My way or the highway," Ariel insisted. "What you learned on the street isn't near enough. I learned how to protect myself before I joined the force, and still was not as prepared as I should have been."

"All right. You're the boss."

Ariel made a call, and half an hour later, she was introducing her Uncle Murray to Chanda. He must be seventy now, Ariel thought when she saw him, but was still powerfully built and far fitter than men half his age.

He worked with Chanda for three hours. Thirty minutes, then a break, another thirty, then another, and so on. His message was simple. "Be alert. Look for signs," he said, "of aggression. No matter what I teach you, if you're taken by surprise, you've lost." Then it was defend, injure and maim, with emphasis on the latter.

"You're going to war, young lady. Do you think you can inflict serious—even deadly—damage to another human being without thinking of the consequences?"

Chanda nodded affirmatively. "I want to live through this."

"The object, then, is not to think at all. Just react," he told her.

When he was finished, he looked at Ariel.

"Work with her as long as she's involved," he said. "There's only so much you can teach in so short a period of time, but she's more prepared than when I walked in."

Ariel kissed the man on the cheek as he made to leave. "How can I thank you?" she asked.

"No need. You turned out good, that is reward enough for me." He looked at Chanda. "She's you with an attitude." He stroked Ariel cheek once. "You know, your father is very proud of you. He may not say so in as many words, but he is. He feels very badly that he and your mother caused you pain. You could be a basket case. Instead, you're a self-assured, directed woman. You've done good. He *should* be proud. So am I. Have faith in that one," he said, looking at Chanda ever so briefly. "She'll do you proud."

He left, and Ariel and Chanda were alone.

"It's time to get some sleep," Ariel said. "Tomorrow, you'll get a cram course on how to handle Shanicha. Promise me one thing, though. Don't be Miss Know-it-all. Anytime you're confused, you tell them or me to press rewind and we start over. Forget your pride."

"Thank you, Ariel," Chanda said.

"For what?"

"For having faith in me."

"Did I have a choice?" Ariel asked.

"You could have told them to fuck themselves. Would have, but you had faith. I won't let you down."

Chapter Forty-six

Shanicha could feel the rush return. Often her elaborate schemes would begin on a whim, or even inadvertently. She seldom knew where one would take her. She'd have to constantly improvise, revise, step back and attack from another direction. That, though, was where the satisfaction lay: in overcoming adversity. If everything was mapped out beforehand, she would long ago have lost interest. She welcomed the risk, opened her arms to the challenge, reveled in every inexplicable twist and turn. Then, as all unfolded, she watched in awe.

The fires in New Canaan. Begun by chance. Who could have foreseen so many people fleeing because of her; generations in the making just up and abandoning hearth and home? So many lives changed irrevocably due to her.

Seeing Mia with Mr. Randolph had initiated a string of events that not only saw the man kill himself, but other girls unexpectedly join her in the allegations. So inexplicable. So satisfying.

And Peter Lyle. She didn't even know the boy, yet was responsible for his death. Even better, the entire city had been in an uproar over the response of the 911 operators. If she *had* planned it, it couldn't have turned out better.

And now, she was manipulating Mia to commit murder. Well, at least push Chanda over the edge, she thought. Even here, though, she was allowing events to dictate what would follow.

Yes, it was better than sex. More powerful than any drug. More welcome than winning the fucking lottery. This was a life she was controlling; the ultimate rush.

Chanda and Mia had spent an hour and a half together Wednesday night. In Mia's room. Shanicha could almost feel Chanda's disappointment when they spoke over the phone.

"I can come by your room and cheer you up," she'd sputtered.

"You don't want to be anywhere near me when I'm on my period, Chanda. *I* don't want to be near me." She laughed weakly. "There are times I've seen a doctor, the cramps are so bad. The medication prescribed makes me loggy. Maybe tomorrow . . ." She let it hang for a few seconds. "After group."

"I won't be going to group," Chanda said.

"Oh?"

"I thought Dr. Isaacs would keep everything confidential, but . . . well, he told Mia about your dream."

"The bastard," Shanicha said, then groaned in mock pain.

"I don't know what to do. If I don't go and see him, he'll call my counselor and she'll call my mother. Then I'll be fucked. I was hoping you . . . but if you're not up to it . . ." She didn't finish the thought.

Shanicha smiled to herself. "I'm sorry, Chanda. I wish I could. Look, talk to Mia. She'll come up with something. She's done it for me a lot. Gotta go now. Take care." She hung up before Chanda could pin her down about Thursday.

Thursday, when she returned from group, she just hadn't answered her phone. It had been a spur-of-the-moment decision. The best kind. She could have blamed it on her period, but she wanted Chanda to feel totally forsaken. No Isaacs. No Shanicha. Only Mia and only one way out.

She'd answered the phone an hour and a half later, at 8:30, picking it up and saying nothing. If it was Chanda, she'd hang up. Shanicha almost wished it had been her. Imagine how she would have felt.

But it was Mia. Tomorrow, she thought as Mia filled her in, she'd pick up the phone and hang up without uttering a word. Not worthy of Shanicha's attention; that's how Chanda would feel.

"She's utterly miserable. Listless," Mia said. "Talks about *you*. Asks about *you*. Where is Shanicha? Why won't Shanicha talk to me? I think she has a crush on you," she said, and laughed.

"It's like pulling teeth to get her to open up to me," she continued. "But she always does," Mia said proudly. "She's close, but we need something—"

"To push her over the edge," Shanicha finished for her. Then, as always, unbidden, it came to her.

"Tomorrow, Mia, you tell her you overheard Isaacs talking. He's going to call her high school counselor. Then it's just like dominoes. She *can't* go home with her mother knowing what she did. And she can't stay here. You've planted the seed. Only one option left."

"It's not too early?" Mia asked.

Shanicha smiled to herself. Mia was playing for time. She

didn't know if she could do it in just one more day. No, Mia, she thought, *I* control the timetable. Play by my rules or not at all.

"It's got to be tomorrow. If she goes home, you'll never see her again. If she doesn't go home, her mother will report her missing. You want the cops breathing down your neck? No, we're out of options."

"I'll push hard, but I can't—"

"You *will*. Make it happen, Mia. Tomorrow. Our bond will be sealed with her death. *You* have no other options."

Mia was silent.

"Do it in Monique's room," Shanicha said, the thought coming out of nowhere.

"Say what?"

"It's vacant. Just think of the mood you can create. Monique had the stones to go out her way. To a better life, blah-blah, blah-blah, blah-blah. You still have the key you told me about?"

"Sure."

"This is how we play it. You give me the key, and while Chanda's with you, I'll unlock the door."

"Why? I don't understand."

"Think, Mia. Why would you have the key to Monique's room? Details. It's all in the details. You don't want Chanda thinking about how you got the key. You want her totally focused on her hopelessness."

"I see," Mia said listlessly.

"You tell her the room hasn't been locked since Monique died. The lock's broken, or some shit you come up with. I shouldn't have to think of *everything*. Then lay it on thick."

In the end, Mia agreed, as Shanicha knew she would. The question now was, could Mia convince Chanda to jump? Shanicha felt a rush as she pondered the answer. She didn't know what would happen; just as it should be. The pressure, though, was squarely on Mia. It would be gnawing at the girl all night; weighing on her all of Friday. Her stomach would be doing belly flops. She'd have the trots; journeying back and forth to the bathroom all day long.

Damn, Shanicha thought, it felt good to be in control—*as always*.

Chapter Forty-seven

They sat in Commissioner Desjardins's office Friday morning, wondering what the fuck had gone wrong.

"It's like Shanicha's avoiding me," Chanda told them.

"Could you have tipped her off in some way?" McGowan asked. Just as Ariel had said, the man was always trying to lay blame at the feet of others, Chanda thought as he spoke.

"How? I only spoke with her once, by phone, since the first night. *You've* heard it all. I didn't drive her away."

Chanda didn't feel she had to be tactful with this asshole. She wouldn't jeopardize Ariel, but she wouldn't be bullied or cowered by him either. After all, they wanted her; needed her.

"What I don't get," Desjardins said, "is why this girl Mia keeps suggesting you commit suicide. Could she be in cahoots with the Wilkins girl?"

It was the same question Chanda had asked Ariel. As before, Ariel dismissed it out of hand.

"Shanicha works alone. Look, Commissioner, I've gotten into this girl's head. She doesn't leave behind any loose ends. Mia would be a monstrous loose end."

"Maybe we have the wrong suspect?" Desjardins threw out for debate.

"No!" Ariel said vehemently. "Shanicha may be using this girl somehow, but she's running the show."

It was so frustrating, Chanda thought to herself. Maybe it was because she wasn't suicidal, but Mia seemed so transparent. She had all the subtlely of a train wreck. Could someone actually succumb to such nonsense? She could tell the others in the room had doubts she could continue with this farce.

"Should we fold our tent?" Desjardins asked. "Bring the Wilkins girl in for questioning and hope for the best."

"No." This time it was Chanda protesting, though she did so respectfully. "What if I tell Mia I'm going back to group? I know you've spoken to Dr. Isaacs, but Shanicha doesn't know. She's playing with my mind. Trying to stress me out. Remember, I've got no one to turn to. If Shanicha doesn't show, I'll call her. Tell her I must return to group or Isaacs will report me to my high school counselor. We push her."

"Go on the offensive," Ariel cut in. "Force her hand." Ariel closed her eyes for a moment. "It's sound thinking, but it puts Chanda in imminent danger if Shanicha panics."

"Chanda's wired," McGowan said dismissively. "There's no imminent danger." He paused. "Of course, it's up to Chanda."

Chanda saw Ariel give McGowan a looked of unveiled hostility. McGowan had laid down a challenge, and Ariel knew Chanda wouldn't back down. Yes, the man was manipulative, but Chanda could see no real danger.

Moreover, Ariel had honed her defensive skills daily. Besides repeating her Uncle Murray's lessons until Chanda considered herself a killing machine, Ariel had also taught her police defensive tactics. Then, to test her, Ariel had come at her when she least expected. Once, in the shower, Chanda had almost wet herself, but used her soap-slicked body to get away from Ariel.

Then, while shopping, Ariel had attacked and Chanda had

almost lost it. It was so embarrassing. But she'd reacted instead of thinking, and soon they were at a standoff. Ariel had flashed her shield to a harried store manager, and they'd gone home.

"Are you going to come at me in my sleep?" Chanda had asked as they left, all eyes on them—on *her,* she thought.

"I would, but you need all the rest you can get."

She *was* prepared. She was focused. And she didn't want to give up yet. For if she did, her involvement would end.

—Over.
 —Done.
  —Finished.

"I want to go on," Chanda said confidently. "Push her a bit. Act, not react. If she doesn't bite . . ." She shrugged, and didn't finish the thought.

"All right, then," McGowan said, getting up. Chanda had seen him do this before. It signaled all discussion was over. A decision was made, one he endorsed. He was a bastard, Chanda thought. If something happened to her, he'd grieve all of two minutes. Tops. And then pin the blame on Ariel. It was a lesson, she thought, you don't learn in school. She didn't ever want to be a fraud like this man. She was, though, and before she confronted Shanicha that night, she'd have to remove that blemish.

Ariel was back working the four-to-midnight shift, so the two of them went home after the meeting. After breakfast, as they were washing dishes, Chanda broke a long silence.

"Ariel, I've been living a lie since we first met."

"Is now the time for self-introspection?" Ariel asked. "You've got to maintain focus. It can wait."

"No, it can't. I've seen the fraud your boss is. In a way I'm no different. How can I maintain focus when I'm living a lie?"

"All right," Ariel said, sounding resigned. "Let's to go the living room and you can tell me what you want to get off your chest."

Sitting on the couch, looking at Ariel, Chanda wondered if this was such a good idea. What if Ariel felt so deceived she didn't want Chanda to stay any longer? Could she take another rejection? Fuck it, she said to herself, and began.

"I was never raped by my father. Didn't run away because I cut him and his friend."

Ariel closed her eyes for a moment. "You just got pissed at your parents and ran away then," she said.

Chanda could hear the sadness in her voice.

"Not at all," Chanda replied, "but not as bad as I made it sound. I was desperate. So I exaggerated a bit. Well, a lot. My father abandoned my mother and me when I was an infant. She was fourteen, he sixteen when she got pregnant. He ran away, rather than get married."

One of her fingers made little curls with her hair. It was a nervous habit. She hadn't done it since the night at the police station when she'd met Ariel.

"My mother wasn't too pleased having to tend after a rug rat. That more or less became my name. 'Come here, rug rat,' 'Look at the mess you've made, rug rat,' 'I've got no life, rug rat, with you underfoot.' We stayed with my grandmother, but she insisted my mother take responsibility for me. No partying. No staying out late, hanging with her friends. Go to school and come home and take care of the rug rat."

Chanda paused.

"Look, I need a cup of coffee. You want some?"

Ariel said no, and Chanda made some instant. Back on the couch, she went on.

"Mom ran away when I was five. I got up one day and she was gone. No note. No calls. No letters. Nothing. My grandmother took care of me until she got cancer. From the time I was eight, I was taking care of her. She wasn't an invalid, at first, but my life revolved around school and coming home to be a mother to my grandmother. Eventually, when I was eleven, I was literally taking care of her physical needs. She died the day I turned twelve."

She took a sip of coffee, and remained silent for a few moments.

"I was in an orphanage for about six months, and then in a series of foster homes. There was no overt abuse, but I was no model foster child, so I never stayed with any family long."

"What do you mean, you were no model foster child?" Ariel asked, breaking her silence.

"I'd had no life. My grandmother dying was like being released from prison. I had a lot of catching up to do. I experimented with drugs, sex and booze. Cut school and stayed out when I should have been home. Hung with kids most parents would frown upon."

"What was missing?" Ariel asked. "I mean, the girl you're talking about and the girl talking to me are two different people."

"Love, I guess. I've been thinking a lot about it lately. My foster parents ranged from indifferent to understanding, but maybe because I was no toddler, I never got any love. And, as I got older, rules were set that had to be adhered to, or it was back to the orphanage."

She got up and began pacing, thinking to herself she was mimicking Ariel when she was keyed up.

"See, I was never viewed as a person. I was always made to feel I should be grateful they were willing to take care of me. It was like I was a rug rat all over again. That's all they did; took care of my physical needs. Food, clothes, shelter. You weren't like that, which is why I'm not the person I was."

"Why were you on the street when the pimp was stabbed?"

342

"I finally ran away. Living on the streets was preferable to the prison foster homes had become."

"Was the guy who got knifed your pimp?"

"No. You gotta understand, I was maturing. I'd stopped experimenting with drugs. The street kids I hung with were decent people. We ran scams, usually for food and a place to crash. It's easy, especially for a girl. The old 'I live in the suburbs, my purse was stolen' ploy worked real well. I made eighty dollars one day. At worst, I'd pull in at least ten."

"But you did nothing overtly criminal?" Ariel asked, her voice accusatory.

Chanda knew she couldn't bullshit Ariel now. If she was going to make this work, it had to include warts and all.

"I did a lot of shoplifting. And a bit of hooking. Not often," she added quickly. "I swear. And I always made sure the dude wore a condom. I knew about AIDS, but I was more scared of becoming pregnant. Then I'd be no better than my mom."

"How old are you, Chanda?" Ariel asked, her voice clearly weary.

Chanda looked away. Jesus, she thought, this is difficult.

"Fifteen. I'll be sixteen in two months. You've got me enrolled as a junior in high school. I should be a sophomore. Makes no difference, though. I was good in school, and even at Central, half the kids in my class are several years behind academically."

"Jesus, Chanda, *fifteen*," Ariel said. "I've got a goddamn minor working a police sting operation."

"Age is just a number, Ariel. It's one thing I've learned. I'm fifteen going on twenty. Some kids in my class are seventeen, but when it comes to life skills they're infants. I've lived on my own. I got my diploma on the streets. Pisses the hell out of me I need a piece of paper to validate what I've learned so I can get a job."

343

Barry Hoffman

Chanda fell silent, deep in thought. Ariel, for her part, did nothing to break the silence.

"You want me to clear out?" Chanda asked. "After we get Shanicha?"

"For someone so smart you're pretty stupid," Ariel replied. "No, I don't want you to clear out. I've come to know, trust and rely . . . shit, love—yes, *love* the girl who's been staying with me. You lied to me to get in, but you haven't been living a lie since. Why would I boot you out?"

Before Chanda could answer, Ariel went on.

"Doesn't mean I'm not pissed. Not disappointed. I do have to digest the new—*the real*—Chanda. But it's history. And I'm glad you finally trusted me enough to tell me about the real you. You want to stay, you've got a home. Nothing changes. *Except* from now on it's all on the up and up. No secrets. No cons. No going behind my back. You got a problem, tell me as a friend whatever it is. I'm not going to boot you out. Now, any other bombshells?"

"That's it," Chanda said quietly.

"Then let's practice our takedowns. No distractions tonight. Focus and vigilance."

"Thanks, Ariel," Chanda said before they began. "I mean, no one's ever fucking cared for me. . . ." And she burst out crying.

Ariel hugged her, teary-eyed herself. "I care for you, Chanda. More than you'll ever know."

Taking a shower after a two-hour workout, Chanda, for the first time, felt at home. Layers of despair and suspicions washed off with soap. She knew Ariel cared for her, but in the back of her mind, this had been just another rest stop on a road to nowhere. Now, though, she thought she might have a home.

Shit, she thought to herself—*a home*. What the hell is a home? I've never had one. It's the people that make the home, she decided. A place you could bare your soul and not feel the fool. A place you could fuck up and still be loved. A place you felt needed. Yes, she thought; most of all, a place you felt needed.

Her life had been a mess, but maybe all wasn't lost. She hadn't lied to Ariel, but life on the streets had been no picnic. She had omitted the constant hassling from cops, junkies and other street people who would steal the clothes off your back without giving it a second thought.

She had glamorized it for Ariel. There was just so much she could tell her at one time. Some other time, though, she'd tell her about life on the streets. It *had* taught her a lot. She hadn't been shitting Ariel about that. At times she felt old beyond her years, especially at school. It was one thing to plan a hypothetical budget for yourself, like she had to do in class, another altogether to live it. She had, and while her lifestyle wasn't to be envied, she'd survived.

No way, she thought, Shanicha was going to slip something by her. Shanicha thought she was hot shit, but the girl had never encountered anyone like her before.

At seven o'clock, Chanda was back in Mia's room. The girl looked nervous, Chanda thought.

"You speak to Shanicha today?" Chanda asked before Mia could launch into one of her tirades.

"No. Try calling her, if you want."

Chanda called, and this time the phone was answered.

"Shanicha? This is Chanda. I was wondering—"

Shanicha hung up without saying a word. Chanda called again; swore she could hear someone breathing on the other end, who then hang up after Chanda identified herself. What the fuck? she thought. Plan A was out the window. Maybe she should go by Shanicha's room. Her thought was cut short by Mia.

"I hate to lay this on you, but I overheard Dr. Isaacs talking today. He said he was going to call your high school counselor. He was really concerned and felt he had a responsibility to do so."

What the hell is this? Chanda thought. She knew it was a lie, since Isaacs had been briefed. Ariel had already spoken to her high school counselor, telling her Chanda had confided in her. Why the lie?

"What are you going to do, Chanda?"

"What do you mean," she said, flustered.

"Can you go home with your mother knowing about . . . your being sexually active?"

"Shit, no," Chanda said, playing her part. Stop thinking, she decided, and just go with the flow.

"And won't your mother go to the cops if you don't go home?"

"I hadn't thought of that," Chanda said. Mia was leading up to something, but what was it? And she was jumpy. Wouldn't make eye contact with her. Something was definitely up. Mia was trying to put her in a corner; leaving her no option except what? Suicide? Somehow Shanicha was involved. The girl had hung up on her. It had been intentional. Focus, she thought. Don't think. Just remain vigilant.

"Wanna go to the room where the last girl jumped?" Mia asked.

No, Chanda thought. It's perverse. But she remembered she was supposed to be suicidal. So she shrugged, indifferently, and let Mia drag her along. Act miserable, she thought. But watch your back.

If Mia wanted to depress her, she succeeded. The door to Monique Dysart's room was unlocked and the room was bare: a bed with no sheets, empty desk and bureau with nothing on top. No sign at all anyone had occupied the room. Chanda felt sorry for the girl who'd jumped. It was bad enough to die, she thought, but to be totally forgotten . . . She didn't know what to expect. A plaque wasn't appropriate. Who the hell would want to live in a room where another girl had committed suicide? But it was so barren. Dust had settled on the desk. She saw cobwebs in a corner. The air smelled stale.

Mia led her to the window and opened it.

"She did it here. Some people think it's a cop-out, but I admire her. She took control of her life. And, like I told you, it's not an end; just a new beginning. A better life, a fresh start. Imagine starting over, but with the knowledge of your past life. So many mistakes you could avoid."

She droned on, and Chanda tuned her out. What a crock of shit, she thought. She looked outside and saw trees in bloom, not the gloom and doom Mia prattled on about. Her life had been pretty hollow only months before, yet she'd never seriously thought of suicide.

She vividly remembered giving a john a blow job for a measly ten dollars. He hadn't want to wear a condom, but she'd insisted. He'd been abusive. He'd wear a goddamn condom, he said, but he slapped her around a bit to show who was boss.

It had been the low point for her. As she roamed the streets afterwards, she'd thought of stepping in front of an oncoming SEPTA bus—for all of ten seconds. Yeah, it had been degrading—and a bit frightening, but with the money she could take in a film and get something to eat. Tomorrow . . .

She'd been so lost in her own thoughts, she didn't see, until it was too late, Mia raising her hand with something white and flat; wasn't aware until it was too late that Mia was going to strike her with it. She instinctively stepped back, but not quickly enough to elude her completely. Mia didn't hit her flush, but the whack to the side of her head sent her reeling to the floor. She saw Mia raise her hand to strike again.

Move your feet, she said to herself. Use them to knock her off balance.

Before she could, Shanicha appeared from nowhere, grabbed Mia's hand, and the two of them grappled. Chanda's vision was blurred, but she saw a look of surprise on Mia's face, then terror as she lost her balance and fell out the window. One minute there; the next gone.

"Are you all right?" Shanicha was asking her. Shanicha began talking to her, but Chanda could only focus on fragments.

". . . passing by . . ."

". . . door open."

". . . Mia hitting you . . ."

"You're bleeding!"

". . . call the campus police."

But she didn't have to. Two officers burst into the room. Chanda saw a look of surprise on Shanicha's face, then a smile; just for an instant. She even thought Shanicha winked at her as one of the cops led her out of the room.

A few minutes later, Chanda was lying on what had been Monique Dysart's bed when Ariel entered. She looked pale, haggard and upset.

"Desjardins had to literally hold me back," she sputtered. "Shanicha couldn't see me. When I heard you were hurt . . ." Ariel began, then closed her eyes and visibly shuddered.

"I'm all right," Chanda told her, and smiled weakly. She still felt woozy, but a paramedic had arrived and stopped the bleeding. He'd said something about taking her to the hospital. She had protested, but he'd insisted. Then Ariel had come in.

"You're going to the hospital anyway," Ariel said with a weak smile of her own. "Don't want you passing out on me at home."

Home, Chanda thought. Yes, she wanted to go home. To Ariel's—no, to *their* home.

"Mia tried to kill me," she finally said. "I don't understand."

"Me neither," Ariel said with exasperation. "She hit you with a piece of marble that goes with a calendar. Could have killed you if it wasn't for Shanicha." She shook her head, as if she still couldn't comprehend the chain of events.

"It was Mia all the time?" Chanda said.

"I still refuse to believe it, but she did try to hit you. She would have thrown you out the window and it would have looked like a suicide."

"Where is Mia?" Chanda said, trying to get up, but falling back as a wave a nausea hit.

"Before I tell you, do you remember anything?"

"She's dead, isn't she." It was a statement. She told Ariel what happened.

"Shanicha didn't push her?" Ariel asked.

"Mia was raising the piece of marble, turned halfway towards me and halfway toward Shanicha. Shanicha grabbed her hand. She lost her balance . . . I think."

"What a mess," Ariel said. "It doesn't add up. Who the fuck is this Mia anyway?"

Chanda smiled. "If I know you, you'll have answers pretty soon."

Another paramedic arrived with a stretcher. Ariel grudgingly moved aside.

"I'm going to wrap things up here. Doug's here, and I'll have him do the grunge work," she said with a wink. "So, I'll be at the hospital in a little while."

"What about Shanicha?" Chanda asked.

"For now, Doug's taking a statement. I'm not done with her yet, not by a long shot. But I'm not going to turn up the heat on her just now. There are too many loose ends that need tying up."

As she was carried out, it occurred to Chanda that her part in all this had come to an end.

—Over.
  —Done.
    —Finished.

For once, she was glad.

Barry Hoffman

Chapter Forty-eight

Shanicha hadn't known until the two campus cops had burst in—too soon. *Much too soon.* And then, she'd looked into Chanda's eyes. She'd been set up, but it had all gone awry— *for them.* They must be pissing in their pants, she thought. They'd used the girl to entrap her, and she'd saved the bitch's life. Instead of a felon, she was a fucking hero. And she didn't have to worry about Mia anymore.

It hadn't gone exactly as planned, but that made it all the sweeter.

With the key Mia had given her, Shanicha had unlocked the door to Monique's room. She'd then returned the key to Mia's room; put it in her desk, under some papers, where she wouldn't spot it that night. Then she'd hid in Monique's closet and listened as the two girls entered.

She had heard Mia's spiel. Would Chanda go for it? She opened the door a crack, so she could see. Mia was going on, but Chanda wasn't responding. There was nothing subtle about Mia, but her explanation did seem to put Chanda in a corner. At a crossroads. Which path would she choose?

Shanicha felt her breath quicken. Make a decision, Chanda, she almost said aloud. But Mia made it for her. She saw Mia take something out of her back pocket and strike Chanda with it.

What the fuck? she thought. How could she expect to get away with . . .

There was no time to think it through, though. Instinc-

350

tively, she knew she had to stop Mia. Knew if she did nothing, it would place her in danger. She bolted from the closet and grabbed Mia's hand before it struck Chanda again.

And without thinking, she saw an opportunity and seized it. Mia was off balance. A push, a gentle push, was all that was needed. Mia must have read her thoughts, because her look of confusion turned to horror. And then she was gone. Out of Shanicha's life.

She hadn't planned to kill Mia—at least not then. She knew she'd have to get rid of Mia, of course, but an appropriate way would have to come with time.

She laughed aloud, lying in her bed, her roommate long ago asleep. *Mia would have to go at the appropriate time.* Well, the appropriate time had come and Mia had gone. And with Mia, all Shanicha's problems. The police would hone in on Mia. Her work schedule; being out of The Quad when Officer Friendly was attacked; her conversations with Chanda and subsequent attack on the girl.

Shanicha wondered if Mia had hit Monique, too. Mia had told her Monique was *hers,* but did Monique go willingly or had Mia given her a little help? Fascinating, but really no concern of hers . . . any longer.

The irony of it all enveloped Shanicha like a cozy blanket. The campus cops had entered too soon; giving themselves away. Mia had barely hit the concrete and they were through the door. She had looked at Chanda and known instantly. It had *all* been a fucking trap to ensnare *her*. Unknowingly, she had made Mia a suspect, and all that followed made perfect sense. Chanda hadn't jumped because she wasn't suicidal. Her whole story had been a sham. A crock. It was almost too good to be true. Shanicha couldn't have orchestrated it any better, which was its beauty.

Her other self beckoned, and Shanicha let her out. Long and slow tonight, she thought as she played with her nipples.

For the first time she had dodged a bullet. Actually been under suspicion, and now *they* had egg on their faces.

So good.

Her hand snaked down toward her genitals. She felt the bristles of her pubic hair. She hadn't shaved since she'd learned Mia had set her up. No need to. And now, there would be no dreams of spiders. No need for vigilance. Once again, she was in control.

Her other self began to probe.

So good.

Chapter Forty-nine

Ariel had decided to backtrack once again. Only this time, Mia was her quarry, not Shanicha. Somehow Mia fit into this puzzle. Somehow Mia and Shanicha were intertwined. Ariel was determined to learn how.

McGowan and Desjardins had been bewildered, but at the same time elated, at the turn of events. As far as they were concerned, Mia had attacked Lucius, possibly killed three coeds, and had attempted to kill Chanda. A public-relations coup. In their mind, Shanicha was in the clear. A hero, no less, though the girl herself wanted no part of it.

Typical Shanicha, Ariel thought. Killed yet another, then disappeared into the crowd. The girl had style, Ariel had to admit. But Ariel fully intended for her to fall.

She decided to start at the beginning. She called Tyler Conover in New Canaan.

"Was just about to ring you myself," he said with a laugh when his secretary patched her through. "I heard about the ruckus last night at the University, and it rang a bell."

Ariel had Mia's admissions records to Penn. She was originally from New Canaan. Ariel felt a fool for not checking earlier. As soon as Shanicha had become evasive and foisted Chanda on the other girl, when Mia had gone on about suicide being the only answer, Ariel knew something was amiss. She hadn't looked into Mia's background, though, because she couldn't admit to herself someone other than Shanicha was responsible for the assault on Lucius. Fucking lousy police work, she thought to herself. Tunnel vision.

She was so certain Shanicha was responsible she had blinded herself to other possibilities. Like Chanda, she had lost her focus. It could have cost Chanda her life.

Even now, with the proverbial smoking gun of Mia's attempt to murder Chanda, in the back of Ariel's mind this smacked of Shanicha's handiwork. Mia was just another victim; albeit a not-so-innocent victim. Shanicha, as always, had been the puppet master.

"You're aware, of course," Conover said, cutting in on Ariel's thoughts, "that Shanicha made the initial allegation against Tom Randolph. But he was pushed over the edge by the *other* girls who came forward with similar stories. One of these girls was Mia Fahey."

"I suspected as much," Ariel responded when Conover had paused to let the news sink in. "But not until *after* Mia's death."

"Something else, which may or may not be relevant," he said, then paused.

"Go ahead, Sheriff. I've already made an ass of myself to my superior. I'll take anything, no matter how inconsequential it may appear."

"Well, before calling you, I checked out the dates folks left New Canaan after Sarah Turner's death. Shanicha went with the first bunch. Remember, I told you there was one other fire?"

"The one that burned itself out on its own."

"Right. Well, Mia was still in town. Her family moved out a few days later. No other fires after. Puts a new spin on our arsonist, wouldn't you say?"

Ariel concurred, thanked him, then rang off. She sat at her desk, a legal pad in front of her with a chart of how Shanicha and Mia had come into contact with one another.

Shanicha made the initial allegations against her teacher. Mia followed suit. As for the fires, her take—which she hadn't run by Conover—was the last fire might well have been set by Mia. The *only* one she set. And a dud at that.

A picture of Mia Fahey was beginning to emerge. *A wanna-be*. Wanted to be like Shanicha. But always followed Shanicha's lead.

Ariel went to West Philly to test her theory out.

Luther Woodson was there, almost expecting her.

"Thought you might be around," he said with a swagger. He was high, Ariel knew. She had the feeling he'd soon be dead from an inadvertent or intentional overdose. For a young man with Luther's enemies, he took no precautions. Moving to West Philly offered no protection, especially if he kept a high profile. Warning him would do no good, though. Maybe he knew his days were numbered. Maybe he didn't care.

"Heard on the tube that bitch Mia What's-her-name bit the dust last night. Saw your friend Shanicha did the deed, trying to save some young thing."

"So why do I care?" Ariel asked. Let him confirm your premise, she told herself. Don't say it for him.

. "The white girl that got fucked and beat up; the one that caused all the shit that led to that white boy's dying, you know? Well, that girl was Mia. Whatcha think of that?" he asked with a big glassy-eyed smile.

"Mia told you she had sex with a black kid?" Ariel asked for clarification.

"Mia didn't say shit. Never did. *Shanicha* told some friends who told some friends and, you know, soon everybody knew."

"Last time we spoke, you told me you didn't know who started the rumor. Why now?"

"You was hassling me then. Didn't want to give you squat."

"Now you want something, right?"

"No, man. Don't want jack. Just heard about Mia being offed by Shanicha and, shit, why clam up now? Shanicha a fucking hero. Saved a little white girl's ass by killing Mia." He shook his head.

"She's no saint," he went on. "Fucked me up good. If she'd told us about Calvin, that white boy would still be alive."

He started laughing. Ariel turned to go.

"Ain't what I told you worth something? Token of appreciation, you know?"

"No Luther, you don't want jack, so no token of my appreciation's going up your nose."

"Shit, lady. You a bitch, just like Shanicha."

Ariel wheeled around and got into the youth's face.

"I got something for you, Luther. I wouldn't stay in one place too long if I were you. Some of your friends doing serious time probably want to see you hurt—*hurt bad*. You hang around here, the next time I come out, it might be to escort you to the morgue, if you get my drift."

"Got no enemies. Everyone knows I was set up," he said, but he wasn't convincing. "Everyone knows I wouldn't dime on my homeboys."

Ariel gave up. Luther was still talking to himself as she was leaving.

Next was a trip to the coroner's office.

"Oh, oh," Ed Cawley said when she entered. "You don't

like the Fahey autopsy. Want me to see if she was poisoned *before* she fell," he said with a wink.

"Smart aleck," she said, but she was smiling. "No, but I do have the same question from before. Monique Dysart."

"I'm supposed to remember all my stiffs?" he asked.

"The University of Pennsylvania coed who jumped," she said, hoping to jog his memory. "The one from the same fucking room as the Fahey girl. I asked—"

"If the wound to the back of the head could have been someone playing baseball with her noggin," he finished with another wink.

"More or less," Ariel said. "Though I didn't wax poetic like you," she added with a smile.

Cawley went to a table and brought back the piece of marble Mia had used to hit Chanda.

"You're asking, Detective, my professional opinion if the deceased might have clobbered the Dysart girl with this miniature two-by-four?"

"As an expert, of course," Ariel said, playing the medical examiner's game.

"Haven't the foggiest," he said, deflating her. "Won't say she couldn't have," he added. "Remember, there was no blood on that wound. The only hair samples forensics found on this baby was the girl she took a swing at last night."

He paused, looking at the weapon.

"On the other hand, it is entirely possible Miss Dysart was given some assistance with this. Unofficially, of course. And, Detective, I checked the photos of the first two girls. No similar head wounds. No head wounds at all on the girl who hung herself."

On the way back to homicide, Ariel remembered what bothered her about Monique Dysart's death. Only one week after Jocelyn Rhea. No suicide note, though Lucius said she was a prolific writer. It hadn't seemed like Shanicha's handiwork. Too soon after the second.

Almost a botched job. Like the last fire in New Canaan. Like jumping aboard ship *after* Shanicha had accused the teacher of molesting her. To Ariel it looked like another Shanicha wanna-be. Mia somehow knew Shanicha had convinced two girls to kill themselves, and had wanted a piece of the action. Only, Monique might not have been cooperative. Similar head wounds on Monique and Chanda. None on the two others—Shanicha's victims.

How, though, would Mia know Shanicha was responsible for the other two suicides? Something tugged at her mind. Something Isaacs had told her. No, she remembered, something on the tape Isaacs had played; his conversation with Lucius.

Ariel found what she wanted on the tape. Lucius was honing in on Shanicha, but unlike her, he hadn't discounted the possibility another was responsible. Mia had been a receptionist at Psych Services. Been there the night Lucius had spoken to Isaacs. But the girl hadn't been here the two times she'd visited the shrink.

She called Isaacs and asked if he could help her get Mia's work schedule.

"I still can't believe she was responsible for all this mayhem," he said after telling her he'd fax what she wanted within the hour.

Everyone, Ariel thought, was giving Mia all the credit: three murders and the attacks on Lucius and Chanda. It was truly ironic—Mia had achieved in death the notoriety she had never gotten while alive.

More significantly, Ariel decided she could use this against Shanicha, for she wasn't about to abandon her plan to interrogate the girl. All the credit going to Mia. None to Shanicha.

And the assault on Lucius fit Mia's pattern. A botched job. She'd meant to kill Lucius. For the moment, she'd failed.

Ariel also thought she knew the motive for the attack on Lucius. Doug had found bugging devices in Mia's room, along with downloaded computer instructions on their procurement, placement and use. Mia had heard Lucius's conversation with Isaacs. The tape proved she was working that afternoon. A conversation she'd overheard in which Mia's name had been brought up by Lucius. The girl had panicked, fearful if Shanicha was exonerated, she would be next.

If Ariel read Mia correctly—and she was getting into the girl's head—she assumed she'd come under suspicion, and had staged a preemptive attack.

The faxed work schedule that followed was damning. Mia had worked every Tuesday and Thursday when Isaacs's group met since late January. Then, right after the assault on Lucius, she'd never again worked the late-afternoon shift.

"You even bungled your cover-up," Ariel said aloud softly. The pattern was all the more glaring with the sudden change. You're no Shanicha, Ariel thought, which is why you're on a slab in the morgue and Shanicha feels she's home free.

If Mia were alive, Ariel would have questioned her parents and numerous others to learn the motivation for her desire to emulate Shanicha. But there was no compelling reason, other than her own curiosity. And McGowan wasn't going to let her satisfy her curiosity.

As she rifled through a manilla folder with her evidence against Mia, a paper fell out. She'd almost forgotten. *The note* that had started it all. Why the note? It was a question only Mia could answer. Was she trying to draw attention to herself? Bait the police? Catch-me-if-you-can? Or was there something deeper? One thing was certain; Mia had sent the note. Shanicha certainly wouldn't have. Never had before. Another mistake, for it set everything else in motion. Wannabe like Shanicha, Ariel thought, but Mia was a rank amateur.

Doug trudged in at three. He'd been canvassing the students at The Quad to crack Mia's alibi the night Lucius was attacked. After telling him what she'd learned, Ariel asked if he'd had any success.

"Nothing conclusive *if* we had to go to court, but there was a period of time that night her friends remember she was gone. Thought nothing of it. Kids popped in and out while studying all the time."

He then produced a gym bag.

"This, though, might wrap it up. One girl remembered she had a gym bag. Our Mia was a pack rat. The only thing she didn't keep was a diary. The bugging devices and down-loaded material are bad enough. There was also the key that opened Monique Dysart's room. And I'd bet my pension we get something from the jogging suit in here: fibers of Lucius's hair, possibly, or blood. But something. I'm going to bring it to forensics."

"Why not have someone from forensics come and get it? We should see McGowan." She paused in thought. "Any keys . . . anything *at all* linking Mia to the first two suicides?"

Doug shook his head.

"So they could be Shanicha's doing."

"C'mon, Ariel. We've got squat on her. Less than squat with Mia tied to the attack on your ex, and Monique Dysart."

"You don't know Shanicha. You don't know Mia. See, Mia had no mind of her own—at least when it came to fuck-ing with other people's minds. Everything she did, Shanicha did first. No way Mia kills Monique and makes it appear a suicide unless she's emulating Shanicha."

"So what are you going to get Shanicha for? It's no crime to suggest someone commit suicide. Even you think Shanicha was someplace else when the other girls actually killed them-selves. The attack on Lucius was all we had."

"We have Mia's attack on Chanda. Conspiracy to at-tempted murder. Shanicha planned it, got Mia to participate and was outside listening when Mia took the easy way out. Doesn't matter that she stopped Mia. They planned it together. Shanicha's as guilty, under the law, as Mia."

"It's a stretch," Doug said, shaking his head. "Back to square one. Break Shanicha or she walks."

"Well, I want to at least give it a shot. If nothing else I want to scare the shit out of her. Want her to know *I* know what she's done."

"I'll support you with McGowan," he said dubiously. "But—"

"What I thought," she interrupted, "is *you* suggest it to McGowan. You tell him I'm a woman—*a black woman*. I can relate to her. If it comes from you, he'll go for it. If I suggest it . . ."

Doug raised his hands in surrender. "Okay. You've made your point. C'mon. Let's get this over with."

McGowan was in a particularly good mood. What could have been a fiasco—a career-breaker if Chanda were killed by Mia—had turned into a triumph. One for which he took full credit, while grudgingly acknowledging the "interdepartmental cooperation" of Commissioner Desjardins and the campus police department.

McGowan, at a press conference with Lieutenant Schumacher—his presence unusual in and of itself—intimated Mia was the prime suspect in what had been ruled three suicides, but were actually murders, as well as the assault on the campus patrolman. Any mention of Chanda was conspicuously absent, for which Ariel was grateful.

It was self-serving on McGowan's part, she knew, for if it were learned a fifteen-year-old had been used as a decoy, McGowan's head would be on the chopping block. It looked, though, that a promotion might not be too far off. He had plenty of reason to be in a festive mood.

His mood brightened further as Doug outlined what Ariel had discovered, and what he had found in Mia's room.

"Right church, wrong pew," McGowan said when Doug had finished. "You had the Wilkins girl all but tarred and feathered," he added, looking at Ariel but not quite making eye contact, "when all along it was the other girl. We'll want to feed all you've got to the media: 'Our investigation has now tied up all the loose ends, etc.,' " he finished, paraphrasing the spin to put on the findings.

When Doug mentioned bringing Shanicha in, it dampened McGowan's cheerful frame of mind.

"C'mon, Doug, you're not still claiming complicity on the part of the Wilkins girl?" he asked, without acknowledging Ariel's presence, which suited her fine. Again, she thought, a chapter meeting of the Boys' Club. As Lucius had said when referring to Desjardins, she was no more than a house nigger they could talk around, as if she were invisible.

"We need a statement from her anyway," Doug said, "and my gut tells me she was somehow involved." He then suggested Ariel interrogate her.

"No offense," Doug said, looking at Ariel, "but she's black and female. Shanicha will relate to her better than a white male. Why not go fishing and see if we get a nibble?"

McGowan was pensive as he seemed to mull it over. Ariel knew why he was reluctant. As it now stood, everything was cut and dried. All wrapped up, just waiting for a ribbon. All blame at Mia's feet, with the girl unable to defend herself. Shanicha's complicity would be an unnecessary complication that might raise unwanted questions.

"Bring her in for a statement, Doug," he finally said. "Ariel can have a shot at her, but anything short of a confession ends this investigation. Is that clear?" he asked, making eye contact with Ariel.

They both agreed.

Outside, Ariel beckoned Doug to the locker room.

"Thanks, Doug," she said, wanting to say more, but not quite finding the proper words.

"You deserve your shot," he said, flushing slightly. "Tell

361

you the truth, I don't like how everything is being swept under the carpet. It's just all too pat."

"I want to apologize for the way I've treated you," Ariel said, almost having to force the words out.

"Get out," her partner said, but flushed even further.

"No, hear me out," Ariel said, taking a deep breath. "I'm not one to easily admit mistakes. We're not ideal partners. We both know that. But I took you for granted, and that was uncalled for. You've backed me up more than once during this investigation, when you could have earned Brownie points kissing McGowan's ass. I want you to know it's appreciated."

"We were both at fault," he responded. "Butting heads all the time. But you've opened my eyes to how the Department—well, how the McGowans of the Department operate. Maybe every team needs a maverick. All of us are so intent on staying the course with McGowan, we've lost sight of our real job—catch the perp, even if it ruffles some feathers. You're kind of the conscience of the squad. A pain in the ass, sometimes," he added, "but one I can live with."

"Should we hug now," Ariel teased, and saw Doug turn crimson. He'd taken it seriously, she thought.

"Kidding," she said, shaking her head. "We've most definitely got to work on that sense of humor of yours."

He laughed, but she could see he was still uncomfortable, so she turned to business.

"I'm going to plant some stories with the media," she told her partner, and explained her rationale. "Unless you feel otherwise."

"No, the spin you suggest would thrill McGowan, if he knew. Do it. And good luck tomorrow."

Ariel made her calls and called it a day. She wanted to get home. Chanda would be there. No more "Out doing stuff." Someone to go home to for a change.

Chapter Fifty

Chanda lay on the couch, pretending to be Shanicha, as Ariel rehearsed her plan of attack. Ariel had been going at it for over an hour, stopping only to get input from Chanda. It was exhausting, but Chanda saw Ariel relying on her judgment, and couldn't think of anything more satisfying.

Chanda was still feeling the aftereffects of the evening before. It had all caught up with her at the hospital, before Ariel had shown up. Kind of delayed shock.

She could have been killed. She cursed herself for losing her focus and dropping her guard. All of Ariel's badgering for what? At a crucial moment her mind had been miles away. Ariel had been right; she wasn't trained. She wasn't ready. She'd finally felt at home, and could have been killed because of an inflated ego.

Her stomach had erupted, and she'd thrown up for a good fifteen minutes, until she felt her insides totally flushed out. Her head pounded as she tried to reconstruct Shanicha's sudden appearance. Why hadn't Chanda heard her enter? Why hadn't Shanicha called out when she saw Mia wallop her? And had Mia lost her balance, or had Shanicha helped her out, just a wee bit?

Like Ariel, Chanda believed Shanicha had orchestrated it all. What had she expected to occur? Did Shanicha think Mia would convince her to jump? Or, for some reason, had she set Mia up to take the fall—figuratively or literally?

She accepted the fact that Mia had attacked Lucius, and that Mia had probably been responsible for Monique's death.

Barry Hoffman

But what she remembered most of all was Shanicha hanging up on her twice that night. You had an agenda, Shanicha, she thought to herself. And I think you accomplished just what you set out to do.

Lastly, there was the fleeting smile on Shanicha's face when the campus police burst in; then the wink. Of the smile, she was certain. She thought Shanicha had winked at her in silent communication, but it might have been her imagination.

With her mind abuzz with thoughts and unanswered questions that scampered around like mice in a maze, but never caught the elusive cheese, she had fallen into a fitful sleep.

She'd awakened to Ariel at seven the next morning.

"You look like shit," she'd told Ariel. "You been up all night keeping a vigil over me?"

"Dozed a bit, but yeah, pretty much," Ariel said, stifling a yawn. "Talking about shit, you don't look so hot yourself. How are you feeling? Don't bullshit me," she added.

"Better. Still a bit weak, and totally humiliated. I forgot everything you'd taught me—"

"No recriminations," Ariel cut in. "No one was prepared for what Mia did."

"But I should have been prepared for *anything*."

"It's water over the dam. What's important is you're all right. Doctors say you've got one hard head. A slight concussion, but you can come home—if you're up to it."

"Home sounds good," Chanda said. "Real good."

She'd slept off and on most of the day, and knew she was finally over the hump when she woke up at three and was starving. She raided the fridge, and was watching MTV when Ariel returned.

Now she was doing her best to be Shanicha; deflecting Ariel's questions and reacting as Shanicha might to surprises thrown at her.

"This is really important to you, isn't it?" Chanda finally asked when they took a break.

"I've got just this one shot."

"That's no answer. This is personal, isn't it?" she asked. "Not just another case."

"Maybe I feel my integrity's on the line," Ariel said. "It took me a while to grasp Shanicha. It took me all of an hour to know what made Mia tick. I can't buy the party line that Mia was the mastermind behind it all. Because this wasn't the work of an amateur, and Mia was a rank amateur. I want my shot at Shanicha because she's killed. She'll kill again, too. That's what's driving me. She'll kill again and again and again, unless I stop her now."

"And if she doesn't crack?" Chanda asked. "Are you going to be a basket case?"

"I don't expect her to crack, if you want the truth. I've got to try, though. So, no, I won't be a basket case. I'll be pissed, but it's not like I've got much ammunition. I'm resorting to mind games, because there is no real evidence against her."

"It's incredible," Chanda said, "that with all she's done, she may have the last laugh. It's not fair."

"Life's not fair, Chanda. We've discussed that before. You just hope you win a few more than you lose. It's the only way to cope with life's inequities."

Chanda knew Ariel was right. Her head could accept Shanicha getting away with murder. But her gut said otherwise. Shanicha had hoped she would jump. The only reason Shanicha had interceded on her behalf was because Mia fucked up. Her gut told her Shanicha wanted her to jump to her death. Her gut couldn't accept Shanicha getting off; a hero, no less. She'd give Ariel her shot, but she wasn't through with Shanicha.

She owed Shanicha. Big time.

Chapter Fifty-one

Ariel and Doug kept Shanicha waiting in a cramped interrogation room for thirty-five minutes. It was 11:35, and they had no intention of giving Shanicha anything to eat. As the day wore on, hopefully this would further weaken the girl's resolve.

Doug would take her statement, with Ariel in the background, little more than a prop. They'd let her sit a while longer, and then Ariel would ambush her.

Ariel looked at the girl from the two-way mirror. She had to hand it to Shanicha. She showed no nervousness. No impatience. No *nothing*. Skin so dark, she could lurk near Tia Hughes's house at night without being spotted. So beautiful, she should be spending her time fending off young men rather than plotting murder.

Lucius was very much on Ariel's mind as she looked at Shanicha. For while Mia had attacked her man, if it weren't for Shanicha, they would have been exploring the possibilities of a second chance. And, even if it were purely physical, with no long-term future, after just one night she sorely missed what only Lucius could provide.

Funny, she thought, to be thinking of sex with Lucius when her total concentration should be on Shanicha. But then Lucius, lying in a coma, fueled her anger, and she had learned long ago to channel her rage during interrogations.

Doug came and stood by her.

"Cool as a cucumber, isn't she?"

"For now," Ariel responded.

"I wouldn't want to be that girl," he said. "You're on the prowl. Only a kill will satisfy you—figuratively speaking, that is."

Ariel smiled wickedly.

"Show time," he said, glancing at his watch. "My turn for the prelims."

Shanicha answered all of Doug's questions tersely, but her eyes kept wandering to Ariel. Shanicha *was* good, Ariel thought. She never elaborated, just answered his questions in as few words as possible. One would have thought the girl a career criminal; one who knew the ropes.

As Doug was wrapping up, Ariel left the room, then returned a few minutes later.

"Sarge wants to see us," she told Doug, totally ignoring Shanicha.

"We'll just be a few minutes, Shanicha," Doug told the girl. "I apologize, but . . ."

One of Doug's hanging sentences, Ariel thought, and smiled to herself. Sometimes it was a lack of confidence on his part, but other times, like now, he'd start a sentence and literally didn't know where to go with it. Getting into your head, Doug, she thought to herself. You're more complicated than you seem at first blush. And *definitely* not the fool you sometimes seem.

Ariel entered the interrogation room alone fifteen minutes later. Shanicha gave her a smile. Could it be she knew Ariel had intentionally kept her waiting and was letting her know?

"Do you want a lawyer, Shanicha?" Ariel started, hoping to get her off balance and wipe that damn smile off her face.

"Why would I want a lawyer? You don't think I lied to the other detective, do you?"

"I think your statement's a crock of shit, Shanicha," she said, leaning across the table so their faces almost touched. "To be honest, maybe you should have a lawyer."

Shanicha pondered the question a moment, then smiled.

"Thanks, but no, thanks. Nothing to hide. No need for a lawyer."

Ariel saw the girl's eyes were no longer smiling. Shanicha welcomed the challenge of wills. To humiliate Ariel on her own turf, that would be a turn-on for Shanicha. Ariel knew this girl. Shanicha looked forward to this unexpected duel. No lawyer. No Doug. No interlopers.

"See, Shanicha," Ariel began, "I plan to charge you with the murder of Mia."

"You got to be kidding. Chanda was right there—"

"And says you *pushed* Mia," Ariel interrupted.

"Chanda was half zonked," Shanicha said sullenly.

"You can't have it both ways, Shanicha. Either Chanda saw what happened, or was seeing stars. Which is it?"

Shanicha said nothing.

Crafty bitch, Ariel thought. She was going to have Ariel make the choice.

"Chanda knows what she saw. Mia was off balance, and you pushed her. That's murder. You and Mia were a team. You'd target girls at Dr. Isaacs's group sessions, and you'd both work on their frailties. Only, Mia was the boss. Like in the buddy movies. The white guy—the Mel Gibson—was the brains, and Danny Glover—the black dude—the trusty, but not overly bright, sidekick. You were jealous, so when the opportunity arose . . ." She shrugged. "Good-bye, Mia."

"That's crazy," Shanicha said, no longer smiling.

Ariel slapped down copies of newspapers she had brought with her on the table. "Look at them, Shanicha. 'Mia the Master Manipulator,' says the *News*. And 'Warped Mastermind,' the headline in the *Inquirer*. No way a nigger could plan and execute the deaths of three coeds to look like suicides," Ariel said, raising her voice.

"The white girl gets the credit. You were just along for the ride. That the way you want to be remembered, Shanicha? Just along for the ride?"

"I could have planned it, you white bitch," Shanicha shot back, "but I didn't." The smile was back.

"Child, I may look white, but my ass is as black as yours, so call me a bitch if you want, but it's black bitch, if you don't mind."

She could see she'd caught Shanicha off guard. Now she pressed.

"Look, Shanicha, these newspapers are full of shit," she said, tossing them across the room like confetti. "I know you were behind it all. Why should Mia—that white bitch—get all the credit? You admit you pushed Mia, so why not tell the world how big and bad you are?"

"I didn't admit nothing," Shanicha hissed. "Mia and I fought over that marble doodad she had. Mia lost her balance—"

"Bullshit. Remember, we have a witness," Ariel said, her eyes glaring at Shanicha. "Who are they going to believe; a fifteen-year-old white girl who's been attacked, or a nigger—especially with your history."

"You're talking in riddles. What history? I've never been in any trouble."

"Sure you don't want a lawyer, Shanicha? You do have your rights, you know," Ariel prodded.

"Don't need no fucking lawyer," Shanicha growled.

"Whose idea was it to accuse your teacher of molesting you? Yours? Mia's? The press—*the white press*—will say Mia, but I don't buy it."

"What teacher?" Shanicha asked, appearing bewildered.

"The one in New Canaan. The name slips me. Mr. . . . Help me out, will you?"

"That man *did* molest me. Mia and all the rest of them, too."

"And what of the fires? In New Canaan. Your handiwork."

"Bullshit."

"Getting testy, Shanicha? Can't handle the heat." She sat

369

down, directly across from Shanicha. "Sure you don't want a lawyer?"

Shanicha balled her hands into fists. "I didn't start any fires in New Canaan," she finally said, and Ariel could feel her venom.

"Mia did. You want me to believe that?"

Shanicha shrugged, but said nothing.

"My Sarge and my partner and everyone else thinks Mia's responsible for everything. Not me. She botched everything she did. I know she attacked the campus cop. Couldn't kill him, though. Couldn't kill Chanda. You masterminded the accusations on that teacher. You started the fires. But that white bitch Mia set one *after* you left New Canaan. Didn't know that, did you? See how it looks, though?"

Still no response.

"You going to tell me Mia was responsible for Peter Lyle, too?"

Shanicha glared at Ariel, but held her tongue. Closed her eyes, then asked, "What are you talking about now?"

"What about your good friend Tia Hughes?" Ariel pressed, ignoring Shanicha's question. "Can't pin that one on Mia. Don't spread rumors about Shanicha or you get burned to a crisp. Right, Shanicha?"

Volley after volley, Ariel pressed her attack. She didn't want Shanicha to respond. She wanted the girl to know just how much *she* knew.

"See, I know all about you, Shanicha," Ariel said when the youth remained silent. "Know you drove Simone and Alexis to commit suicide."

She took out a small diary from her purse.

"Take a look. Simone kept a diary. That S in the diamond is you, Shanicha. Look what she says you told her; there's a better life for her. Similar, I'd say, to the suicide notes of Sharon Ingster and Jocelyn Rhea."

"You're talking gibberish," Shanicha said quietly.

"Tell you what, Shanicha. We can play this two ways. We can charge you with the murder of Mia Fahey. We have an eyewitness. Or you can tell me about the other two suicides—the ones at Penn—and you'll be charged only with being an accomplice to the attempted murder of Chanda. What with your coming to her aid, you'll probably get off on probation. What will it be, Shanicha?"

Shanicha smiled. "I think neither, Detective." She sat back in her chair. "Very impressive, Detective, *if* I were guilty. But why such a . . . what do they call it, reduced charge *if* I admit to two murders I didn't commit."

"Because proving those murders would be difficult."

"Then charge me with the murder of Mia. You have your eyewitness." Shanicha began to laugh. "It's all a sham."

Now she was leaning across the table, right in Ariel's face. "If you could you would, but you have squat. An unreliable witness, because she was hit on the head. She couldn't have seen me push Mia because I didn't. If she says she did, she's either lying or groggy from the blow to her head."

Shanicha put her hands out in front of her. "Do it, Detective. Arrest me. Charge me. Try me. Do it. Do it. Do it . . . *or leave me the fuck alone.*"

"You're free to go, Shanicha," Ariel said.

"I thought so," Shanicha said, getting up. She came over to Ariel's side of the table, and leaned close to her.

"I've gotten under your skin, haven't I, Detective?" she said derisively. "Kind of an obsession. Don't let it eat at you." And she laughed again as she started to leave the room.

Ariel had one last card. It wouldn't crack Shanicha. She'd lost that confrontation, but she'd rehearsed it with Chanda the night before with that expectation in mind.

"You've got a problem, Shanicha," she said, and Shanicha stopped.

371

"Really? Pray tell."

"I'm not going away. Going to hound you. Like flies on shit. A flea on a cat. Or maybe I'll be your spider, spinning my web around you. Ready to pounce when you fuck up. Pick your cliche, but you're through. No more fucking with other people's minds. I'm on to you and you know it. Can you live fifty or sixty years without the thrill you get with your fires, convincing people to commit suicide or stirring up a hornet's nest, then standing back to watch the havoc you've created? Maybe it's better than a confession, just like life imprisonment is worse for some than the death penalty. There's so much you want to do, but I'll be there dogging you, so you can't. The thrill is gone, Shanicha. Can you live with that?"

Ariel opened the door for Shanicha, and before the girl could respond, gave her her most sarcastic smile. "Now get the fuck out of here." And walked away.

Chapter Fifty-two

Shanicha should have felt triumphant. She'd won the battle of wills with the bitch detective. But she felt drained. Walking from the interrogation, she felt sweat dripping from every pore. The smell made her want to gag.

How did the bitch know so much about her? she thought. The fires in New Canaan, her teacher there, Peter Lyle, Tia, the two white girls she'd helped.

And the spider.

Born Bad

It was like she had crept into her mind in the middle of the night and camped out, reading her thoughts by flashlight. She had never felt so exposed. Naked. Vulnerable. She wanted to tell this cop it was all true. Wanted to lord it over her, because nothing could be proven. Wanted to come clean. And, dammit, she wanted to share the thrill of it all with her and claim her glory.

It was all spoiled for her at the end. She knew the last promise was no hollow threat. The bitch would be dogging her every move. Could she go on with her wanton destruction knowing this cop knew her as well as she knew herself? Did she dare? What would she do if she couldn't?

The thought made her skin crawl.

Back at the dorm, she showered; long and hard. With a washcloth, she rubbed herself raw. She must rid herself of the fetid smell. With a razor, she shaved her pubic hair, just in case. There must be no hiding place for the spider.

She lay in bed, naked, the entire afternoon and evening. She willed her other self to appear. She caressed her breasts, tugged at her nipples, fingered her genitals—all to no avail.

Her other self was in hiding.

She kept at it, even when her roommate entered.

"That's disgusting. *You're disgusting,*" her roommate said under her breath, but loud enough for Shanicha to hear, then left the room.

Shanicha didn't care, though. She summoned her other self. Commanded her appear, then finally lay limp with despair.

The phone rang an hour later. Her roommate had returned, without even looking at her, and was asleep. Shanicha answered it.

"Shanicha?"

"Who is it?"

"Watch out for the spider," the voice said, and hung up.

Back in bed, she closed her eyes, but the voice echoed in her mind.

—Watch out for the spider.

—*Watch out* . . .

She didn't sleep.

Wondered if she ever would. Ever could.

Epilogue

(One)

A week after Ariel's interrogation of Shanicha, Ariel was still going through what Chanda labeled "Shanicha Withdrawal." Once Shanicha walked out the door, the investigation was closed. Coming to terms with that finality had proven more difficult for Ariel than she'd imagined.

Back on rotation, she and Doug had *investigated*—for lack of a better word—three routine homicides; Doug's type of case where the perp could have left bread crumbs as tracks saying, "Follow me."

The lack of challenge, more than anything, kept her flashing back to Shanicha. Intellectually, Ariel knew almost all homicides were no-brainers, but all the same, every time the phone rang, there was the possibility she might have to match wits with someone like Shanicha.

Part of the lethargy she felt, she knew, was a result of the unfinished nature of her investigation. She had promised Chanda otherwise, but there was no getting around it; she had Shanicha on her mind.

The girl *had* become an obsession, *had* gotten under her skin. It's bad enough, she thought, when a case ends without leading to the perpetrator; worse still when you have the guilty party walk out of an interrogation without any possibility of arrest or punishment. Shanicha had beaten her, plain and simple.

The absence of closure gnawed at Ariel daily.

So, she walked through her job, because nothing more was required at the moment.

Every day, she and Chanda would stop by the hospital to see Lucius. Each day she expected to see him sitting up in bed, hoping Chanda would leave so he could jump her bones.

Each day she was disappointed.

Dr. Kaplan was sympathetic, but could offer little solace.

"He's alive," he said with that ever-present gleam in his eye. "I know that's of little comfort, but it's better than being dead."

"Alive, but a vegetable; I don't know," Ariel would counter bitterly.

"Wrong, child," he'd tell her almost daily. "He's no vegetable. He's not brain-dead. He's asleep. Whether it's due to brain damage or he's just holed up within himself, I can't honestly tell you. But a vegetable, he's not. You talk to him like he's alive. I hear things," he added when Ariel looked at him in surprise. "I think he listens. We must believe he does."

"Little comfort, as you say," Ariel responded.

"His vitals are good, and he's healing. Maybe he's waiting for the day his other injuries are fully mended. It would be easier that way for him. Maybe he knows it." The doctor shrugged.

"You'll call—"

He didn't let her finish. "No, I'll hold a press conference so you can find out about it from friends."

He shook his head in exasperation.

"Of course, silly girl. I've got all the numbers you've left—home, office, beeper. Now go, spend some time with him. Talk to him. Let him know he's wanted—*needed*. By both you and your young friend," he said with a wink at Chanda.

Both Ariel and Chanda filled Lucius in on their day; nothing exceptional. Neither had mentioned Shanicha *after* Ariel told him about the ill-fated interrogation.

"You were right on the mark from the start, Lucius," Ariel had told him. "Something troubled you from the get-go. You felt personally responsible. Well, that's one less item to fret over. Shanicha killed the first two, Mia the third. You had Shanicha pegged. Unfortunately, I couldn't turn her."

She had replayed the confrontation like a videotape. Odd, she thought, how she remembered almost every move, every gesture, every glance.

Now, with the investigation completed, she worried even more about Lucius. Before, she'd been so focused on Shanicha, she'd consciously—and without remorse—relegated Lucius to the back of her mind. Now, though, several times each day, his face swam before her eyes, followed by vivid images: he and Ariel before their marriage; the two of them just married and supremely happy; he and Ariel in bed the night before he was attacked.

She knew it was sanitized—if X-rated—and an incomplete picture of their life together, but how she longed for a second chance.

She was grieving for Lucius, she knew, and felt guilty, for she didn't dare share Dr. Kaplan's optimism. At times the grief was overwhelming. There were days she visited Lucius a second time, alone without Chanda, when she gave vent to her emotions and just cried. What a stupid bitch she'd been. Not the divorce; they hadn't been right for one another—at least then. But, she regretted the bitterness she'd felt over the last eight years. She knew divorced couples who remained close after their breakup; some with a stronger bond than when married. She was so angry at Lucius, she had totally divorced him from her life. It was wrong. Worse, it was stupid. The time lost could never be recovered. So she cried for him and for herself, too. Cried, because she desperately wanted another chance; if only to be Lucius's friend.

377

Barry Hoffman

Chanda had been her only solace, helping her cope during the week. Before, when she got a choice case assigned by Phil Donato, she'd dealt with her depression alone, when the case was finally put to bed. It was like a drug, she recalled telling Chanda earlier. And withdrawal could be a bitch. Before Chanda she'd drink too much, prowl around the house like a caged animal, was loathe to clean and consoled herself *with* herself.

Chanda wouldn't have that. The girl was like a sponge. No matter how many times Ariel repeated her confrontation with Shanicha or second-guessed the investigation, Chanda listened patiently, often adding her own spin. She forced Ariel to get out of the house, dragging her to the Valley Forge Music Fair to see Luther Vandros. Chanda had only squirmed a little as Luther crooned steamy ballads; not at all her type of music.

After that, Ariel had to come out of her shell.

The next day, Ariel suggested they go down to the shore. It was still a bit brisk for the hordes that normally descended, so there were only a few brave souls there. The tranquility amidst the violence of the pounding surf was welcome. They hit Cape May, Wildwood, Ocean City and Atlantic City. Four very different beaches, all cleansing to Ariel's sludge-filled soul.

Even Chanda had a ball; venturing into the water up to her knees, only to return shivering.

Life could have returned to normal, if only Lucius awoke from his coma.

A week to the day that Shanicha left her life, McGowan called her into his office—*alone*. She had no inkling why.

He got right to the point.

"I want you to request a transfer. Not out of homicide," he added quickly, "just out of my squad. I'd be perfectly justified in requesting an Internal Affairs inquiry to get you booted out of homicide, if I desired, you know. Having a

378

fifteen-year-old do research on a criminal investigation was more than just inappropriate. What were you thinking? And then, because of your irresponsibility, she took it upon herself to become an active participant in the case. If she had gotten seriously hurt or killed . . ." He stopped, as the rest was evident.

Ariel was stunned and pissed. The typical McGowan approach. A transfer, but also the "I-could-have-really-fucked-you-if-I-wanted-to" approach, to make her feel grateful. And he wanted *her* to take the initiative. He conveniently forgot, she knew, that he'd more than willingly agreed to allow Chanda—the fifteen-year-old—to become bait, something she'd opposed.

"Why the transfer? I'm a good—no, a *better* cop than most of the men in this unit."

"But you're not on the same page as the rest of us," he said, as if that should have been evident. "Take this case. We *had* Mia Fahey, but no, you wanted the Wilkins girl. For purely selfish reasons, not for the good of the unit. You constantly put your personal agenda above that of the team. And I want this unit functioning as one."

For one of the first times, he met her eyes.

"And don't think I'm not aware you briefed Commissioner Desjardins behind my back to get what you wanted. I demand total loyalty. It's foreign to you," he said, his voice filled with rancor. "I've given you a lot of leeway, Dampier, but it's best for all of us if you leave here gracefully."

"And if I refuse and file a grievance if you have me transferred?"

"That's a no-win situation, and you know it," he said with a knowing smile. Again, he made eye contact with her, challenging her to make good on her threat. "Air your dirty laundry in public and you'll be ostracized, win or lose."

It was true. She knew many cops who filed grievances, won, but came out losers. You get a reputation, and then it's like you're a leper. And women were under suspicion under the best of circumstances. You got no balls if you filed a grievance, she'd heard more than once. And a woman without balls is no police officer.

"And you happen to know of an opening," she said. It wasn't a question.

"As a matter of fact, I've been looking for a unit where your individualism would blend in. Sergeant Morales lost one of his men to a chronic back injury. He already has a female detective, and from what I hear, only cares he gets a good cop. You're a good cop, Dampier; not my kind of cop, but you're no slouch. You're thorough. Your instincts are good. You just don't fit in here. Morales can live with your style."

"You've talked to him?"

"We shoot the breeze. Talk about a lot of things. With an opening, I mentioned one of my detectives might be happier with his management style. He checked you out and he'll have you."

Ariel smiled bitterly. "You've been laying in wait. I was fucked the day you got here."

"Draw your own conclusions, Detective. I was willing to give you a shot, even with what I'd heard about you. You just confirmed what I'd been told. Capable, maybe even superior, but a maverick. To me, that's a cancer."

"What about Doug? Is he next?"

McGowan looked surprised. "He hasn't become infected with you as a partner. More credit to him. And lately, he's shown real initiative. I had my doubts, I admit, but he stays."

"So, I don't have a choice," Ariel said with resignation.

"You don't want to be here. You caught a good case by accident. If you stay, you *and* your partner would be consigned to cases you abhor, domestic disputes, ODs and the like. I can make it happen, you know. The wheel is random, but just like at a casino, the game can be fixed. You'd come up with shit until you got so sick you'd want to puke."

"That voluntary transfer is beginning to look pretty good," Ariel said without a smile.

McGowan smiled. "I knew we'd come to a meeting of the minds."

He rose, the signal, but she stopped him.

"I do have some vacation time coming," she said. "I'd like a week before I start with Morales." It wasn't a request.

He looked at her sharply, then softened. "As long as you're outta here by the end of the day." Then he turned his back on her.

In the locker room, she tossed a trash can against the wall. Why did she care? she thought to herself. She didn't want to be on McGowan's team. She should be grateful.

No. She stopped herself. *It should have been my decision.* That's what pissed her off. The bastard forced her out, and was slick enough that she had no recourse.

Maybe she should quit the force altogether and join the University of Pennsylvania Campus Police. And do what? an inner voice asked. Become buds with the kids on campus, like Lucius? No, he was a people person. She was an investigator. A homicide detective.

The only comfort was knowing someday McGowan would fall on his face. His smooth style—covering little substance—could only take him so far. One day the shit would hit and wouldn't slide off. Teflon corroded with time. She only hoped she was around to witness his downfall.

(Two)

Chanda was worried about Ariel. First the futile interrogation with Shanicha. Then Lucius—just lying there for . . . until he decided to awaken, if his brain wasn't so addled he could awaken. And now the transfer.

Ariel was working the eight-to-four shift, and she'd come home exhausted from doing nothing. She'd shower, then nap, then gaze at the tube, seeing nothing. Chanda didn't know if it was self-pity, natural depression at a case ending, or if Shanicha had really gotten to her. On the second night, Chanda sat down in front of the television to see Ariel's reaction.

"What are you doing, girl?" Ariel asked without much feeling.

"What were you watching?" Chanda shot back.

"You know, that show . . . the one with . . . Shit, I have no idea," she said with a weak laugh.

"That's 'cause you weren't watching anything. You were staring at something with your eyes, but your mind is miles away. Time to talk about it."

"Not now, Chanda. I appreciate—"

"Don't give me that 'I appreciate' shit," Chanda said, trying to stir some emotion in Ariel other than apathy.

"I'm being a pain in the ass," Chanda added, "Why not say it?"

" 'Cause you're not. You're concerned and I—"

"Appreciate it, right, Ariel?" She turned the TV off and sat on the couch. Ariel was forced to turn away from the television to look at her.

"I don't know how you handled being down before I got here, but I'm here now. Here as much for you as you are for me. I know what your problem is."

"Tell me, Miss Know-it-all," Ariel said with just a hint of a smile.

"Shanicha Withdrawal. It's not just that a case is over. You told me about the natural letdown, how a lot of guys down their depression with booze. Your problem is the case *isn't* over. You know who committed the crime, but you're handcuffed. And it's eating at you, tearing you up inside."

"You're fucking wise beyond your years, pardon my French," Ariel said. "Shanicha Withdrawal. Yeah, I'm going through Shanicha Withdrawal. She taunted me, Chanda. Said she'd become my obsession. She was right. I lived in that

girl's head. Knew during the entire interrogation it was fruit-
less. She doesn't want notoriety. She's bad, and just wants
to be bad."

"Born bad," Chanda said.

"What?"

"A crack baby, you said. Maybe it did something to her—
like fried a part of her brain."

"Her conscience," Ariel said. "Like that commercial about
drugs. You know, 'This is your brain. This is your brain on
drugs.' And for that portion they show the egg cooking in a
pan."

Ariel was excited now.

"The crack did fry a part of Shanicha's brain. She gets
pleasure from the pain of others. And she's without remorse.
You don't break a girl like that. You need rock-solid evidence to convict, and we had nothing of the kind."

They talked long into the night, Ariel doing most of the
talking, purging Shanicha from her system.

The next night they did it again.

Ever so slowly, Ariel was coming to terms with Shanicha's
apparent triumph. It was destined from the outset. There were
no buttons to push with someone like Shanicha; with no conscience, no feeling of remorse, no desire to hog the spotlight.

Ariel even began to talk about Lucius, and how he was
preying on her mind. All her regrets. Again, it had a cleansing effect on her.

By the third night, Ariel was far more lively. She willingly
went with Chanda to Rittenhouse Square, a small neighborhood park, and giggled as Chanda chased the pigeons.

"You know one of the great questions of life, Ariel?" a
winded Chanda asked.

"Tell me."

"Baby pigeons. Have you ever seen a baby pigeon? They
seem to be born as adults."

Ariel laughed.

The next night, they went to the Valley Forge Music Fair to see Luther Vandros. Chanda had bought the tickets at a Ticketmaster outlet, so Ariel couldn't beg off. At the concert Chanda saw Ariel almost snuggle into the man's songs of love.

Chanda, for her part, had to pinch herself to stay awake. The Cranberries, Alanis Morissette and REM did things for her. This man was putting her to sleep. But the look on Ariel's face as they left made it all worthwhile. Ariel was coming out of her funk. Driving home, Ariel sang some of the man's songs, but with her own interpretation. It gave Chanda goose bumps.

"I envy you, Ariel," she said.

"Why? Because I like good music?" She laughed.

"You *make* good music. You make music come alive. That's a gift."

Finally, there was the junket to the Jersey Shore. Ariel seemed acquainted with every goddamn beach in creation. And, as she pointed out, each had its own unique personality.

Walking along the shoreline, Ariel began to sing a gospel-inflected version of a Whitney Houston song, "The Greatest Love of All."

Chanda let her sing, her a cappella voice rising above the surf.

When she was done, she sat cross-legged on the beach and Chanda joined her.

"That song meant so much to me when I had no identity," Ariel said. "Like it says, I had to learn to love myself. Easier said than done. There's irony in it, too. It was written by a white woman, Linda Creed. She died of cancer a few years back. Anyway, the song is about Muhammad Ali, a black man. It was for a movie about his life. See, it fit me perfectly. Neither white or black, fish or fowl. To exist day-to-day, I had to learn to love myself. It took me a while, but I do."

Out of the blue, she gave Chanda a hug. "You're my Linda

Creed. You've helped me come to grips with the demon that is Shanicha. I was so into her mind that I couldn't escape, yet I didn't know it. I've always worked out my problems by myself. Even when I had Lucius. Until now. You've been my tonic. My cure."

Ariel wiped her eyes. "Damn salt water," she said, and they both laughed.

Then Ariel's boss had to spoil everything by transferring her.

She came home with all her belongings in a cardboard box. She wasn't depressed. She was mad. Ranting and raving at that SOB McGowan as she paced the room.

"You tell Doug yet?" Chanda asked.

"He saw me packing. He took it hard. Funny, we'd just seemed to have become sort of comfortable with one another. He was on his way to becoming a real mensch."

"Mensch?" Chanda asked.

"Yiddish for man. He was beginning to see McGowan as the bastard he really was, and it made him uncomfortable. He stood up for me twice, even though he wasn't certain I was right. Partners do that. I'll miss the little shit. Nobody to watch his back now. A misstep and McGowan will know I've poisoned his well, and Doug will be out on his ass."

Chanda listened, letting Ariel pour out her frustrations.

"What pisses me off most is I didn't leave on my own my terms. Deep down I know it's for the best. I want to get as far away from that ass-kissing McGowan as possible. I know I had no future there."

She shook her head, and looked at the ceiling.

"Yet I was fighting the transfer. Can you believe that? I've got a fresh start—still in homicide—with a Sergeant who I hear is a human being. And I was fighting it. It defies logic. I should have kissed the schmuck."

"It's because you didn't make the decision," Chanda said. "He forced you out, and that goes against your nature."

"I can be a real ass sometimes."

"Join the club."

They were at the point where they were sharing everything. Chanda began telling Ariel about what it was like living on the streets. Being robbed by homeless men. Being raped by one. Giving a blow job to a cop who promised to protect her in exchange.

Chanda kept just one secret from Ariel. Unlike Ariel, she hadn't finished with Shanicha. The bitch had almost gotten her killed. She'd learned on the street to never let anyone get the best of you. They do it once, they'll be back again, just like blackmailers. She hadn't told Ariel—not yet anyway—that the day after she'd been robbed, she'd whacked the man in the nuts with a two-by-four while he slept, then hit him upside his head when he opened his eyes. He'd steered clear of her after that.

And the bastard who'd raped her. She'd set his clothes ablaze while he slept. When he got out of the hospital, two months later, she'd confronted him and he fled.

As for the cop, the next time she saw him, she'd told him she'd tested positive for the HIV virus. He didn't protect her, but he never propositioned her again.

Now Shanicha had messed with her. Chanda could well justify her actions as avenging the attack on Lucius, for Shanicha was ultimately responsible for his lying in a coma. She also owed Ariel, who had to live with the knowledge that a killer walked the streets.

But, in the final analysis, she went after Shanicha because the girl had fucked with her. Chanda had a conscience; she felt remorse; *but* she lived by the Code of the Streets. Always exact revenge, lest you forever become a victim. Two eyes for an eye; two teeth for a tooth.

That's why Chanda called Shanicha that first night after the interrogation, and told her to watch out for the spider. For unlike Ariel, she had seen the look of undisguised terror on Shanicha's face when she told her story at group. It wasn't some made-up bullshit. Shanicha had her own demons to contend with, and Chanda was intent on making her confront her worst nightmare.

She called the next night and repeated the message, then remained silent. Shanicha, too, said nothing, though Chanda could hear her breathing.

Finally Shanicha spoke.

"Stay the fuck away from me, you hear."

It was music to Chanda's ears. She'd hit her button, and would do so again and again and again.

The next night, halfway through the message, Shanicha hung up. Chanda waited ten minutes, then called again. As before, Shanicha hung up before she was through.

You don't get rid of me that easily, Shanicha, Chanda thought to herself. She waited half an hour, then phoned again. The phone was snapped up midway through the first ring.

Chanda smiled. Shanicha had been waiting. Past midnight, and she hadn't been able to fall asleep. This time Shanicha didn't hang up until Chanda had completed the message. And when she hung up, she didn't slam the receiver down. Gently replaced the receiver in the cradle.

You're learning, Shanicha, she thought.

It bothered Chanda a bit that she was enjoying herself so much. She wondered if this was how Shanicha felt as she hatched, then implemented her schemes. This was payback, and she shouldn't relish it the way she did.

The fifth night, the phone rang a dozen times before Shanicha answered. Maybe Shanicha was out, she'd thought, but as she was about to hang up, Shanicha was there. Before Chanda could begin, Shanicha was talking.

"Leave me the fuck alone."

Not a command, Chanda thought. Shanicha was beseeching her. And the girl's breathing was labored, as if she were physically ill. Chanda felt no sympathy whatsoever. She delivered her message, then hung up.

She thought of telling Ariel, but knew she'd make her stop. Knew, too, it would upset her. Ariel had too much on her mind; was just now emerging from Shanicha Withdrawal. And that night, she'd told Chanda of her transfer. A transfer, from what Ariel had told her, that was inevitable, *but* Shanicha was the direct cause. Ariel mustn't be bothered, and Shanicha must continue to pay.

Saturday, Ariel was having lunch with Doug. Her transfer had really upset him, and Ariel hadn't wanted to talk about it at work.

Chanda went on a trip of her own. She took her backpack and a number of jars: jars that had held peanut butter, jelly and spaghetti sauce. Jars she'd been hoarding since that first call to Shanicha. Ariel had commented on her suddenly voracious appetite, and she'd shrugged.

"I wanted nothing to do with food after getting hit upside my head. Now I'm ravenous. Just catching up."

One thing Chanda had learned long ago was that Philadelphia had an abundance of abandoned buildings. Some were havens for drug addicts; others home for squatters. All havens for creatures of every sort, roaches, rats—even spiders.

On the western end of South Street, just before the river, it didn't take Chanda long to find a dozen spiders of every sort; including one that was particularly hairy. Each she put in a bottle, dotted with tiny holes on their lids for air.

She slipped out of the house at ten. Mercifully, Ariel had come home exhausted. Lunch with Doug had taken its toll; then he had insisted they go back to his house. Ariel had never met Doug's wife, and she felt guilty. Closure, he'd said.

"Muriel's wanted to meet you for months. I'd always come up with a lame excuse not to have you over." He'd blushed.

"You're ... much more attractive than Muriel, and I knew she'd be even more jealous, more suspicious, more paranoid than she already was if she saw you in the flesh. But with the transfer, you're no longer a threat to her. So, please come on over."

Muriel had cooked dinner and doted on Ariel; surreptitiously glancing at her "competition" at every opportunity. Ariel thought the two were made for each other; just as dogs often resembled their owners.

She'd returned home dead to the world, and was asleep by nine-thirty.

Chanda got into to The Quad using Mia's student ID. She'd "borrowed" it that last night, thinking it might be of use if Shanicha evaded her, as she had previously. She'd completely forgotten about it until she had returned from the hospital. It was in her purse. She'd been right; it had come in handy, as Shanicha had eluded arrest. She had worried that the card might be scrutinized when she entered, but trailing three other girls, she was ushered through without a second glance.

At Shanicha's room, she opened each of her jars and watched as the eight-legged arachnids, once free of their glass prisons, scurried into Shanicha's room; sometimes with a little nudge from her hand.

Her task complete, Chanda left. She had no idea what, if anything, she'd accomplished. She couldn't bring Shanicha down. Wouldn't commit a willful crime against the girl. Wouldn't continue to obsess over her. After tonight, Shanicha would be looking over her shoulder nightly for a long time, waiting for the next attack. Each time her phone rang, the words "Watch out for the spider" would echo through her mind.

Chanda could live with that. She could go home to Ariel and put this behind her.

Shanicha, tough as she was, hadn't read her at all. Shan-

389

icha was no street kid. She might have been born defective, but she hadn't grown up with the desolation and despair Chanda had experienced.

"You should have never messed with me and mine," she said in a whisper as the last spider made its way into Shanicha's room. "I don't forgive and I don't forget."

As she walked out of The Quad, she tucked Shanicha into the back of her mind, with the bastard who'd raped her, the cop who'd betrayed her and the shit who tried to rob her; along with a host of others who'd done her wrong. Not forgotten, just distant memories for cold lonely nights.

Maybe, just maybe, with Ariel those nights would be far fewer. Maybe she could even purge some of them altogether.

Home. She was going home.

Home to Ariel.

(Three)

Shanicha should have been studying. Finals were the following week. But it was like Mia had returned from the grave. Only, she knew it wasn't Mia. The first call had truly terrified her. *Someone* knew about the spiders. She'd talked about them in group. . . .

—A mistake, a voice within spoke.

Everyone could know her greatest fear; her only fear. Even that black bitch cop had mentioned them. Knowledge of the spiders, in itself, didn't faze her. Deep within, though, she felt the spiders themselves—especially the one who wanted her for a nest—were using someone to send *their* message. It didn't matter then who was calling her. That person was only a vehicle. Find her. Deal with her. Then what? *Another* would take her place.

For the first time in her life she felt totally helpless. She slept in fits and starts; awakening at times *knowing* the dream was about to begin if she continued to sleep. She went to class, but couldn't focus on her professors. She tried to study, but saw phantom spiders as she turned the pages of her text. She felt hungry all the time, but couldn't keep anything down. Her stomach would quake and she'd vomit her meal. Then have to dash to the bathroom with the runs.

Twice, Isaacs called her, asking why she'd skipped group.

"Leave me the fuck alone, all right," she'd finally told him. "You betrayed me. Betrayed us all. We spoke to you in confidence, yet the whole fucking world knows our secrets. Do me—*all of us*—a favor and fuck off." And she'd hung up before he could respond.

Each night she awaited the dreaded phone call from a female who disguised her voice. They were closing in. She could feel it. Even her roommate could. Without saying a word, she packed her belongings and moved into another girl's room.

Shanicha tried to hang up on her tormentor, but she wouldn't let her be. She'd call and call until she let her have their say. Deliver *their* message to her.

She stopped answering her phone, but it rang incessantly. With each ring she felt their presence grow stronger. They were in the walls. She could hear them scampering about, probing for a way in. She checked for cracks where they might escape, covering them up with glue, tape, even toothpaste. She saw the walls pulsate as their frustration mounted. They were trapped, and didn't like it one bit.

Showers were her only solace. Half a dozen a day now, to keep them at bay. She shaved three times daily, so they couldn't hide if they breached her defenses. She sprayed her entire body with deodorant, then with a stick deodorant, coated her body again a second time to mask her odor.

Alone in her room, she spent hours searching, commanding and beseeching her other self to emerge. Her other self was her true barometer. Once it was present, she would have nothing to fear. But her other self was even more attuned to the vile creatures than she. If her other self hid, they must be close.

Now she closed her eyes, fatigue having totally sapped her of the will to remain awake. She felt a tickling sensation, and opened her eyes to see one of the little fuckers tap-dancing across her stomach.

Somehow, they'd broken through her defenses. Try as she might, she couldn't awaken from her nightmare to flee. Then, to her horror, she realized *she was awake*. The spiders had escaped from the wall and were everywhere. Hundreds, thousands all around her; one or two already on her.

She reached for her genitals, as if her puny hand could repel their attack. But it was too late. She felt a squirming in her womb. Could see, with eyes from within her, the queen nestled in her womb; laying hundreds of eggs and protecting them with a silky protective web.

She stifled a scream that arose in her throat. She couldn't allow them to hatch. They would devour her from within, as they sought nourishment.

She laughed aloud.

"You fuckers. Think you've won," she said aloud.

No one controlled her. She could still defeat them. Keep them from hatching. Then they and their queen would wither and die and she'd be free of them forever.

She went to the window, opened it and without hesitation stepped out.

All their effort in vain, she thought to herself, as she plunged toward the pavement below.

She could feel her other self emerge, and smiled.

She had nothing to fear.

HUNGRY EYES

BARRY HOFFMAN

The eyes are always watching. She can feel them as she huddles there, naked, vulnerable, in an iron cage in a twisted man's basement. Someday she will be the one with the power, the need to close the eyes. And she'll close them all.

___4449-8 $4.99 US/$5.99 CAN

Dorchester Publishing Co., Inc.
P.O. Box 6640
Wayne, PA 19087-8640

Please add $1.75 for shipping and handling for the first book and $.50 for each book thereafter. NY, NYC, and PA residents. please add appropriate sales tax. No cash, stamps, or C.O.D.s. All orders shipped within 6 weeks via postal service book rate. Canadian orders require $2.00 extra postage and must be paid in U.S. dollars through a U.S. banking facility.

Name_____
Address_____
City_____State_____Zip_____
I have enclosed $_____ in payment for the checked book(s).
Payment <u>must</u> accompany all orders. ☐ Please send a free catalog.

BITE RICHARD LAYMON

"No one writes like Laymon, and you're going to have a good time with anything he writes."
—Dean Koontz

It's almost midnight. Cat's on the bed, facedown and naked. She's Sam's former girlfriend, the only woman he's ever loved. Sam's in the closet, with a hammer in one hand and a wooden stake in the other. Together they wait as the clock ticks down because . . . the vampire is coming. When Cat first appears at Sam's door he can't believe his eyes. He hasn't seen her in ten years, but he's never forgotten her. Not for a second. But before this night is through, Sam will enter a nightmare of blood and fear that he'll never be able to forget—no matter how hard he tries.

"Laymon is one of the best writers in the genre today."
—Cemetery Dance

YOU COME WHEN I CALL YOU

DOUGLAS CLEGG

An epic tale of horror, spanning twenty years in the lives of four friends—witnesses to unearthly terror. The high desert town of Palmetto, California, has turned toxic after twenty years of nightmares. In Los Angeles, a woman is tormented by visions from a chilling past, and a man steps into a house of torture. On the steps of a church, a young woman has been sacrificed in a ritual of darkness. In New York, a cab driver dreams of demons while awake. And a man who calls himself the Desolation Angel has returned to draw his old friends back to their hometown—a town where, two decades earlier, three boys committed the most brutal of rituals, an act of such intense savagery that it has ripped apart their minds. And where, in a cavern in a place called No Man's Land, something has been waiting a long time for those who stole something more precious than life itself.

___4695-4 $5.99 US/$6.99 CAN

BRASS

ROBERT J. CONLEY

The ancient Cherokees know him as *Untsaiyi*, or Brass, because of his metallic skin. He is one of the old ones, the original beings who lived long before man walked the earth. And he will live forever. He cares nothing for humans, though he can take their form—or virtually any form—at will. For untold centuries the world has been free of his deadly games, but now Brass is back among us and no one who sees him will ever be the same . . . if they survive at all.

___4505-2 $5.50 US/$6.50 CAN

Welcome Back to the Night
Elizabeth Massie

A family reunion should be a happy event, a time to see familiar faces, meet new relatives, and reconnect with people you haven't seen in a while. But the Lynch family reunion isn't a happy event at all. It is the beginning of a terrifying connection between three cousins and a deranged woman who, for a brief time, had been a part of the family. When these four people are reunited, a bond is formed, a bond that fuses their souls and reveals dark, chilling visions of a tortured past, a tormented present, and a deadly future—not only for them, but for their entire hometown. But will these warnings be enough to enable them to change the horrible fate they have glimpsed?

___4626-1 $5.99 US/$6.99 CAN